The Evil Men Do...

"It's coming," a soldier called as the timer rolled away from the warhead.

"No time to wait," Jestak shouted. "Just lift it out of here before it explodes to trigger the other device. We'll throw it over the side and pull this boat away."

They tugged at the heavy device, swaying and grunting, straining to hold it as men above looped ropes around it to help. Finally it grated and rolled up onto the deck, but caught on a cleat and hung there.

"I'll get a pry," Stel shouted, running forward ahead of the wheelhouse. A horrifying silence followed...the timer had ceased.

With a roar and a flash, the device blew up...

THE PELBAR CYCLE
Also by Paul O. Williams
Published by Ballantine Books:

The Sword of Forbearance

Book Seven of
The Pelbar Cycle

Paul O. Williams

A Del Rey Book

BALLANTINE BOOKS • NEW YORK

A Del Rey Book
Published by Ballantine Books

Library of Congress Catalog Card Number: 85-090751

ISBN 0-345-32504-4

Manufactured in the United States of America

First Edition: October 1985

Cover art by Darrell K. Sweet
Map of Urstadge by Chris Barbieri
Map of East Urstadge by Shelly Shapiro

For the people of Elsah, Illinois, who have made the last two decades of my life fascinating, varied, and remarkably active.

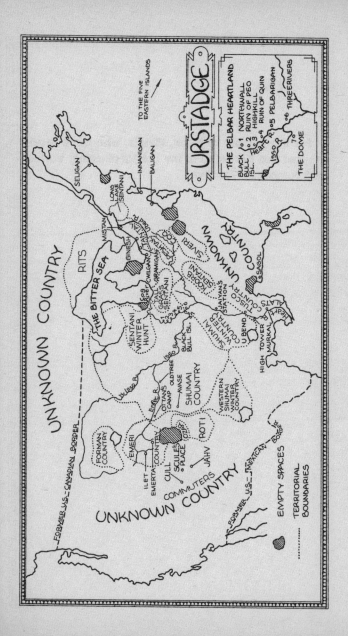

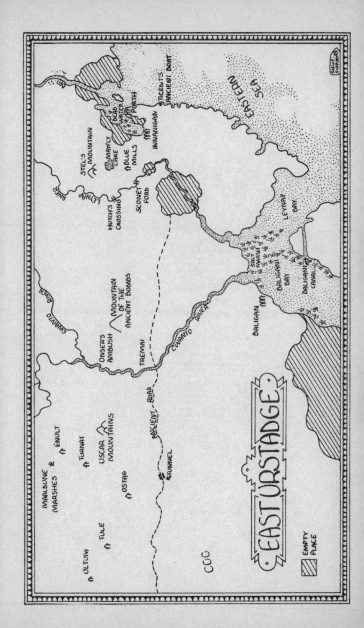

I

THE cold fall wind blew crowds of dry leaves past the entrance of the tent—like fleeing soldiers, Exalt Peydan thought. He hitched his cloak around him again and shivered slightly, glancing over at the legislative observer. "I think we've come far enough, Borund."

"You've said that before. Enough times," the heavy-browed observer replied. "The scouts haven't encountered anyone. Anyone. It would appear the Peshtak have abandoned the region."

"Or that they are simply entrapping us."

"With this force? Come, Peydan. You've conducted successful thrusts with less than half as many men."

"We don't know what this Heart River Federation means. It may mean allies. Observer, this is a military decision. I feel the legislature is forcing us into a disaster."

"Ah. Yes. So you've said. But the position, if I must repeat it again, is that even if we refuse to provide a western border, we deposit their scruffy messenger as far west as possible. When dealing with savages, one must treat them as such, one must . . ."

Borund paused, looking at a man in scout's tans who had just appeared at the tent flap. Peydan silently beckoned him in. "Yes? Any contact?"

"Yes and no, Exalt," the man said, throwing his right arm up smartly, palm forward, in a salute.

Peydan returned the salute with a slight wave. "Explain."

"We went as far as the Peshtak village of Ostag, Exalt. It was wholly abandoned."

"Then they have fled!" Borund slapped his knee.

"Have they fled?" the exalt asked, raising his eyebrows.

"We don't think so, Exalt. They stripped the houses and storerooms. Nothing was left. They've taken every freaking bone and stick they could move across the mountains westward. And before the last rain."

1

"Four days then at least. Well, Observer, we have made contact then. Are you satisfied?"

"Contact? I hardly see it as contact."

"People don't abandon homes at the start of winter. They know we're here. They've begun taking action, and with some considerable effort and resources."

"They've simply fled us. We have time to go farther before the close of the season. We can make a forced march eastward before the weather closes."

The exalt looked at the scout, who continued to stand at attention. "Is that all? Is there more, then?"

"I . . . don't know, Exalt. It's the land ahead."

"What about it?"

"This broad valley turns south. Continuing west, we'll have to cross a high ridge into a narrow valley. Then the next north-south ridge is even higher, and rocky. To go around the ridges we'll have to travel at least twenty-five ayas southward. It . . ."

"Yes?"

"It has a bad feel to it. For some distance this is the last place we can defend at all easily. Ostag may have been abandoned to sucker us farther. Retreat may be very difficult once we've crossed that ridge. And the tracks—at Ostag—there were queer ones. Some large animal, heavy, used to pull drags—and even carts, I think. Left a strange track like a moon, but longer. We distinguished at least fourteen of them, all different. It's strange. The Peshtak with carts is strange enough. All very orderly. I sent Ocul and Zard on ahead. Told them to be careful."

"Some large animal pulling carts?" mused Borund, laughing.

"Yes, sir," the scout murmured.

Outside a deep horn sounded in short bursts.

"General alert," Peydan shouted, rushing out, shading his eyes westward across the clearing his men had made, squinting at the brushy area by the stream. Another scout was running from the stream toward the camp. On the far side of the stream two men sat on the backs of large animals as big as wild cattle—small-eared beasts with long heads, which they shook and tossed as the men waited. One carried a pole from which a maroon flag waved lazily in the light wind. The other, even at this distance, Exalt Peydan could see was extremely tall.

"Here's your contact, Observer," the exalt remarked, advancing between flanking guards to meet the scout. "Move up a line of men, Lieutenant," he added to a short, dark man who had rushed up to him. "Set flankers and a rear guard."

"It's Ocul," the first scout said.

The other scout finally ran up, the gathering soldiers parting for him, then slowed, panting to a halt in front of Peydan. He threw up his hand in a weary salute.

"Catch your breath," the exalt said. "What is this, then?"

"They have . . . Zard, Exalt. They say they'll return him when we give . . . back their messenger."

"Swine!" Borund spat.

"Have they hurt him?"

"No. Fed us. Talked to us. Brought me back on the . . . horse— that animal."

"How many?"

"I couldn't tell, Exalt. I saw maybe a hundred, and about thirty of these horses. A mixed group. Not all Peshtak. Mostly not Peshtak. They call themselves the Heart River Federation. They . . . over there . . . have asked to talk with you."

"Invite them in."

"They say to pull your men back to the camp itself and set up a table near the stream. Then they'll come."

"Within bowshot of the brush on the far side, no doubt," Borund said.

"Observer, you're interfering. Tell me, Ocul. What do you think?"

"I think they'll not engage us, Exalt, if we're cautious. They insist they only want the messenger back. They've seen the caged cart. They don't like that. They said . . ."

"Yes?"

"Only . . . the savage and benighted would behave like that, Exalt."

"Double swine!" Borund yelled. "Who are they—child stealers, harvest burners, faceless pustules—to say that!"

Peydan shot him a look. "That tall one. What's he?"

"His name is Arey. He is a Shumai horse guardsman, in the Heart River Federation. He has an arm wound just healed. Said he got it at the Bitter Sea Portage, where they engaged the Tantal."

"Where's this Bitter Sea Portage?"

"I don't know, Exalt. He says the Peshtak destroyed Ginesh, with Pelbar help. He says the Peshtak have joined their federation and are even now speaking to the Coo."

"Snakes. They are welcome to all of them."

"Yes, Observer. But we can get along without your sputterings. What of the other man?"

"He is a Sentani from someplace called Koorb. He's young. His name is Igna. His mother was Pelbar, but of Shumai ancestry."

"Mixed breeds," Borund muttered.

Peydan paused, tapping his leg with his stick. "And the flag?"

"The Heart River flag. Maroon, Exalt. With a heart at the center, divided by stripes into segments, one for each society."

"How many segments?"

"Seven. Soon there may be more."

Peydan turned his back and let his eyes sweep the camp. It was not a good place to be, even with over eight hundred men. He turned back again. "Tell them we'll talk, Ocul. Lieutenant, get a table and four chairs. Borund, you may come, but I'll talk. This is a military matter."

"Hardly. It is a border dispute."

Peydan sighed. "I think they'll be easier to deal with than you, Borund."

"I shall report your remark to the legislature."

"Provided we ever get out of here."

After some delay several Innanigani soldiers brought the wooden table and chairs and set them up. Peydan used the time to firm up his perimeter and ready his men. Finally he and Observer Borund walked slowly out through the low brush and grass toward the table, followed by a young aide. All this time the two horsemen sat their animals impassively waiting.

Only when the two Innaniganis were seated did the riders urge their horses forward through the rocky stream and up the bank to the table. Arey, the big Shumai, dismounted, handing his reins to Igna, the flagbearer. Turning, he approached the table. The handle of his sheathed axe lightly slapped his leg as he walked.

The exalt felt his hair rise as the Shumai approached, unsmiling, and quietly sat down opposite him. He was big-boned, light blond, and heavily muscled, with penetrating blue eyes. His reddish beard stood out, curled and wiry, but neatly trimmed.

Arey smiled slightly. "You didn't have to bring our messenger this deep into Peshtak country," he said, rubbing his hands. "I'm sure he could have walked."

"It has not been established that this is Peshtak country," said

Borund. "We certainly have not agreed to that. No western border has been set."

Exalt Peydan shot him a look. "Our scout has told me that you are a Shumai? Arey by name? I am Exalt Peydan, commander of this defense unit, representing the military of the three eastern cities and, in specific, Innanigan. This is Borund, the legislative observer assigned the unit. We are not empowered to make border agreements. We—"

"Are you empowered to return diplomatic messengers who have been treated like criminals?"

"The old Peshtak? Of course. We shall return him. But it would be more regular, you must admit, if we knew what group we were addressing. Might you inform us of that?"

"Surely the message he carried gave the basic information. You're talking to the project commander of a mixed defense force gathered on information of your move westward into the territory of the Federation. Your observer may say what he likes, but this area has been used by the Peshtak for generations. In spite of Innanigani invasions. You've never stayed. They have, as I understand it. We're curious—"

"You would have us believe, Commander, that you have come all this way after our little group gathered itself for this walk westward? That the information was taken to you far in the west and it brought you here? I think it is fortuitous we came since you must have been planning your gathering of hostiles for some time."

Arey smiled frankly. "You may believe what you like. I am talking to you in a final attempt to prevent hostilities. You can't go much farther without coming to Ostag. The Peshtak think you'll burn it. Naturally we would regard that as a hostile act. We could not merely let it occur without response."

"Whose lives are you saving?" Borund asked.

Arey's expression went hard momentarily, but he smiled again with a hard glitter in his eyes. "Perhaps yours. Maybe mine. Maybe both. Look. There's an easy way out. You give us the messenger, in good shape, and we'll give you back Zard. We don't want anybody hurt. Then you can go home for the winter and we'll take your answer back to the Federation."

"Suppose there is no answer?" Peydan asked.

"No answer? Obviously one'll have to come. Two peoples have to have a border. There's empty land enough. No need to argue. Only to agree."

"What if we set it here, then?" Borund asked, looking at his neatly clipped fingernails.

Arey hesitated a long time, stared up at a circling hawk, and said quietly, "You mean would we fight for all the land between here and Tremai, or here and the Leynap? I can't say. We'd have to consult. It'd be a real expense for you to hold it. But no great joy for us to fight for either. I don't think I'd do the fighting. I have a family in the West. It would be a larger force I would guess. The Federation simply wants order. Not much chance of it, seeing you caged our messenger. But there is a chance. My Shumai soul says we should come screaming in here and tear your force apart, but the Federation is . . . somewhat milder."

"More prudent, no doubt. A hundred savages could not scratch this force," Borund remarked.

Arey's reply was a silent, glittering smile, then a low, throaty chuckle. The hair on Peydan's neck rose and the feet of a small shudder pattered down his backbone.

"Borund may not speak for us, Shumai. He is an observer, though sometimes he thinks he observes with his mouth. But what he says is basically true. I am a military man, as . . . in a sense you are. I see the point in trading men clearly enough. We will not take that as an acknowledgment that this is our western border, however. That is something the legislature refused to commit themselves on."

"Fine with me, Innanigani. No doubt you see that the Federation will simply set a boundary then, and inform you of it. Then you'll have to deal with their view of the matter."

Exalt Peydan raised his eyebrows. "We are able enough to deal with it when the time comes." A slight edge had crept into his voice.

"I wish you knew what you were saying," Arey returned. "I've had enough fighting with misguided attackers for one year. It isn't fun burying people—even the enemy."

"The Tantal? The scout said you had a brush with the Tantal."

"Yeah. A brush. In Heart River country by the Bitter Sea."

"And you defeated them. At much cost?"

"Yeah. We defeated them. At some cost. There's always a cost, isn't there. But they were the ones who paid dear."

"You used these animals?" Peydan described a circle with his forefinger.

"They played some part. Not that great." Arey laced his fingers behind his head, leaning back.

"And you mean to tell us that you came on these animals all that distance this year?"

"No. Of course not. But we came. We are here." Again Arey smiled his quiet, glittering smile.

"That makes no sense," said Borund.

"Were I Stel, I would say that you must allow me my little mystification, but not being him I'll just say I'm here. Now. The point is the trade of men, isn't it. But there's another matter. If we can make the trade here, we'd as soon you turned around and went home."

"This is home enough," said Borund, with a deep chuckle.

"Home is where you die in? At any rate, we'd as soon you made no attempt to burn Ostag. It would be inconvenient to rebuild it."

"For you."

Arey looked at the two for a long time. "For you, too," he murmured.

"You intend to defend it then?"

"We intend to make it costly to burn it."

"But not impossible."

Arey frowned slightly. "No. I imagine you could do it. I know I could with a force of eight hundred men with recurved bows and swords, even if they are mostly townsmen already footsore and ill fed. Even though you already have sickness enough and are not equipped for winter fighting. Of course . . ."

"Of course what?"

"It's not in your back field."

"No. But close enough."

Arey stared. "So," he said, slapping his hands on his thighs. "Are you prepared for the exchange at least?"

"Bring the scout to the stream edge. We will bring the Peshtak. Then we'll make the exchange here. Agreed?"

"Agreed," Arey said abruptly, then stood, turned, took his reins, and mounted in one swift flow of motion. The two backed their horses away for some distance toward the stream, then turned and trotted back through the water into the brush beyond it. The last thing Peydan saw was the top of the flagstaff bobbing through the thick scrub.

"The flea-bitten bastard," Borund said. "The cocky savage. Are you going to give him the Peshtak? Just like that?" He snapped his fingers.

"I don't know. They would be furious anyway when they saw his condition. He hasn't had good care. I wonder, though."

"Wonder? What now?"

"He practically dared us to burn Ostag."

"I thought he told you not to."

"Of course. Is he saying that they would defend that as a border? We shouldn't do it, of course. He's right. It isn't in our back field. He knows the number of our men and their arms. He knows their condition. He didn't really dare us. I think he meant it."

"Meant what?"

"He meant he didn't want a fight. And I think he warned us."

"He's weak, then. Gave himself away. We should have shot them both. Could have. The men had the range."

"We are just as close to that brush over there. I'm sure they have men there. Now."

Borund raised his hands in momentary panic, then composed himself. "They're gone. We'd best pull back. Quick."

"No need. They want the Peshtak."

"Even so . . ."

Exalt Peydan strode slowly back to his perimeter and gave orders to bring the Peshtak and retrieve the table and chairs. Then he stood tapping his leg with a stick.

"What do you mean to do?" Borund asked.

"I don't know. We have to think. Lieutenant, form up the best long-range bowmen. I mean the best. They have to be able to pick the enemy out from among us if need be." He waved the men away. "Still, I don't like it. They picked their place. It'll be hard to trick them."

"You have to. We have our name and pride. We can't give in to a scruffy gang."

"That Arey. I'd . . . hardly call him scruffy. He's . . . a little hard to pin down. I think he clearly has something in mind."

As though in answer a long arrow arced out from the far brush and *wunk*ed into the ground some fifteen arms ahead of the perimeter. A note was tied to it. A soldier retrieved the message and brought it to Peydan, who unrolled it and read, "Do not reposition your bowmen. This is an exchange, not a fight. You are certainly free to lie about our agreement. But you will lose."

"Pus faces!" Borund spat.

Peydan sighed. "Bring the Peshtak. There's no help for it."

"If you dare—" Borund began.

"I dare. They have picked the situation. And now Zard is of more use to us than the old man. Besides, we may still be able to exploit this. You, Lieutenant. Get two men with a stretcher and take the Peshtak to where the table was. Set him down and come back quick. Then we'll see. Bowmen, look sharp for my orders. Do nothing that will endanger the Scout Zard."

The Innanigani did as ordered, the gray-haired old man tossing and flopping on the stretcher as they rushed him out. But as they neared the spot, a force of five riders trotted out of the underbrush, splashed through the stream, and mounted the bank. They carried something between them. The panicked stretcher-bearers shied away, accidentally dumping the old messenger to the ground. They turned to look at him, and were knocked aside by the rush of horsemen.

The first two stooped and grabbed the old man's arms, jerking him upward as he cried out with pain and fear, the man on the right releasing him to the other, who flung him across his horse ahead of the saddle, as they both turned and raced away through the brush with wild, trilling wails.

The other two men trailed the scout between them, completely tied up. They dropped him by the stretcher-bearers and followed the other riders.

The fifth man, the flagbearer, had already turned, as Borund yelled out, "Shoot. Shoot the bastards."

"No!" Peydan shouted, but the bowmen quick-drew and released. A series of flashes and explosive roars replied from the bushes to the west. Eight bowmen went down, along with Borund.

An arrow had taken the flagbearer through the side as he reached the stream. He cried out and wavered, his horse splashing on through as two more riders burst from the brush, one grabbing the flag, the other rider, retreating in a boil of water and animals.

The bowmen on the southern perimeter then released, taking the man with the flag out of his saddle, though he clung to the stirrup and dragged up out of the stream into the brush, trailing the flag, which caught and tore on the bushes.

"Hold!" Exalt Peydan shouted. "Pull back. Now look, you gull-gutted garbage eaters. Lieutenants all. Follow orders. Now!"

As the Innanigani began to back up, they heard an order sung out from the brush to the south and saw forms moving vaguely there. Then a wail like that of the horsemen sang out, and as it cut off, again the flashes and explosions came from the brush, and over a dozen bowmen dropped. The southern perimeter broke and ran until beaten forward by the officers, who set them to digging in as the wail again came, and the roaring flash again, and more men fell and cried out, the lucky clutching wounds. Then the brush and woods made little sound, though the Innanigani could hear distant shouting.

"Well, Borund, so much for the wisdom of legislative observers," Peydan remarked, staring down at him as two men worked to cut the legging away from the observer's bleeding thigh.

Borund cried out, then said, "Lieutenant. Lieutenant Eplay! Now. Show the exalt your orders."

The thin lieutenant reached into his side pouch and presented Peydan with a folded and sealed document. The exalt broke the seal, opened it, and read it, frowning. "So," he said. "That's it, huh? I'm relieved when Borund requests it." He turned and sighed, tapped his stick against his leg, and added, "Very well, Lieutenant Eplay. It's yours. You and Borund may command the force. I—I suppose I must have anticipated something of the sort, Borund, with all your interference. Even wounded you haven't given up your incredible stupidity. Look at my men. The Federation has some cannonlike weapon we don't. Look at your own leg. Now what . . ."

"Commander Eplay," Borund muttered, "take over now. Show the exalt due respect but isolate him. And get me some medical help. Please." He paused, shuddering and groaning from the pain in his leg, then added, "It's clear now."

"What's clear now, Observer?"

"We have to go burn this Ostag and then march eastward. Quick."

Eplay stared at him. "Burn Ostag? After what we've just seen?" Then he swallowed. "Yes, sir. I see." His eyes swept the scene. Then he turned and walked rapidly away, shouting orders to the sergeants' messengers.

"Look there, Peydan," Borund said, rolling over. But he didn't finish, seeing the exalt was gone.

II

FOLLOWING the scouts' directions, Lieutenant Eplay moved his force out well before dawn, packing all the supplies and establishing a new camp on a rocky, easily defended hill two ayas west of the former one. Then the main force climbed the ridge and marched rapidly toward Ostag. They met no resistance.

Dawn came gray, with the winter's first flakes of snow, a low wind moaning hollowly through the bare branches. In late morning, as they came out into a stream valley, harvested fields lay ahead of them, and beyond, the low rows of house tops of Ostag. The whole area appeared deserted, and a scattering of crows on the houses and in the street increased that impression.

"We went as far as that line of trees," Ocul said. "After we examined the whole area, Commander, they cut us off with the beasts—the horses—then men in the woods took us as we ran toward them. They were hidden in the trees."

"You ran to them. I wonder. Is that what we're doing?"

"Maybe."

"We have an army, though. With this many, we could handle what we saw. No brush here. Almost seven hundred men here. Things seem clear back to the supply guard, and that's easily protected. Besides, Borund insisted."

"Borund may still die from his wound, Commander."

"It wouldn't matter. There are two other legislative people here. Legislative control of the military is our longstanding tradition." Eplay shook his head.

"Never before to the point of dictating strategy, Commander."

"Enough. You and Zard go ahead of us as we move down. Don't worry. We'll be close behind you. Be careful. We want this fast and safe. Just burn and go. We'll be back to maincamp before night."

Ocul looked at him but said nothing, then jerked his head to Zard and trotted down the valley. The whole force followed, trotting slowly, in across the fields, splitting up, moving behind the houses and storage buildings as well as down the main street. Then they kicked down doors, burst in, weapons ready, but found all deserted. As the lieutenants and subdirects commanded, they fired the buildings, withdrawing into the street, then back as they came, as the village bloomed into flame, sending gray smoke and clouds of sparks up into the raw air.

The whole operation took less than twenty sunwidths. Its ease made the Innanigani force jubilant and relieved, but also very nervous.

"It was a bluff, then," Eplay remarked to a lieutenant as they entered the trees again, rapidly retreating. "Borund was right. We even might have occupied the place."

"Not enough supplies to—"

A heavy concussion and explosive roar cut the lieutenant short, as dirt, men, and arms flew into the air ahead of them. The officers ran up toward the cries of the men and fallen debris. A long steaming trench had appeared along the path, and the area was obscured by patches of pungent smoke and littered with fallen and torn men. Others stumbled around, dazed and covered with dirt.

"Form a perimeter!" Eplay shouted. "Aid men! Come, come!"

Order slowly formed out of the confusion. The Innanigani had lost seventeen men, with four others disabled.

"It's a Tantal technique, Commander," one of the lieutenants remarked. "Hidden explosives. We should have brought the cannon."

"Over that hill? We'd be still coming. Form up now. We've been delayed. We need to move out. There still is time—"

Ahead a line of successive sharp explosions, like the ones from the last fight, moved along an arc in the trees. The officers formed a defense line, then moved forward with bowmen in the lead. They found no one. The force had lost six more men.

"Commander," said Ocul. "We'll have to keep moving to get back today. I think—"

"Yes?"

"This suggests they are attacking the forward camp. As Peydan said they might."

"It's a good position with nearly a hundred defenders. You've seen more of the terrain than any of us. What do you suggest?"

"Nothing. We came the best way. We'll have to—"

Another volley of fire sounded from the south, and more men

fell. They saw the enemy this time, running back through the trees.

"The savages have a fearsome weapon," a lieutenant remarked to Eplay as they surveyed a wounded man. "It's a miniature of our cannon, looks like."

"There was a rumor of something like that. From the Tantal. We're working on one now. It's an ancient weapon. There's one in the museum. We'll have one better soon enough." He sighed. "But now—"

"We'll just have to freaking fight our way through."

"That's right. No other way. Well, let's get on with it."

It was a nightmarish day for the Innanigani. Six more times they received Heart River rifle fire, losing more men each time. It was well past nightfall before they reached the rocky rise where the forward camp had been set up. They smelled the heavy smoke long before they arrived. The place had been overrun and destroyed. All the supplies, the cannon and its ammunition, tents, and food had been taken or burnt. The Innanigani dead lay lined up—sixty-nine in all. Near them eleven wounded men lay in their blankets, with five other men who had been left to care for them.

They were very sober. It had been a sharp fight, they explained, but the westerners had advanced behind wooden shields that protected them almost wholly, firing their explosive weapons around them. Eventually it had been hand to hand, and the Innanigani had fought well. But it had been no use.

Finally Peydan, who had assumed the command when the fighting started, surrendered. The westerners had taken Peydan, the wounded Borund, and four men to carry him. They had treated the wounded and gathered the dead. Then they brought carts and hauled away all the supplies they didn't burn, along with their own dead. One man said at least thirty enemy had been killed, including nine of the blond horsemen, who fought with a kind of gleeful abandon. Most of the rest were Peshtak, he thought.

Eplay ordered the dead carried to the maincamp and buried. He then commanded that the perimeter be strengthened and dug in deeper. As snow had commenced in earnest, he ordered a large, guarded detail to cut hemlocks by the stream to make shelters since the tents had all been lost. That work took much of the night.

Once a large shelter had been set up for the officers, he called them to a meeting. They sat on the cold ground in a circle around a smoky fire. All of them looked tired and grim.

"I don't need to tell you how bad our situation is," Eplay began. "It must be a hundred and forty ayas to any supplies. If we hunt for food, we'll be in danger. We'll have to build shelters every night. The men don't have blankets. If the enemy is determined enough, we could lose the whole force."

"No, Commander," one man ventured. "We are bad enough off, but not that bad. Only about two hundred men attacked the supply camp."

"We thought they had only just over a hundred. Maybe more were held in reserve. Or maybe they'll be reinforced. Borund was contemptuous of them. I think we can't afford that. They have horses, the explosive weapons, and the hidden explosive charges. We've seen that they are shrewd and not afraid to fight. Besides . . ."

The men waited, looking at him in the flickering firelight. Then one said, "Besides, we are on their land. They warned us, and we broke the truce."

"None of that is established," another man hissed.

"Take what position you like," Eplay said. "It may not be established that this is their land. But we arranged an exchange and then shot arrows at the men who attempted to carry it out. At Borund's command. That is a fact."

"They are savages," the second man said.

"But it's us that acted like savages," the first returned, stirring a ripple of resentment among the others.

"Enough. We'd better leave all that. We need to decide what to do. There are no really good solutions. But we can minimize the bad ones. The bad ones are starving, freezing, getting sick—"

"And engaging the enemy."

"That might not be so bad. We might defeat them."

Again the officers argued, all talking at once, though in low tones. Eplay clapped his hands for silence. "I'd rather engage the enemy when the conditions are more of our own choosing. Now. What are we going to do about food?"

The men sat silently. "Fish," one finally said. "March east until we hit a river and then fish."

"Too far. That's the Cwanto, north of Tremai."

"The scouts will have to hunt. We'll send a squad with them."

"The enemy'll pick them off."

"Nobody said this would be a vacation."

"Some did."

"Stick that, too."

"Want to try?"

"Enough!" Eplay held up his hands. "Let's not win their fight for them. We'll send out the scouts in the morning. The whole force will move east by midmorning. We'll set up a new main-camp in late afternoon. Ask the men. There must be food here we could forage for if we knew it. Now. Let's use what's left of the night to sleep. No questions now. To it."

The men stayed by the fire a few long moments more. Then one left, the others stirred themselves, and all but one followed. He squinted at Commander Eplay. "The fact is, Commander, that Peydan called it right all the way and Borund put us in this mess. The men know it. They know you are Borund's man. You'll have to do something bold and decisive. Or this will shift power right in the heart of the legislature."

"Put that up your left nostril, Sharitan. You think I don't know that? Right now I don't care much about the legislature. We've lost almost a hundred and fifty men, and more wounded. I have to get these men out of here."

"Listen, Commander. I have an idea. It might work. It's bold and it might mean another disaster. But it may turn things around, too."

Eplay sat up, sighing wearily. "Let's hear it, Sharitan. I can't sleep anyhow."

EXALT Peydan tried to sleep but could not. Despite the blanket under him and the fur robe over him, he was not comfortable lying on the ground. His wounds were light but irksome, and it was nearly morning before a silent Sentani hunter came to bind them up. The savage was an old, slightly bandy-legged man, nearly bald, with bushy white eyebrows.

A Peshtak boy knelt and held the flickering lamp while he

worked. His mouth stayed tight and downturned the whole time. When he had nearly finished, a young man in a maroon coat came and leaned down to him.

"Mokil," he whispered, as though not trusting his voice.

The old man closed his eyes and said, "No. No."

"I'm sorry," the man replied. "Want me to finish?"

"No."

"I'll wait for you."

"Don't wait. Too many to take care of."

"All right. Atou will sustain us." He lightly touched the old man's shoulder.

"Whatever."

The young man stood up and left in the dark, his feet making barely any sound on the frozen leaves. Mokil turned to watch him a moment, his hands trembling as he held the tan bandages. Then he returned to his job.

When he finished, he looked over at Borund, who lay in a fever, his leg swollen. Then he stood and turned.

"Aren't you going to help him?" the exalt asked.

Mokil turned and came back, squatting down by the exalt. "I was there," he said in a husky voice. "I saw Igna holding the flag at the exchange. I saw this fish bait give an order to shoot. I saw the arrow find Igna, and I helped bear him here. Now I'm told he has just died. That didn't need to happen. None of this did. This drip of cow slobber set it off just the way you can light a prairie fire and watch it roar downwind in the fall, to the destruction of everything. No. I won't help him. All he will feel, no matter what happens to him, is just a shaving of the pain he's caused. To our people. To yours. You're Tantal all over again. Your fate will be the same."

"People of civilization do not act that way."

"Trucebreaking is civilized, then?" Mokil squatted silently for a long time. "When I was much younger," he began in a far-off voice, "I led a starband on the winter hunt. One of my men hurt his leg. Through unusual events he was taken to Northwall, a Pelbar city, and there made well. We were enemies at the time, though for no real reason. Strangeness. Difference. Custom. He met a Pelbar woman. Her name is Ursa, a blondish woman of Shumai ancestry abandoned there as a baby. Winnt and Ursa were married at Northwall in the spring, with the whole starband there and all of Northwall. Before the celebration was over, some

Shumai came. There was no fight. One of them knew Jestak the Pelbar. Another . . . had been helped by Ursa and Winnt.

"The next morning we left in our boats. I always felt that Igna began that wedding night, the first child of a new peace. That began the transformation of the whole Heart River Valley. Igna. He had his mother's eyes. How will we tell her?"

"He took his chances, like the rest."

"He carried a flag. He was unarmed. This one . . . well, when the two Koorb starbands come, Winnt will be with them. He has the right, the claim by Sentani law, of this one's life."

"No," Borund murmured. "No. I am a prisoner taken in war."

"Igna was a flagbearer killed in peace. That is the point."

"You will find any savagery to prisoners inadvisable," Peydan said. "We are not helpless."

"In the morning I will show you the old Peshtak messenger you returned. You must think savagery to prisoners is all right. You were the commander."

"I was acting under strict orders. You already know I was replaced."

"By this one, the killer tanwolf leading the pack."

"It is a political matter. We have a right to defend ourselves."

"And burning Ostag does that? Deep in Heart River Federation land? Huh."

"We do not acknowledge any such thing. This place is held by the Peshtak scruff. Invaders. Torturers. Murderers. Harvestburners. Ambushers."

Mokil stood abruptly. Without another word he jerked his head to the Peshtak boy and they left.

After daybreak two men on horses trotted into the camp and dismounted. Peydan could see them talking and gesturing. He could see the big Shumai, Arey, his arm in a sling, limp up to them. Others gathered. Something was up. A tall Sentani blew a long, mournful call on a cow horn, then a series of spaced notes that were returned by horn calls from over a rise.

Peydan sighed and shivered. He looked at Borund, who seemed sunk in a morose contemplation, his forehead beaded with sweat. "What do you think it is?" the exalt asked.

"Our people. Our people come to get us," the observer gasped out.

Shumai horsemen approached from over the rise, the breaths of the men and animals puffing and trailing behind as they disappeared. The exalt began to count, but they started passing in clusters, at a trot, going northward. Surely he saw over a hundred. All of them had that explosive weapon—except Arey, whose axe lay down along his leg. Somehow Peydan felt unutterably weary. He knew he had good men, but these were good men, too. There would be more death. The whole expedition could be shattered, even if his Innanigani held and fought well. He wondered at what the old man had said—the Sentani called Mokil.

A group of Peshtak followed the horsemen, trotting briskly, and after them a mixed group of Sentani and those others in maroon coats—they must have been Pelbar. The whole camp began to empty out except for guards and those tending the wounded.

Peydan lay unfed and uncomfortable until late morning, when he heard another succession of spaced horn-notes and a large band of Sentani trotted into the camp, clearly weary from a long run. But they moved out in bands setting up a circle of smaller camps. Peydan watched as the old man, Mokil, talked to a tall, thin man and gestured in his direction.

The man hesitated, then walked toward the two prisoners. Peydan twisted on the ground, tugging at his bonds, and as the man approached, he felt a strange terror worse than that at his capture the day before. The man came up to them, glanced at the guard, nodding, and gazed down at both of them, flicking his eyes from one to the other.

"You must be Winnt," Peydan said in his calmest voice. The man said nothing. Borund groaned and stirred. Winnt turned and stared at him a long time. Then he turned and walked away, soon returning with a bowl of warm water and bandages.

He knelt by Borund, drew back the furs and uncovered the wound in his leg, which was dark and angry. Borund wrestled on the ground and cried out.

"Mokil," Winnt called.

The old man hobbled up, looking grim and quizzical, then without a word held Borund down by the shoulders, bearing his whole weight on him. The observer shrieked out in agony while Winnt worked on his wound, lancing, bathing, and binding it. Then Winnt checked the ropes that bound him and covered him up again.

"Harzas pig guts," Borund spat at him, gasping. "If you're going to kill me, just do it. Do it. I'm not afraid of swilling Peshtak lovers."

"Stick it, Borund," Peydan said.

Winnt just sat on his heels, looking down at the observer. Then he flicked a glance at Peydan. Somehow their eyes caught and held for a few moments. "I . . . " Peydan began, but found himself unable to continue.

Winnt stood and turned his back on the two, standing motionless a long moment. Then he walked away through the dry leaves. It had begun to snow again, big flakes slanting down in the cold wind. From far to the north came the faint popping of the explosive weapons. Winnt never hesitated nor turned as he walked toward his point band, the wind flattening his fur collar.

 IV

THAT morning, well before daybreak, Eplay had called his weary officers together at the maincamp. They huddled near a fire his men had surrounded by a hastily made windbreak of hemlock. "The situation is this. We have a long and hungry walk home if we go now. We will have lost the whole harzas campaign. We may lose more men to hunger than we did to the savages. Now. Ocul says there's another Peshtak village, Turnat by name, about thirty-seven ayas north of here, up this same valley, which bears some eastward.

"The enemy went south. We know they were hurt some. We think there weren't all that many of them. They didn't engage our whole force but lured us into splitting it.

"Now I'd like to split it again, but to some purpose. If we take half the force and follow them south, we can engage them, hold them. If the other half makes a forced march north, we can raid this Turnat and get their winter stores. Then we can rejoin and go home. Well?"

After a silence, a subdirect, an older man with a fringe of gray hair around his bald head, said, "The men are near used up, Commander. Tired and hungry. I'm not sure . . ." He drifted into silence.

Another man stood. "Lieutenant?" Eplay asked.

"I don't know. If we all force-marched the same distance east, they might let us go. We practically made them engage us. But if we really can get supplies at this Turnat . . ." He also trailed off.

"We might blunt their victory," another lieutenant said.

"We might," said another subdirect. "But what if we don't?"

"Then we'll burn another village anyway. There are too many of us. They won't stop that."

"What if they know how to use the cannon? Too bad we lost the cannon."

"They have these horses. They can warn the Peshtak."

"Not if we split and engage them. Not if we leave now."

"That assumes a freaking lot," the old subdirect murmured. "I've fought the Peshties a harzas many summers, but they never were like this. This is too harzpiz much. We could lose the whole filthy force."

"Indeed," said Eplay. "We may anyhow. I regret seeing so little enthusiasm for what must be done. But if I can't rely on your ardor, perhaps I can count on you to follow orders."

"Of course," said the old subdirect. "We'll do our filthy finest, sir."

"Good. I expected as much. Now. Lieutenants. Stay a bit. Subdirects, form up the men."

Before dawn the Innanigani southern force had engaged the Heart River scouts, all Peshtak hunters set out in a fan to guard the northern approach to the camp. The Innaniganis forced their way ahead, gaining a ridgeline before the resistance, with scattered rifle fire, stopped them. They continued to move forward, though, slowly, covering each other, using the trees, moving with great caution, guarding their flanks and rear, using their over four hundred men to create a tough challenge to the westerners.

As Arey sat his horse on the ridgetop to the southeast, he found slight chills trailing down his spine. "This has a bad feel to it, Garet," he muttered to the young Pelbar guardcaptain who rode beside him. "I don't understand . . .

"Why are they doing this? It can gain them nothing but more death. Is it those two—Peydan and the other, the foulmouth— they want that bad?"

Garet said nothing. He knew the Shumai needed silence to

allow his surmises to gather and braid themselves into a cord of perception.

"Garet," Arey finally said. "Take four riders and send four around the other side. Stay well back. I want to know how many of them there are. Be careful."

Garet looked, nodded, and touched his horse, moving off.

"Be careful," Arey shouted after him. "We want a report, not a fight. Avoid a fight." He frowned after Garet. He had sent the Pelbar to accompany the scouts in hope that his presence would help prevent impetuous Shumai riders from chancing a skirmish. They were angry from the losses of the previous day. Too many were of Shumai horsemen, who had strained, shrilling and yelling, up the rocky slope to the forward camp, only to be met by the one firing of the Innanigani cannon that occurred before the gunners were shot away from it while reloading.

Arey went over the tactics the Innaniganis might be undertaking. His scouts had sent back very sketchy reports. Some were still out and overdue. He was glad the two Shumai starbands had arrived. They weren't any more worn out than the enemy must be—and they had eaten.

Once again Arey and his command post had to move back from the advancing easterners. He sent a directive to pick up the base camp and move it farther south.

To the north he heard shouting and sent two riders to look. They sent back a long, ululating call for help, and seven more riders set off toward them. Ahead they could see a horse down, with arrows in it, and a Shumai rider under it as it thrashed. The Innaniganis advanced from the west as the Shumai riders swung east, spurred around and raced toward the easterners, rifles ready, passing a Peshtak scout, lowering their rifles, and shouting back for more help. An arrow took one man off his horse. A second horse went down. The other five aimed and shot. One jumped off, spanked his horse, and heaved at the downed horse as the man beneath grunted and struggled. An arrow went through his sleeve, then another through his leg. He crouched briefly behind the horse, rose for another shot, and found a line of men advancing on him.

He dropped one, took an arrow through the neck, gurgled and thrashed, then lay still, half on the Shumai under the horse. That rider couldn't get free, but he reached for the dead man's rifle and reloaded it. The other Shumai had dismounted and dashed for cover, firing their rifles as they could. But the line of easterners came on, now at a run. As one rushed by the downed horse, then turned, the trapped Shumai shot him through the midsection. Another easterner jumped over the horse then knelt and stabbed the Shumai repeatedly. Another Shumai shot the man, but they had to fall back, and one went down between trees. Other riders appeared on the slope above, but with a shout the Innaniganis halted and held their line, digging in.

One crawled forward and grabbed the two rifles then turned to run them down the slope, but a Shumai shot took him in the back, and he flung them down. Another subdirect scrambled to recover the weapons and raced down the hill, dodging in the trees.

Arey rode toward the Shumai horseman who had taken the Peshtak up behind him. They palmed briefly, and Arey dismounted to talk to the Peshtak.

Still panting, the man managed to say, "This is only . . . half of them. The rest are . . . marching north. Toward Turnat."

"What's Turnat?"

"A village. Like Ostag."

"How far?"

"Forty-five ayas . . . from here."

"How far are they?"

"Left early. Must be twenty or twenty-five ayas north. From here."

"Anybody warn the villagers?"

"No. I don't think. I was alone. Came here."

Arey stood silently awhile. "That's what it was." He gestured to a Shumai. "Call the riders in here," he said, and as the man took out his curved cow horn, Arey turned to the Peshtak. "Can you ride a horse?"

"Never have."

"No time to learn. You'll have to. My men'll help. I don't know if we can make it in time. You're going to have a sore rear tomorrow—if you're still alive." He turned away, then back. "What will your people do at Turnat if they come?"

"Fight. But they're few. Only a farming and hunting place."

"The Innaniganis want supplies then. Would your people burn their own village?"

The man frowned. "No. Never."

"What if we did it?"

The man looked angry. He looked down.

"It's up to them. Shame to let all their work go. Worse to

give it to the Innaniganis. If we can deny them food, they'll soon be spent. I've lost a third of the horsemen already— We can't hold such a force. But we can deny them their goal."

A rider galloped up. "Arey, we'd better move back again. They're coming."

Arey mounted and took the Peshtak up behind him. He turned his big buckskin and nudged him with his heels, calling to the man with the horn, "Summon the starbands to form a line. While you do that, get some charges. Five packs anyway. I want all but ten riders to go. Get Elson's horse for this man. It'll need an extra pad—for the horse's sake," he shot over his shoulder. The Peshtak laughed.

Arey rode off southward, a man with him calling the starbands in horn talk. "I think the Innaniganis are going to buy it dear," Arey said. "Because of Igna. Ride ahead. Tell the bands to form up on the side ridges like a funnel. Keep 'em in. We want two lines, the front one with bows, to retreat slowly to the riflemen as the Innaniganis advance. Then we'll pour it to them. We'll have to watch. They may not come in hard. They may think to hold us and then begin to pull back. If it's that, the flanking men should move ahead and keep with 'em. Like a moving U. Look for officers. Single them out if you can."

The man grinned and raced ahead, again talking on his horn, as Arey turned to survey the scene behind him. He felt the thrill of battle flirting down his spine. Already the horsemen were headed north to Turnat. He hoped they would skirt far enough around the enemy. He hoped they would pick up Garet's men. The Innanigani force had a big lead on them. It looked bad for Turnat—and for all of them. Mostly, Arey decided, for the Innaniganis.

V

EPLAY took the rifle and turned it over in his hands. "Huh, Lieutenant. Well made. They have foundries, fine skills with steel. We'll take this and—"

A heavy explosive roar from the south startled him. "The cannon," Ocul said. "If we mass, maybe we can retake it." He looked at Eplay, who nodded. Then he raced off in the direction of the sound, but when he was only about two hundred arms off, he spun, stumbled, and fell.

"Pig's eyes!" Eplay spat. "Listen to those weapons now. We have no chance to push in and take it. They must have more men. Subdirect, sound the horn for a slow pullback. Slow. Remember. Slow."

A heavy, balding man put a curled horn to his mouth and sounded a long, mournful note. It was echoed from four points ahead and then seemed to merge with the horn signals of the Sentani footmen, all punctuated by distant shouts and sharp rifle fire. Eplay stood on a fallen trunk and shaded his eyes forward. His men were trotting toward him in a closing loop, with their officers trying to hold them.

"Sound hold!" Eplay yelled.

The subdirect pulsed out the notes, then turned, only to find Eplay fallen over the log, a long arrow in his left eye. The man cried out and ran to him, but instantly saw it was no use. "Lieutenant!" he yelled.

The officer turned and gasped.

"Take over, sir."

The young man looked panicked. "Me?"

"Yes, you. You rank. Don't yellow out on us now. Come on, man, keep your brains in your skull."

The lieutenant gulped and swallowed. "All right. Sound hold again, then slow retreat. We'll move up to that ridgetop."

"The scum have it now, Lieutenant."

"Then we'll take it away from them, Subdirect. Now sound!"
The subdirect did, but the men kept coming.

"Sound it again. Keep sounding. When they get in tight enough, they'll hold."

The subdirect stared at him. Then he raised the horn again and sounded. The men slowed, the officers and subdirects shouting at them, as the lieutenant shaded his eyes around. A longbow arrow went through his pants, slicing into his calf. Absentmindedly he snapped it off. Then he raised his staff and pointed.

"Now, Subdirect, sound advance, double time. We are going to take that ridge." He turned to the men and shouted, "Keep your circle. Give it everything, men. We're going up that filthy, hog-sniffing, barn-bottomed, garbage-perfumed ridge. The last one up has got snake's legs. Watch all sides. Now, now, now. We are going. Sound advance, Subdirect."

The lieutenant swept the scene with a desperate, freckled grin and headed northeast on a run, limping slightly, his staff raised, and yelling. The men glanced at each other and followed, also yelling.

The ridge was held by Sentani and Peshtak, a thin line, which gave back as the Innaniganis ran and stumbled toward them. The officers held the rear men in check, looking back, preventing a rout. In a few sunwidths the Innaniganis had taken the ridge and set up a perimeter, using the plentiful rock slabs for hasty barricades while the westerners pecked away at them with rifle fire. Shading his eyes, the lieutenant could see two horses hauling the cannon through the brushy trees at the bottom of the narrow valley below.

"Lieutenant Oberly, we've lost the initiative," said another lieutenant at his right elbow.

"We never should have taken it, Ungo. We've held them anyway. Sharitan's men are out of reach now. They'll resupply at Turnat."

"We'll never hold this place that long. This gang'll set up a perimeter then go and engage them."

"They don't have the men, Ungo. They can't do both. Eplay saw that. But he didn't count on these others. What are they? Sentani? Not Lake Sentani, I think. But look how many. They're sore-pickers. Deadly. Not like the horsemen. The combination would've wiped us out."

"So what do you intend to do?"

Lieutenant Oberly grinned boyishly. "Talk," he said. "Everybody keep his head down. You, Subdirect Athfal. You carry my scarf on this staff. We'll wave it. Then you and me—we're going to have a talk."

"Hold that!" said Ungo. "Not on your scruffy neck are we going to surrender."

"Who said anything about surrender? I said talk."

"That'll mean surrender. No sane man surrenders to Peshtak. Or Peshtak lovers."

"Yeah, Lieutenant Ungo. You have a better plan? Eplay's idea stunk like an old carcass when he brought it up."

"Listen. It wasn't his. It was mine. Watch it, fungus eater. I can take you and this whole force away . . ."

Two subdirects crouched beside him, long knives pointed at his sides. One, an older, bald man, said, "We have order in this force, sir. Lieutenant Oberly is in command."

Oberly grinned. "Subdirect Athfal, wave that staff." He looked at Ungo. "I might've known it was your plan. What did you do? Hypnotize him? Split the force so that two weaker forces could be taken one piece at a time. Nice. I joined the force just to avoid work, and even I know better than that."

He rose, took the staff, and stepped over the jutting rock they had been behind. A Sentani round spanged off the rock, but after flinching, Oberly continued. "Come with me, Athfal," he called over his shoulder. An enemy horn spoke, then the shouting and rifle fire ceased. Athfal came up beside him. "I don't like this, Athfal. Not a thimbleful."

"What do you have in mind, Lieutenant?"

"I have no vague notion. But at least they'll be back there digging down like woodchucks. Below cannon-fire level. That thing's the worst. The longer we talk here, the farther Sharitan will walk north. I think that was his idea anyhow. We were the thumbsuckers all along. Sharitan used Ungo to help cosy Eplay into this. I think. All stupid."

"Sir?"

"Ungo isn't capable of even this bad an idea. He's good for carrying things out—a kind of rule book on legs. For doing the bidding of that underregion of the human system, Borund."

"Sir, I don't want to hear this."

"Oh? Fine. Let's say then that there are men up on the ridge who'd like to see their families again. Is that freaking all right?"

"Yes, sir."

"Ah. Here's somebody. And the cannon. Different when you

look it in the eye. It's their man on the animal—from the first truce. A little frayed, looks like."

A line of Shumai riders awaited them at the bottom of the hill, with Arey ahead of the others. A young Sentani came up and took the reins from him, then went to help the big Shumai, but Arey waved him away with his good hand and stiffly swung down. The buckskin put his ears back until Arey scratched the near one. He walked forward and stood, right hip cocked.

The Innaniganis approached. "Ready to give up?" Oberly asked. Athfal glared at him.

"Just about," Arey said. "Thought we'd practice on that hill with this big rifle of yours awhile."

"It ought not to be hard. To hit the hill, I mean."

"After a while I think we'd get it. We might send some men up there to see how we'd done."

"I wouldn't. Place is crawling with poisonous snakes, I hear."

"They'd all be underground by now. They're cold natured enough. Their bellies full of mice and rats."

"Always room for a few more rats."

"While we talk, you ought to get a few men and send them to pick up the ones you left around here. Careless, you know, scattering men all over."

"Well, you gave us the example."

Arey grinned. "Ten men will do. We'll help you with them. The ones far away. Kind of clean the refuse out of the woods. You can have water for them. Unless you've dug a well up there already."

Oberly flushed, but gulped back his retort for fear Arey would then refuse to help the wounded. "Athfal. Get ten men," he said.

"We have plenty of time," Arey said, as the subdirect trotted wearily up the hill. "We'll get your man, Peydan, to arrange your surrender."

"What surrender?"

"This one. Don't play any more games. We're some tired of all this. If your mother strews babies all around your pigyard, maybe you won't surrender. You've got men to squander. No need for it, though."

"We want to negotiate. Not surrender."

Arey turned. "All right. Sound the horn to form up the men. Bring that wheeled rifle up." He turned to Oberly again and said, "You. You'd better get up that hill. Never mind the ten men.

Your wounded'll just have to lie there. We'll wait until you're out of sight up there."

"No. Wait. All right. My terms are these. A truce. We keep—"

"You don't set any terms. We'll let Peydan do that."

"No. Don't. Keep him out of it. He'll . . ."

"Yes?"

"He'll talk the ears off a barn owl. He'll spend these men . . . the wounded . . ."

"You mean to give the other crowd a better chance to raid Turnat? No point to that. We've got that all taken care of."

Lieutenant Oberly looked crestfallen. "Even so. Better talk to me."

"That'll go hard with you later. He won't like it. Fine with me, though. I'll tell you my terms. You may keep one set of weapons in ten. We'll collect the wounded and help you with them. You'll have to eat downed horses for now. We don't have the food to give two hundred men. We—"

"Three hundred."

"Look around. We don't have the food. We have wounded of our own, and our own to feed. We'll need the two rifles back . . . the ones you recovered. We'll keep the cannon. We'll escort you back to your land and send ahead for food. Most of you. We'll keep about sixty to rebuild Ostag."

"No. We'll take them all."

"You agree to the other terms? Winnt, are you back there? Get a Pelbar guardsman to draw up a paper. Here, Atlan. Take him up behind you and get us a guardsman."

"Wait," Lieutenant Oberly said suddenly. They all paused and looked at him. "You agree to feed us? You agree that nobody will be left behind to rebuild Ostag?"

"You agree to the rest?"

The lieutenant paused a long moment, then said, "Yes."

"Winnt, get the guardsman. All right. We'll let you all crawl home." Arey turned and winked at the horsemen. He turned back. "Ah. Here. Your men for the wounded. Remember, young one. We didn't tell you about Peydan. Right?"

Oberly dropped his eyes. "Right," he murmured. "You guarantee our safety, then?"

"Don't worry. They didn't like it, but we got the Peshtak to promise. Not to torture you, I mean . . . Well, don't look that way. It was the Pelbar. We're all turning into Pelbar, looks like. In the old days I'd of sworn at you like the bloated blue salamanders of Koorb's caves. We're all getting very tame. But not too tame. Maybe not tame enough to pet." He laughed, then coughed. Then he turned and said, "Destri, you stay with this man. I have other things to check on. I'll come back for the signing."

The horsemen could see the smoke from Turnat's burning several ayas off. They had been too late. The young Peshtak rose wearily in his saddle and shaded his eyes. "The filthy pig's ear eaters," he spat out. "To come so far . . ."

"Too bad," Garet said through his teeth. "But it isn't over. This is the middle of a bad time. We'll be able to do some things. Look out for some of your own people who escaped. And for *them*. We'll have to move in closer. But walk now. The horses are spent."

At Turnat, Sharitan stood on a table to direct the destruction. From a hastily erected scaffold seven Peshtak men hung by the neck, swinging and turning in the cold wind. Others were lined up to take their turn. The center street was littered with bodies, some of women and children. The Innaniganis had set up a perimeter of men around the town, well out into the fields. Others stripped the harvest, packing what they could on drags and burning the rest. Near the trees the Innaniganis dug four graves, and nine wounded men lying in Peshtak fur blankets showed the invaders hadn't gotten off unscathed.

The Innaniganis were obviously spent. They chewed dry ears of maize as they stripped others and soaked them in pots over fires. Men threw in strips of dried squash, onions, and assorted seeds as others stirred. Those who could sprawled near the fires, some covered with furs and mats from Peshtak houses.

A subdirect, short and stocky, walked wearily to Sharitan's table and saluted, palm forward. "All the supplies are gathered, Lieutenant. This operation has been a complete success. We have enough to get us back. If we start in fifty sunspans, we can move a few ayas south to that stream valley and set up a camp."

"We're not going back, Upay."

"Not . . ."

"We stay here tonight and head northeast tomorrow, early. One more village there—Enult. Zard scouted it two years ago. If we don't hit it, they'll have raiders on our trail in a day or two. And they'll bring others."

"What about Eplay?"

"They'll have to hold out. I'm certain they will. The enemy didn't have that many men."

"What about food? Shelter?"

"They'll hang on until we get back. These scruff can't hold them. They've probably retaken our old supplies by now. Now, Upay, get Risan and have him direct the hanging and disposal of the enemy. I'll see to the supplies."

Sharitan leaned down and jumped to the ground, wincing slightly with his stiffness. Then he strode toward the piles of supplies his men had gathered. A man handed him a steaming cup of stew as he passed by. He held his hands around it, shivering a moment, then threw off the feeling. His raid had gone perfectly. Even though the Peshtak knew they were coming, they could do little about it. He had lost, including two killed on the trail, only six men, with nine wounded. Few of the Peshtak had escaped. He was sure to gain a promotion from this, even though the other force may well have been lost.

He had sent Zard back to scout out the results of that conflict. If he reported success, they would arrange to meet eastward because Eplay would have supplies. If they had failed, then there was no reason to return, and every reason to hurt the stinking Peshtak even more. Sharitan shivered again and glanced at the gray sky. If the weather would hold off . . . He turned and looked to the table where Risan was directing the hanging of the last four Peshtak, all old men.

Garet and his men stood on the ridge to the southwest, looking down on the scene. Icep, a wiry Shumai, had a firm grip on the young Peshtak, who was cursing in anguish.

"Let go," he said, without struggling. "I can at least distract them. Look. Look what the stinking snake sheddings are doing. Let go."

"We can do nothing," Garet said, at the same time drawing his rifle from its long boot.

"It's almost a half ayas," one of the men said. "You can't hit anything."

Garet snuggled in against a rock and muttered, "What would you call the wind, Kendo?"

"About ten ayas northwest. Remember the slope. Won't be so much down there."

They all held silent for a long moment as the far figures arranged their victims. Garet's rifle jumped with a roar. A man on a table raised his hand, staggered, then pitched off the table and lay like a rag on the ground. All the Shumai rode up onto the ridgetop and raised a long trilling yell, then wheeled back and disappeared down behind it.

Garet rubbed his rifle against his sleeve. "I don't know if that was smart or not," he said, shaking his head. "The men'll hang anyway." He stopped to reload. "We'll ride back southwest and rest the horses. Kendo, you keep watch. We'll relieve you in fifty sunwidths." They palmed.

"I'll stay, too," said the young Peshtak.

"So long as you don't run down there."

"I can't. My butt end is raw as an old sow's teat at weaning."

"Ah. Well, keep this up and it'll be as calloused as an Innanigani heart." Garet mounted his horse and urged it slowly after the others, thinking of the weariness of all they had to do, wondering how they would manage it. Still thinking, he reined in the horse. Then he turned and walked it back up the slope. Below he could see the easterners had all taken cover, except for a line of men facing the slope from the wood's edge.

"Arbin," he said to the young Peshtak. "I know you're tired. Is there anything at all left of you?"

The young man looked at him. "What?" he asked.

"The horses are near spent. We'll need them. Can't kill them. Can you . . ."

"Whatever, I will do it, Garet. Butt or no butt."

"This place you told me about—Enult?"

"A village. Like this one—a little smaller."

"How far?"

"Twenty-six ayas. Northeast."

"Can you go there? On foot? It's asking too much, I know, but—"

"I can. I'll tell them. They'll come."

"Wait. Not to come. I . . . what if this gang goes there next?"

"They . . . Fishguts! You think they will?"

"Nothing to stop them. Even with half the force. The other half could take the supplies south. They need to watch. And we can use some men to harass these. At night. From far off. To keep them tired. Until it snows. I feel a snow wind."

"I'll go. You'll be west?"

"Yes. With a watch here. Wait! Take your foodsack. No.

Really. Take it. Walk. They won't move tonight. Swing west. They'll have scouts out."

Arbin held up a palm, but Garet reached down and gave him a tight hug with one arm. "Aven go with you, Arbin." He then turned his horse away.

VI

"YOU just handed them the whole force—like that!" said Peydan, snapping his fingers. "The whole force, Lieutenant. If we ever get back, you'll have a lot to answer for."

"Exalt, I didn't hand them the whole force. We had half to start with. We'd lost over a hundred men by the time Eplay was killed. They had more men. They agreed to terms—to get us home. I signed. I gave you my copy. It seemed better than getting us all killed."

"Swine's breath!" Borund growled from his pallet. "When I think . . . of what you did, I can't believe . . . my whole insides feel like erupting right out of me."

"They're feeding the men. They've worked on the wounded."

"They're Peshtak and allies of the Peshtak."

"All right. It's done," Peydan said, waving his hand. "We'll sort it out. Borund, I might remind you, now that you are vituperating again, that none of this would have happened were it not for your overruling me. I can't believe Eplay split the force. That's what comes of having mud-sucking legislators and their relatives involved in the military."

"You'll sing a different tune when—"

Peydan made a sudden lunge, seized Borund by the shoulders, and said through his teeth, "Go ahead. One more threat. Just one more. I'd be very pleased to . . ."

The Peshtak guard took him by the hair and threw him backward on the ground. "Over there," he said. "If there's killing to be done, we'll do it."

"I'm sure you will," Peydan said.

"If it was me, we would. Have a pig roast of you. A little at a time. The soft-bellied Pelbar wouldn't like it. They haven't dealt with sore-running swine before."

"They've dealt with you, haven't they?"

The Peshtak smiled. "Looks as though they've done all right by us. Them and the others. Too bad for you. No more raiding. No more burned villages, broken promises and truces, robbing the miners, raped women."

"You! You talk about all that! You're defining yourselves," Borund spat out.

"Enough of this," said Peydan. "I wonder if you would see if I could talk to the one called Winnt? Please?"

"Winnt?"

"A Sentani. Older. Thin. Father of the man with the flag."

"Oh. Why?"

"I wish to. Isn't it a frequent custom to accord captive commanders some rights?"

"You never did. I'll see."

The Peshtak whistled, walked back from under the cloth fly, and talked to a Sentani, who glanced at the prisoners, then left.

It was dark in the woods as Arbin moved wearily toward Enult. Suddenly, as he stepped around a thick hemlock, something swept his legs together and snatched his whole body upward. He cried out, finding himself hanging in a noose trap, upside down, swinging. A shadow moved out to him and took him by the hair.

"What?" a voice said. "Who are you?"

Arbin sagged inwardly. "Arbin. Going to Enult. The Innaniganis have burned Turnat. I'm . . ."

"We know that. We're from there. What is this?"

"Let me down. Slow. I'm stiff enough without this. Careful. My leg."

On the ground, Arbin explained the situation to the four shadows who squatted around him. He ended by mentioning Garet's fear that the easterners might try to take Enult. "He even would prefer burning the town to their getting the supplies."

"Burn our own town! The freaking Pelbar may do that. Not us."

"What if they burn it for you? And take what they want?"

"We'll die preventing it. We'll take a big enough litter of them with us."

"Garet says we can harass them and let the winter eat them."

"Unless it eats us first. No. Oppose the filthy sowsuckers. Wound for wound. Arrow for arrow. Three for every one of us."

"Wait, Sistan. Is this freaking Garet worth all this? What is it about him?"

"He . . . I don't know. He sees things . . . big. He's fought before. His mother is . . ."

"His mother? A fishsucking Pelbar bigwoman?"

"Sistan. Let him. Listen, Arbin. What would he have us do?"

"Warn Enult first. Let them decide. He'd have us all harass the Innanigs, wear them down, let the winter take them when they decide to go home."

The group fell silent. Far off to the south they heard the tiny crack of a rifle shot, then heard it roll and fade from the surrounding hills.

"Keeping them awake," Arbin said. "You wouldn't believe that shot of Garet's. Kahdi is nearly as good."

"They'd better watch themselves. The Innanigs are all right in the freaking dark, too. Some. The harzas scouts."

"They'll watch. Now. We'll send you back. With Esul. The rest of us'll go to Enult. Bord must be there by now. We'll talk. Decide what to do. You think the Federation's force'll send anybody?"

"Don't know. They had almost four hundred men to fight. With not that many."

"But they had the animals and the rifles."

"And the Innanigani cannon."

"That piece of filth."

"The Innanigs killed about ten Shumai and their horses with it. With one blast."

"Huh. Never thought to hear of Shumai dying for us. That's filthy amazing. All right. Go now."

In the dark, among the flickering lights of the Heart River Federation camp, Peydan became aware of a shadow quietly emerging from the blackness into the firelight. It was Winnt, who looked at him, then squatted down. His right hand was thick with a bandage. He cradled it in the other.

"You are Winnt."

The Sentani made no reply.

"Look at Borund again, please."

Winnt glanced over at the sleeping Innanigani. "In the morning maybe," he said, and stood.

"Don't go. I . . . need to talk to you."

Winnt squatted down again.

"Your son. I'm sorry about your son. It . . . was an error. It should not have happened. You have to understand how it is with the Peshtak. How they've raided us, burning, pillaging, raping."

"Raping here?"

"No. It's been necessary to keep them driven back."

Winnt looked at him.

"How . . . what will become of us? Will you keep your bargain?"

"Bargain?"

"Your terms?"

"Yes. It depends."

"Depends?"

"On the other force. What they do. We won't free you here. If they come back. We'll have to be free to fight them."

"Then you'll kill us?"

"We'll probably try to talk. First." Winnt picked up a twig, bent it, and snapped it. "But they aren't coming back. Not now. They are still at Turnat."

"How? You can't know that now."

"We do. They may go on. They burned the village, killed everybody they could. Even hanged men by their necks to choke. Prisoners. Like you."

"You can't know that."

"We do. We won't do that to you, though. We'd be as bad as you. Might do it to some of them. When we take them."

"If you . . . " Peydan began, then found himself unable to continue.

"It'll snow by morning," Winnt said, standing. "I'm going to lower this fly some. Warm enough?"

"Not overly," said a voice from the shadows.

"Not overly, Oberly?" Winnt said with a whiff of amusement. Then he stooped and felt the man's face and the bonds on his hands. "That'll have to do. Get closer in together."

He finished his adjustments and stooped again near Peydan. "You'll have to understand one thing," he said. "We may well hang as many men as your other force did. From among them, though. You see, we can't allow your barbarism to continue.

Shooting unarmed flagbearers during an exchange. Hanging villagers you've captured. You have to see there are consequences. In the absence of agreements, that'll save lives in the long run."

"Do it. Do it if you wish. We'll be avenged. Remember that."

"You've been avenged. You like vengeance? Maybe the Peshtak do. We used to. Before the Pelbar alliance. The trouble with vengeance is there's never an end to it. Each act breeds the next act. Every time the avenger feels elated. He's inviting the death of others he loves, though. I wish I could convey to you how much better things have been since we gave it up. Until now. This isn't so good. You think it's good? Why don't you tell them when you get home? It doesn't have to be this way. Not at all. Hasn't been for us."

"You underestimate the power of the eastern cities."

"No. But I did underestimate your barbarism." Winnt stood and snugged his coat up around his neck. "Good night then, Exalt. Is that what they call you? We'll start walking tomorrow, I imagine." He turned away into the dark.

At Turnat a small circle of men huddled around a fire behind a hastily erected earthwork.

"You get wood this time, Mase."

"Not me," he said, laughing. "I don't want to get shot. I'd rather be cold. Tomorrow at least we'll freaking see them."

"Maybe. I hear tomorrow we're going north."

"North! No. We've got to relieve Eplay."

"Sharitan wants to raid another town."

"I've got a cousin with Eplay. What's he supposed to eat?"

"Birdbarf, Lasy. Snowflakes. Oak leaves. Shale. Dig for worms, maybe."

"Not funny, Mase."

"Really? Not funny, is it? Huh. Is that snow?"

"Freaking snow. What we really need."

"Don't know about you, but I'm getting some wood before it's all buried," a heavy man said. He peeked over the edge of the earthwork, squinting, then quickly rolled up over it and ran away in the dark.

"Just like Sharitan," said Mase. "Burn all the houses when we could sleep in them."

"Keeps you tough, sleeping out here. Wouldn't want you soft."

They heard quick footsteps, and the heavy soldier dumped a

load of wood over the edge of the earthwork. A rifle shot flashed out of the dark, and he cried out and fell over among the others, clutching his side. The others crowded around him as he writhed, panting and groaning.

Sharitan, in the center of the clearing, winced slightly at the shot, and at the sound's careening around the hills. "In the morning we'll send patrols. We'll keep ahead of them. Only a few now. We'll force the issue."

"The men are still tired, Lieutenant."

"They'll have to endure it. This is our chance to sting the snakes back."

"It's starting to snow."

"Then they'll leave tracks. Everybody knows where we are."

They heard the sound of running feet, then Zard stumbled, panting, into the middle of the group, squatting down behind the earth and logs. A man handed him a cup of hot stew. He cradled it, catching his breath, worn out completely. Finally he said, "All taken, Lieutenant. They've taken the whole force."

"Taken it? Killed?"

"No. It must have been a surrender. Couldn't get too close. Those Peshkies are patrolling."

"A surrender? Never. Never. You must be mistaken."

"No mistake, Lieutenant. Saw it. Them. Lined up. Guarded by the enemy."

"They had more sense. Nobody surrenders to Peshtak."

"Not Peshtak, Lieutenant. These others. Saw they were eating. Burying. Tending the wounded. Had to come. We could relieve them if we leave now and march south."

"They would only kill them all before freeing them. No. Tomorrow we burn Enult."

"We could split the force again," a subdirect called. "Then we could do both."

Sharitan flashed a look at him. "Never. Only a fool like Eplay would do that. We'll hit this Enult and make for home. We have to go back with the new weapons. Next time it'll be different. Maybe we can take another village or two on the way home."

"You're writing off the whole force? Just letting them go?"

"Me? No. They did it themselves. By their foolishness. Zard, are there any other villages to the east?"

Zard looked at him wearily. "No, Lieutenant. No. None. Only camps and fields. We've pushed them freaking back in the past. Sir, maybe volunteers could go to relieve Eplay."

"No. We stay together. Only a fool divides his force that way."

To the south Arey lay at his ease in a brush and canvas shelter as an old Sentani redressed his arm. Igant, the Peshtak's chief delegate to the Heart River Federation Convention the previous summer, squatted with him.

"I say we kill them all. They'll only be back, with others. With rifles. They'll find a way to make them even if we have recaptured the ones they took. They'll be even stronger. We know what they did at Turnat."

"We made an agreement, Igant. They signed it. We both have copies."

"Only words. Made to be burned."

"Not quite. We know even now what sticklers they are about law. They themselves'll argue about that one. They'll turn blue arguing over any minor point, Jestak says. They wouldn't acknowledge the messenger. Now they have signed a document of surrender. It says we exist. They'll have to deal with that."

"We'll have to bear the weight of them."

"Where are we? Look. I'm a thousand ayas from where I'd normally be. Some of us came here to stay. Our bones anyway. Come on, Igant. I won't say we won the battle for you—but all of us together did."

"You don't know them. They won't take this loss without wanting vengeance."

Arey watched the fire a long time. "Vengeance . . . Pity runs easily in the blood of a gentle heart, Ahroe says."

"Ahroe. She's a woman."

"And a good military commander. And Garet's mother."

"I can't sway you, then. What about this? Brand each one— a small brand on his hand—and warn them that if they come back and are captured, we won't hold them alive."

"Brand them?"

"With the touch of a hot iron."

"Will you settle for that, then?"

"Yeah. It's not fribbling much. But we will."

"All right. We'll tip an iron with their own star insignia. In the morning maybe." Arey held up his good palm, adding, "Wrong hand. Sorry."

The Sword of Forbearance 39

Igant smiled at him. "You won, of course. But thank you for the concession. Rest well."

As he turned and left, Arey looked at the old Sentani, who rolled his eyes upward just slightly.

 VII

IN the morning the prisoners had to break camp in a full hand span of wet snow, packing their gear on drags, shivering in the cold wind. Only then were they given hot hemlock tea and cups of porridge with horsemeat. One group had left earlier, under guard, and now another, also guarded, was to clean up.

The Innaniganis had no winter hats and mittens, and no proper shoes for snow. A detail of prisoners buttered grease on the boots of the others as they passed in a line, but it didn't help much.

The tracks of the advance party bore southeast, away from the line of march coming westward. Peydan mused that this might be an attempt to avoid the other force. Surely Winnt was wrong and Sharitan's men were coming to the rescue. Peydan looked over at Borund, swinging in a litter carried by four men. The observer's eyes seemed to have sunk with pain and shame, but he had looked better that morning when Winnt had dressed his leg.

At high sun they paused where a part of the advance detail had built a fire, heated more tea, and handed out flat cakes folded around a piece of meat, horse for the prisoners, something else for the westerners, Peydan noted. But he ate it with pleasure, and warmed his hands around the cup of tea.

By late afternoon they had made about twenty-three ayas. The men were worn out, grim, cold, and silent. When they caught up with the advance detail, they found the beginnings of a camp laid out on a field near the curve of a stream thick with hemlocks. The men had already felled several hemlocks for the brush and had made drags to clear the area of much of the snow. The prisoners were put to work finishing the camp. Some of them were gloomy and rebellious, but to stop moving meant to begin to shiver, so they kept busy. When the shelters were finished, with a double line of fires, and a supper of boiled grain and meat had been cooked in the Innaniganis' own pots, most of the men felt resigned and even strangely content. They were on their way home. The enemy was wary but not cruel.

In the dark, the Pelbar guardsmen sang hymns from the hill overlooking the camp as they buried two of the wounded prisoners, who had died during the day. The easterners were familiar with four-part harmonies, but not anything as involved and melodious as the Pelbar songs. The drifting voices, mingling with the snapping of the fires and wind in the weeds and branches, had a lulling effect. No one whispered of escape. There was nowhere to go, and even if they did make it out of the camp, they would leave tracks.

As evening fell to the northwest, Sharitan and his force looked down on Enult from a hill to its east. They counted fourteen hexagonal log houses along a central street. Each house had two log outbuildings behind it. At the north end a public building, slightly larger than the others, stood at the head of the street. Smoke rose lazily from six chimneys, but they could see no one in the streets, nor did lights show from cracks in the shuttered windows. A track worn through the snow led northwest. The Peshtak had evacuated.

"We might as well walk in," one subdirect said. "At least we'll have someplace warmer to sleep tonight. And out of reach of those weapons."

"If they're still here. We haven't been attacked since we left in the morning."

"Don't be so flipping sure," Sharitan said. "Something is going on here. You can wager on it. The Peshkies are bad enough, but with these others—we have to be careful. Zard, what do you think?"

The scout sat on the snow nearby and had to be shaken awake. "Huh? I'm faded out, Lieutenant. Haven't been paying attention."

Sharitan looked at him in the dim light, then turned away. "All right, tell the men to ready their weapons and we'll walk in. Spread out, four deep. No noise."

The easterners walked into the village, finding it deserted except for one thin dog, who ran away, tail down. The houses and outbuildings had been stripped of almost everything. But woodpiles lay stacked nearby. The fires were all still glowing, and over two of them pots of water hung steaming. The soldiers were overjoyed, and moved into the buildings without asking permission. The subdirects said nothing. Sharitan called a meeting.

"I'm more uneasy than ever," he began. "This was too easy. They stripped the houses but left us a place to sleep. We know the Peshtak reluctance to burn their own houses, but when have we ever left one standing? They have something nasty in mind. You can wager on it. Divide the supplies evenly among the houses and tents. We'll set tents against the houses, on alternate sides. The men can draw lots for who gets to stay in the houses. Set a double guard and change it often. Cook a light meal now. We'll eat more heavily in the morning. Zard, assign me two scouts and ten others to follow that trail for a couple of ayas. Where do you think it leads?"

"Don't know, Lieutenant. Out of here is all."

"Yes. All right. Let's get on with it."

The men settled down slowly, worn out with their walk in the snow. Some arguments flared over who got to stay in the houses, but these were quickly silenced by the subdirects. Sharitan seemed tireless, walking throughout Enult, checking on everything, stirring the sentries to wakefulness.

Some time passed before a soldier in the third house north, on the east side, thought to make more room by moving a water barrel toward the corner. The house erupted in a sudden roar, scattering logs and men up and out, raining pieces of both in a circle on the snow.

Men raced from the houses, some only partly clad, to claw through the wreckage for wounded. They found only two men alive. Both had been asleep in the corner opposite the blast. Both were seriously hurt. After torches had been brought and the area completely searched, the Innaniganis found they had lost nineteen men.

"All right," Sharitan shouted. "All you men. Pull out of the houses. Get your gear outside. We'll set up camp out in the field."

A general moan brought him into a rage. "You want to stay inside and get what those men did? We've lost nineteen men. You want to be next?"

"More like thirty-two," said a subdirect.

Sharitan whirled on him. "Who? Where?"

"The scouts should have been back by now," the man said.

"You don't know that!" he shouted back. "Now. Follow your orders. Get the gear. Outside! Outside!"

The weary men turned away to follow his command. As they were dragging things from the houses, another one roared up into the air. The men stood stunned, lethargic. Again they gathered the wounded, four this time, and counted the dead, six this time. The rest of the men didn't want to return for their gear. Sharitan had to order one man from each group to pass out the gear. No others were lost.

They built a large fire from remains of the shattered houses and a circle of smaller ones near it. As they were setting up tents, a rifle flashed on the hill to the west and another man dropped. Four more shots followed in quick succession, wounding two men and killing a third. The rest ran for refuge behind the east sides of the houses, but then a rifle shot flashed from the woods to the east, then another. One more man was hit.

Sharitan ordered out large patrols. The men reluctantly climbed the hills east and west of Enult, with an occasional rifle flash harrying them. They took and held the hilltops, with periodic reliefs, for the rest of the night, losing two more men to rifle fire. The rest slept fitfully in their tents.

Before sunrise, Sharitan assembled the men in the central street. "All right," he said. "We'll fire the houses and move out following the tracks northwest. They have women and children, and all the goods of a town. They can't have gotten very far. We can't give up now."

The men, even the subdirects, stood stolidly, staring at him. "Now!" he shouted. "Not after high sun."

"What sun?" a man said. "It's going to snow again."

"Who said that?" Sharitan yelled.

None of the men said anything. "Subdirects, do your duty," Sharitan shouted.

"It's no use, Lieutenant," Zard said. "We're about used up. If we stay around much longer, the Peshkies will be gathering. Who knows how many more Sentani and Shumai and Pelbar and who can freaking imagine what all else will gather? If we're going to survive at all, we'd better move our butts out of here. And it *is* going to snow again."

An older subdirect stepped forward. "It's like this, Lieutenant. We're losing men steadily. We don't have proper clothing. We don't know where we're going. Some of us have relatives with Eplay and think if we're going to fight, we ought to be trying to relieve them. No telling how they're being treated. Here we don't even see the enemy."

"Let me tell you something. We've always just toyed with the Peshtak. We haven't rooted them out. You're from the city, aren't you? I grew up on a farm. Until . . . that is, until the Peshtak butchers came. They burned the whole place. Killed my family. I watched it from where I was hid in an old well. I saw them do the usual to my mother and sister. I can still hear their shrieks. Not a night goes by that I don't. I vowed then that those butchers would never live any longer than I could help it. You saw me given proper command. I haven't given it over to anybody. We've destroyed one village. Another one is in our hands. We have the supplies from Turnat. You can't think they'll survive the winter without them. We've suffered losses. But so have they. If we can take out two or three more villages, we'll have done a good season's work. We'll . . ."

Behind a shale outcrop to the west, Garet was watching through a field telescope. "What's going on?" a young Peshtak asked.

"Don't know. I think they're arguing with the commander."

"Why don't you kill him? Think you can from here?"

"It's a long shot. But he's a hardhead. He's holding them to all this. If he holds them much longer, he may have a revolt. We don't have the men to attack them. I have a feeling . . ."

"Let them alone? To burn the houses?"

"They'll probably do that no matter what. It'll snow again soon. Where are they going to go from here? Can't see anywhere much. If I kill the commander, then they may march south and pick up the trail of the other force. They may make trouble there. We're better off if they stumble around here while our forces continue to gather until we can confront them. Maybe I can help him out a little. Hold the telescope. I'll try for the man he's fighting with."

Garet leaned the rifle against the rock and sighted a long time, scarcely breathing. Then he fired. Seconds later the subdirect fell in a heap. And those around him turned toward the shot. Some took cover, but a crowd bent low and ran toward Garet and his companion. Garet reloaded and shot one of the lead men, then he and the Peshtak ran to the horses, where two Shumai waited. Weapons ready, the four of them waited for the easterners to charge over the ridge, then, one at a time, they fired, dropping three more men and sending the rest to ground. At Garet's signal, his men mounted and rode off at a trot through the snow, listening to the shouting behind them.

Once the easterners had regrouped, after posting sentries in sheltered groups on the hills, Sharitan again commanded them to move out northwest, following the tracks of the villagers. The men gathered, with only the protest of their obvious reluctance. They fired the rest of the houses and outbuildings, threw trash in the wells, and headed slowly along the tracks of the fugitives from Enult.

Zard, still tired, hung back, using hand gestures to others from the Opwel draft, and as the column of easterners climbed over the ridge northwest of the village, they dropped away, trotting across the valley and straining hard up over the eastern ridge. Zard counted the men who had come with him—forty-two in all. He posted a sentry on the ridgetop and gathered the others.

"You'll think this is a rash and mutinous action," he began, "but I assure you it isn't. I'm nearly sure that trail will lead through the Maaldune marshes. I know I'd never convince Sharitan to turn away from them. That's where we'd be just plain helpless. This sort of expedition was never planned. Sharitan hopes to bring home a record that will excuse his reckless improvisations in the field. He even thinks he's cautious. There's no question that he convinced Eplay to divide the force. Now he's succeeding in killing it all off. I never minded accepting danger for Innanigan, but I have no intention of dying for a mere child of an officer. Are you with me?"

"You don't even have to ask," one man said. "But what are we going to say when we get back?"

"Blame it on me," Zard said. "I may take it very hard for this, but I'll take that chance. And I'll get you back home, if we're lucky. Let's hope the Peshkies are following Sharitan."

"Don't count on it," one man said. "They'll watch us as well. We're done geese unless we swivel our legs out of here."

"Horse coming," the sentry on the ridge called out. "He has a flag. Standing in the field."

The group climbed the hill and stared down. "It's the Pelbar guardsman," Zard said. "Met him before this whole thing started. All stay here. I'll go talk."

He loped stiffly down the hill through the snow to where Garet sat his horse waiting for him. Breathing hard, Zard came near and stood, legs apart. "Well, what's it going to be?" he asked.

Garet regarded him silently. "Had enough?" he asked.

"We're going home. Let us alone and we'll not give you any trouble."

"No you're not. Think you can burn a town like this and then walk away from it? You're going to stay and help rebuild it."

"Not likely. Let the Peshkies kill us off?"

"No choice. You broke away from the others. We have you outnumbered and outweaponed. Either you help or you die. That's all the choice you've got."

Zard unsheathed his belt knife with a quick sweep of his hand but found himself staring into the muzzle of Garet's rifle. "Hand it over," Garet growled. "Easy. You kill me and we'll fry you slow—maybe over one of those houses you fired. Make it last. You people must always break truces. Come to talk and then kill, huh? That's the way it is?"

"You call this a truce? What choice did you give us?"

"Of living. We're sick of this. Turn around, then. Go on up your hill. We'll wait until you rejoin your people. Then we're going to wipe you all out. This is your chance to surrender. There won't be another. We have things to do after we clean you up."

Zard paused, glanced at the trail the main force had followed, and handed over his knife.

"Now call your men down here," Garet said.

Zard turned and beckoned the others down. Garet dismounted and stood by him watching them come. "Don't forget," he said. "I'm not alone. Others are watching. We well realize that Aven will never let a man thrive who shuts his eyes when he should be looking."

"Meaning us, no doubt."

"Meaning Innanigan, I suppose."

"You . . . you aren't going, are you?"

"You mean are we leaving you with the Peshtak? No. Not yet."

"Not yet?"

"They aren't yet truly integrated into us. And they are justly furious. You've just burned them out."

"You'll protect us then?"

"Yes. Until you finish rebuilding and we send you home. Tell your men to lay down their weapons." Garet cocked his rifle and held it at ready.

Zard looked at him. "No need. We've seen it work. We'll play along." He advanced toward his men.

Meanwhile, Sharitan's men had come upon the remains of his advance scouts, all thirteen swinging from the ropes they had been hanged with. A soldier unpinned a note stuck to one of them and brought it to Sharitan, who read it to himself:

> This is fur the men you hangd at Turnat.
> You still ow us 8 men and we wil hang them to.

He crumpled it up without reading it to the others. Then he spat and gave commands to bury the dead men. They found, though, that they had no means of digging in the frozen earth and ended up taking the bodies to a rock outcrop and piling stones on them.

Sharitan watched the men quietly as they worked. Then he gathered them, posted sentries, and addressed them from a jutting rock near the burial. "Men, we leave here our faithful comrades, who died in obedience to the orders of Innanigan in protecting our borders and citizens from these barbarians. We must not feel frustration or futility in this. They have fulfilled their lives in a just cause. At this moment we are the westernmost guardians of true civilization in all of Urstadge. We are entering a dark time, in which we will be tested to the bone.

"We must meet that test if we are to survive as a culture and a city. After we follow the enemy and destroy him, we will return to our homes and duties knowing the joy of loyalty to our constitution, the legislature, our sacred honor, and our families. We will be back here without doubt, for there will be much to do in the future. Yet we will prevail. Never doubt it. While this rising tide of trouble has almost washed away our force, it would seem, yet it will ebb, and the sea-beaten rocks of our firm resolve once again emerge triumphant. Now let us devote ourselves, and all our remaining energy, to tracking down this enemy and avenging our companions."

A voice called out from the far edge of the body of men, "Have you seen the harzas tracks? Most of them are women and children."

"Who said that?" Sharitan shouted.

"I did," a tall, red-haired man replied, stepping forward.

"These are brave words, Lieutenant, but mostly hogwallow. Our enlistments ended five days ago and we want to go home."

"Seize that man!" Sharitan shouted to a subdirect.

The man turned and took the red-haired man by the arm.

"What have I done, Lieutenant?"

Sharitan was livid. He looked briefly at the loose ropes cast in the snow, then said in a level voice, "All right. Your enlistment is over. Go. Now. Back down the path." The man hesitated. "Subdirect, see that he goes. Watch him out of sight. You are no longer one of us. You are on your own."

"Give me my share of the food then," the man said.

"The food belongs to the soldiers. Go. Now!" Sharitan yelled.

Without another word the man turned and tramped off down the path they had just come up.

"All right, men. Forward," Sharitan called.

The trail led downhill toward a marsh, then turned along its edge, going north nearly four ayas. Then it struck out across the marsh, the drags of belongings sinking deep into the ooze in places, then mounting onto slight, dry rises and plunging back into the wetland. As the Innaniganis followed, their feet grew sodden and chilled. It began to snow. They came to a narrow, rickety bridge across a small stream.

At that point, a young subdirect called a halt and said, "Lieutenant, it seems to me we're getting into a trap. They could easily come behind us and destroy this bridge. Then we'd be at their mercy. I'd freaking well like to go back now. We know they're here. You've been in enough Peshtak traps before to filthy well know the signs. They aren't going to abandon their harzas women and children. And what about the horses and westerners? They've got to be around somewhere."

Sharitan turned on the man, but before he could say anything a rifle shot spat out from the distance, sounding strangely muffled in the falling snow, and the subdirect spun, staggered, and fell into the water. The men dragged him out, and Sharitan ordered him buried by the stream.

"A man who talks when he should keep his mouth shut will never get along," he said. "Fortune herself has ears."

The men grew even more sullen, but they followed orders and advanced across the bridge again sinking into the wintery bog. Moments later the advance men shouted that rising ground lay ahead, on the other side of another narrow bridge, but as the Innaniganis got nearer, they saw the bridge floor had been taken up, and on the other side of the sluggish water stood a rough-hewn barricade. As they pulled to a halt, rifle fire flashed from between the logs and several men fell. The others ran through the marsh as Sharitan and the remaining subdirects strove to halt them. Finally they drew up on one of the islands of higher ground. The snow fell harder, and afternoon began to wane. Sharitan ordered scouts out and commanded the rest of the men to set a camp. "If we're in a swamp, then the swamp will protect us tonight," he said. "It's just as hard for them as for us."

Two of the scouts returned to announce that the bridge behind them had been destroyed as well.

As night descended, the westerners under Arey showed no signs of halting the mass of prisoners moving southeastward. In fact, they lit torches and started up another very steep ridge. Peydan sought out Arey and protested.

The big Shumai looked down from his horse and said nothing.

"You're breaking your conditions to see us home safely," Peydan said. "The men are nearly destroyed with fatigue."

"It's going to snow. We'll rest tomorrow, probably," Arey replied, then touched his horse and moved off.

"Move on now," a Peshtak said to the exalt. "Move your hog bones."

Peydan ground his teeth in anger and stumbled up the hill.

It was well into the night when the crowd of captors and prisoners stumbled down a steep hill and found a flat shoulder on the side of it. They turned eastward, following the winding ancient road, then entered an ancient tunnel, partly collapsed, piercing a mountain. There the westerners already had fires built near the entrances. The prisoners sank down onto the damp floor until the westerners roused them, forming details to cook and gather wood and bedding. It was after high night before they settled down, prisoners in the middle, captors at both ends. Guards by the fires directed rotating squads of prisoners in drying their sodden boots near the fires.

Inside the tunnel, as he listened to a slow drip from the roof, Peydan settled down in a bed of hemlock boughs. A shadow came near and squatted by him. "We may be here a day or two," Arey said. "Looks like a heavy, wet snow. May turn to rain. No need to go out in it."

"What is this place?"

"It was part of an ancient road. Looks like it. The road was broken and ruined hundreds of years ago, of course, but it leads eastward, and they say it's easier than the raw woods."

Peydan mused a long time, then said, "It was worth it then, coming here. I thank you. I owe you an apology."

"No. It was a long pull. Didn't like it myself. Hard on the horses, too. Hope I can find another way back. Not used to these mountains."

"I don't understand—what you're doing here."

"I don't myself sometimes. But it has to be. We're all one people. Even yours. It may be your people and mine passed through this tunnel together so long ago. On those fast ancient vehicles. Besides . . ."

"Besides?"

"Something I hope you'll learn. It's easier joining up with the Peshtak than having them raid. They came as far as the Heart. You people pushed them out. Had to go somewhere. They aren't so bad. I could do without their shamans, but now the disease is gone, they've relaxed a whole lot. Used to be as snaky as a dried bull hide. Not any more. Not that way much at all."

"Much?"

"You'll find out about that part. You'll have to remember how it is to be a commander."

Arey rose and walked slowly among the sleeping men toward the tunnel entrance and the three fires there.

 VIII

As Arey had predicted, the night brought snow, then by midmorning of the next day, rain. In the tunnel the captors and prisoners settled down to a routine of waiting, combined with the necessary work of cooking, wood gathering, and other chores. The westerners seemed to stiffen their organization and regulation of the prisoners, refusing any interchange except what was correct and necessary.

Except for chores, the prisoners had little to do but watch the

Shumai play na na, their hands moving with remarkable speed as the chant picked up, always ending in shouts of laughter when one of the players finally missed the rhythm. The big, blond horsemen carried themselves with a cocky offhandedness. The Sentani, with their close-cropped hair and formal manners, seemed more withdrawn, though they incessantly played a board game with counters set in rows when they weren't working on their gear and weapons, which they kept in perfect order. The Pelbar were the handymen and coherers of the group, comparatively subdued, always busy, aware of the needs of everybody. The Peshtak, whose country this was, seemed somehow alien in it, silent, clannish, and wary, though shyly pleased to be with the other westerners. As Peydan found himself astonished to perceive, they were all, taken together, a single society in the process of being fused into a unified culture, each section different, yet each contributing something.

Toward evening of the first day of rain, Winnt made his way through the area of the prisoners to look once again at Borund's leg, bringing his old Sentani companion with hot water. He removed the dressings in silence, washed and checked the wound, and rebound it. Borund held his hands over his eyes, returning silence for silence. As Winnt finished, Mokil came and stood behind him, hands on his hips, watching.

"I know now," he said. "It's Stel's book, isn't it?"

"Let's not talk about it here," said Winnt softly.

"I can see it. It will destroy us," said Mokil.

"We all need what resources we have to deal with what we have to," Winnt said. "But let's not talk about it—not here, old starleader. Remember what the Pelbar did for me."

"Different. Huh. I remember. You think these people would rescue Northwall from the Tantal? Not worth a bull's hoof. They'd make stew out of somebody else's hide scrapings, then sell it to him as prime meat. You can see it. They don't even have respect for each other."

"You don't even know respect!" Borund spat. "You're nothing but a gang of dirt scratchers and murderers."

"Borund, if you don't mind," said Peydan. "The dirt scratcher has just worked on your leg."

"Don't have to any more," said Winnt, stretching. "It's pretty much all right." He turned to the lieutenant. "Hello, Odorly. You all right?"

"Yeah, Winnt. I see *you* are—as all right as a Sentani scraper can be," he replied with a smile.

"Lieutenant Oberly!" Borund called. "We'll see where you stand in Innanigan."

"Oh, I imagine we will," said Lieutenant Oberly. "They're going to love to know how you started a war all by yourself. Not many people can say that."

"Lieutenant!" Peydan said.

"Yes, Exalt?" Oberly was suddenly more sober.

"Hold your peace!"

"A good idea," Mokil said. "For all of you to learn. I hope there's some chance of it. I'd wanted to finish my years at Koorb. Lazing around. Fishing. Singing the great sagas. Dandling grandbabies."

"Where you going to get the grandbabies?" Winnt asked, grinning.

"Borrow some. I . . ." he began, then caught a look in Winnt's eyes and fell silent.

"It's all right," Winnt said. "Igna came as a soldier, and he took a soldier's death. Like so many. Atou gives us strength to see that."

"It was treachery," the old Sentani said.

"That, too. A part of war. This is war, isn't it, Overly?"

"Don't answer, Lieutenant!" Peydan said.

"Why not?" Mokil asked.

"Because where there is admitted war, there has to be a formal treaty of peace. That's not always simple. Sometimes things can be more easily settled."

"Ah," Winnt said. "I see. But peace is, after all, a state of mind."

"*That's* Stel's book," said Mokil. "Come on. We've been here too long." They sauntered away.

Watching the retreating Sentani, Oberly asked, "What in fortune's cards is Stel's book?"

"Who knows?" Peydan said. "Perhaps something we can turn to our advantage. They certainly are psychological simpletons. Full of fear and superstitions. I imagine the science of psychology is wholly lost to them."

To the northwest, in the Maaldune marshes, the snow had obscured the tracks of the fugitives from Enult, and the rain following it turned the already bleak campsite of Sharitan's force into soggy misery. The men had made hemlock shelters, but they were not keeping out the steady drip of frigid water. Smoky fires helped some, but fought with the damp, which prevented the men from drying their bodies and clothing. On the second morning, Sharitan reluctantly ordered a retreat through the marsh eastward.

The men's spirits lifted as it seemed evident they were at last going home. They had to ford the stream where the first bridge had been torn out behind them, and as the lead men waded up out of the water on the far side, they blew high into the air with a flashing roar and a shower of cold mud. Those behind looked across the stream at their broken comrades with dismay, until a subdirect shouted out, "Cross now, men, and charge ahead. If the enemy is there, let's take them on."

With trilling yells the body of men ran through the water and up into the bog beyond, continuing their run until they came to an island of higher ground. No enemy appeared. They paused, milling around, catching their breaths, but glad to be farther along. Sharitan had said nothing, but had waded through the water with the rest.

"All right, men, move it forward," he finally yelled, and the force again began to march, warmed by their run. Someone started singing, but after a few moments a single rifle shot, from far off, took him through the midsection and he pitched forward.

"Now there's an enemy!" the subdirect shouted. "Now. Move, men, in the direction of the shot." The force again began to stumble and trot through the bog hummocks and finally up out of the marshes altogether. The subdirect raised his cased bow and shrilled out a yell, twirling his body in a dance on the rising ground. He ran backward encouraging the men, then he, too, was blown into the rain-wet air by the last of the landmines the westerners had brought with them. He landed with a sodden thud. Three other men went down as well. Two lay still, the third, groaning, held his ears. The men close behind caught some of the blast, but were comparatively unhurt.

Sharitan came up and said, "All right, men. We'll carry these and put them with the scouts the skunks murdered. We'll stay off the trails all the way."

When the bodies had been covered with rock, Sharitan again called his force together. "Men of Innanigan," he began. "This may seem at first a defeat. Do not take it that way. We've learned. We'll be back. The might of Innanigan has driven the Peshtak and their scruffy friends back this far, and we'll continue. We'll spread our steel hand so far west they'll never come again. Now. It's time to march eastward, heads up. Think of it as a preparation for next year. This whole advance was not properly planned, but we have succeeded in engaging the enemy in force, and while Eplay met with a reverse, I'm certain he hurt them bad first. Now the citizens will be alerted and see the necessity of supporting—"

Sharitan's speech was chopped off by a rifle shot from far to the southeast.

The Innanigani lieutenant spun and dropped off the rock he had been standing on. "Thank fortune," said one man. "Let's bury him with the others. Who's left? Subdirect Kaynard? Looks like you're it. Let's go home."

"Me? Lollar, you take it. You've got more time in than I do."

"Not on your pig whistle, Kay. You're it. I suggest we blow out of here."

"We'll bury the lieutenant first."

"Pitch him on the rocks. He'll guard it all. It's blowing up cold. It'll freeze all this rain before long."

Not waiting for further orders, four men threw Sharitan's body on the rock pile and started walking eastward through the woods, shouting for the others. Kaynard looked at Lollar and shrugged. The whole crowd followed, shouldering their supplies.

Meanwhile, the red-haired soldier Sharitan had ordered to leave strode steadily eastward, several ayas ahead of the others, alone and scared. He shivered and looked for a rock shelter for a rest. As he walked, he gnawed dry corn from Enult. A farmer, he was not dismayed by the unbroken woods, but anxious to move away from the Peshtak. He was relieved to be far from Sharitan, whom he felt to be a madman.

The wind had turned northerly and cold. Before long, back in the Maaldune marshes, the standing water acquired needles of ice in the shallows, and these extended themselves outward to lace and join. The dripping rain slowed and congealed. The four bodies of the men killed by the third mine, which the Innaniganis had left behind by the stream in their haste, having given up their heat, slowly hardened like the mud they lay in, merging with it, a part of the marsh churned and smeared by the passage of the force.

* * *

About this time to the southeast, at the tunnel, the prisoners became aware of five Sentani, runners come from the west. The newcomers conferred with the westerners, and several Pelbar guardsmen set out at a trot. Soon a pack train of twelve horses arrived, with fifteen more Sentani on foot and four more people on horses. Two of them were women. Mokil went out and embraced them both, then Winnt embraced the younger one and held her a long time. Igant, the older Peshtak, also embraced the elder, and Arey, standing bemused, laughed and palmed her.

"What's all that?" Oberly asked.

"Women for the soldiers," Peydan remarked.

"No. Not those," said Oberly. "They're family or something. Ooo. Look at the young one."

"Traitor." Borund spat. "Pond scum, both of them."

"The one is a pond lily."

"May I remind you, young man, that they are the enemy?"

"Ah, Exalt, that one—that one. I wish all my enemies were like her."

"Be amused. She may be bringing your execution notice."

"They do have some kind of papers. *Hsst!* The Shumai's pointing this way."

"Patience. We'll learn—too soon, I imagine. That one is Pelbar. So we'll be seeing how the Pelbar governors operate. I hear they run this whole gang. She doesn't look easy, either."

The easterners had to wait while the new party settled themselves and had tea and cakes. It was blowing cold, and all of them warmed their hands around the mugs. Oberly watched with some impatience.

At last Peshtak guards separated the Innanigani officers from their men and walked them down the long tunnel some distance. The guards set log seats for them. Arey and a Peshtak guard brought the two women and Igant forward to seats facing the others. The elder woman seated herself and looked from one of the Innaniganis to another. She was very straight-backed, her hair black, but streaked with gray. Her high cheekbones modeled a face once obviously very lovely, but hardened and aged some with thought, care, and weather. She looked at them unsmilingly.

By her stood the younger woman, tall and slender, lightly freckled on her face, Sentani, carrying a shoulder bag with all the papers. Oberly saw grace like fire flow from her, brightening like the sky behind her head, which caught the straying hair below her cap and made it glow. Her eye swept over his, came back, and dropped to where her idle fingers rested on the band across her breast.

"Your name?" Oberly asked. She flashed a look at him. "I understand you've come through all that rain," he said. "I see you haven't melted, though." She moved away, glanced back. He grinned and said, "Don't go. Please. Stay."

The other woman coughed and, coming back to himself, Oberly saw Peydan glaring at him. He drew back and seated himself, looking at the Pelbar woman, who arranged herself and the young woman, then glanced at the easterners and cleared her throat.

"My name is Ahroe Westrun," she began. "I am a Pelbar from Pelbarigan, but empowered by the Heart River Federation to speak for us all. I take it you are Peydan, the commander of the invading force. And you must be the legislator, Borund, whom we have most directly to thank for this war."

"Conflict," Peydan said. "It is a conflict."

Ahroe regarded him silently.

"As I understand it, it doesn't matter what it is but what you call it." Arey chuckled. "If you call it a war, then it is more difficult to settle an end to it. Something to do with the arcane politics of the easterners."

"Oh," Ahroe said. "I see. I had heard that you cared more about words than essences. A common enough problem. I trust you can understand my dialect. Is it all right?"

"Difficult enough," Peydan said, "but we are used to provincial speech."

"Ah. If you eventually become less parochial, then you will learn a number of modes of speech and the superiorities of each. But to the purpose. We have been given to understand that you did not acknowledge our recent messenger, in fact grossly mistreated him and did not answer our inquiry as to your western border. Is that correct?"

"It is correct that we do not choose to inform you of our border," Borund growled.

"May we inquire why this is?"

"We see no need of it. Our western provinces are inhabited by savages, and we see no need to accord them any special consideration. They are there only because we have not chosen as yet to take possession of those lands."

"I see. Then any land to the west, inhabited by anyone, is to you simply . . . land not as yet inhabited by you?"

"I decline to answer that question."

Ahroe looked at Lieutenant Oberly, who stood back to the side. Oberly was looking at the younger woman, who sat busily writing down the conversation. Ahroe turned again to Borund. "And yet this young man signed a paper of surrender, which Arey has shown me. And such an agreement of necessity includes your acknowledgment of our existence as a legal body."

"He was not authorized to do that."

"Was he not the commanding officer of your army at the time, the others having been all killed or captured?"

"Our legislature would never agree to such a document, and so it would never have force for us."

"You mean our care of you, and our . . . returning you safe, mean nothing? We will keep our side of things, and you will then renounce your side?"

Borund said nothing.

"What should keep us, then, from lining you all up and killing you here so you, at least, will not invade us again? What, that is, but our own civilization, which would not permit such a thing? We are, I must point out, obviously able to defend ourselves."

"Now, perhaps. We Innanigani are a peaceful people, so far inclined only to defend ourselves. But we have seen your weapons and will be readily able to make our own and better them," said Exalt Peydan.

"No doubt," said Ahroe. "That has been our own experience in the last two decades. Ever since the Tantal invaded and laid siege to Northwall with their tube weapons, which they got, I take it, from you. I wish I could see the point in all this. It seems to make little sense."

"The superior never bows to the inferior," Borund said evenly.

"Superior in what way, Legislator?"

"In intellect, civilization, rule of law . . ."

"And numbers," Peydan added.

"That's a curious question," said Ahroe. "I'm glad you're so sure. I gather that your force here was about eight hundred men. No doubt all you could conveniently spare, without cutting deeply into your economy. You have about twenty-two thousand people?"

"You underestimate us. And there are Seligan and Baligan. You may have heard of them."

"Yes. About nine or ten thousand each. And not inclined to

make war on their neighbors. Not long ago the Peshtak mounted a force of about a thousand and invaded us with it. You see, we are involved. You cannot push from the east without pushing everyone west. I might remind you that the Peshtak have been hurt, but not eliminated as a culture or a military power, by your invasions or by our destruction of that invading force. You do not know how many Peshtak there are. Neither do we . . . nor do they themselves, living as they do in loosely knit groups scattered about these mountains. I suspect you have little realization of what power can be brought against you with a bit of organization.

"I must stress that we have no wish to do that. We would like to arrive at an agreement, even . . . an accommodation, if it comes to that. There are few people in this vast land. Surely there is room enough for all. We could gather all of the Federation in a single, small area if we wished to. You must see that we would all benefit from peace and tranquility. Other projects are far more worthy and interesting than war. Is this not so?"

"Every nation has its rights," Borund said.

"If it came to that, Legislator, we would have no trouble. The basic problem is that you will not acknowledge that we are a nation. You will not accord us even an eastern border. Is that not so?"

"I was speaking of our nation."

"No doubt. Are you at least willing to take the matter up seriously with your government?"

"I am the representative of the government, carrying their message to you."

"And that is it, then?"

"We have given our answer."

"Your answer is no answer. Even after what has happened here?"

"You will have our answer soon enough, but not in words."

"In more death, then? In explosions, and arrows, and knives, and misery? I wish I could understand your recalcitrance. Is it vaunted superiority? Pride, refusing to bow even to decency?"

"Our superiority is not vaunted. A simple visit to Innanigan would show even you that."

"And Commander Peydan—you agree to this?"

"He is the legislator. I am the soldier. I have been pained enough by his interference with my business not to interfere in his."

Ahroe looked at her nails, then over at Igant, who smiled grimly. "You were right," she said. "I would not have believed it. A people without a sense of honor or truth or justice. Only argument, conflict, and power. I see now how the ancients destroyed themselves, and I regret that some of that spirit has survived even now."

She turned to Oberly, who was looking at Ahroe's secretary. "You," she began. "You are the one who signed the agreement of surrender, are you not? Ah. I see we must digress. What is your name?"

"Lieutenant Oberly. I cannot answer your question. Borund speaks for us."

"But you did speak—at the surrender."

"I was the only one able to, being the chosen commander. That is no longer so."

"Yes. But I have digressed from my digression. Lieutenant Oberly, I failed to introduce my secretary. This is Miggi. She is Winnt's daughter and the sister of the flagbearer that your legislator ordered killed during an exchange of prisoners. Your face has fallen. Well, every act has some price, you must see."

"Ahroe," Miggi murmured.

The Pelbar guardchief grinned girlishly for a moment, then her serious face clouded back over her amusement. "Legislator. If my assistant makes a copy for each of us of what has been said here, will you sign each of them—provided you agree that the content is accurate?"

"Of course not. I will sign nothing."

Ahroe pursed her lips. "Then will you carry a copy to your legislature unsigned?"

"I see no need of it. I can tell them what happened."

"Your version. Lieutenant Oberly, if I can tear you away from your preoccupations . . ."

"Ahroe," Miggi murmured.

"Yes, Miggi. Lieutenant, I am making it a condition of your release that you agree to return a copy to the legislature. Will you accept that?"

"But we have an agreement which does not include that condition," Oberly said.

"Of course. But Borund here has renounced it. That means, of course, that we can set any conditions we want, doesn't it?"

Oberly dropped his eyes, then glanced at Peydan, who nodded almost imperceptibly. "All right. I agree to that," he said.

"I will have that agreement drawn up for both of us to sign— two copies. And you will see to it that this sanctimonious vulture does not prevent you?"

"I can do little or nothing to . . ." Oberly paused. "Yes, I will do all I can unless of course arrested."

"Which of course will occur, for your traitorous act," Borund said.

"Without which we would all be dead," said Peydan. "He will carry the message without your interference, Legislator, if I have to put the whole armed force to seeing it done. We wish to get out of here alive, and you are jeopardizing that eventuality."

Borund stared at him.

Ahroe smiled. "You are thinking, Legislator, that you will agree to anything here and have it your way when you get home? Well, of course we can do little to stop that, except one thing. We plan to announce to all your soldiers all that has transpired here. No. Don't object. I know they are loyal. And completely trustworthy. And they have no families. And they are deaf and dumb. And there is only one political party in Innanigan, and all are as recalcitrant as you. Correct?" She laughed in a silvery voice.

"Perhaps," she added, "we can have some tea together even though we cannot agree immediately. No, Miggi, don't leave yet. There is plenty of time to make the copies. Tea will do you good."

"Ahroe," Miggi murmured.

 IX

As Sharitan's force trailed eastward, trying to move beyond range of the westerners, the day waned, the wind rose, and bitter cold bit into the men like thorns. They found no sheltered place before nightfall, and finally settled for a hollow in the woods in which they built large fires in spite of their fear of the Peshtak and their allies.

Subdirect Kaynard set out sentries in twos on the hills around the camp, sending them stew when it was finally ready. They tried to dig ankleroot in the low, marshy center of the hollow, but the ground grew stone hard as they worked on it, so they got little.

On the ridgetop to the west, one of the sentries set down his mug of stew for a sunwidth or so, only to find it freezing over when he picked it up again. He scooped out what he could with his knife, cutting his lip while eating it. His companion had sat down to eat and seemed to be growing drowsy. He shook the man, saying, "Hey. Hey. None of that. You know what happens when people get sleepy in the cold."

"I'm not sleepy. Just resting here."

"Get up. Come on. Up. We got to walk. This is no party. This is enemy territory—a grave undertaking."

"You're worse than that bonehead Sharitan."

The standing guard jerked his companion to his feet and began marching him around a tree, counting steps.

The other man began to laugh. "We're supposed to guard. We're freaking announcing to them where we are."

"They're all harzas safe and snug someplace. Now. Walk."

They continued walking around the tree for a long time, fitfully joking about the lack of feeling in their feet, which, though their boots had frozen hard, were still damp from the Maaldune marshes. After a time they stopped for a rest and leaned on the tree, talking. One fell silent while the other talked on through strangely lethargic lips. Gradually it seemed less important to talk. He couldn't remember why he had been doing it. It wasn't so bad out here. Like home, behind the house, lying at length, listening to the summer insects grit out their tunes. There was no real worry. No Peshtak would be out on a night like this, cold to the marrow.

When their replacements came up the hill, they searched through the dark for some time, calling, before they found the two beneath the tree, frozen like memorial statues. The new sentries carried the others back to the fires and then refused to leave. Kaynard didn't argue very much. But as they discussed the matter, a rifle shot flashed in the distance. One man standing close to a fire cried out then pitched backward.

The others ran back out of the light and shivered there. They heard the soft call of an eared owl from the north, another answering on the south. One man ran out into the firelight shouting, "Come on ahead, you slimeskulls! Go ahead. Shoot. Get it over with." Three other men dragged him back away. But no more rifle shots came.

Lollar took his horn and called in all the sentries. Only four returned, slowly, from the north side of the hollow, limping on numb feet.

Behind them, well swathed in winter furs, Kendo and Garet watched from the hill. "I can hardly stand to do this," Garet said.

Kendo didn't reply.

"There are too many to cosy up to, though," Garet added. "If they got any ideas, we couldn't handle them."

"Even with the thirty-two new Peshtak and twenty-eight Sentani?"

"The Peshtak have no rifles, we are low on ammunition, and the Sentani added to what we've got still aren't enough. We've got no more than ninety-three. They're still over two hundred twenty, counting the men who must be freezing tonight. Not counting our prisoners."

"Well, then, we'll have to let the winter swallow 'em."

Garet stood silent a long time, then asked, "Will you be all right alone here? I'm going to get Zard."

"Zard?"

"Make an agreement. He leads them home if he agrees not to do any fighting or raiding on the way."

"He's Innanigani. Can you trust him?"

"I don't know. We'll see, I guess. He hasn't seen much of our strength anyhow."

"I'll be all right. You go."

"Kendo, you come, too. They aren't going to get away."

Kendo shivered then nodded. "I'm not going to argue with you," he said.

They slipped away along the slope, over the ridge, and walked a full ayas west in the next hollow to where the horses, blanket covered, were tied. The patient animals protested mildly, and walked stiffly through the dark, led by halter.

It was sunup before they reached the logging camp where the Innanigani captives were cutting and trimming trees for the new Enult. Morning fires were burning, and tea heating. The two led the horses to hemlock windbreaks and fed them ankleroot and dry grass gleaned from the marshes. Then they drank tea and ate cornmush, squatting near a fire where prisoners and westerners mingled freely, watched by a detail of guards.

Garet hunched with weariness, but he beckoned Zard over and motioned for him to sit. The Pelbar looked slyly at Kendo, who smiled slightly. Then he began, "Zard, that one, Lieutenant Sharitan, is dead. He led his force out into the Maaldune marshes, but we held him there. They are now retreating—going home, I think."

Zard looked at him but said nothing.

"They are poorly led, not well clothed, and ill provisioned."

"They're freezing, then."

"Yes."

"What are you going to do?"

Garet took up a stick in his mittened hand, flexed it, and laid it down again. "I don't know."

"Why are you telling me this?"

"There are too many for us. We can't really help them."

Zard looked at him. "You mean they'd kill you?"

"Yes. They might. I thought we'd let the winter destroy them, but now that it is happening, it is obviously not right. Would you . . ."

"Negotiate with them?"

"Lead them home. They seem to know little. We could probably find a wild cow and drag it in to them. They could eat it, dry what was left. It might help. I don't think this cold will last long—too early in the winter. Would you do that—with no tricks?"

Zard regarded Garet silently. "I can hardly do that—all the way," he said. "I left Sharitan's force and brought the men of the Opwel draft. We had a story all made up. I thought the others'd all be killed. When they get home, they'll tell what happened. I deserted when I saw you were killing anybody who might rival Sharitan. Letting him lead us in deeper."

"We were. We did."

"But you had no force."

"We could have destroyed the entire force. We still can. But only by harassing those men and letting the winter do most of the work. The Peshtak are gathering, though. If you don't leave, I promise you none of them'll make it."

Zard looked at the fire a long time, then took up the stick Garet had laid down, bent it until it snapped, and threw the pieces in the fire. "I'll do it—get them far enough to make it on their own. Then I'll have to get out. Come back here."

"Not back here."

"No?"

"Never. Never return to Peshtak country. Go somewhere else. Baligan maybe."

Zard looked at his hands, which were dirty and chapped. Then he put them back in his coat. "Baligan? That wouldn't be safe."

"Somewhere. Up to you. I can't think of anybody else but you."

One of the other prisoners, who was listening, said, "Better do it, Zard. It has to be done. We'll let them know you did what you had to—when we get back."

"If you get back."

"They'll get back," said Garet. "If I do."

Dawn came to what had been Sharitan's force with men rousing themselves slowly, wraithlike, to gather more wood. Some hobbled, some cried out that they couldn't walk at all. Other forms lay huddled together, wholly unmoving, no more to care about arctic wind and desolate woods, beyond conflict, beyond the slight warming of the slant sun on their gray faces. The wind still moaned high in the bare trees, which tossed their skeletal limbs stiffly, monotonously.

Kaynard gathered the men, counted them, and found that twenty-nine had frozen and thirty-two others could walk only with great pain. Others couldn't use their hands, and gray patches on noses and cheeks revealed more frostbite. The normally meek subdirect almost gave up, but he sighed and began a rigorous direction of the men.

Halfway to high sun Garet and Kahdi appeared with Zard, all on horses. They stopped outside the camp until Lollar walked out to them. Kahdi held his rifle. Garet had none.

"You surviving?" Zard asked.

"Not very well. You with them now?"

"They're letting me go to take you home. If we can make it. That all right?"

"I'm sure. It's too far, though. We've lost a lot of men already. Got any provisions?"

"No. They don't have much. They're hunting a wild cow for us. They'll bring it. Now. We'll have to move this camp to some better place. There's one south of here where we can wait out the cold spell."

"A lot of the men can't walk."

"Then we'll have to carry them. Bad? We may lose some more?"

"I . . . I don't know harzaz anything about that. I'm a shoemaker taken in the draft."

"All right. This one is going to stay with us if we can promise him safety. With his horse. His name is Garet. He's a Pelbar. His getting back is a condition for the release of much of the Opwel draft back there."

Lollar nodded to Garet. Kahdi took the reins of Zard's horse. The scout slid off as Kahdi backed away and turned his mount, then touched it into a trot. Zard looked at Garet, who said, "We'd better get started."

Arey's force, with its prisoners, stayed in the tunnel all day because of the bitter cold. Ahroe was restive, wanting to return west before the Oh River froze over. But the river was a good five days away, even with the ancient road to help. Nevertheless, she worked on the documents with Miggi's help, drawing them up and checking them with Igant and Arey.

The following morning the wind had died down. What breeze there was came from the southwest, bringing warmer air. Arey's men organized the prisoners and marched them out the east end of the tunnel, then formed them up into rows. Ahroe, sitting on her horse, addressed them, explaining her conversation with Borund and Peydan, and their responses. She showed them the document which recorded that conversation and discussed with them the fact that their representative had refused to acknowledge it as accurate. Then she paused and drew out another paper she had brought with her.

"This document is my main reason for coming all this way in this season," she began. "We have asked you for a statement of your western border, but your reply is, in essence, that you will not declare one, because all land west of you is yours to have when you choose to settle it. We cannot, of course, allow that. Your view that we are mere disposable savages is not one we can adopt. In fact it is historically absurd, because we know that one nation inhabited this whole section of land, from the Eastern Sea to the Shining Sea of the West, some three thousand ayas beyond you here. We all are the survivors of that one ancient nation, formed unhappily into separate societies.

"Therefore, we are here giving you our interpretation of the matter. We are declaring the eastern edge of the Heart River Federation to be the Leynap River, as far north as the border between the Long Lake Sentani and the city of Seligan, which has settled the issue with them. This gives you all the land that is traditionally yours, and enables the Peshtak to return to the land from which you have driven them.

"In return, we guarantee you that we will not permit any raiding across the Leynap. We invite you to trade with us. We reserve the right to use the western half of Leynap Bay as our path to the Eastern Sea, but we will not interfere with your use of any portion of that water.

"If you wish to negotiate these matters, we will certainly be willing to do so. However, if you insist on using our territory for raiding, we will be forced to defend ourselves, and in this eventuality, we shall of course not limit the fighting to our own land but will take it to yours if that seems the best way to handle the problem.

"Thus we will defend what is ours and not invade what is yours until some amicable arrangement can come about and we can become neighbors. I must add that we do not contemplate any union with your state at its present level of law and morality.

"As I leave you, may I wish you well and hope you have a safe journey home? I hope and trust that you will stay there. In order to insure that, we have decided to mark you all unmistakably, though slightly, and inform you now that we will not pardon and release you again if you invade our country, but will dispose of you. Thus our release is conditional on your promise not to return."

A murmur of fear and anger washed through the prisoners. They turned their heads and saw the nearby fire with irons in it, and began shouting protests. Then they watched as a gloved Peshtak brought a hot iron to Ahroe. She held up her hands and said, "We anticipated a protest. However, I propose to join you in this mark, in fact lead you, so you will see that if I, a mere woman, can bear it, surely you, the soldiers of Innanigan, will manage."

Ahroe held out her left hand, and the Peshtak gingerly touched the tip of the hot iron to its back, near the wrist. Ahroe winced slightly, then held up the hand and said, "See? Now I bear your insignia. I assume you are all able to bear it yourselves. Now again I bid you good-bye." She turned her horse and walked it back into the tunnel, as the westerners herded the lines of men toward the branding fire. They were still angry, but clearly Ahroe had disarmed them.

Lieutenant Oberly broke from his line. When a Peshtak stood across his path, he said, "I wish to speak to the Pelbar, Ahroe."

"Back in line."

A Pelbar guardsman stepped forward. "All right. I'll take him."

Back in the tunnel, Oberly found Ahroe grimly tying up her case of documents. "Does it hurt?" he asked.

"Of course."

"You didn't have to do that."

"You know I did. This is the wrong time for a rebellion."

"I'm sure your people could handle it."

"Yes. I'm sure they could."

"I wish to say good-bye to Miggi."

"No. She does not wish it."

"I . . . Why?"

"It is upsetting to her. You killed her brother, you know. During a truce. It has been hard for her."

"I? I have thought this whole invasion was a fool's parade from the beginning. I'm the 'traitor' who surrendered, remember?"

"Why did you come on the fool's parade in the first place?"

"I . . . never did that well in school. The family wanted me to be a lawyer. I thought guarding the river would be easy enough—an occasional raid. Never amounted to much. Then they began stepping it all up. Fools."

"Well, maybe you'll get out of it then."

"They'll boot me out now. I may be imprisoned."

Ahroe laughed ruefully. "Well, Oberly, you'd better go now. Get your mark. Under better circumstances . . . What?"

Lieutenant Oberly was staring over Ahroe's shoulder. She turned. Miggi stood there, slender in her furs, a braided belt cinched tightly round her waist. She held a travel flute, and as she faced him, both seemed frightened, paused, then traded stares before the easterner said, "Miggi, I have wished so much we met another way, but no one can avoid reality. What's done is done, and so I'll say good-bye—but let me add, nor am I made ashamed by this, you are more lovely, more the kind of woman

I've envisioned in my mind, than anyone I've known. You may have blamed me for your brother's loss. Could I replace his death with mine, that's something I would face with pleasure if it would remove your pain."

She paused, said, "Words won't bring him back again, nor any of the others. I wish no one's death. Now go away, back to your city. Invest your interest in more profitable dreams. I'm sorry. Why complicate things so?"

Ahroe put her arm around Oberly's shoulder and led him back toward the east end of the tunnel, then gave him to the guard with a final smile.

"I hope your hand doesn't hurt. Too much," he said.

"Soon you'll see how much," she replied. "Good-bye, then."

Turning back she found Miggi crying. "People don't say such things to me," she said.

"Most of them aren't as open as he is," said Ahroe. "Otherwise they would. They surely would, Miggi. Now, are you ready?"

The prisoners and their captors passed through another ancient tunnel not far to the east and followed the ancient road nearly all day, except for those places at which the whole configuration of the structure had gullied away or washed down a slope. They made nearly thirty ayas before stopping for the night.

The prisoners remained sullen and angry because of the branding, sometimes shouting insults and jibes at their captors, but none of the guards answered, not even the Peshtak. That night the prisoners were fed and ordered to construct a single large hemlock shelter, in which they all were to sleep. From inside they could hear the Pelbar singing their hymns, softly and melodically. Then the Peshtak sang some more earthy songs, this mingling with the Shumai na na games and Sentani music. Late at night they heard the shouts of the Shumai playing their star-naming game from outside the camp. Finally all fell silent, and those still awake could hear only the winter wind in the treetops and the hushing rumble of a rocky stream in the background.

They next day they walked on, turning southeastward after high sun to skirt around the dead land south of Tremai. When they came to the Cwanto, the westerners built rafts and ferried everything across the river, even though they worked at this until well after dark. Then they insisted that the prisoners build a hemlock shelter like that of the night before, though the weather had turned much milder.

A Peshtak hunter had killed a wild cow, which they dragged into camp, dressed, and cooked, giving each prisoner a thick piece of meat when all had finished working.

While he was still eating, Peydan looked up and found Winnt standing over him. The Sentani squatted down and asked, "You have some message system in Innanigan?"

"Message system?"

"We never really had one until the Federation. Just arranged signs the hunters would leave, or told people to pass things on, mostly. The Pelbar had their message birds and all. But now we have a Federation system for sending messages. You have that?"

"Why do you ask?"

"How will we communicate?"

"Is there a need to?"

Winnt regarded him with some disgust. "You still upset over your hand? You have to think about it. We're a Federation. We have to take everybody into account. All the wishes. It isn't so bad. Ahroe wears your emblem now. I'd be happy enough to wear the Sentani crossed snakes. A memory. It had to be done. Saved you some."

"Saved us?" Peydan frowned. "Oh. The Peshtak. I don't . . ."

"They used to torture us, you know. Like you if they captured you."

"You mean this is a symbolic torture, then. Huh. So they are satisfied? I . . . " Peydan raised his eyebrows. "You want to be allied to them?"

"Better than fighting. They aren't so bad. Good cooks. Good hunters. Some sturdy women, too."

"You like sturdy women?"

Winnt dropped his eyes. "If life is hard . . ."

Lieutenant Oberly, who was near, moved near and interrupted, saying, "Winnt."

"Yeah."

"You have a message system? Where is the east end?"

Winnt laughed. "You want to write to Miggi then? Leave Miggi alone. You're marked. You can't go west. She wouldn't want to live in Innanigan."

"How do you know?"

"She has more freedom. A greater hope of justice. Besides, you just saw her. What kind of a basis is—"

"You married a Pelbar, didn't you?"

"Mokil tell you that?" Winnt asked, slightly amused. "So you want to write Miggi? Well, we'll talk about it later."

"Be patient," Peydan said. "Innanigan is not powerless. We will rule all the area some day."

"Never," Winnt said. "You don't know the realities. Remember—if you somehow managed to conquer us, you couldn't hold us. We would have memories of ancient liberties to sustain us against you. There are only three ways you could handle the situation. The first would be to destroy us all. That might be possible, but impractical. It would gain you nothing. Besides, we have so much wilderness to flee into, and so many untapped allies, that it would all swallow you up. The second way is to send your representatives to live among us and administer things. Again the problem is too complex for you. The territory is too vast and communication too difficult with so few people. We would slip from your fingers like greased fish. The third way would be to send a ruler and let us live under our own laws and administration, which we are used to. What would that gain you? Taxes? Perhaps. But we are an energetic people and would soon throw you out. There would be more bloodshed, and much of it would be yours. Besides . . ."

Peydan had been regarding him with some astonishment. Now he said, "Yes?"

"If you settled among us, we would fuse into one people again, so it would not matter much who ran things. We would soon anyhow. We hear stories enough of your administrations, your laws, your squabbling, your attempts to run a society with fine nets of rules but no insistence on justice, no social pressure to do right, but only to win. I think many of your people would prefer our system and would flock to it."

Peydan smiled slightly. "Our system came down from that of the ancients, though we have weeded it out. It was enough to maintain a society vastly more complex than ours."

"And to allow its destruction."

"You will argue that forever," Lieutenant Oberly said. "Now, Winnt, where is the eastern end of your message system?"

Winnt laughed. "I'll describe it tomorrow," he said. "I'm too tired now." He rose and left.

"Oberly," Peydan said. "Here in the biggest mess Innanigan has been in in my memory, you're still thinking about the girl? How did you ever get to be an officer? It's beyond belief."

"We'll take care of that harzas detail when we get back," Borund rumbled.

"I simply saw the jewel in the mud," Oberly said. "You see only the mud."

The guards began to rouse the prisoners and herd them into the shelter. After they were bedded down, again they heard the Pelbar singers, and the Peshtak, mingling with the Sentani na na games. The camp quieted down sooner, though, and eventually only the star namers could be heard laughing and shouting from outside the camp. Finally the fires died down. The guards slipped away from the ends of the shelter, closing the brush doors. A single Sentani travel flute continued to play, but far off enough so as not to disturb the men. Eventually that too ceased.

When the light began to filter through the hemlock branches, and no guards roused them, the prisoners began to be alarmed. One parted the thick brush and looked out. "They're gone!" he shouted. "We're free."

Peydan rolled upright and shoved through the brush wall, calling behind him, "Oberly, form up the men and get a detail to look at our supplies. This may be some trick. Inventory the weapons. Now." He shaded his eyes back toward the Cwanto and saw one of the rafts caught in the shallows on the west bank. "Huh," he said to Oberly, who came up by him.

"Winnt didn't take my message," the lieutenant muttered. Then he looked at the exalt and said, "Don't say it. I'm going. Look. They left us the rest of the beef."

As Peydan organized his men, far northwest of him, the other Innanigani force lay in much sorrier shape. Garet had long since given up his furroll and traded his winter furs to men who needed them to shield their frostbite. He had helped to amputate toes and finger ends. He had fed stew to men whose hands were too swollen to hold a cup and had helped pile stones on others who had died.

He had shown them how to gather dry leaves and squirm in groups down into piles of them to sleep, how to snare rabbits, how to dig ankleroot in the cold, and how to lead the horse, dragging a travois with three frostbitten men on it. He taught them to drink tea or even hot water to put heat in their bodies, and he showed them how to weave rush mats to hold masses of leaves over them. He had helped Zard keep their spirits up and had even put an Innanigani arrow into a wild heifer from the back of his running horse.

The party moved eastward slowly, some days making only ten ayas, and winter now began to set in in earnest. Since Garet had joined Sharitan's force nine more men had died, but the remaining Innaniganis were healing slowly, eating better, and enjoying a freedom from fear.

But Garet was still worried. "Zard," he said one evening, "we're going to get a real snow soon—one that will lie a long time."

The eastern scout grunted noncommittally.

"Aren't your people sending out a relief force?"

"How would they find us?"

"The others must be back by now."

"Think so?"

"Must be. Think you should go on ahead and look for them?"

"Me? You know I can't."

"Want me to?"

"You? No. They might just kill you. Then the men from Opwel would never get home."

"You're worried, aren't you? About what they'll do about you."

Zard threw a twig in the fire. "I never should have pulled out. But that nether eye, Sharitan, had set out to be a hero and avenge his family. I was sure you'd have killed them all."

"I suppose we might have if he kept on. The Peshtak would have formed a big enough party."

"What if they catch us now?"

"They've been behind us for three days now."

Zard jumped up and looked out into the dark. "What?"

"Only a few, I think. Watching. I think they are watching out for me."

"You've seen them?"

"They let me. For reassurance, I think. Don't worry."

"Wonderful. Just when I needed some sleep. How do you know you can trust them?"

Garet laughed. "My father showed them how to burn down the Tantal city of Ginesh and free a big body of Peshtak the Tantal had enslaved. They made the bad mistake of running across my little sister and stealing her."

Zard stared at him. "What?" he said.

Garet told him the story of Stel Westrun's trip to Ginesh and its aftermath. Before he was well into it, a number of the men had gathered around him to listen.

When he had finished, one of them said, "How much did you add to that?"

"Nothing."

"The ships, then. We'd heard of them but hadn't believed it."

"From the Tantal? I suppose you would. They must have settled with you."

"Most of them are at Seligan. We got a few."

"You'd better watch them. Nasty people."

"If we said the same about the Peshtak, would you believe it?"

"Not now." Garet laughed again. His big bay, hearing the tanwolves in the distance, nickered slightly and moved in closer among the men. They had grown used to her. One rubbed her nose. She butted him lightly with her muzzle and reached toward his pocket looking for a treat. The man laughed and reached up to rub her ears.

"I smell snow again," said Garet. "How far to the Cwanto?"

"About twenty-two ayas now," said Zard. "A hard march tomorrow for these invalids, and we should be there. Just north of Tremai."

But they didn't make it the next day. A number of the men were ill, and walked slowly, and Zard wanted to stop early to build more elaborate shelters because the raw wind continued to bear signs of snow.

That night, as they lay together snugged down in leaves, under a thick shelter of hemlock boughs, Garet suddenly sat up, listening.

"What?" the man next to him muttered.

Garet was silent a long time. Another man turned to look at him, but could see nothing in the dark. "Lie down, Pelbar," he said. "You're making it cold."

Garet grunted and lay down but stayed awake a long time, listening to the tanwolves howling. It was different. He knew more Peshtak lingered behind them, and had spread out, but now he sensed in the wolves' voices some people ahead as well. He hoped they were on the other side of the Cwanto.

Garet rose early and stirred up the fires. The first flakes of snow drifted lazily down through the bare twigs. Zard came beside him. "Only three ayas or so to the river now," he said.

"We should cross it this morning—if we can. We may have to build rafts."

"Where is this Tremai from here?"

"South. About eight or nine ayas south of where we'll cross, I judge it."

After they ate, Garet put the weak man who was wearing his fur coat on the horse, and got another man to take the bridle and walk ahead. A third man walked beside him to be sure he stayed in the saddle. He asked others to drag the travois, saying the horse was weary, hungry, and footsore, and would give out if overworked.

He himself helped with one of the drags, lagging back as they always did, because of the brush and the weight. The snow seemed in no hurry, but continued to drift down, flake by flake, on a chill wind.

Someone passed the shout back that they saw the river ahead, and the whole force began angling down a gully to get to it, when suddenly three arrows went through the man on Garet's bay horse, and an Innanigani horn sounded. In an instant Garet dropped the drag and ran west past the last few stragglers and back up the path they had come. Looking over his shoulder, he saw no one pursuing. He stopped and sent back a long, clear whistle.

His horse jerked free from the milling confusion around the struck man and set out after him at a gallop. "Catch him," one man shouted.

But already the horse was off at a run, flashing by the stragglers. Garet whistled again and the bay came up to him. Garet caught the bridle, ran alongside, and swung up into the saddle, cantering away from the shouting behind him, then slowing to a trot when he was well away, scanning the woods for the Peshtak. One waved, and he turned his horse toward the man.

Far behind, an Innanigani lieutenant in winter uniform came up to the crowd around the dead man. "You're safe now," he said, grinning. "Borund sent out a whole fan of patrols. That's the last of the Peshtak scum around. We've got plenty of food and blankets."

"That's Unfor, from the Runswik draft, you idiotic sow-swiller," Zard said. "The Peshtak scum—or rather Garet the Pelbar—gave him his winter coat because of his frostbite."

"Well, he won't harzas need it any more now," a man said from one of the drags. "How about giving it to me?"

"No good," another called from the center of the circle of men. "It's all cut through and soaked with blood."

"Fortune! If I ever get back to Innanigan, I'm never going to leave."

"Hey, easy now," the lieutenant said. "We'll have some order here now. Form up and let's move out of here to some place we can defend."

"All right, men," Subdirect Lollar shouted. "We're forming up and moving out to someplace we can defend."

Several men laughed. "Lieutenant," one shouted. "Bring any cookies? I need a cookie." More laughed, and the subdirect from the relief force sounded the horn for order again and again.

 X

THE ancient stone Judgment Room at Pelbarigan was crowded with an assembly containing not only the full city council, but a body of representatives from the ministry as well. Flanked by two guardsmen, Alance, the Protector, sat on the dais. All bowed in silence as the sun-light slanting through the window moved slowly across the marks on the floor, timing out the opening prayer. Finally the senior guardsman rapped the heel of his short-sword on the table announcing prayer's end.

The chamber stirred. Alance cleared her throat. "We are here, as you all know, to settle the present vexed matter of Stel's old book. As I understand it, there is even difference of opinion on the matter among the ministry itself. Is that correct?"

Dessic, a tall elderly minister, stood. "Protector, I wish to speak to that."

"Yes, Dessic. Speak."

"Protector, while we must acknowledge some dissension among us, it would hardly be accurate to call it a difference of opinion. It is probably more a generally accepted view with some variations."

"I protest that characterization, Protector," a younger woman said.

"All in good time, Isend. Now, Dessic, would you summarize the problem from your point of view?"

"It is the heretical book, Protector. The one Stel brought with him from Ginesh. He claims it is an ancient scripture, and he and his friends are making copies as rapidly as then can. It bears some resemblances to the writings of Pel, though it has corruptions, and it is through these corruptions that it is undermining the authority and piety of our practice. It's a terribly mixed book, with some violence and horror, and some rather interesting and useful moral instruction. Its inspirational character seems wholly reckless, advocating a reliance on deific help wholly beyond prudence, ignoring entirely Pel's axiom that prayer is an aid but operates always in accord with practical considerations, being, as it is in part, a discovery of the natural logic of things. One does not start a long winter journey without supplies and then pray for them. And it is, as one might expect from a heresy, dominated by males."

"Ah. Can you give us an example of some of the things in it you find objectionable, Dessic?"

"They are myriad, Protector. But let me simply read a corrupt version of a familiar Pel text. Stel's heresy puts it this way: 'Let wives be subject in everything to their husbands.'" A general murmur drifted through the room.

"The book is often self-contradictory, as well, Protector. For example, in one place it says, 'I make weal and create woe, I am the Lord, who do all these things.' By the Lord it means Aven. Then later it says of this Lord, 'Thou who art of purer eyes than to behold evil and canst not look on wrong.' That seems to mean that Aven can't see evil, which elsewhere it says She created it in creating woe."

"Ah. And what does Stel say of those things?"

"Not much, Protector. He sees it like a net in the river, drawing up some valuable things, some to be thrown back. He's not concerned at all with the welter of confusions he is dumping into Pelbar worship, which has the virtues of clarity and consistency."

"And limitation and domination," Isend said, "begging your pardon, Protector."

"You will have your opportunity to speak provided you do not interrupt someone who has the floor, Isend."

"Yes. I regret it, Protector."

"Protector," Dessic continued, "in Stel's book, the central teachings of Pel are garbled and placed in the mouth of a man who is supposed to have been killed and returned to life again."

"Perhaps he is a metaphor, Dessic, the way an idea may be forgotten, but when remembered, comes with all the power of its truth."

"Not so, judging from the latter part of the text, Protector. And from it we see traces of the pernicious practices growing among some of our distant friends, the Atherers, who now find complete submersion in water as necessary to goodness, and threaten a terrible afterlife to all who disagree."

"As I have heard it, Dessic, that is only one opinion among them."

"Yes, Protector, but one causing great dissent among a formerly united people, some good people claiming to be the only just ones and rejecting the true friendship of the others."

"Ah, Dessic, if this is something to deplore, then why do we have these proceedings? Is that not what you are doing?"

"Not really, Protector. They are basing their odd views on this wholly strange and jumbled book, and not on good sense, charity, and the solid tradition which underlies Pelbar scripture."

"May I speak to that, Protector?"

"Will you yield to Isend, Dessic?"

"If you wish, Protector."

"Proceed, Isend."

"It is precisely this point that seems to some of us vitally important, Protector. Looking at this text, and the writings of Pel, and even some of Ollo, it seems very clear that the Pelbar tradition started in Stel's book, but was pared down and reedited by Pel to conform to her views. Thus if there is any authority in the writings of Pel, it may truly be traced back to the older and fuller book. We appreciate the fact that Pel did a masterful job of editing and producing consistency, and that her text has served us for many hundreds of years, but nonetheless, it is surely derivative, and we do not see what harm can come from having, at last, the source text that hers has come from. Furthermore, Stel's text is sometimes like lightning in its depth of insight and purity of expression. Pel's book is remarkably limited in scope and grasp by comparison."

A gasp rose from some of the council members at this point, and the Protector raised her hand to still it.

"Protector, it is precisely the loss of that consistency that will bring us such great harm," Dessic rejoined. "The leadership of woman, which Pel proclaimed, has not only ordered Pelbar society but has been an obvious help to the peace of an entire region, smoothing our relations first with the outside tribes, now with the Federation. If we lose the consistency, we lose our nurturing influence."

"And yet it may be based on a falsity, Protector."

"Only," Dessic countered, "if you assume that there was some prophetic authority in the writers of Stel's book but not in Pel. We have long taken Pel to have been a prophet, and her accomplishments seem amply to have justified that characterization."

"Protector, I do not contend against that point, but only feel that an attempt to suppress Stel's book arises from a fear that our minds must be directed by others and are not to be free to see for ourselves."

"But, Protector, no society constituted as ours has been for so long can really permit subversive inquiry like that," said Dessic. "We must have the unity of order."

"That may have been true of the old days, when we were locked away from all other peoples, Protector. But it is no longer true. Now ideas roam as freely as the migrating geese, and cannot be walled out except by control and oppression."

The debate continued in mild but definite tones for some time, the full council listening and eventually questioning both parties. Dessic read a passage from Stel's book that advocated and praised the total massacre of an entire city, and even of its domestic animals, as something pleasing to Aven, though the action seemed clearly one of tribal conquest by a marauder. "Such a passage," she remarked, "could just as well be taken as proposing to justify the overcoming of Northwall by the Tantal when I was a child. I cannot see such material as worthy of theological study."

The council itself took up the debate, and added to it the present conflict in the east with the Innanigani invading force and the weakening effect that strong internal dissension might have on it.

Eventually, as the winter sun turned the western sky into a brief, dull red in its cold lapse into twilight, Alance called for a recess until the first quarter of night, charging the body to ponder carefully what they had heard. "The decision, it would appear, is mine. I dread it, and am going to ask for an advisory vote first, the results of which only I will know. I invite the

voters to include position statements with their votes. I will
ponder the matter and give you my conclusions in the morning."
The guardsmen by her sides rapped their staves on the floor, and
all stood while the Protector retired to her private chamber, with
only one slightly whimsical backward glance.

The rest of the council members filed out with an extraordinary silence.

After the evening session, which was short and largely taken
up with the vote, the Protector again retired, calling for her
attendant to bring a pot of tea. The assembly watched her go
gravely, knowing that she would occupy much or all of the night
pondering her decision. They knew also that not only the immediate city of Pelbarigan would be deeply affected by her conclusion, but the relation of the city to the Federation would also
be altered. It was a serious time.

Alance was a fairly young Protector, elected only that summer
to replace Sagan, the mother of Stel, who had precipitated the
crisis by bringing the book back from his expedition to the north
and east.

Leaning her head on her hand, Alance first read over all the
opinions, laying them on the plain wood table between two oil
lamps. Then she reread them, smiling to herself as she recognized
the personalities of their writers, as well as their handwriting at
times. Then she took the vote statements and split them into two
piles, woefully noting that they were nearly equal in number.
Taking each pile, she sorted it on the basis of whether the replies
were thoughtful or merely prejudicial. Again she noted the rel-
atively even weight of the results. Making one pile again, she
sorted the replies according to whether she felt them progressive
or traditional, reading very carefully, and found an entirely different mix.

Rising, she stood by the window and looked out at the night
for a long time. Across the river she saw a light in the window
of one of the Shumai houses that had lately sprung up there.
Perhaps a birth kept the family up so far past high night.

Then she sat again and sorted the votes once more into those
that had religious concerns and those that had libertarian or
political ones. Her eyes glazed over, the pages before them
hazing and blurring. She left the table and sat for a time in the
easy chair near the window, but feeling the chill of the stone,
she stood, paced, and eventually opened the door to the Judgment
Room, which lay wholly dark except for slight ribs of light from

its tall, slender windows. She grated back the Protector's chair and sat in it, gazing out into the well of darkness so full of life the previous day.

When she finally retired again to the Protector's chamber, she saw the fire had been tended and fresh tea placed on the grate. She stood by the window and watched the stars grow pale with morning, then turned and sat down to write her decision, marking out the letters in firm strokes of her goose quill pen, as though she could be made more certain by the wide flows of ink. When she was done, she went to the window and read her words by the coming light of day. She took the paper to the fire and reached it out toward the flame, then drew it back and slipped it into the drawer in her plain table. She sighed and left by a side door for a little rest before the meeting.

The Judgment Room filled again at the third quarter before high sun, the tiers of seats making neat rows of maroon winter dresses and piled hairdos. All faces turned to Alance as she entered, sat, and ordered the opening prayer.

The silence of the prayer persisted after it was completed, and Alance looked around at the grave faces of her fellows with a slight internal tremor. She raised her hand, though the room was already plunged in stillness. "As you well know, I have pondered your collective comments on this matter with all the care that time has allowed. I was startled to see how deeply this new book has cut into our religious life, and how disruptive it has proved to be. However, I am also aware of the passion with which some people are reading the book, and how much of real use they are finding in it.

"Pelbarigan as a city and a society has been built on long traditions of unity and order. Northwall has departed from those traditions and found what has seemed to them a successful compromise with the views of the other peoples. Threerivers, as you well know, has ceased to exist as a typical Pelbar city, and is now wholly reconstituted as a mixed society, devoted to trade, manufacture, and especially now the providing of services to the Federation governmental proceedings. Only Pelbarigan remains, as a city within walls, governed in more or less the traditional manner, even though we too have seen a great many changes.

"Somewhere, Pelbar society needs to have an anchor, and it seems to me that the religious practice of Pelbarigan might, for a time, be braced up by the decision I have made here. Yet I hope it will not be seen as arbitrary for those of other views, and that their needs will be met as well. Therefore, I have composed the following directive, which I shall read to you:

"'I, Alance, Protector of Pelbarigan, in response to the advisory votes of the council, decree that for a period of two years from this date, no copies of the Tantal book brought to this community recently by Stel Westrun be in general circulation; that no further copies of the book be made; that the copies presently in circulation be gathered and kept for their owners by the ministers of the city, who will be responsible for their care and safety; that those wishing to read the Tantal book be permitted to provided this is undertaken under the direction of the ministers, in the city library, and in conjunction with religious teaching by those ministers.

"'I direct that in two years from this date the question shall once again be raised in this chamber and decided once more, assuming the conflict with the East shall be at an end and time for sober reflection shall have ordered and informed our reaction to these new ideas. I order the guardsmen to proceed immediately to collect the existing copies of the Tantal book and further order complete cooperation with the guardsmen on the part of the citizens. Thus shall we hold fast to the good we have and yet not oppress those among us who wish to inquire into these new doctrines.'"

Alance laid down the directive and rose. "This meeting is at an end. May I request two sunwidths of silence before our departure from the Judgment Room." She herself spun and entered the Protector's chamber, the door shutting with a deep and hollow knock. The council members stared at each other. Then the senior guardsman set the timer. As the sun moved across the floor, with infinite slowness, a slight and increasing restlessness began to pervade the room, and when the guardsman signaled the end of the silence, the room emptied with astonishing swiftness, the counsellors' voices rising in debate when they reached the halls.

After high sun, Raydi looked out the window of the Westrun cottage, which stood on the bluffs outside the city walls, and remarked to her father, "Someone's coming. Guardsmen."

"Guardsmen?" Stel looked up from his reading, his eyes swimming out of their concentration.

"Five of them. Coming here, Father."

Stel rose and came to the window as the maroon-clad men reached the terrace and strode across it. They knocked before

Stel could reach the door. He opened it and stood in it. "What?" he asked.

"Ah, Stel. May we come in?"

"Something's wrong? Is it Ahroe? Is—"

"We have come to collect your copies of the Tantal book. Protector's orders."

"My . . ." Stel began, stopping. He gripped the door frame. "Just like that? My copies of the book?"

"They will be kept safe for two—"

Stel turned slowly, then slammed the door and bolted it and ran through the room yelling, "Come on, Raydi! Quick." The guardsmen were already pounding as the two vanished into the back room.

"I thought as much. You two, take the sides. Rulf, take the back." The guardsmen deployed as the guardcaptain pounded on the door with the hilt of his short-sword. There was no answer. He peered in the window, seeing only a sparsely furnished sitting room with papers strewn around it. He tried the window and found it open, then eased in, went to the door and unbarred it. The two guardsmen searched the house and came up with some partial copies of the book, but no original. They could not discover where Stel and Raydi had gone.

They stepped outside, and the guardcaptain called the three standing outside. As he turned, Stel came and stood in the door. He held out a copy of the Tantal book, saying, "Here, Guardcaptain. For you. My copy. I would like a receipt, please."

The guardcaptain looked at him, took the book, riffled through it, and remarked, "Stel, we know you've done a great deal for this city. We don't want any trouble. We suspect you have other copies. We would like them as well."

"You are welcome to search the house, guardsmen. Raydi is preparing you some tea."

"No tea. Just the copies."

"What about the receipt for this one?"

"No receipts. The ministers will keep them. They'll give a receipt."

"Wonderful. It's as good as gone then. Why not burn it here? Use it to start fires. Make a net weight of it. An anchor. Or stuffing for the cracks of stonework."

"They are enjoined to protect all copies for two years, when the matter will again be taken up by the council."

"At which time they will be enjoined by all those hickory-nut brains to pickle all the copies in a barrel and lose it in the river."

"You'd better come with us, Stel. I see trouble here. Too bad, but we will have order."

"No tea?"

"Funny. Come."

"A moment." Stel turned. "Raydi," he called, then added, "You'd better go down to Aintre's, Pumpkin. Don't know how long this tangle will take to unsnarl."

Raydi appeared in the door to the kitchen, her mouth hard. "Father, come back soon," she murmured. "I don't want—"

"To Aintre's, Pumpkin. With Garet gone, she can use the company. But not of such a clamped mouth. Give us a toothy smile, child." Stel laughed, but Raydi caught the mirthless quality of it.

"Father," she said. He looked at her. "All right. I'll go."

"All right, Guardcaptor, do your worst," Stel said.

"Be decent, Stel. At least try."

That evening, after the guardchief had questioned Stel, he was brought before the Protector and an abbreviated council. Alance was still weary from the previous night's vigil, and slightly short-tempered. Stel continued to maintain that no copies of the ancient book remained in his house and that he had not been hiding them after the guardsmen arrived.

"How do you explain your behavior, then?" the Protector said, sighing.

"Merely a deception, to throw you off the scent, Protector. A decoy. A ploy. I enjoy befuddling oppressors. You may search my house till the geese fly north if you wish. I give it up to you for searching."

"Perhaps we should take the house apart, stone by stone, Protector," the Northcounsel remarked. "We know he has odd passages in it."

"You might do that," said Stel. "But remember it is also Ahroe's house, and she is absent on a diplomatic mission. I'm sure she would not be overjoyed to find a pile of rocks for a house when she returned."

"Stel," said Alance. "I am tired of this. I know you have done many good things for this city. But this time you have done a very bad one in the eyes of many of us. We know you have been copying the Tantal book. I am beyond patience. You are right that Ahroe does not deserve to find her house destroyed. So you may simply await her return imprisoned. She will let us know of any hiding places we could not find. Guardsmen, take Stel to the detention chambers. Stel, if you change your mind, you may let us know." Alance rose.

Stel smiled. "I am not angry, Protector. You see how sweet and mild the old book has made me? I am not at all inclined to compare your brain to a hickory nut, as I formerly might have been tempted to do. Now, guardsmen, let us go. To the prisons below. Such honors you bestow to people who choose to be free.

"But one word more, Protector. You might as well try to stuff the light back into the sun. Or when I was a child, I saw a hive dropped when the beemen were moving it. There were bees everywhere. They couldn't be put back in the hive. You all are mistaken, you see. Ideas let loose are like those bees. They have taken flight. You can't stop that. They may bring you honey or they may sting you, depending on your treatment of them. But the old hive is a gone structure."

"Guardsmen, take this drone."

"Spoken like a true queen, Protector. I shall have time to brood, but my thoughts will gather pollen from all of Urstadge."

"Your thoughts will gather dust, Stel. Enough. Take him."

Three days later, in the early morning, a guardsman knocked at the Protector's door. No answer came. She knocked again, and heard a faint voice from within. Soon the door opened. Alance was in her night robe, her hair bound in a cloth, her eyes puffed.

"Protector, a problem," the guardsman murmured.

"Yes? It is Stel? Someone has let him out?"

"No. Someone has beaten him severely. He is in the infirmary."

"Ah. How badly?"

"Very."

The Protector stood, head bowed, for a long moment. "I was afraid of something like that. The city is split already. I hope . . ."

"Yes, Protector?"

"Nothing. I'll dress and come. Wait, please."

"Yes, Protector," the guardsman said to the closing door.

Meanwhile, in the city of Innanigan, the legislature was discussing, in extraordinary early-morning session, the disastrous expedition to the west. The Chair recognized a delegate from the Ariston sector, a short, bald man with a fringe of black hair, Ason Koster by name. "Mr. Chair, Borund's report seems to me to indicate clearly that we are faced with savage fanatics, who have armed themselves with weapons enough better than our present ones to have made the difference in producing this disaster. His proposal that we now arm ourselves better than they seems a sound one.

"We have the models in the museum. We can indeed miniaturize our cannons. We are easily capable of producing the set explosives. We can no doubt produce weapons of the same type superior to theirs, and hence carry the fight to them, wiping the west clean of Peshtak and their allies. But it will take time and expense. Surely our safety, and the sanctity of our families, is worth it. This is a threat we must meet aggressively and promptly. The hegemony of Innanigan is at stake."

The delegate proceeded to outline a program of expenditures and procedures designed to take three years and produce an army capable in his eyes of patrolling the west and clearing it of Peshtak for two hundred ayas west of the Leynap River.

A clamor ensued, from which the Chair recognized the Atham sector delegate, a ponderous old man with a sweeping shock of white hair. His name was Lume Budde. In his earlier years he had been a military officer, but was one of those nudged aside when a more aggressive military policy had taken form fifteen years earlier.

He hunched over, staring at a paper in his hands, tugging at his forelock. Then he squinted around the room and said, "I've never heard more arrant nonsense in my years as a legislator. I have here a copy of the conversations between Borund and the Exalt on the one side and the westerners, especially the Pelbar, Ahroe, on the other. It makes clear—"

"Point of order."

"Yes, Legislator Crupp."

"That material has never been signed or acknowledged by Legislator Borund and hence is not accurate nor germaine to this discussion."

"Nonetheless," Budde continued with a sigh, "the material was brought by the exalt and is stated by him to be substantially accurate, as well as by the lieutenant who was present—Oberly."

"Point of order."

"Yes, Legislator Dupon."

"This lieutenant is presently under arrest for surrender of his force to the enemy when others maintain that he could have fought to a victory. We do not feel that his views should be allowed in this assembly."

Budde sighed. "Mr. Chair, I will strike reference to Oberly, though I might point out that of his half of the force, two hundred and nineteen men returned home safely, under the nurture of the enemy, while from those of the similar number under that raving Sharitan, only one hundred and seventy one made it, many of them suffering severely from frostbite and in poor condition generally, and that only happened by the grace of the enemy as well. I tire of the badgering of the industrial Hegemonists, who hope to gain from higher taxes for armaments. I only wish to make my statement in peace, but their devotion to conflict is so extreme that they will not even permit that."

"Mr. Chair."

"Will Legislator Budde yield to the legislator from Lanfeld?"

"Must I?"

"No, but it is the usual courtesy."

"All right, I will yield for a single turn of the sand clock."

"Very well, Mz Vans."

"I think it highly unseemly for the legislator to impugn the patriotism of some of our most steadfast legislators and military people. Legislator Borund has suffered immensely, doing his duty to all of us, and I here denounce the remarks of Mr. Budde with all the force that a just regard for our city inevitably brings to the hearts and minds of its upright citizens. I have no intentions of remaining in this chamber if the legislator chooses to continue such abuse."

The Chair raised his hands. "It would appear, Mz Vans, that you wish to admit only one set of views to this body. We have never operated in that manner and will not begin now. All members are free to speak. While this procedure may be cumbersome, it seems to have worked over a long period of time. I shall now rule that Legislator Budde be permitted to complete his statement without interruption except for legitimate points of order or questions. The harassments of the Hegemony Party are not aiding our considerations today."

The Chair cleared his throat and regarded the retreating back of Legislator Vans. "Proceed, Mr. Budde," he said.

"Yes," Budde said, again tugging his hair. "As you know, I served for some years on our western border, when—"

"Point of order," said Legislator Subish.

"Yes, Mr. Subish," said the Chair. "You wish no doubt to point out your view that we have no western border because we have refused to describe one for the westerners, who have now assigned us one, the Leynap River, which was our traditional border during Mr. Budde's military career. You know as well as I such a point is unnecessary. You also know that the vexed problem of the border will come up. You are being, in the view of the Chair, tiresome. Of course you have a perfect right. Proceed, Mr. Budde."

"There hardly seems much use, Mr. Chair. However, I wish to make several points, and I shall endeavor to make them without rasping the industrialists against their coarse grain. However, having sat silent while listening to the blatherings and vagaries of Mr. Borund, only to be interrupted in this manner, I and those of my views will know how to hinder them in their speeches in the future.

"The first point is that these are not merely the Peshtak and their allies. It is clear from the exalt's report that we are faced with a new situation. Not savages. People with education comparable to our own. With a superior social organization. With inventions we could well use. With markets we could well sell to. With materials we could trade for. With the hard-footed animals which could well aid us in our agriculture. That is, with peace rather than war.

"The second point is that they have cured the Peshtak of their disabling disease and ended Peshtak raids across into our farms. We might well accord them the same courtesy.

"The third point is if we need their coal, we could as easily trade for it as fight for it. Such an action might well stimulate our economy in producing goods to offer them. It certainly would save lives.

"The fourth point is that we might well open our west all the way to the Heart River, wherever that is, and beyond. One of the westerners even described to one of our soldiers a great sea far to the west of where they live. Some of them have been there. With friendly relations, we also might go.

"A fifth point, and one brought up by the Pelbar, Ahroe, is that in ancient times there seems evidence that we were indeed all one people. Instead of seeking to dominate, we might restore the old unity. We could still maintain our sovereignty, and perhaps contribute to their knowledge. When it is possible, good will is always cheaper and easier than fighting.

"A sixth point is that if we gain friendly terms with the westerners, we will not need to develop weapons superior to theirs. Not only will we not need them, but they will probably give them to us for our mutual defense, though against what I cannot imagine at this point.

"Finally, I wish this legislature to discuss at length the nature of the westerners with the officers and survivors of our western expedition, including both branches. It appears to me that we dealt with the westerners bestially and were treated with remarkable fairness in return. There is the matter of the branding, but as I understand it, already the third corps has taken that mark as an emblem, and all recruits receive it with pride. The Pelbar, Ahroe, bears it as well. It would appear to have been possible for them to eliminate both branches of the force totally, hence a small burn on the hand seems by comparison not something to be very excited about.

"I have talked to survivors and found them grateful to have returned and interested in the westerners. One Sentani explained in some detail to the exalt why we could never beat them militarily. Peydan was astonished at the cogency of his analysis, and he seems to agree with it. I am not sure about it. We seem to have some other options, but none so attractive as peace.

"In conclusion, I wish to thank my detractors for their silence at least. I know we do not have agreement."

Budde sat down. The discussion and debate resumed, but without any sign either of a motion or any movement toward agreement. By the time the meeting recessed for a noon meal, several legislators had resolved not to speak with one another.

Many perceived that the issue at hand would shift the main direction of Innanigani government for some time, and none was in a mood to shrug it off. The Hegemonist Party, of which Borund was a member, saw the issue as their chance to bind the economic efforts of the city into a bundle, both military and industrial, held in their hands. The Popular Party, to which Budde belonged, perceived an opportunity for growth of trade and individual enterprise, and a relaxation of the military initiatives of the recent years. They welcomed an influx of new ideas and products, and resisted the concept that the central control of the Innanigani government ought by rights to be extended westward, by force if necessary. But they clearly lay in the minority.

Hegemonist promises and the fear of the West drew people to those who claimed strong leadership. And yet the veterans of the recent campaign were talking. Even Zard, who now lay in prison, had talked to some legislators. His word was to go slow. "This one, Garet," he told Budde, "is a model warrior and doesn't even know it. If our officers took care of us the way he took care of us, his enemies, we never would have stumbled into all that trouble. And he isn't even a commander. They have the horses and the explosive weapons, but their best weapon is their men and the regard of the men for each other. Even the Peshtak feel drawn into their one society. I saw that when I was a captive."

Exalt Peydan told the legislature much the same thing. "Each of the societies has something," he had said. "I saw it when we waited in the ancient tunnel. They have merged these talents. The Shumai ride happily into danger, but they are backed by the systematic Sentani. The Peshtak add a fierceness and a refusal to conform, a fire that burns deep and will not go out. And the Pelbar, well, the Pelbar take care of them all with a persistent gentleness that is not present in the others. Somehow they all look to the Pelbar, who assure them of their great strengths. I will be a better officer for having seen all this. But not if I have an extremist interfering at every step. If that is what you wish, I would like you to be frank about it, so I can resign my commission."

"Mr. Chair," Borund shouted, jumping up, "I move that we ask the exalt to resign his commission now, so we can be commanded by a person of strength and resolve."

"Second," came a voice from the back.

"Legislators, you are out of order to present a motion in the middle of this report from our western commander. Later, if necessary, you can introduce your motion. Please be assured, Exalt Peydan, that you have our support."

Peydan looked at the Chair and laughed a long, bitter laugh.

The Protector leaned over Stel's bed and examined his swollen face. He opened his eyes and smiled slightly. "Alance," he whispered. "Come to pretend concern, to yearn for Pelbar unity, burn for justice, discern the enemies of Pelbarigan."

Alance closed her eyes in a slight frown.

"Looking stern," Stel croaked.

"Stel, will you never learn?" she replied.

He started a light laugh, but it turned into a groan.

Alance studied his face for an unbruised spot, then leaned

down and kissed him. "You needn't worry. I'll put my own guard on you. This won't happen again. Who did it—did you see?"

"It doesn't matter."

"They have discredited themselves, and partly me."

"You did that yourself, Protector. It is more than me, more than Pelbarigan that will chastise you."

"The book will, then? The book itself."

"A book can't chastise. But a book that's shut can't instruct. And the logic of events will take care of itself, no matter what you or I think. What I think is that I'll lie here and let my face try to resume its normal size."

"Very wise. Ah, Stel..."

"Yes?"

"I cannot go until you let go of my hand."

"Ahroe is not here, Protector. You'll have to sit with me a moment or two longer."

Alance dropped her eyes. "Stel, will you never learn propriety?"

"Or Pelbar piety?"

"Certainly, in spite of the beating, not sobriety," Alance said, laughing. "But seriously, Stel, in spite of all we owe you, you may have torn Pelbarigan apart."

"Seriously, Protector. That depends on you. Remember Threerivers. Remember Udge. No, I mean no insult, no comparison of people. But there is a parallel in method. I hope you will see no parallel in result. I...regret all this, Alance. Have you ever read the old book? No. I see it. You ought to. Some of it. So you can judge."

"Ah. It would capture me, then? Now, let go. I must leave."

"Yes, for the day breaks."

"What? What do you mean?"

"Nothing. I will let you go if you kiss me again."

"What a wretch you are," Alance muttered as she bent to kiss him. Then she stood and smoothed her robe. She glanced at her personal guardsman, who erased a grin. Then she looked back at Stel and said, "You didn't fight back, did you?"

"In what way do you mean, Protector?" Stel whispered. Then he smiled slightly and shut his eyes.

XI

BEFORE Ahroe reached Threerivers, ice closed the river to her small steamboat, and soon after, the heavy snowfall made all travel cumbersome. But she was eager to report on her meeting with the easterners to the small group of Heart River Federation delegates still at the new city, so she pushed on upriver on snow sliders, accompanied only by four guardsmen.

Besides, she found it exhilarating. It reminded her of the time, so many years ago, she had left Pelbarigan in winter in search of Stel. The moan of the wind in the bare branches, the hushed gliding of the wooden sliders, the flow of snow around their upturned points, like water parted by a ship's prow, all set up a rhythm she responded to, her body willingly accepting the shock and steady pressure of travel.

She was also worried. Stel's book had already begun to stir ill feeling before she had left, and she had a strange premonition of a trial ahead. He was so blandly stubborn about it. His wishes in the matter would have to suit everybody. He never seemed to see things in societal ways. In fact, he seemed to see a society as an assemblage of individuals happening to live together—this in spite of his rigorous Pelbar upbringing. Her old irritation with him had returned. He seemed so perverse.

About this time Alance, returning to her rooms, found a note pinned to the door. She took it down and read, "All scripture is inspired by God and profitable for teaching, for reproof, for correction, and for training in righteousness, that the man of God may be complete, equipped for every good work." She crumpled the paper, the fourth she had found in the last two days. Pelbarigan was not accustomed to this kind of rebelliousness. Already an old couple had left for Northwall, ostentatiously, it seemed to her. Though they claimed to be going on a visit only, they took or gave away all their possessions. Alance was uneasy. It was too much like Threerivers, which broke up almost completely under the heavy thumb of the former Protector, Udge.

But the conservatives and ministers also had been strident, and there seemed more of them in this matter. And Alance's old love for Stel, which was widely known among those with whom they had been young together, had made her hard on him to avoid any charge of favoritism. He himself had never seen any woman but Ahroe, or so she thought.

The following morning a guardsman summoned her to the window to see a statement tracked into the snow on the river ice. It read:

> You shall go out in joy,
> and be led forth in peace.

Alance said quietly, "Have the guardsmen tramp it out, Sard. Do it now, while it's still early." She continued to watch, hands behind her, and saw another small party dragging three sledges leave the city and start to trudge north through the snow. A small crowd stood on the riverbank to say good-bye.

Taking her bell, she summoned the guardsman by her door and said, "Bring me a representative from that departing group, please. I wish to talk to her."

Alance continued to stand by the window, though she heard a knock and called behind her to admit someone. "Come up here," she said. "I'm at the window."

It was Jun, a minister. "It is all over, Protector, like an infection, this book of Stel's."

"Yes. Do you feel I didn't act appropriately?"

"You gave them access at the library."

"Have they taken it?"

"A few. Very few."

"I have been told the ministers have given only reluctant access to the book, and then only with a heavy overlay of instruction."

"We felt that came within the outlines of your directive, Protector."

"Look down there, Jun. Do you see the guardsmen erasing that statement? Look. They've started with the ends of the lines."

"Yes." Jun paused. "I don't understand, Protector."

"Those words were 'joy' and 'peace.'"

"So you see that as of significance, Protector? It seems more to the point to me that Pel's original read, 'You shall hold fast in joy and rest protected in peace.'"

"What difference, but for the joy and peace? But you must leave me now, because I have to interview someone. I will talk to you later if you wish."

"But, Protector—"

"Go."

Alance was alone a short time later when Eger was admitted. She was a middle-aged woman, a ceramicist by trade, short and inclined to be heavy. Her gray hair was parted in the middle and lay tightly bound in two braids in the Shumai manner. Alance motioned her to a chair and offered her tea.

"The others are waiting, Protector. I must not keep them in the cold while I drink tea."

"They can come in. They can stay. It is the book, isn't it? Is it really worth your whole life at Pelbarigan, then?"

"The book? No. We have Pel's writings, for what they are worth, Protector. It's the manner of its suppression, mild as it may be. We have agreed. The world is opening. Stel should have a right."

"Stel?"

"And Cwire, my husband. And others. Besides, things are happening at Northwall. They have a use for us. The book may have been a flint that lit a pile of dry dissatisfaction, Protector. With always having lived here. We want to look. There are so many possibilities."

"But this is midwinter."

"As good a time as any. There are no hostiles. We can keep warm enough. We've been told there's room and work."

"So the book is a flint."

"For some. Others are the kindling. Good-bye, Protector. I must go. I have committed no crime."

"No." Alance looked around for something to give Eger and idly picked up an inlaid box. "Here, take this. A gift for your journey." She opened it and took out a scrap of birch bark, then put it in the still-mittened hand of Eger. They embraced, and only as she was leaving did she recall that the small box had been made by Stel, for her, and given a special symbol of crossed Shumai lances, bound by inlaid ropes of dark wood. Well, too late to ask for it back. She glanced at the birch bark. On it was a note that read, "Stel made this to celebrate your election as west quadrant council member. He is restless here on the Isso and eager to return, but I am enjoying the rest. Raydi eats solid food now so I am free of that, too."

Alance's hand trembled. It was an old letter, an old gift. She threw the bark in the fire and watched it burn like an old friendship, ignited by political necessity, and even now turning to ashes.

She turned toward the table and noticed for the first time a scrap of paper there. Frowning, she picked it up and read, "You must face your adversary squarely, while you are at the point of confrontation, when you know you are right. Remember that your view is founded in your truth, like a city of rock built on rock, which rain and flood cannot remove. This is where your strength lies. Pel, Roll 7, Ch. 18."

So now the conservatives also had begun to strew quotations around. Alance knew she had sought a middle ground, with a nod to the faithful, but it wasn't turning out that way. Perhaps the city would crack and break like the others. Perhaps that was a necessary aspect of the new age, difficult as that might seem. But there had to be a better way. With the trouble in the east, the Federation could ill afford cleavage at Pelbarigan.

Alance rang for her guardsman. He appeared instantly. "Sard," she said absently. "I wish to speak to Stel. Bring him here, please."

"I—I'm not sure he can walk that well, Protector. Perhaps you could go see him again."

"No. Never mind, then. It will have to wait."

"Yes, Protector." Sard bowed and retired. Alance wondered if she detected an unwonted coldness in his tone. He was an old man, extremely loyal. What did that mean? She sighed and felt her teapot. Even beneath the cosy, it was dead cold.

Late that night Stel heard a scuffle and muffled voices outside the room where he was confined. A small light flared, then snuffed out, and the bolt grated slowly back on the door. At the first sound he had slid painfully from the bed, as he had planned, rolled up the blanket and spread the thick puff back over it, and moved behind the door, holding the end of his trip cords. His arms still ached, and one black eye still opened only halfway.

Three dark figures glided into the room and toward the bed. As they approached it, Stel pulled up the trip cords behind them, sliding them behind the chair leg he had wedged against the wall, tying them off instantly and making for the door. One figure said, "A trick. He's not here."

Two of the figures turned as Stel slid around the open door. As he slammed and bolted it, he heard them lunge and fall inside. The two guards lay bound and gagged in the hallway. Stel stooped and patted each one on the cheek, then ran limping down the hall and disappeared up the narrow, stone steps.

"Six of them, three dressed as women," Atch said to the Protector, who sat by her table in her night robe.

"I thought you were better than that, Atch. My own guardsmen. The best."

"They were women, their hair piled in tiers. We came to attention and bowed, Protector."

"Huh. A simple ruse. Well, we'll soon enough learn who the other three were."

"You will question them, then? The ones we caught?"

"The ones Stel locked in. He must have had it all planned. Didn't trust us. Fortunate for him. Where is he?"

"It is barely morning, Protector. We don't know."

"Assign some people to find him. Look at Garet's. Ahroe's house. Get Raydi to show us the passages. No tricks. Tell her we'll take the house apart if she doesn't."

"The prisoners. You didn't say—"

"They will be brought before a full council, Atch. No. No frowns from you. I'll put you to night watch on the woodpile."

"All have ministerial connections, Protector."

"So much the worse. It was some of the Protector's own guardsmen they overpowered, you may recall."

"Yes, Protector."

Stel lay on the bed of Eolyn, the Dome woman, in her small house, a part of her laboratory and academy behind the city. "All this nonsense about old books," she muttered as she examined his eye. "Well, it looks all right—or it will be. When will you settle down, Stel? It seems as though you can't avoid trouble."

"Yes."

"All right. I know that some of that trouble was getting us all out of the Dome. But . . . Listen, Stel, you can't stay here, you know. I have to have some home. I can't go wandering off on the ice like those people who left. I don't care about your religious politics."

"I know. Today. Can you put me under the bed for today? I'll be out of here tonight. I can't make it now."

"Under the bed?"

"Don't worry. I won't poke you through the mattress tomorrow night. I'll sneak off at high night."

"Stel."

"Come on now. I know you wish . . . Well, never mind."

"I don't want to be teased, Stel. It hasn't been easy."

"All right. Not another tease."

"Smile again? They chipped a tooth."

"That's the truth. Cut off in its youth."

"Well. Will you be all right under there?"

"Yes. Just get me some food. Anything will do. I need a two- or three-ayas start on after dark and I'll be all right."

"I just don't understand. None of this makes any sense."

"No. It doesn't. It's just one of those things one has to do."

"What will become of Raydi? And what of Ahroe?"

Stel shut his eyes. "I don't know, Eo. I don't know."

At Threerivers, Ahroe was up and preparing for a meeting with the delegates later in the day. A light tapping brought her to the door. Dahn, a young Peshtak woman, stood there leaning back from her pregnancy. "Ahroe . . . I was on the radio, and a message came from Pelbarigan. It said if Stel came here, they were to take him and hold him. It was confidential, but I thought—"

"Did they say why?"

"No, Guardchief. How could they do that to Stel? I don't understand at all. He—"

"It's the book, Dahn. Something to do with that fisheating book. Thank you for telling me."

"You will—"

"Yes. I'll keep it muffled. Don't worry. And don't worry about Stel. I've done that for enough years." She laughed lightly. "I suppose I needn't quit now." She embraced the young woman guardedly and patted her shoulder, then shut the door and sat back down on her narrow bed. She roused herself later, her arms chilled. She had been staring at the gray winter morning out the window. She knew this visit would have to be short. She would push on tomorrow.

The full council filled the side seats when the Protector entered the Judgment Room. Three men, heads held down, stood on the open floor, hands bound, flanked by four guardsmen.

"And so, Triner, Redo, and Idged. All married to ministers,"

Alance said. "Yet all of you saw fit to counter the law of this city and do violence to the Protector's own guardsmen. Only you and Aven know what you intended to do to my prisoner. Now we have the task of finding him again and learning where the original book is. I'm sure that is not what you intended. Please tell the council what you did intend."

"We have nothing to say."

"That is not our custom, Triner. Citizens brought before the full council are expected to give truthful and full answers to questions put to them by the Protector. Are you not aware of that?"

"We still have nothing to say."

"You are from the west quadrant? Does Triner's counsel have anything to say to him?"

A short, thin woman with pure white hair rose and cleared her throat. "Triner, the rule is clear. If what you have done is defensible, it will be defended. You must speak. Otherwise the ministry which you clearly represent will be shamed."

"We do not represent the ministry. They knew nothing of what we did."

"Why did you do it, then?"

"You must see the wreckage that wretch has made with his book. The whole city falling apart. The word of Pel flouted, garbled, twisted," Redo said.

"Redo!" Triner hissed.

"There is no help for it. I will speak."

"We agreed."

"A mistake. Protector, your decision gave comfort to the enemies of Pelbarigan and Aven. We only meant to hold Stel and free him in exchange for all the copies of the book. Your plan did no good."

A murmur went through the Judgment Room. Alance stood and put her knuckles on the table in front of her. Then she laughed and sat back down. "I see," she said. "I made such a bad job of it that you had to correct me. Well, you are not alone. It seems everyone in the city is dissatisfied, writing their slogans on the walls, on paper, on snow, leaving, attacking the guardsmen, and all for different reasons. Each of you will have it your way. For everybody. And that way only. I tried to compromise. It seems to have been a failure. You—prisoners. You may sit, please. You may listen to your first council meeting. Who wishes to speak to this subject?"

Eleven council members stood and waited to be recognized.

It took until well after high sun to listen to them all, and their opinions represented a complete spectrum of views. Finally Alance raised her hand and said, "Well, Triner, now that you have heard all that, what would you do? The same?"

"Ban the book. It is the only way."

"Stel said I might as well try to stuff the light back into the sun. The ideas are out."

"They will fade without the book."

"And you are so sure of your ideas that you are willing to make all accede to them?"

"For their good, yes. The rule of Pel has sufficed for this city for hundreds of years. Why throw away our birthright?"

"Then you have not moved from your position?"

"No. I see no need."

"Do you two agree?"

"Yes," Redo said.

"Protector, I have a suggestion," said Idged. "I've listened to all the talk, and I see now where we were wrong. I regret doing what we did. I—"

"Idged!" Triner hissed.

"I suggest that all agree to drop the question while a committee compares the new book with Pelbar scripture. Where the two agree, that part of Stel's book may be allowed. Where they disagree, that part of the new book must be censored. That way, Pel's work will be intact and the new book will simply support it."

Alance looked at him, idly drumming her fingers. "Thank you, Idged. You have tried. I doubt that would satisfy many. Guardsmen, take these men and put them in the room Stel was in. We will care for their case later."

After they had left, she said to the council, "You see what we have come to. I fear for the city more than for religious truth, which will take care of itself, perhaps. We have reached an impasse. Here is what I propose. No one take any action for a period of six days, while we think this out. My original decision stands, except I propose to modify it in one way. Clearly we cannot subject to the ministers those people who wish to read the book in the library. Therefore, all who wish to read it may, and they must only agree to read an equal amount of Pelbar scripture and to attend standard services. I'm sure that can be monitored. I will put that in writing. Now. I have no other solutions at present, but I will entertain any further thought you might have. We will meet again on the matter in six days. Let us close with two sunwidths of prayer—in the Pelbar manner."

After the prayer Alance swept the assembly with a glance as she turned to leave. The faces she saw were sober and in some cases angry. Alance sighed as she entered her private chamber.

Meanwhile, in Innanigan, Borund sat in his home with a circle of men and women. "It is agreed, then? We will analyze what we know of these westerners and counter each of their strengths and exploit each of their weaknesses. The most obvious weakness we have found is their tendency toward compassion. Surely we can exploit that. Another is the fact that they are several societies. Perhaps we can split one off from another. Now, Subish, explain to us your views on our promotion of new weaponry in the legislature."

"Yes. We have seen they have the set explosives of the Tantal. They have the animals—the horses. We must get some of them. They must have Tantal rockets, though they did not use them. They have our cannon and their own smaller explosive weapons.

"So far we have discovered in our investigation that we can make the smaller weapons, which the ancients called rifles. And we can better them because Erret found in the museum archives a version that can shoot one projectile right after another—an advance over their technique. We can spray an area with projectiles. We also have remarkable improvements on the cannon, which we should really have made all along. Odd we hadn't. There's nothing like war to advance technology.

"We also found a hand-thrown explosive called a grenade in a scrap of the ancient encyclopedia. We are sure we can reproduce it. It can be launched from the rifle, too."

"Given the appropriation, can you manufacture these devices?"

"With time, yes. And a proper compensation."

"A problem, of course. The legislature must agree. I have a plan. The westerners have said that the Leynap will be the boundary. If we disagree, and get the legislature to push for the Cwanto, backing this with all possible patriotic fervor, then the westerners will fight to defend the lost territory. Then of course we will have to have the new weapons. Once we have established them, we can move west as far as we like, because they will have caused it."

"It might work."

"Have you a better plan?"

"No."

"Then it will have to."

 XII

As night fell, snow followed, on a rising wind from the northwest. Eolyn finally freed herself from her students and returned to her room. She knelt by the bed and whispered, "Stel."

"Time to go?"

"No. Soon. Here. Some food. I couldn't bring much. The guardsmen are still looking for you, and if I noticed correctly, the ministers' people, too."

"Better to be taken by a guardsman—but best by neither. Thanks, Eo, for taking this risk. You'd better leave me quiet here and be busy elsewhere. I don't want you troubled."

"All right. How will you make out? I don't understand."

"No need to. I will. Trust that. I wish Tristal were here to take care of you, Eo."

"Tristal? Yes, he would fend off present dangers. But..."

"But he is not your own."

"Yes. It humbles me to say it. I wish..."

"You wish Tor were here."

"Ah, Stel. Why must you always bring him up?"

"Because it's true. You know it's true. I've seen you turn your head when someone talks of him. You know you and Tor were always meant to be together. It was obvious enough to me—and him, too, I'm sure."

"Ah, Stel. It's so insane. But you're right. I thought I had ample reasons to shove him away—the wild man, the eternal hunter. But you've been my friend so long—my oldest Pelbar friend, really. Too late now. How many nights here alone—I've grieved for him. For what I did to him. Besides..."

"Besides, wild as he is, he's a match for you, a complement

to you. He completes your logic with intuition. Don't worry. As intuitive as he is, he'll feel your yearning and come back."

"If he's still ali—what's that?"

"Someone at the door."

Eolyn rose and went to the front door of her quarters. She opened it, finding three men, muffled against the cold. "Yes?" she said.

"May we come in?"

"Yes. Who are you? What can I do for you?"

"We have a message for Stel—to help him," said one, pushing through the door.

Eolyn hesitated. "Stel? I . . . I don't understand."

"Don't worry. We're from his brotherhood. We saw some stray tracks. They told us he came here."

"Here? Who are you?"

"What have you done with him? If you've hurt him . . ." The largest man grabbed Eolyn's wrists and shook her.

"Stop! You're *hurt*ing."

"Tell us where he is, then," the same man hissed, then threw Eolyn against the wall.

In the bedroom, Stel slid a slat from under the bed. It was oak. He recalled Tor's advice on confronting a group. *Plan your swings so you graze vital areas. Don't slug it out.* He rolled from under the bed as he heard Eolyn scream, then heard the sound cut off, probably by a hand. He heard blows and slaps as he limped toward the door, then a gasp and tearing cloth. Suddenly he was overcome by fury and burst through the door.

Stel found one startled man waiting for him motionless, short-sword drawn. Stel swung fast, catching the fellow across the bridge of the nose. He whacked aside the second man's hand, catching him on the ear on the return, then swung for the third, connecting solidly with his throat. Stel turned and felt the tip of a sword thrust into his side as he caught the first man's wrist and sent his weapon spinning. The second man was on him then, and Stel spun, rushed him backward into a doorframe, threw him over his head, and rapped him hard across the shins with the oak slat.

The first man had recovered the sword and charged him with it again, but Stel ducked under the thrust then tripped, and the attacker fell on him. Stel grabbed his sword arm at the wrist as the man strained and bore down on him. The second man had rolled over and was crawling toward them.

In desperation, Stel heaved upward, twisted and rolled away, hearing a cry as his opponent fell on the sword point. Stel staggered to his feet as the other man did also. But Eolyn had recovered the slat and swung it down on the man's head, buckling him.

They looked at the third man, who was gasping for breath, looking blue. Eolyn examined his throat and tried to readjust it with her fingers as the man cried out.

"I'd better go for the guardsmen, Stel. This has gone too far."

"You'll be in trouble—for keeping me."

"Yes."

"No other way. I've got to go. I can't think of a convincing lie." Stel grinned slightly.

"Stel, you're bleeding!"

"Not bad. I *have* to go. I won't get my long start, but the storm'll help. Are you all right?"

"I hurt. Nothing too bad."

Stel reached out and rearranged her torn clothes. "It's no use."

"No." She turned and rummaged in a drawer. "Here. A fresh radiation detector. Improved. You may need it. No telling where you'll be. Good-bye, Stel. If there is an Aven, may he protect you."

"*She*. Aven is a *She*."

"Who cares? Go. Take care. Where . . ."

"Never mind. You take care. Let me tie these men. That one is really hurt. Better get help soon. Good-bye." He kissed her cheek lightly.

She reached toward him, took his hands a moment, and whispered, "Oh, Stel. Good-bye."

He swung the door open and plunged out into the snow.

In a wayhouse Ahroe sat by the fire listening to the storm. The four guardsmen with her played a quiet game of Sentani stones, knowing she was troubled. She rose and stepped outside into the wind and snow. She had a bad feeling about the trouble at Pelbarigan, though she knew little about it in detail. The radio messages received at Threerivers sounded grim. She shivered. What was it about Stel that he always seemed to be at the focus of trouble? She could barely see the trees swaying in the blue-black darkness.

* * *

Aintre sat by Eolyn's bed in the morning watching the Dome woman sleep. A mouse under one eye and a swelling of the opposite cheek showed the rough treatment the three intruders had given her. Yawning Raydi walked into the room and stood by her side, hearing the movement, Eolyn woke with a start. "Don't go, Aintre! Don't go away!"

"I won't. Are you feeling better?"

"Some. Where is Stel?"

"Gone. Vanished. So far not a clue. It's all right, Raydi. He'll be all right."

"Not this time. He can't come back this time."

"Can't come back?" Eolyn asked.

"The wounded man. He's expected to die."

"But he almost killed Stel. It was only his own doing. His own sword."

"But Stel was a fugitive, and by law fugitives cannot exert force against any arresting person, even a private citizen."

"But they broke into my rooms and beat me."

"A separate issue. All of you are guilty. You of harboring a fugitive, they of assault, Stel of escape and resisting arrest."

"What are you guilty of, Aintre? It would appear everybody has to be made guilty of something."

"I? I am guilty of being both a guardsman and the daughter-in-law of the fugitive. I span both sides of the issue."

"What will they do to me? For harboring Stel?"

"I don't know. They may exile you."

"But what of my work?"

"I haven't even a muddy notion. They'll think of something."

"I don't see what else they would have expected me to do. Stel stood by me. I owe him my life."

"Yes. But they will go by the law and the Protector's judgment."

Eolyn sighed and shut her eyes.

About twenty-three ayas to the southwest, across the Heart River, Stel dismounted and gave the reins to the young Shumai who accompanied him. He untied a pair of snow sliders, a small pack, a furroll, and a short bow and quiver. "Thank you, Alwar."

"Don't go far. You aren't in shape for it. Rest. Be careful crossing the Isso. Maybe you ought to go back to Black Bull."

"No. I'll be all right. I'll build a frame to cross the river. But not yet. Rest first. I know a brake near the river. It'll be fine."

"At least you have the book to read."

Stel laughed. "I don't know if my arms are long enough."

"Father's getting that way. Did you bring a glass?"

"No. I'll get along." Stel pulled off his mittens, as did Alwar, and they palmed good-bye in the Shumai manner, the young man leaning down from his horse.

Stel watched the Shumai go, the second horse following at the end of a lead. The Shumai would stay out until he could find a wild cow to kill and bring in on the horse. Or finding none, he would put a stack of wood on its back. In any case, he would ride in to the family farm from the northwest, across the river from Pelbarigan.

Finally Stel knelt and put on his snow sliders, his legs so sore and weary he could barely stand again. He started out through the wind-driven snow, slowly but steadly. The sky had brightened. By high sun, he hoped, he would be looking out at blue sky from a small shelter in the thick brakes by the Isso.

He wondered for a moment if he should have given them the book and let it all go. No. The bastards. They might run the economic life of Pelbarigan any way they chose, but every man was free to think what he wished about Aven and the way of things. Something would come of this book. It was too good a body of ideas to fail out of Pelbarigan wholly. Besides, it was abroad already—at Northwall, among the Atherers, among some Shumai, perhaps even among the Sentani, though their stoic and disciplined worship of Atou seemed sufficient for them.

Stel heard the distant barking of a tanwolf, but paid it little heed. Nearby a crested redbird flitted through the brush, *chip*ping repeatedly, brilliant in the white landscape.

XIII

AHROE stood before the full council at Pelbarigan, giving her report on matters in the East. Her voice showed no tremor, but it also showed none of its usual liveliness and slight, wry humor. The council questioned her at length about the Innaniganis and the likely expenses of dealing with them.

"Peace is better than war, of course, and cheaper," said Ahroe. "However, as I have said there is a party that seems eager for war. I saw it in that doughface, Borund. For him it's an axiom that everybody west of Innanigan is a savage, and it's his right to remove them when he sees fit. Fortunately, there are voices of reason as well, and some of them may prevail. We can only hope."

"I don't understand," one council member remarked. "How can people be so doctrinaire?"

"How? Look around you. When I left, I had a husband at home, but he was detained for the crime of having a book, or being suspected of having one. He was attacked in prison twice, the guards not protecting him. The second time he escaped, probably to save his own life, only to be charged with the crime of escape. Then he defended Eolyn against the Borund faction in this city and is charged with violence and resisting arrest. Borund is no wonder if we judge by ourselves."

"But all this is very different, Ahroe," Alance said gently. "You have put a bad face on a very vexed matter. We must have the rule of law. Law has the right to decide matters. You have spent your life enforcing that concept."

"Yes, Protector," Ahroe murmured, dropping her eyes. "And no one knows better than I how troublesome Stel can be—and how effective, as he recently showed at Ginesh. You may well fear what he has let loose. I myself think there are more practical matters to worry about than these . . . words. I understand though that there are those who wish to tear apart my house, stone by stone, in order to be sure these words are not in it."

"Your assurance will probably suffice, Ahroe."

"My assurance? I will look and report to you. But if Stel said the book was not there, then it was not. It is not a matter of his being beyond lying. It is simply that he would have to be stupid to have left it there. He probably acted as he did to fool you. It proved easy, Protector."

"I regret your hostility, Ahroe," Alance replied, with a forced reserve. "It is not desirable."

"Indeed. Not desirable, Protector? It is my view that you all have done . . . very badly. You may feel I do not have the right to say that, and perhaps you are correct, but the facts seem to support me."

"What we have done is supported by much precedent, Ahroe."

"Yes, of course, Protector. But we are living in unprecedented times. However, this discussion goes nowhere. I have a proposal. I will go to look for Stel, and if I find him, I will return the book to you if he has it. As to the house, you may tear it all apart if you choose. I care nothing about that."

"I—I don't understand, Ahroe."

"It is my duty to return the book, Protector. I will do that if you wish it."

"And then?"

"And then . . . this Federation has more important work than quibbling about books, Protector. I intend to contribute to that work. May I go?"

"You have not rested. Do you wish company?"

"No."

"No?"

Ahroe sighed and rolled her eyes. "No, Protector of Pelbarigan. I do not wish to rest. I do not wish help. I wish to settle this matter—or my corner of it. All of it will never be settled. I have been told what Stel said. He was right. You will never stuff the light back into the sun, just as Borund will never prevent the people of good will and economic sense from eventually ending his drooling desires for conquest. It is just that many people will have to endure much and some of them will likely die before that question is decided. May I go?"

"Yes."

"Then good-bye all." Ahroe spun on her heel and left. For a time Alance sat very still, lips pursed. She felt the insult, but it had all been done very correctly, and there was little she could do about it without seeming petty and peevish. Well, Ahroe would eventually take too much on herself, and the cautious path that Protectors generally followed would triumph in the end.

Alance called for a full four sunwidths of prayer. This time she did pray—for Stel, for the peace of the city, for safety against the East, for relief from her turbulent feelings about Ahroe, for some way to resolve the present issue without seeming too stupid.

Ahroe assumed that Stel had returned to the area around the Dome, as he had on a few occasions when he wanted quiet. Here, some years earlier, he had, with little help and much work, freed the people who had lived in that structure ever since the Time of Fire, all on the hunch that the rod which rose out of the Dome at every equinox was guided by a human agency inside. It had been a close thing, since the structure was on the verge of collapse into a ravine, and the arrival of the Dome people, Eolyn and Celeste, with their knowledge of technology, in Pelbarigan had done much to change the city.

Ahroe crossed the river and traveled southwest, then crossed the Isso on the ice and turned south. She was angry at the absurdity of the situation, and the parochialism of Pelbarigan, and had to remind herself that its people had traveled little. Most of the council had accustomed itself to viewing the world from the windows of the city, even though safe travel outside Pelbarigan's walls had been possible for years.

And she was angry at Stel for causing the disturbance. It seemed so gratuitous. True, Pelbarigan was probably due for an upheaval, but why had *he* brought it on, and at such a time when resources would be needed for the trouble in the East?

Ahroe was entering middle age, but she glided easily on her snow sliders and felt comfortable alone in the vast winter though there seemed more tanwolves than usual. Twice when they came too close she had to unstrap her rifle and shoot one to dissuade the others. Once she slept in a tree because of them.

At last she approached the familiar jutting outcrop under which Stel and his companions had lived the summer they opened the Dome. She was by then about eighty ayas southwest of Pelbarigan in a wholly unpeopled area of stream-cut hills of woodland and long grass prairie.

Yes, there were his tracks. She rested for a few sunwidths before gliding in toward the old, familiar shelter. It was near dusk. She held herself still, hearing something. It was Stel's flute playing a familiar Pelbar hymn. Ahroe stopped to listen as the sun sank further, spreading the west with a dull winter red.

He finished the hymn and began to improvise. Ahroe caught a new aspect to his music, rich and sad, yet somehow satisfied and contented. No, not really contented. The music seemed to yearn, but for nothing easily attainable. It reminded Ahroe of thrushes in the deep evening woods in summer, as though the whole rich green maze of shadow had found a voice, and the thrush had become the woods itself speaking its upwelling life. She choked a little. What did she sense? Stel had become a stranger in a way. He had found a dimension she had not yet explored, and she sensed herself . . . afraid to plunge into it.

Finally he stopped, and she realized her feet had gone numb as she had stood still.

As she came around the last bend in the overhanging limestone, Stel looked up from his fire. "You're in time for supper," he said. "I made plenty."

"Are you a Tor, then? You knew I was coming?"

"No. I've been making plenty for three days. Enough for a couple of guardsmen, should they come."

"I am the guardsman."

"I know, Ahroe. I've known that a long time. You are the quintessential guardsman. Are you tired? Cold?" He handed her a wooden bowl, steaming with stew. "We can eat inside. I haven't fixed a proper fireplace in there yet, but it's out of the wind."

Ahroe slurped off some of the liquid that hung at the brim of the bowl. It burned its way down her throat, causing her to blink. Stel had stooped into the shelter, and she followed.

A small pottery lamp burned there, and as they settled down in their furrolls to eat, Ahroe saw in Stel's underlit face the marks of his beatings. Beside that he looked pale and moved with a tentative stiffness.

"I've come for the book, Stel," she said.

"I know."

"It is important now to settle the issue as much as it can be settled. The city is tearing itself open."

"Yes. I see."

"You didn't need to do this. Your willfulness has gone beyond the walls."

"A metaphor from the old times," he said, chuckling.

"Stel, I don't care where the metaphor is from. This is a

practical matter. We must show some gesture of conciliation to the conservatives and obey the council."

Stel stared at the lamp. "We? You mean I."

"You quibble over everything. I'm talking about big issues."

"Isn't trying to understand the nature of things a big issue?"

"Are you going to give me the book?"

"Ahroe, I don't know. I might. But I think somehow I can't give it up."

Ahroe sighed and closed her eyes, trying to hold down her fury, but it seized her. She threw the rest of the stew in Stel's face. Scrambling out of her furroll, she jerked him to his feet by the hair and shook him. "The book. I will have that book."

"Look around for it," Stel said dully, wiping at his face.

Ahroe slapped him sharply on the cheek. "I mean it," she said.

"Yes. Hit me again. You look wonderful with stew on your hands."

Ahroe did hit him, as he stood and reeled around, and when he covered his face, she swung wildly at his body. As she struck his side, he cried out and fell, crawling, still half in the furroll, into the corner, not moving.

At his cry, Ahroe's anger was spent and shame mingled with her frustration. She knelt by him and put her hand on his back. He didn't move, though his back heaved and shuddered.

"What's the matter with you?" she hissed. He didn't reply. "I've spent more trouble over you than any three husbands should give anybody. And this doesn't change anything. I must have the book."

Stel still didn't reply. Ahroe moved her hand on his back, but he shuddered away from it. She sat back, keeping her hand on him, and watched the lamp burn. Guilt crept into her. She had never hit him before, though this had been fairly common among Pelbar wives in the old time when the cities were closed. Still, she knew the best of them didn't do it.

"I'm sorry, Stel. That it has come to this." Still he didn't reply. The night wore on, as Ahroe watched the lamp burn in the small shelter, its light revealing Stel's neat but simple carpentry. His body had not relaxed into the slumber she was so familiar with from having slept by his side for so many years. Occasionally she spoke, but he never replied. Finally the lamp flame flickered and faltered, burned lower, smoked, and went out. The darkness seemed entire.

Ahroe eased herself back, weary with her day on the snow sliders and the emotional trial of the evening. The weight of her guilt struggled with her sense of duty and necessity. Finally she went to sleep, pulling the furroll over her, keeping her hand on Stel.

She came awake suddenly, with full daylight streaming in the scraped hide window. Stel was gone. She scrambled outdoors and saw the tracks of his snow sliders leading away. Again anger rose in her. She would have to walk him down again. She stooped back into the shelter to prepare herself, eating a little of the remaining stew, and only then noticing, in the corner, Stel's underblouse, soaked with dried blood. She picked it up and saw the sword slice in it. So. She had hit him on his wound. He could have told her, let her help him. She could have rectified her mistake. She dropped her head and her whole body trembled with conflicting emotions.

Finally she opened her eyes and saw sunlight pouring through the open door across her hand, with its neat burn scar in the shape of a star, gripping the cloth with its clot of dark blood. She stared down at it a few moments, then laid the underblouse aside and prepared to find Stel.

By high sun she could see his tracks were faltering. He stopped to rest more often. The trail eventually curved in to the base of a high limestone outcrop, led into a notch, then vanished into a small, low hole.

Ahroe squatted down and peered into the blackness. She slung off her pack, leaned her snow sliders by the gap, and crawled in, repelled by the darkness, which looked strangely pink to her snow-dazzled eyes. She waited until the darkness assumed its true depth. From the light of the entrance, she could see several passages. She drew in her pack and rummaged in it, but she found nothing to light her way but her flint and steel and a small bundle of the matches Eolyn had given her.

She struck a match and held it up. A tangle of tracks in the dust, human and animal, fanned from the entrance into several tunnels. Stel's led to all the passages. The match burned to her fingers and she waved it out. She looked around, relieved to see the rush of light in the entrance. She called out for Stel, but heard the sound deaden in the rock fissures, receiving only one small, distant echo, "Stel."

She moved into the passage with the echo, feeling her way,

glancing back at the entrance, and yelled out again, hearing in reply, a faint "Stel, tel, el."

She returned to the entrance. There was no help for it. She would have to go back to the shelter for the lamp and enough oil to sustain it. Again she felt rage and frustration, knowing that Stel could easily depart while she was gone. But if he could, she also knew he would never get far in his present condition. Ahroe crawled out and prepared to follow her own trail.

By traveling rapidly, she made it back to the cave by sunset, carrying the lamp and the small pot of oil Stel had saved from cooking at the shelter. Again she crawled in the entrance and lit the lamp. Without much thought she picked the tunnel with the echo again and plunged in. It wound downward, sometimes narrowing, finally opening out into a large room that stretched black and still beyond the power of her lamp to illuminate it. Ahroe hated it.

She had left a trail of X's drawn in the clay and gravel floor of the cave, but somehow this enormous cavity, with its methodical dripping sounds and strange flowstone formations, frightened her. She shouted again, "Stel! Stel! Stel!" The room seemed to soak in the sound, returning only the slightest of echoes.

As she began to explore the cavity, she ran into several blind tunnels and finally began to feel disoriented. She returned to the big room, retraced her X's, and found Stel's tracks, along with several other pairs, some with strange soles and a raised heel, and one that printed a pattern of squares with each step. She realized suddenly that those had been there since ancient times, and had been left undisturbed by wind or weather. A shiver ran down her neck. She decided to retrace her marks to the entrance and try again after a rest.

On the way she noticed Stel's tracks entered a side passage, so she ducked in, seeing where he had knelt, then following his tracks down to a small pool. She found where he had sat down. Ahroe's lamp lit the small chamber, with its pointed, hanging rock pendants and thicker stakes of rock rising to meet them. Suddenly she realized how tired she was, and wished to sink down there on the wet rocks and sleep, then felt a wash of fright at becoming lost so deep in the Earth.

She scrambled back up to the main trail and began to retrace her steps again. Somehow it looked different, though she could see her X's firmly drawn in the cave floor. Eventually she realized that she seemed to be following the same way she had when she entered, with all her footprints going her way. She turned and retraced her path, eventually finding her own tracks in both directions. She sat down, thoroughly confused, and attempted to sort out her way. Then she turned again and retraced her steps, saw where she had turned, and went beyond that point. Soon she came again to the big room.

Ahroe sank down in despair. She added more oil to the lamp and turned once again, plunging back. Forgetting to look, she found herself in a tunnel that showed none of her X's on the floor. She turned again and retraced her way, finally finding where she had angled aside. But her tracks lay in both directions, and now she had no idea which way to go. She selected one and walked down it, then came to a place where there seemed to be her tracks but no marks.

Again she sank down, on a rock shelf sheltered from the dripping. She was unutterably tired and decided she must sleep to regain composure. Arranging herself, she took the bundle of matches in one hand and, then, almost unable to force herself to do it, she extinguished the lamp. The darkness was total, and after the ghosts of lamplight ceased racing through her head, she felt more completely alone than she ever had. She forced down her feelings and shut her eyes, listening to the slow dripping of water from the cave ceiling. Eventually she slept.

When she awoke she was for a moment wholly confused and sat up wildly. Then she remembered, by the matches in her hand, where she was. Undoing the bundle, she took one out and struck it against a coat toggle. The flare momentarily blinded her, but she shaded her eyes and carefully relit the lamp, filling it once again, noting that her supply was growing low.

Retracing her steps, she began to recognize some places, but once again became disoriented. She began tracing side passages, carefully marking them to return to her former way. In edging her way along one wet rock shoulder, she slipped and tumbled down an incline about ten arms high. Miraculously, her lamp stayed lit, but the jar of oil crushed in her pocket. She sat up and saw below her a gaping shaft, dripping with water. She threw a rock down it and heard it hit far below. Painstakingly she climbed back up to where she had been and found the tunnel leading back.

At that point she saw a light. "Stel!" she yelled. "Stel!" She looked across the chasmal shaft as the light grew clearer. It was

Stel, walking haltingly down a passage toward the shaft. He shaded his eyes against his lamp and squinted across the gulf.

"Ahroe. How did you get there?"

"Following you, you numb-livered riversnake. Stel, get me out of here. I—I don't have much oil left."

"Where you are, it will take awhile. A long while the way I am. Go back out that short tunnel and wait. You might douse the lamp. It will likely run out before I make it. Don't go far."

"Are you all right?"

"All right?" Stel laughed dryly. "Just don't go far."

Ahroe watched Stel's lamp fade away across the shaft and again felt wholly alone. She retraced her steps, found a smooth rock, and sat down. Setting the lamp down, she took out some travelbread and dried meat, chewing them methodically. She could not bear to extinguish the lamp, but after an interminable wait, it slowly died out. Again she lay in darkness. She knew then that Stel had tricked her. He meant to leave her there. She tightened her jaw. She would find her way out even if she had to crawl in the dark, feeling for the X's she had cut in the floor.

But she knew that was impossible. She could only wait. The weariness of it grew on her and again she dozed and finally slept.

She awoke with a start to find her lamp lit by her, and a small pot of oil, next to a knotted-up cloth she knew would contain food. She opened it and ate the travelbread inside, and cold, cooked ankleroot. Stel was nowhere around, but he had left a trail of arrows grooved in the cave floor.

Ahroe scrambled up and followed the path. Eventually it turned aside from her footprints and mounted a rocky incline. Here Stel had tied a green string, which she recognized as his old undersweater he must have been unraveling ahead of her. She climbed the rock, wondering faintly if Stel meant to lose her completely and then leave her there. But no. He could have done that before.

The path leveled off, and Stel returned to using arrow marks to show the way. At one point the marks turned down a side passage. Ahroe was puzzled because she saw them reemerge again, but curiosity made her follow them. Where the passage ended lay a large skeleton of some heavy beast, with long claws and teeth, curled in a reposeful snarl. Ahroe shuddered and scuttled back out to the trail again. Would Stel never be serious? She was not on a pleasure trip. She desperately wanted to get out.

The path again ascended and then suddenly met a set of crumbling stairs, of concrete, with a rusted iron handrail. This part of the cave was dry, and everything lay in powdery dust. The stairs curved up toward a squared doorway. Ahroe paused there, then entered a strange room.

Rows of circular tables, each with four chairs, occupied most of the room. One end was dominated by a long counter with stools in front of it and shelves of glasses and plates behind it. A sign above the counter read "Lunch at Smedley's Cave," and behind that faded, framed pictures dimly showed features of the cave below. Also on the wall hung a crumbled paper diagram with numbers on it. Ahroe read "November 2009" above the chart, and saw after the number 22, in fierce but clear handwriting, "And here it all ends, inside as well as out!"

Ahroe coughed in the dusty dryness. Her eye scanned the room again, and on the far side she saw three long objects lying in a row. Stel's tracks led to them, and as she approached, she could see where he had knelt in the dust. She drew in her breath. Shriveled and mummified, the bodies of a woman and two children lay face up on the floor. Farther on, in the dimness, Ahroe saw another grotesque figure propped in a chair behind one of the tables.

Only then did she note that Stel's green yarn led across the room to this figure, which also lay mummified in the dryness. The forefinger of one hand pointed to some scattered rectangles of heavy paper. Ahroe could see where Stel had brushed away the dust from some of them. Three of them had 8's on them. The others she could not understand.

Stel had tied a fork in the yarn. One part led toward the man's pointing hand and went over it to be tied neatly around the ancient book she had come for. The other branch went to the man's other hand, which clutched a strange metal object. In an instant Ahroe recognized that it was a short version of the rifle they had recently developed again. But this one was held in the hand.

Ahroe's glance went up to the mummy's head. Its teeth grinned horribly at her from between shriveled lips, and she could see how he had used the weapon on himself—probably on the others as well.

Shivering, Ahroe pried the weapon from the man's hand and dropped it in her coat pocket. Then she reached for the book. As she picked it up, a note fluttered out. She squatted in the dust and read it by lamplight. It was written in blood, no doubt an ironic thrust from Stel.

> Ahroe. Here is the book you so much wanted that you were willing to do anything for it. Having you act this way has made me weary of the whole thing. I still think it must prophesy again to all the societies. It is no doubt a troublesome book. I think I know some of the essence of part of what it says, though it is worth much more study. I can't read it anymore anyhow. May you and the Protector enjoy it. Please read some from the latter part before you give it to her. Now. To get out, go back down the stairs but take the left branch. When you get to the rubble, crawl over. You have been in here three days. Have a good trip back. I am not going. Good-bye my love. Stel.

Just that? Good-bye my love? Was he gone then? Not returning? Ahroe reread the note, took a last look around, and left the room. She found where the stairs branched, took the fork, and climbed up a slide of rock as Stel had instructed. As she worked her way over the top, she could see light ahead. She scrambled and slid down into the same entrance chamber she had been in before. Her snow sliders stood neatly against the wall and a bowl of stew, still slightly warm, lay beside them. She took the stew and sat in the entrance to eat it where she could see outside. It was near night on a dull winter day. The snow was turning slushy in a steady rain, and it seemed to Ahroe that the whole world matched her present mood of dejection.

XIV

AHROE slept in the cave mouth that night and remained there the next day, watching the rain outside and listening for Stel. But toward evening, feeling oppressed by the place, she wrote Stel a note, arranged her backpack, and set out for the other shelter.

It was past dark when she reached it. Finally hungry, she heated some grain mush over the lamp and sweetened it with a few spoonfuls from a pot of honey she found on a shelf. Then she made tea and decided to keep off the silence by reading the old book.

As Stel suggested, she started toward the back. It was heavy going at first, but she became curiously fascinated to see Pel's word gnarled and twisted this way, yet somehow speaking with more authority than Pel herself.

In the morning she went hunting, setting snares for rabbits and shooting two of them. The rain had stopped. After high sun she decided to return to the cave, but when she got there, she found her note untouched. She stood in the entrance room and called repeatedly for Stel, then again ventured down one of the tunnels, but when she got out of sight of the entrance and again heard the slow dripping of water from the roof, she felt panic swelling inside her and retreated once again to the entrance. She sat down and added to her note, printing carefully with a sharpened stub of charcoal. Then she left once again for the shelter.

Evening found her roasting the rabbits on a spit and reading again by the firelight. She took care to catch the drippings from her supper to replenish her oil. At this season they were scant. After eating and washing, she again settled down to read. At every sound she looked up expectantly, but it was never Stel.

Toward evening of her fourth day there she was surprised by distant barking, then the arrival of a big Shumai dog, galloping up and fawning by her to be petted. A tall figure followed, fur swathed, giving her a Shumai greeting yell. It was Tristal, the bridegroom of Jestak's daughter Fahna, recently back from his long adventure in the West.

They palmed in silence, Tristal grinning. "It brings back memories, this place," he said.

"Stel isn't here."

"Ah. Too bad."

"But he was. He's in a big cave southwest of here about nine ayas. But he won't come out."

"Is he all right?"

"I . . . don't know. Not all that much, I think. Why did you come?"

"I came to Pelbarigan with Jestak, who wants the council to work out some compromise. He's alarmed by the arrival of refugees from—"

"They aren't refugees. They left by choice."

"Yes. Anyhow, he sent me when you stayed so long. I see you have the book."

"Yes." Ahroe told him frankly and fully of her experience, watching his face grow more grave. Finally he unlaced his backpack and took out travelbread and dried apples, laying them down near the fire. Then he added two rabbits from his coat pouch and set to work preparing a supper.

Neither spoke for a long time. Then Tristal said, "I see you've been reading."

"Yes. The book in question. The cause of so much trouble."

"What do you think?"

"Much of it is culturally so distant it's impossible to understand. A lot seems like garbage to me. Or beside the point. Then there are good things. Extremist, but good things."

"Huh."

"I think I see why Stel would like it. All its heroes work against the governments they exist under—this Elijah, Jeremiah, Jesus, Paul. They all harass the authorities. Even, who is it? Moses. Until he became the authority. Then he knocked everybody around keeping them in line.

"Stel, in case you didn't notice, is against authority. He must find confirmation of himself here. None of them seem to understand what you can accomplish through social organization. The book makes the governments seem bad. Very bad. I wonder how accurate that part is. All these heroes wander off, though, doing everything on their own. Just like Stel now. He must see himself like this one, Elijah, running from Ahab's wife."

"I don't know that part."

"Don't bother. The Stels always win. The government is always wrong. I've worked for just government and order all my life. It isn't that easy."

"I see it another way, Ahroe. I know I'm young, but I've been some places. I didn't grow up your way, the Pelbar way. My uncle Tor absorbed some of it. I took in some of it from him. What I've read of the book is like the spirit of Pel."

"Not really. Pel wanted peace. She taught us to wall ourselves off from war, even when it cost us dearly. In freedom, in prosperity. This one says he came not with peace but with a sword."

"Not a literal sword. Tor used to quote Pel, 'Strike with the sword of forbearance.' I think that saved my life this past autumn. You've seen how raising the level of violence calls up violence on the other side. That's how the Innaniganis lost so many men just now. Their level of violence caused a comparable response. It didn't need to."

"We didn't strike with any sword of forbearance," said Ahroe, drawing the old short-sword she still carried, flipping it up, catching it on the end of the handle, idly and expertly twirling it, point up, on her fingertip. "We gave them violence for violence and beat them at it." She dropped the sword into her hand and resheathed it in a casual motion.

"Look at your hand. You took the burn to ease their way into it. They must have known that was a symbolic torture to satisfy the Peshtak a little without hurting the prisoners much. We guided them home and let them go. That was the sword of forbearance."

"I have little trust in it. If you saw that bug, Borund, you'd know by instinct he'd be back as soon as possible with an army like the wild cattle migration and all the force he could muster. We couldn't do any differently. We had to let them go. Because of who we are."

"That can't be lost on all of them. It has to have its effect. It is a weapon. They can't all be blooddrunk."

"They don't have to be. Only the leaders. The others'll do as they're told quick enough. It's always that way."

"Maybe they'll have a Stel or two."

"No doubt. But look what happens to the Stels."

"He hasn't done so bad, Ahroe."

"Not bad? He won't compromise at all, Tris. And look at

him. He won't let me see him. He's lying somewhere in that wretched hole in the ground, wounded in the side. He's aggravated it by running off, then I made it worse. He's lost to me now. It didn't have to be that way."

"Didn't it?"

Ahroe glared at him, but he simply smiled slightly at her, not intimidated. Finally she dropped her eyes. "It can't be helped, I think. I've always been the arm of authority. It hasn't been all that nasty, Tris. We've done a lot of good. Look at what we've done. He's always stirring up stews I have to eat. Or piling up rocks I have to build into walls."

"Maybe. There are other ways to look at it, Ahroe. You both are the two ends of a balance beam that weighs a lot of important things."

"That's little comfort. The forces on a balance always work against each other."

"But when they act in harmony, everything is held at the very tip of exactness, and when they pull against each other equally, that's when they are most together, most useful."

"Huh. Most analogies can be taken too far, Tris. You just did. Is the rabbit ready?"

Tristal prodded it with his knifepoint. "Just about."

After they ate, he wandered off in the dark to see the empty area around the old ruined Dome. Ahroe returned to her reading. When Tristal came back, she was asleep in the shelter, curled up in the cold. He spread his furroll next to her and squirmed in. She stirred and turned, putting her arm across him. "Tris, I can't leave him here."

"Yes you can. He wants it. Who knows? You may be in your best balance right now."

"Don't talk foolishness. Not now."

"I'll look for him in the morning. I'll see what he says."

"I'm afraid of what he will say. And I'm sick of the whole thing. Maybe I should go back there and lose myself in that black hole and—"

"Never. There is too much work to do. Work only you're tough enough to do. Let Stel do what he has to do."

Very quietly, Ahroe began to cry, and Tristal turned to her and tucked her head, still in its winter hat, under his chin. They lay very still, but the dog, feeling the cold, slowly wormed his way up between them, thrusting his nose under their crossed arms, squirming and rooting, finally sighing, as all three fell asleep. Far off, in the renewed cold, a tanwolf barked and another answered, then a third.

Even as they lay asleep, Jestak addressed the council about the question of the refugees. It was a late-night meeting, and the Judgment Room was not full, but all the principal politicians were present.

"I remember when I was young," Jestak resumed, "and training for my trip to the East. About three ayas downriver from here, high up on the bluffs, is a ruin from ancient times, mostly covered with vines and dirt. Some of it is astonishingly well preserved. Somebody really knew how to work with artificial stone. It might make the basis of a branch of Pelbarigan. Why not invite those who are uncomfortable with the ministers' views to go there? Help them settle it. Build with them. . . ."

"Split the city up?"

"It's split now, Protector. This way the crack doesn't become a canyon. There's cooperation. Interaction. You could start now. I'll show you where it is tomorrow. We—Brus and I—dug down into one of the foundations right on the river bluff. It's eroding out, but well based. A shelter could be made there very quickly."

"It's winter, Jestak."

"With this thaw the ground won't be frozen, Protector. It could be done. It's a good time to cut timber. Not bad to dig wells. It's high ground and some of it all right to clear for gardens."

The debate on the issue continued until finally Alance summoned several known dissenters and asked them what they thought of it. They were amazed and, though hesitant, willing to undertake the work.

"You will have help, of course," the Protector said. "Now. It's late. We have done enough. Set the timer, Linge. One sunwidth. We'll finish our prayers in bed." The guardsmen rapped their swordhilts as the Protector left, rapidly, through her private door.

XV

TRISTAL did not return from the cave the day he left for it, but arrived by high sun of the second day. As he approached Ahroe, he held his hands out, palms out, in a gesture of resignation.

"The note was gone, Ahroe," he said. "I searched the cave, but I don't think he was there. I found a room he had used to sleep in. Nice place, high and dry, on the other side from the room with the dead ones. Some cave. Beautiful. Never been in a place like that."

"Not there? Where, then?"

"I don't know, Ahroe. Gone. Too bad. I had some glasses Celeste had made him. He can't read easily anymore. Too farsighted. I left them in the cave. In the entrance room. Maybe he'll come back."

Ahroe studied a redtailed hawk circling lazily to the north. "Let's go, then. Back. I'll give them their book. I think it's going to turn cold again."

"Yes. Maybe some snow, too, eh?"

"Why did he have to do that, Tris?"

Tristal looked at her, surprised, but said nothing.

Before they returned to Pelbarigan a cold front bore down from the northwest with driving snow, halting Jestak's new community in the planning stage. But the idea had been planted and had germinated in hope and interest.

It took Tristal and Ahroe four days to get back, and though they arrived chilled and weary, Ahroe went immediately to the Protector's quarters and knocked on the door. When the old servant, Linge, admitted her, she found Alance awaiting her at the circular table in her sitting room.

"Your book, Protector," said Ahroe, laying it in front of Alance.

"You found him, then. Is he all right?"

"To imprison, you mean? No, I didn't really find him, but he left me the book. And this as well." Ahroe drew out the ancient revolver and laid it beside the book.

"What is it?"

"An ancient weapon left in a cave. Like the rifles but held in the hand. I think it should be studied and reproduced. We may need it before we are through with the bloody Innaniganis."

"Hmm." Alance took up the revolver and moved the cylinder. She drew back the hammer and snapped it, as Ahroe jerked back, alarmed. "I doubt we need to worry, Ahroe. It's been around a long time."

She laid the weapon down on the table and glanced at it just as it fizzled and flamed, sending up a gout of smoke. Alance jumped back. "Did you load it, then?" she asked tremulously.

"No," Ahroe said dryly. "It's been waiting all that time to go off. One shot left now. Might not work. Then it might. Don't fool with it, though."

"Don't worry. I'll give it to the guardsmen. Now. What do you intend—"

"To move to Threerivers. I wish to talk to Jestak first."

"To move? When?"

"As soon as possible."

"I have a job for you first."

"A job? I—"

"See Jestak about it. Don't go until spring. You can help with the new settlement on the bluffs."

"I don't wish to—"

"Ahroe, you are an officer of Pelbarigan. This is your duty. I won't hold you beyond it."

"My duty?"

"Yes. You can organize it as well as anybody. Jestak will be free to go then."

"I'll see him. Must I escape then, too?"

Alance laughed. "No. Not after you've helped set this up."

Ahroe found Jestak bent over a table with a circle of people, men and women, drawing buildings. Tristal sprawled in the corner, dozing. Jestak greeted her warmly, though the others drew back warily. Soon she was drawn into the project, which now only waited a break in the weather.

It seemed forever before she could talk with him alone, and

she was weary with the journey, but they finally shared tea together in the quarters of the Jestana, Jestak's cousin.

"I've been thinking, Jes."

"As usual. What this time?"

"It's the Coo. I'm worried about them. The Peshtak have drawn them into the Federation, but we haven't met any of them formally or diplomatically. We sent a mission, but its results didn't seem definitive to me."

"I don't understand. They are out of the way enough. A minor problem compared to the Innaniganis. What . . ."

"It all fits, Jes. They are the path to Baligan. It may be that Baligan will hold the key to the whole conflict with the East. That snake, Borund, referred to his treaty with them. If he could bring six or seven hundred more soldiers under his command, we'd have a hard time. We won't get away with what we did early this winter. They will have thought it over."

"Baligan? What are you getting at?"

"We think the Seliganis are essentially neutralized. They've established some ties with the Lake Sentani. They would be averse to breaking them and starting hostilities, even in spite of threats from Innanigan. Did you ever get to Baligan?"

"No. Never did. I know nothing much about them."

"If you could draw in the Coo, and perhaps go with some representative of theirs to Baligan, we could neutralize them. I understand their treaty is of mutual defense. If further hostilities arise, they have to understand that the Innaniganis are not being attacked but are themselves the cause."

"Is this what the Federation wants?"

"I want it. I've just had plenty of time to think about it. I am sure the Federation would go along."

"I see." Jestak stared at the ceiling a long time. When he looked back at Ahroe, he found she had gone to sleep sitting in her chair. But he had no need to ask her why she wanted him to do it. From the beginning he had been at the center of the expanding union of peoples, though for a long time he had not been at its forefront. He still had the name, though. And perhaps she thought he had the skill. Or was she growing weary of it all. He looked at her sleeping face and found it rich and still beautiful, but its developing lines were more those of responsibility and sorrow than of laughter. Only with reluctance did he reach for her hands to awaken her at last.

* * *

At that time Lume Budde, the Innanigani legislator, slowly climbed the stairs to his lodgings in the city. He opened the door to find his wife sewing maroon roses along the edge of a shawl.

"Well," she said, "do we go home now, or is it more freezing and waiting in this scant shinbone of an apartment?"

"Home," he said, sinking into a chair.

"Is it done, then? Did they decide to carve up the westerners with their table knives, then? Make peanut mash of them? Serve them on rolls?"

Budde waved his hand. "No. Almost, though. They decided to send a counterdemand. That the border not be the Leynap but the Cwanto as far north as the long bend westward, then north to Lake Sentani country."

"Is it war, then? More bodies? More expense?"

"Looks so."

"Why? Doesn't look as though it'll really be like swatting mosquitoes. Do they think it?"

"Yes. Probably. But I really think that isn't their point. It's the Industrialists. They're cooking up new weapons. They'll get to sell them. Besides . . ."

"Besides? You mean a cure for unemployment other than working?"

"That area gets them coal of their own. It goes west of the ancient fire in the ground."

"That far? Over all those ridges, then? Like a log road. How'll it be defended?"

"The weapons, Bes. They say the weapons'll do it."

"They'd better be some good weapons. They'd better fly up into the air and smell out the enemy like foxes, then fall on them."

"They won't, you know."

"Oh, I know that well enough. Anyway, in the morning we'll be going home. I'll have Telly put the cover on the wagon."

"Won't help him much with the rain and mud. He'll need help pulling. Maybe we could wait until he got the ox."

"Too much of a wait. He'll just have to do it. I want to get home. There's a pile to do before spring."

"Yes, my dear. So you've been saying. And saying."

"Lumie, is it really going to be a war, then?"

"I don't know. I expect yes, Bes. Unless they give up. It won't be a raid this time."

XVI

THE leaves were just beginning to dust the willow trees with green when the sentry at the Innanigani post at Sconet Ford, on the Leynap River, heard a distant explosion pulse and echo down the valley. He scrambled up from where he had been lounging in his log bastion and shaded his eyes across the river.

A puff of smoke drifted away from a line of horsemen on the bank. He sounded the horn and began counting. A lieutenant scrambled up the stairs saying, "What? What is it?"

"The westerners, sir. A lot of them. On their harzas animals, I think. They have a flag."

As they looked, four men waded their horses out into the stream, slanting upriver toward the long wooded island that stood about a third of the way from the east bank. The channel set on the east side, and ran high and cold with spring melt water. The lieutenant drew in his breath and said, "I guess they want to talk."

He ran down the stairs shouting orders. "Subdirect Tavvy! Roll out the cannon. I want all the men on the walls but for the boat detail. Raze, get me that document—from the legislature. Out of the upper right drawer. You, Sergeant Cathet, prepare the infirmary. We may need it."

Garet handed his reins to Kahdi and dismounted as the first Innanigani boat neared the island. He walked out on the rounded stones near the bank and caught the bow, lifting it a little and easing it ahead until it held fast. Then he stepped back and watched the easterners bring the two boats in and make them fast.

He held up his hand and said, "Garet Westrun, for the Federation. We have prisoners to return and want to arrange an orderly and safe transfer. We propose to bring them over to this island and then let you pick them up from here. You withdraw to your bank before we start. You wait there until we withdraw. All right?"

The lieutenant stared at him. "Prisoners? You mean the Opwel draft? They're still alive?"

"All but one. He died of something about twenty days ago. Couldn't do anything about it."

"Where are they?"

Garet jerked his head toward the west bank. The lieutenant squinted. "I don't..."

"On the horses. In the middle." Garet looked at him narrowly. "Easier than walking. And faster. Now, do you agree?"

The lieutenant drew in his breath. "Yes. We agree. Now. I have a message from our legislature. You will see that it gets to the ... federation, or whatever you call yourselves?"

"We call ourselves the Heart River Federation, as you well know—all of you in the eastern gang, or mob, or conspiracy, or whatever it is you call yourselves. Yes, I will see the Federation gets it."

"You won't like it. And now, according to it, it is my duty to inform you that you are trespassing on Innanigani territory because the legislature claims its border lies along the Cwanto. We will enforce our claim with arms and must request that you return to your own territory." The lieutenant looked at him anxiously.

Kahdi spat noisily on the ground behind Garet, but Garet merely smiled. "You mean you are giving up your claim to everything from there to the Shining Sea of the West?" He laughed. "I'll convey your message, but I think we ought to have an understanding. We're going to patrol this area until we receive a reply from the Federation Assembly. It would be easier on both of us if we let the matter lie until then. Agreed?"

"I can't agree to that. It is our land."

"Bullgills and birdsweat! You mean you want to start fighting now? After last fall?"

"We have no desire to fight. We only want to maintain our claim. That seems reasonable."

"All right, Innanigani. Have it your way. You'll see us patrolling, however. If you want to fight, that's up to you. We'll bring a reply to you here and signal you from this island. Is that acceptable?"

"As far as I have authority, I'll guarantee you safe passage here and back."

"Not like our last messenger—the old Peshtak. He's recovered, largely, from your mistreatment, but not without a struggle. Now, if you'll retire, we'll proceed with the transfer. Agreed?"

"Agreed," said the lieutenant, swallowing hard. He gave orders to his men to reboard and push off. Before he reached the bank he saw the horsemen push out into the water with the prisoners to be exchanged.

"All right, all boats ready!" he shouted, wading ashore. "A full five bowmen in each. When you reach the island, occupy it. We'll move our recovered men back and then supply the men on the island. You will occupy the island until nightfall."

"What in Sam's sweet rabbit ears is that supposed to mean?" one man muttered.

"We're showing our mastery," another said. He had a star brand on his left hand.

Thirty-two days later Sagan read the Innanigani declaration to the Federation Assembly. The Peshtak jumped up and swore, and the others looked grave. A long debate followed as to what course of action to take. Some wanted to invade Innanigani territory wholly. Others wanted merely to defend the disputed land. The Lake Sentani opposed an invasion, because it would jeopardize their relations with the Seliganis, who had a mutual defense treaty with the Innaniganis. However, they agreed to defend the land west of the Leynap.

Finally Ahroe stood and said, "I think what I am about to say will be very unpopular, but I feel we need to study the issue more deeply than we have. What could the Innaniganis have in mind? We've beaten them in the field decisively. Yet we know they are a numerous, resourceful, and advanced people. They would not do this without hoping to profit in some way.

"I think this declaration suggests that they think themselves able to back their move. That suggests new weapons, perhaps better than anything we have. It also suggests pride, of the kind that snake, Borund, sneered out of his face every time he talked to us.

"It may be that the key to our problem lies in Baligan. I gathered from talking to the prisoners, especially Borund, that the easterners rely on their alliances. They hope to call them in at will. This suggests some coercion. I doubt that the Baliganis are all that eager to send off a lot of soldiers to fight for Innanigani conquests. They may have to. It may be economically necessary.

We've just heard from the Lake Sentani about the Seliganis. They don't seem overly aggressive.

"I don't think, either, that any of us are anxious to lose men fighting when we don't have to. For these reasons, I suggest that we give them a counteroffer that will basically accept their terms."

Igant jumped up and shouted, "Traitor! I knew we could never rely on you."

When the hubbub died down, Ahroe said, "Igant, I understand your concern, but you ought to realize that Pelbar, as well as Sentani and Shumai, have already died for your cause. My own son has spent the whole winter on that campaign and only now has returned with their document. In any further fighting, Peshtak and Peshtak possessions will take the brunt of any punishment. If that could be avoided, it would benefit you as well.

"The land east of the Cwanto is not settled now. Obviously the Innaniganis don't need it. But we ought to notice that their declaration does contain a concession—a remarkable one. They have essentially given up their claims to land west of the Cwanto. That is a new thing. If they would hold to the declaration, I'm sure we could live with it—almost.

"We must prepare a reply, I feel. We should hold out for two things. First, we will accept their claim if they agree never to penetrate the land west of the Cwanto. Second, we must gain access to the Eastern Sea by means of the Baligani canal, thus avoiding the dead lands to Innanigan's south. This will mean free navigation of the Cwanto and the acceptance of the Baliganis.

"If they agree to these conditions, then we will be saved a war. The party among them which hopes to profit by a war will be disappointed. Those who hope for peace will be heartened. Our position with the other two cities will be strengthened. If we close our border with the Innaniganis, and the Baliganis prosper by trading with us, it may encourage the others to be more accommodating.

"Therefore, I hope you'll discuss this proposal seriously, and accept it, and send information about it ahead to Jestak so he can include it with his discussions with the Baliganis. We would want, of course, Baligani observers with our patrols along the Cwanto."

"If you expect the snakes to cross the Cwanto, why not stop them at the Leynap?" Igant growled.

"Two reasons. There will be no question that it will be aggression if they cross the Cwanto. We will save ourselves fighting maybe six hundred to a thousand Baliganis if their observers witness Innanigani aggression. And those supply lines—those nice, long, soft-bellied supply lines."

Mokil began to laugh. "You expect them to cross the Cwanto, Ahroe," he shouted gleefully. "You're just setting them up to lose."

"Well," she replied. "No. I don't really expect it. It may be. I would just as soon set it up, though, so they will lose."

Mokil laughed again, and this time Igant joined him, as did some others. The debate continued, but it seemed clear that eventually Ahroe's proposal would be accepted.

The year was rapidly warming toward summer when the Innanigani legislative president summoned a special meeting. He rapped it to order with the ceremonial stone and said, "I have an unexpected announcement that will need your consideration. First of all, a surprise. The Heart River Federation has accepted our declaration regarding the western border. They will accept the Cwanto north to the westward bend, and straight north from that to Lake Sentani land.

"However, they ask some concessions. The first is a promise that we will never move west of the Cwanto. The second is safe and free navigation down the Cwanto to the canal to the sea. They make no other stipulations. They have enclosed with the document a small packet of pamphlets produced by their academy. These pamphlets deal with fertilization of wheat, fish culture, the migratory patterns of waterfowl, the creation of plant hybrids, and the like. So. What do you think? Do you accept their stipulations? Ah. Legislator Borund?"

"Never. We shall never agree not to cross the Cwanto. We may go wherever it is our interest and will to go. I'm sorry. I cannot accept either stipulation. We cannot give those thieves and murderers passage down the river either. They must accept the directive just the way we stated it."

"Thank you. Legislator Zogab?"

"Why would they ever accept the directive as it was stated? All they would get from that would be a loss of territory. If we did not guarantee them safety on their border, they might as well keep the land to the Leynap. Since we've driven the Peshtak from it, *nobody* has settlers in it. It seems to me a marvelous and truly unexpected concession on their part. The only possible objection to it could be the desire to start a war we do not need to have. I suspect that might disappoint some of the Industrialists who hope to profit from one, but most of us—"

Borund jumped to his feet. "I deeply resent that, and—"

"Zogab has the floor." The president pounded the stone.

"Most of us are delighted to have peace. The westerners have even conceded coal land. That ought to satisfy the Industrialists if anything would. No. I think the westerners have once again proved themselves civilized, as they did this spring by returning the Opwel draft without harm and in good condition. No one made them do that."

The debate continued for some time, but eventually the Federation concession was accepted with its stipulations. Borund was consoled privately by a friend, who noted that nothing really prevented invasion. They needed only a pretext, and when the time was right, one could be managed. The westerners' concession did give Innanigan additional land and time to perfect the new weapons. Borund mused on that, and withdrew his objections with a show of reluctance and concession to the general will.

Sconet Ford received news of the legislature's decision by messenger, the lieutenant raising his eyebrows at the fact that another lieutenant—Oberly by name—brought it.

"We have orders to cross the Leynap and begin patrols, Oberly. We will run into the westerners soon enough and give the decree to them."

"I will convey it to the westerners for you, if you wish."

"You have orders?"

"I'm off duty this summer."

"What'd you do to your hand?"

Oberly lifted his left hand. The whole back of it was seared and scarred. "Oh, burnt it in a smithy fire. It's practically good as new."

"Looks horrid. Those stars were bad enough. That get you some time off?"

"Yeah. That, basically."

"We'll gear up, then. Listen, Lieutenant, I'm undermanned. You take a patrol across. Go directly west. Make a lot of noise. Build fires at night. They'll show up. Give them the document and order them off our land. Politely. It would be a good idea to do it politely. We are *very* undermanned out here. It's all stupid anyway."

"I know. Don't worry. I'll be the very grace note of courtesy."

"Huh?"

Three days later, as Oberly's patrol sat around the evening fire eating, one man played row pipes, Oberly thought he caught a faint smell of horses. He glanced up. Two men stood behind him. He jumped up and faced them, his heart pumping.

"What'd you do to the sentries?"

"Nothing. Walked around them. I assume you have a message for us."

"Yes. We've accepted the concession—your stipulations. You are now on our land. I am instructed to ask you to leave, to fall back to the west bank of the Cwanto. Want some supper?"

"No. Thank you. You have the document?"

Oberly rummaged in his shoulder sack, drew it out, and smoothed it. "Here," he said.

Garet took it and stuffed it in his shirt pocket. "Your hand," he said. "That looks bad."

"Oh. No. Better now. Sure you won't eat?"

"No. We have to get our men back across the river. It'll take a while. If you see any on your patrols, it'll be them, though I expect we'll get to them before you. Not many of you over here yet."

"Just us. Say, uh, you . . . you're Pelbar, right?"

"That's right."

"You know any Sentani?"

"Some. We have some along. Want to talk to one?"

"No. Well, no women?"

"No. Just smelly men, looking at each other's hulking bodies in disgust."

Behind Garet, Kahdi snickered.

"You wouldn't have met a Sentani woman named Miggi, would you?"

"Miggi?" A dawning recognition turned Garet's face into a broad grin. He let out a howling laugh. "So. You're Oberly. Ha. My mother told me about you." He laughed again, and seeing the lieutenant's annoyance, he stepped forward and hugged him, chuckling and slapping his back. Oberly pushed him away.

"Look, Oberly," Garet said, slightly sobered. "Let's you and me take a little walk. I need to explain some things to you."

Kahdi rolled his eyes at the subdirect then resumed his noncommital look.

Oberly and Garet strolled away to the edge of the firelight and sat down. "You actually burned your hand to erase the star. Amazing. What did Miggi do? Charm you with potions?"

"You know her?"

"Met her once. Look, Oberly. Do you have any idea of the difficulty of what you are proposing?"

"We're practically at peace now that the border is settled. I could maybe travel west sometime."

"You think we're at peace? For a while, maybe. Until the next Sharitan decides to cross the Cwanto. Or Borund."

Oberly was suddenly sobered. "That won't happen. You can't think . . ." He stopped and stared at the distant fire, waving away the insects.

"Mother says Miggi was embarrassed by all that attention," Garet ventured. "How can you have so much hope that you'd stake your life on it? I really don't understand at all."

"Will you take her a note?"

"I'll send it on. She'll get it eventually if everything goes right."

Oberly reached in his pocket and brought out a folded piece of paper sealed with a glued paper strip. He smiled shyly. "I had it all ready," he mumbled. "In case."

Garet took it and put it in with the document. They strolled back to the fire and the staring men. "Lieutenant, we are a few ayas west of you. We'll pull out in the morning. I'd appreciate it if you give us time," Garet announced.

"Some. Don't grow roots there."

Garet smiled slightly. "No. No roots. Then good-bye. Maybe we'll wave to you sometime across the Cwanto."

"Maybe. I assume any exchanges of information will take place at the ford south of Tremai."

"That will do," Garet called over his shoulder as he turned and walked into the dark. Kahdi backed up with him, then the two vanished.

"What was that all about, Lieutenant?" the subdirect asked.

"Just the document, Wali. I'm glad it went so easily. Hope it stays that way."

"I'm having enough of a fight with these mosquitoes, sir," one of the men remarked.

XVII

JESTAK'S horse trotted down the trail under forest trees, following two young Coo, who ran tirelessly ahead, ran, it seemed to him, for the sole purpose of proving they could exhaust the horse, could lope casually along it until it dropped. Then they would slide one of their long knives from its back harness and slice through the animal's throat, saw into its chest, and plunging a hand into the wound, groping for the scarcely stopped heart, tearing it from the still but warm beast to hold it up in triumph, with a laughing yell.

But he knew that was just a bemused impression. As he watched their easy strides, and their back muscles working under crossed leather straps, he came to see they were tired but unwilling to be bested by the horse, though fearing it.

"Ho," Jestak called, reining in. The men ahead stopped and grinned back. Their front teeth, filed to points, removed all boyish innocence from their smiles, though Jestak thought he could detect a common sort of glee beneath the twin red roaches that ran down the sides of their heads and the black tattoos of their foreheads.

"Easy," he added. "The poor horse is getting frazzled out. You mind if we walk it awhile?"

"Frazzled?" one asked.

"Tired. Weary. Ready to collapse."

"Huh," said the other. "Only Coo can run with Coo. Even Peshtak get tired. Too bad. We will walk for the sake of your bug-ridden animal."

"Good," Jestak said. "How much farther to Baligan?"

"Not far. Forty ayas, maybe."

"We'll be there tomorrow then?"

"With your animal? If it can take it."

"Xarn, I'm not an old man, but I do need the animal. He can

132

take it, but I have to take care of him. If we can make another ten ayas today, walking the horse, that would be good. All right?"

Xarn frowned. "We need to kill supper still," he said.

"No need to worry. I'll take care of that," said Jestak.

"Huh," said Xord, the other Coo. "We will. Fast enough. Another ten ayas then. Come along, Xarn, lazy one. But slowly. For the animal." They were both chuckling silently.

Jestak smiled at their sweaty backs and watched them bunch their arm muscles against the copper bands around their biceps. They reminded him of his own youth and touched him with the fire of its abounding energy. He looked forward with amusement to the thought of the disorientation their presence would give the Baliganis. He wondered how that would skew his mission to Baligan, but perhaps it would help. The Coo were universally feared for their ferocity, and seeing them participate in a treaty discussion would be a new thing to any easterner.

As Jestak and his companions traversed the Baligani path, far to the north, in an old gravel pit south of Innanigan, Borund stood with his hands behind his back watching Subish direct the testing of a new weapon, a machine gun modeled on an ancient one dug up from a ruin some years before.

"All right," Subish commanded. "Load it. Aim it over there. All ready?"

"Yes, sir. All ready," a young man called back somewhat dubiously.

"All right, then. Depress the start lever."

The man squeezed his eyes shut and pulled the trigger. A series of staccato roars exploded, with fire pouring out the breech, along with spent cartridges, then suddenly, the front end of the barrel blew apart, spiraling back in jagged steel petals.

"Efans, what have you done? Stupid! If you want to keep this job, you'll have to do better than that. Efans..."

The young man, who had remained behind the gun, turned slowly, his agonized face a mass of blood as he curled and collapsed.

"You filthy, harzas, harzpaz lout! What have you done?" Subish shrieked, shielding his averted eyes. Efans lay still and did not reply.

"You," Borund said to Subish's four attendant workers. "Don't stand there. Help the man. Evidently there are problems we don't understand yet. Take care of him. We'll work it out. The safety of Innanigan depends on it." Then he too turned his back.

* * *

The following day Jestak and his two companions walked out of the forest and across the field that led to the northwest entry of the city of Baligan. There a small military post had been built: a low stone tower surrounded by a log palisade, outside which sprawled long garden rows, meticulously kept by the bored soldiers and their commander.

Jestak paused and sounded his cow horn in a long greeting blast. The horse shied a little. He saw men in the garden look up, then stampede for the palisade. Xarn laughed. "Look at the beetles run," he said.

"Remember, Xarn, you are a diplomat now, not a fighter. No insults," Jestak said. "There are other weapons than knives and bows."

"Clubs, traps, snares, slings, and fire?" Xord asked innocently.

"Talk. Just talk this time." Jestak chuckled. "Now, hold that flag up, please, Xarn, and let's move forward."

As they progressed slowly across the field, a resonant gong sounded ahead of them. Jestak moved ahead of the two Coo, holding up his hands, palms forward. His horse sneezed and shook its head. The gate opened and a man slipped out. As he neared the man, Jestak swung down off the horse and walked ahead of it, hands still held up.

"Far enough," the man called. "No tricks. You are under our bows. What is it?"

"I am Jestak from the Heart River Federation. These are Xarn and Xord from the Coo. We have come to talk to your government."

"Major Zimon. About what do you want to talk?"

"Peace. Peace and trade."

Major Zimon stared at them. "So," he said. "Come then. You will eat with me in my quarters. I will send word. We will go to the city tomorrow. The beast—what is it? What is to be done with it?"

"A horse. His name is Hammer, but he is old, and most of the temper is out of him. I will take care of him. Do you have a forge? I need to fix a shoe."

Major Zimon looked at him dubiously. "Yes. Supper is in four clock strokes. You will have time to wash. Fix the beast afterward."

Jestak smiled at him, comfortable with his type and sensing his discomfort. "Thank you, Major Zimon." He turned to the two Coo and was surprised to find them slightly diffident and embarrassed. *That's a relief. The less bravado the better.*

☐ XVIII

Two days later Jestak sat in the reception room of the Baligani governor. The two young Coo squatted one on each side of him, having pushed away the chairs set out for them. They remained motionless despite the flies that crawled on the bare skin of their arms and upper bodies. Occasionally they exchanged timed clicks of their tongues. Jestak could not determine if it was a game or some more elaborate mode of communication, but its mysterious originality seemed to suit the Coo.

They had waited a long while, as he had expected they would. He had gone through his papers several times, counted the parquet squares on the floor, and had tried to play a Shumai mathematical solitare game but found himself unable to concentrate.

Abruptly a door slid open and two men in narrow-legged gray uniforms walked in stiffly and stood on opposite sides of the passage. Jestak rose. The two Coo did not move, but exchanged measured clicks.

A heavy man entered, swinging his legs stiffly. His crown was bald and shiny, but the fringe of gray hair that ran around his head seemed to form a complete ring with his fiercely tangled, heavy eyebrows. He too wore a plain gray uniform, more generously cut than those of the aides. A single braid of black piping surmounted his shoulders.

"Governor Entat," one of the aides announced in a loud voice.

The governor waved his hand deferentially and said, in a strangely hushed tone, "And you are ... the Pelbar ... Jestak? And your ... companions, the ... Coo. You have come to talk? There is not much to say, I assure you. Our treaties are set. Our loyalties are drawn. I have considered your document. I see no need of it. However, since you have come so far, I am willing to, uh . . . listen to what you have to say."

"I am indeed Jestak," the Pelbar said, stepping forward, "come all the way from the city of Northwall on the Heart to see you. And these are Xarn and Xord, young diplomats of your neighbors, the Coo.

"I have had some small chance to look around your city in the company of Subdirect Kensing, who was assigned to us by Major Zimon, and I must commend you on its order and enterprise, as well as its fine location and harbor. I live, as you may know, on a great river far inland, a river much larger than the Cwanto, our border now, which feeds into your harbor. But I have been on the Eastern Sea many years ago, as far as the Eastern Islands, where I lived for a time. It is good to see the great salt water again. I also wish to thank you for the accommodations you have put at our disposal and the provisions for my horse."

"A strange animal. I understand that half the children in the city have been riding it," Entat said with a slight smile.

"Some have. It is a gentle animal, and they seemed to want to. I saw no harm in it."

"Indeed, they seem to have found it . . . amusing."

"But to the point you raised initially, Governor. We certainly understand that you have longstanding alliances which you have no desire to disrupt, and that any threat to them would not be taken kindly by your su . . . allies, the Innaniganis. I know you are well acquainted with the border question which has arisen between the Federation and the Innaniganis, and also—"

"But you ought to know that a dispute with the Innaniganis is also a dispute with us. When you killed Innanigani soldiers, you committed a hostile act against us. We always act in concert."

"I see, Governor," Jestak said, pondering with a slight frown. "I may be mistaken, but I thought you had a *defense* treaty with them, and that you had a government of your own, of which you were the chief officer. If you will pardon my inquiry, Governor, was your elevation approved by the Innaniganis? I had thought from Major—"

"There is no need for impertinence. We have a free electoral system here and take no orders from the Innaniganis, though we do act together in matters of dealing with other . . . groups."

"But you were not asked to give approval of the border question, I assume."

Entat did not reply, but mused at the far wall near the ceiling.

"I mean no impertinence, Governor, and am sorry if I may be giving you offense. But last fall the Innaniganis invaded deep into Peshtak territory, burning villages which had stood undisturbed for a great many years, in two cases hanging all the citizens they could catch. Was this also a Baligani act and wish as well as one of the Innaniganis? I had not thought they had consulted with you."

The governor sighed, motioned to an aide, and said to Jestak, "Sit down, please. If this discussion will take a little while, we might as well be comfortable."

The aide brought a brocaded armchair for the governor, who sat. "The Innaniganis did not consult with us. They had no need. It has been a longstanding policy that we each have the right to defend our territory against incursions from the west. If they saw it necessary to pursue their defense by this . . . action westward, it was a military choice and arose from their present policy of pushing the Peshtak far enough back so that their vicious raids would be less possible."

"If you might permit an observation, Governor, you seem to be saying, as do the most severe of the Innaniganis, that westerners have no rights. When they raid, it is vicious, and when you raid, it is defense."

Entat pursed his lips. "No. We do not raid. Your . . . companions, in our experience, have done all the raiding. It has taken a good portion of our economy to defend ourselves."

Xord raised his hand and said, in a slow deep voice, "There is the matter of the burning of Coron."

"That was regrettable, but it was an act of private citizens, not of the government. They were reacting to the theft of five boats."

"Not by us," Xord said.

"At the time that was not known. It fit the pattern of longtime harassment."

"I trust," Jestak said, "that will now be at an end, and that negotiation will straighten out further problems. It is the feeling both of the Peshtak and the Coo that they have been systematically exploited and cheated, and that the general eastern attitude is that what lies in the west is theirs if they choose to take it. The Federation does not hold this to be reasonable.

"But to the point, Governor. Our present desire, as our document mentions, arises from our fear that our concession of territory may not be honored by the Innaniganis, their agreement notwithstanding."

"You do not think them honorable, then?" Entat asked, his giant eyebrows raised.

"Some of them are, Governor. Others . . . Legislator Borund, in particular, gave the impression when we captured him that we had no legitimate rights. In the agreement we made, we conceded territory to keep peace, and they conceded the concept that we indeed have a border. But we are not convinced that the Innaniganis really feel that way. We—"

"You must be aware that I will report this discussion to the Innanigani representative, Owayn, in the near future."

"We had surmised so."

"And that we will make no agreement which is not in their interests."

"I see. We had never hoped that you might abrogate their treaty. It is the maintenance of the agreement on the border that concerns us. It is necessary to the growth of trade between us. It should be profitable to both."

"Trade. Yes. You mentioned—"

"Cloth, hides, furs, coal, tallow, wood and lumber, grain, herbs, knowledge. As well as some copper, ceramics, western cut stone . . . that would have to come by sea, of course. With the aid of the Atherers."

The governor rubbed his eyes. "We would be most anxious to trade in peace," he said. "I am pleased to have met you. You must permit me time to consider these matters. Perhaps you could return in three days? In the morning?"

"Very well," Jestak said with a slight bow. "We are as desirous of peace as you. Quite frankly, if the Innaniganis do violate our territory, we feel that the nature of your treaty, which is defensive, ought not to force your participation. We feel that if this is clear to them, the chance for peace will be greater. They have agreed to the border of the Cwanto, as have we. We would like you to have observers on the border and are willing for them to run and ride with our patrols if you agree to that. Fighting is really absurd when you realize that we were once one people—and there is so much room for all of us."

"One people? I have heard that this is your theory."

"Much evidence supports it. In fact all the evidence I have seen."

"The evidence of culture opposes it, however."

"Some of it surely. That of language seems to support it, Governor. But no matter. We shall return in three days as you wish. Meanwhile, I know I will continue to sample with pleasure the crabs which are so plentiful in your waters."

The governor smiled slightly, inclined his head, and walked ponderously from the room. The aides slid the doors shut and stood in front of them. In unison, in a twitch, the Coo stood, startling the Baliganis. Jestak also inclined his head to Entat's disappearing back, then at the aides, spun around, and left.

On the second evening of his wait for the governor's response, Jestak was wandering on the waterfront in the company of Xord and Subdirect Kensing. The tide was out, and even though the Cwanto had not lapsed to the low water of summer, the broad mud of the harbor beach showed that the water had lapsed out the long channel to the sea.

"It's been a custom for hundreds of years," Kensing said, "for every boat leaving harbor to take stones and throw them across the great bay south of the city. Slowly we have diverted the main flow of water away from the dead lands south of here through the ancient canal eastward. Now we barely have to dredge it. Now the south dead lands seem to be coming alive again. Very gradually. But people are afraid of them anyway and avoid them, except for crab fishermen south of the rock dam."

Jestak scarcely listened. Something was odd. It was flute music, coming from the direction of a jumble of waterside shacks and boats. It sounded so familiar.

"What is that?" he asked.

"What? The music?"

"If I didn't know better..."

Kensing looked at him, puzzled, as the flute stopped, then resumed playing a Pelbar hymn Jestak had heard all his life. He sang with it, picking up the words.

> "So when the river has sunk to dust
> and all its cottonwoods have died,
> the waters on which we have relied
> will run, deep streams in which to trust,
>
> we sink fine roots in these full streams
> of Aven's never ceasing strength,
> we..."

Jestak paused and listened again. "That can be only one person," he said, turning and running down the muddy shore, followed by Kensing and Xord.

They found him squatting in the shadow of a large overturned boat, looking under. A shorter man stooped out still holding his flute, his bowl-cut hair like Jestak's. The two men embraced formally, then looked at each other while still holding forearms.

"Subdirect Kensing, Xord, this is Stel Westrun, of Pelbarigan, by some miracle here so far from home."

Stel nodded. "No miracle," he murmured. "I need glasses—or one of them. I couldn't go home for them and so came here in hopes of getting them. Still working on it. No real success yet."

"One of them?" Jestak asked.

"My eye—the right one was injured when I was in custody—sees only a vague blur now. I don't use it much. The world has grown flat and unreal. It has lost all depth and fullness. I'm all right for labor, but can't do much close work without a lens. So. Subdirect? Xord? I'm glad to meet you. Jes, I assume you're here on some business? Some alliance? Treaty? Something equally meaty?"

"I've heard some rumors, but only from fishermen. I work for fishermen now. We worry more about tides and weather than politics. Tides and weather keep us together. The contrary heart pulls us apart. Come. Don't stand in the mud. Come up on the roof and sit."

The group climbed up some wooden stairs Stel had fastened to the curving hull and sat on a long bench he had attached to the upturned keel. They talked for some time, until twilight dimmed the whole scene. Finally Jestak saw Kensing's uneasiness and drew his party down from the hull.

Stel stayed up on the bench. As the three began to pick their way across the muddy harborside, Stel called after them, "Jes, is Garet still in the east? Patrolling?"

"I don't know," Jestak called back. "Oh. I heard Aintre is ... getting fat in the middle."

"Well."

"I hear that anyhow."

Stel laughed loudly and tossed his flute up into the dusky air, catching it again with scarcely a glance. Then he put it to his lips and played something short and fast. "That will happen, I guess," he called after them, and laughed again.

* * *

"He's no spy. Stel?" The old fisherman chuckled at Major Zimon, who stood with his hands clasped behind him frowning, straight-mouthed, in the early-morning light in the small, wooden official building at the harbor.

"You can be so sure then? You're trained in such things?"

"We found him up the Cwanto, standing on the bank. He said he was a Pelbar and wanted to go to Baligan and asked if we knew how to get there. He said he'd work his way here. Wanted something for his blinkin' eyes. Said he'd had trouble at home. Done top-line work for us—all the dirty stuff without complaining. A lot of the cleaning and drying. Net mending. Hull caulking. No complaints, many jokes. You ain't goin' to hurt him, hey, Major? He's a good friend. Hurts nobody."

Major Zimon shot a glance at Subdirect Kensing. "I can't believe they'd be that naive," he muttered.

That morning Jestak and the Coo had to wait at the governor's house a long time before Entat appeared. Jestak put it down to the usual habit of officials, designed to indicate that they were busy and superior. He also worried some about Stel. Finding him was an unforeseen, and unfortunate, circumstance. Surely the Baliganis would be suspicious. And if they found out who he was, and learned of his knowledge and abilities, it might go hard for the Pelbar craftsman.

Finally two aides appeared as before and introduced Entat. The governor made no pretense of standing for a routine greeting of diplomats, but had his chair brought and sat in it. Then he sighed and looked from one to another of his visitors. "The matter of this . . . Stel . . . has complicated things," he said abruptly. "We had not known you had an agent here."

"Nor did we, Governor," Jestak said, laughing lightly.

"I can imagine," Entat replied. "However, the fact is that he is here. We cannot allow him to return, nor can we permit any further contact with him. We have detained him and will ask you to leave today. The one thing we can agree to is to allow observers patrol with you as you have requested."

"Your spies?"

"Your request. If you wish to withdraw it, that will certainly be acceptable."

"No. We do not wish to withdraw it, for the same reasons we advanced it in the first place. We are hoping for peace, and if there is to be hostility, we would as soon it did not include your people as well as the Innaniganis. We of course assumed your observers would give you a complete report of us and our activities. We have nothing to hide—relative to our patrols."

"Again, I can imagine. You seem not to have mentioned the Seliganis."

Jestak smiled. "No," he said. "They seem to be less under the heel of Innanigan than Baligan is. We will do as you say, then, and await your observers where you ask us to. I hope, Governor, that you will take the time to interview Stel. You will find him an extremely interesting man. He is the despair of many Pelbar. He is too individual. They will be enraged when they learn that his presence has so strongly affected our relations."

"And you are not enraged, then?"

Jestak laughed. "Yes, I am enraged. No. Not really. I am surprised. I am disappointed. However, I know him well from the past. He has a way of—well, you may see. Have you interviewed him?"

"He is not a diplomat."

"Ah. Not good enough to see a governor. His mother used to be the Protector of Pelbarigan, that is, the governor. Indirectly, he . . . well, I suppose I shall leave you to learn, or not learn, of Stel. You would probably dislike him anyhow. I hope you treat him gently. Now, then. Xord, Xarn, are you ready?"

"I have not ended our conference."

Jestak, who had risen, sat down again. "Yes, Governor?" he asked.

Entat hesitated, raised his eyebrows, and said, "It may yet work out between us. We will be grateful, in any case, for a cessation of Coo raids."

"Be sure your men stay on their own land, then," Xord said.

"The location of our border may be a matter of dispute," Entat said.

"It is well enough known," Jestak said. "West of the Cwanto, north of the Reed west to the big south bow, straight west from there to the north rim of the dead lands. You have much room for expansion out onto the east peninsula. The Federation will defend Coo land."

"With hordes of primitives," Entat muttered.

"Not hordes, Governor. We primitives will manage with no more than crowds. Perhaps a small mob. Seriously, let us not allow it to come to that. If you have leisure, please talk to Stel."

Entat did not reply, but Jestak made no move to leave.

His dignity satisfied, Entat rose and retired through the sliding doors, which the aides closed behind them as Jestak and the Coo rose. "Bullguts," Jestak muttered. "A mess. A freaking, mud-flatted, sweat-oozing, scab-scuffing, maggot-tunneled, plug-nosed mess."

Xord stared at him. "Not Stel's fault. He didn't know, I think."

Jestak tugged at his hair with both hands. "No. He didn't know. I—let's get out of here." He laughed ruefully and added, "Ready to run?"

"Not so fast we'd kill the horse," Xarn said, his eyes narrowing in a smile that added an extra wrinkle to his tattooed cheeks.

"Good," Jestak returned. "I need him. It's a long way to Threerivers, but I think I'll take my time."

 XIX

As the late-summer sedges browned and the long-tailed blackbirds began to move in flocks every evening, Major Zimon began to look more anxiously for the return of his son from the summer patrols of the westerners. At least twice daily Zimon wandered out toward the northern bastion, only to receive a glance and headshake from the posted guards there.

Stel had been incarcerated for a time, but after complaints from the fishermen, he was allowed to work with them during the day, returning to the city prison at night. Major Zimon had interviewed him extensively, and recently had sought him out to inquire guardedly about the possibility of danger to Garf. Stel had said there would be none, unless it came from the Innaniganis.

Finally, one afternoon early in the ninth month, which the Baliganis called the Month of Apples, the guards heard a long, rough horn blast and then saw three horsemen and a Coo runner coming out of the forest on the north trace.

By the time the newcomers arrived at the main gate, Zimon was there, looking noncommittal, even severe, as his son and Subdirect Onson rode in with a tall blond man, whose hair hung behind him in a single braid. The Coo was Xord, whom Zimon had already met.

Garf barely controlled his grin during his father's formal welcome, and Zimon could see him splitting with news and the pleasure of his summer. The subdirect, whose bearing was more military, and reserved, also seemed pleased.

The subdirect introduced Zimon to the Shumai, Kendo, whispering to the officer to slap both hands with him. Zimon had to look up at the steady, pale-blue eyes of the westerner as they were introduced. Kendo, he noted, wore a single Coo earring. His summer shirt, neatly embroidered on the collar edges, hung open halfway down, his chest hair bubbling out, bleached nearly white. His manner was loose and easy, as though he was at home anywhere, and his supreme confidence vaguely irritated the major. Kendo seemed almost amused at the military post, but was also reserved and courteous.

"Major," he said in a strange drawl, "here are some messages for you—some to you and the governor, a couple to the Pelbar, Stel, from his son Tareg, along with pamphlets. Those are all unsealed so you may read them. Now. If I may, I need to cool and water the horses. Onson—your replacement here? He might as well help."

"Over there, Kendo. Ikal, come meet the westerner."

Kendo grinned as a lanky, dark-skinned Baligani walked smartly over. As he lifted his hands, Ikal held his own up and slapped them lightly against the Shumai's. "Come, Ikal. I'll show you about the horses. Major? You have a fine son, even if he doesn't know the stars. We had a quiet summer of it. I guess I'll have to go somewhere else to find a war."

Late that night, after the visitors were in their quarters, Zimon and his son sat across the table from each other, two lamps between them, as the major went through the correspondence, questioning Garf about various points in it.

"These—what are these?"

"Pamphlets. Put out by something called the Pelbar Academy. This one was done especially for Stel. It's on aids to vision. They say the ancient name for them is 'glasses.' They use them in place of our held lenses. A woman from someplace called the

Dome wrote the pamphlet and sent that package, which contains glasses for Stel."

Zimon pursed his lips. "Four copies? One for the governor, one for a library, one for Stel, and . . . an extra. All perfectly alike. They must know more about printing than we do. Now. What did you learn? What weapons did you see? Tell me about the rifles."

"There were none, Father. Only bows, swords, even lances carried by the Shumai. The only thing I learned was about the horses—and their maps. They are well made, and they taught me how to make them. And about the West, and the Shumai and Sentani, then the Federation and how it grew. And a whole lot of mathematics and some stories. Some things about cooking and keeping off the bugs. And how the Peshtak make magic and snare rabbits. That kind of thing. Many things. I want to go west, Father, and see more. But they're wary of us and really spooky about the Innaniganis. The 'Ganis are building a fort on the Cwanto south of Tremai, at the ford."

"A fort? They never briefed us on that."

"No. The Federation thinks they mean to move west. They are convinced of it."

"Nonsense."

"Maybe. I'm not sure. We hadn't realized how far west they went last fall. The westerners beat them and then sent them home."

"You've been taken in."

"No. Ask Onson. We've seen too much evidence. We don't have to report that to Owayn, do we?"

"Of course not. Just give me a general impression. What do you think?"

"I don't know. But the westerners seem to want to avoid trouble. It's the Pelbar, really. They're very peaceful by nature, so I gather. But they fight. One of them, a soldier named Garet, told me a great deal about them. He left, though, to be a father. I—I don't know how they travel so fast, but it seems to be by using the boat the Tantal refugees told the 'Ganis about. They can run it up and down the Oh and some of the smaller rivers. Fast. I think. I didn't see one. They didn't talk about it."

"Hmm. You and the subdirect had better talk to the governor. he can brief you on what to tell Owayn."

* * *

At that time a group of people stood on the riverbank at Threerivers amid a circle of torches. Ahroe, addressing the Shumai, Blu, said, "You've tried it then. Can you show us?"

Blu spun the cylinder on the revolver that had been modeled on the one from the cave. He cocked it and aimed across the water at a floating branch. The gun fired with a bright flash and a splash jetted up in front of the branch. He fired again and again, using all six rounds in rapid succession, churning the water near the target.

"It's hard to hit anything with the short barrel," he said. "But I think practice would improve my aim."

"What do you think of it?"

"As a military weapon? It might be good for riders, or in close quarters. I wonder. It's so easy to hide. We might regret sometime we have it."

"What do you mean?"

"All kinds of people will eventually have them. Right?"

"We'll keep a governmental control on it. And educate our people."

"Huh," Blu replied. "Anyhow, that's how it works."

"What about the hand-thrown phosphorus bombs?"

"I don't know anything about them. I don't think I want to, either."

"It's the Innaniganis, Blu. We'll have to be ready. They're an energetic people. They won't take their defeat easily. They're already fortifying the east bank of the Cwanto."

"They're welcome to it."

That same evening, on the east bank of the Cwanto, Exalt Peydan looked across the river from the bastion of the new fort. "Onus," he called.

"Yes, Exalt?"

"The fires on the west bank. There are none tonight."

"The patrol rode north yesterday, Exalt."

"Leaving no one?"

"We have seen no one."

"I don't like this, Onus. Look at the vast tract of land they gave us. Why this fort? Does Borund still have so much power? Will he never be discredited?"

"He lost credit, Exalt. You are the commander. Over his objections. The people know the defeat was not your doing."

"Some. Now, what about this new weapon, this machine rifle?

Am I supposed to use that? How? Why have we built it? So as not to be helpless? If the westerners wanted to, they could have been in Innanigan now."

"Or the other weapon, Exalt."

"What other weapon?"

"Ah. I heard a subdirect telling another he had seen it tested. Simple. It is like a tube a man can carry and plant up at an angle. You drop a projectile in the end and it fires out and up, then explodes when it falls on the target."

"Like a Tantal rocket?"

"Better. Easier to aim. And you don't have to see your target to hit it. Just know where it is."

"A subdirect knows this and yet I do not. You know right now what that means."

"I'm afraid I do, Exalt. Unless we can head it all off."

On the following night, Major Zimon invited Stel to dinner to see Kendo and Xord before they left with the replacement observers. They ate in the officers' retreat in the city, a traditional dining room with carved wood decor. Among the curving wooden fronds of each wall, the major had drilled holes from which observers could scrutinize all of Stel's movements to see if he would signal the Federation men in any way.

Dinner began with a salad, which Xord ate with his own buckle knife, rapidly and neatly. Stel watched him with a slight smile, then rolled his up in its cabbage leaf and calmly ate the roll from one end to the other. He saw Kendo staring at him.

Soup followed. Again Stel observed Xord, who was not used to spoons, attempting to eat like the Baliganis, finally giving up and sipping directly from the bowl, blinking at the heat. Stel imitated him, but added the touch of swishing the soup noisily around in his mouth. Then he blotted his lips delicately on his cuff.

When the dish of three vegetables arrived, Xord would not touch his until he saw what the major did. At first Stel also kept his hands in his lap as Zimon, talking, delayed Xord's eating. Finally Stel carefully cut the squash into the shape of a human face, inserting slices of tomato for eyes and mouth, and adding the pot herb for hair. As the others ate, he made adjustments to his creation, silently, deftly, squinting through his one good eye.

Finally the major said, "I'm sorry. You seem not to like our food. Is there anything I can get to replace it?"

"Ah. No. I am grateful for this, Major, and wish no spectacle on my behalf. It gives scope to the imagination. It's perfect to anyone with an eye to creation. Your dinner bears up under the closest scrutiny. Could I scrutinize, that is, which I cannot, having lost access to the glassmaker with whom I was devising some means of seeing. I could barely climb your stair this evening."

The major flushed. "Should you think my behavior odd, Major," Stel continued, "you may have some sense of my feeling as a visitor to your city. It's all very odd and uneven. Here I am rescued from scaling fish and invited to climb the hill to this excellent dish. I am promoted from gutshoveler to food spooner. I who serve am thus served. The experience of your humblest net mender is thus amended. I've spliced enough rope to make all the connections, of course, but am asked to cast loose and drift with the tide.

"Are my glasses to be peered through by some equal of Owayn's before I am permitted them? You have some conviction that I am guilty of a crime. Or by rights should be somehow wrong. I am heartily tired of beating about the courtesies while seeing through the dark of this visual fog and so I'm sounding my fog warning. Is this discourteous? I cannot see it. I lack social vision, as my wife used to say. True. You are distant enough, Major, so my poor pupil can study your face, but the face on my plate is not so plain. To be plain, may I not have the glasses brought for me?"

This speech created a silence. The major flushed. "They will be brought presently."

"They are indeed a present," Stel said, "though not present."

"Stel," Kendo said, "you could talk your way out of a Peshtak snare, but aren't you talking your way into one?"

Stel chuckled. "In fact I once literally talked myself out of a Peshtak snare, but this is more like one of the fogs on the bay. You can't talk out of it. I am only banging my warning gong to say where I am in it. It is a fog out of the north. The Baliganis import them to make life more difficult for everyone.

"However, Major, I apologize. I have behaved poorly for a guest, and know it. I am grateful to be here. But I can't really see close things. The means are here. I would like them. I am impatient to know if my nails are clean. Or there. Well, I'll admit it. I really want to read again. You can do it with a lens. But lenses lend difficulty. I want to ignite ideas, not the pages."

Stel stopped abruptly and sighed. Then he looked around, smiled, and ate the vegetable head he had made.

Zimon looked at him severely, but tapped a gong and requested that the glasses and letters be brought to Stel. The Pelbar received them with a grin and put the glasses on.

Kendo snorted. "You look like a beetle in them, Stel."

"But not a futile beetle," Stel returned. "A beetle in fine fettle. You can't nettle a little beetle with a needle not of metal," he added gaily. Then he laughed broadly, grinned around the table, and said, "So much clarity has been added to my situation, Major. Suddenly you are my distinguished host. In view of the marked improvement in my perceptions, I shall no doubt be a more discerning guest." He laughed again, then fell silent, looking down at his plate.

"Wouldn't you like to read your letters?" the major asked.

"Letters later," Stel said. "I mean to enjoy the company now. To take note of you all with dispatch. You yourselves are the massive missives of my relief, and I am grateful. Please. Go on. I won't play the wag anymore, nor shall you bark the shins of your sensibilities on any more puns. I mean it. My friends, may we all find a way to get along and see our way forward to a bright future with the unclouded sun that scatters light on every society."

Stel laughed again, smiled around the table, and began to eat. The rest stared at him for a time, until Xord said, "By Morc's blue beard, Stel, you stand words on their heads. Listening to you is like riding a rapids on a log."

Stel grinned and added, "Riding a rapids on a log could be an upsetting experience."

"You promised, Stel," Kendo said. "My shins are smarting."

"Better to smart in the shins than dumb in the head. But I did promise and thank you for your indulgence. Your tolerance is remarkable—now that I can see."

Major Zimon groaned and Garf murmured, "Don't encourage him. He's incorrigible."

"Contagion has set in," the major said, and tapped for the servers to clear the table.

Late in the evening, Zimon found Stel engrossed in the pamphlet Celeste had sent. Stel smiled up at the officer and tapped the page. "This is something we could set up here, Major. There must be vision problems here beside mine. This could be a new Baligani industry."

"I scanned through it, but I couldn't understand much of it."

"I do. I could help, given the chance, Major."

"Hmm. I read your son's letter, too."

"I expected you to."

"All very enigmatic. As also I expected. Who is Raydi?"

"My daughter," Stel said with a rueful smile.

"And you have a son."

"Yes. Tareg."

"How fortunate you are he is safe at home building walls. It is difficult to send Garf out to patrol with Peshtak and Coo."

Stel smiled. "He is safe with them. It's the 'Ganis who keep me awake at night."

OWAYN sat at supper with his wife and daughter, in a small, candlelit room. They were largely silent, as the ponderous Innanigani ate his methodical way through each food on his plate, one at a time, lightly clashing his utensils on the dishes and each other.

"It's snowing again, and not yet winter solstice," said Mz Sovel, Owayn's wife.

"Urrm," he replied.

"But perhaps it will not lay. A warm sea wind should melt it."

"Um."

"Owayn, what of Ferth's eyes?" The girl looked up, startled.

"Ferth's eyes?"

"Yes. You know she has trouble seeing anything over an arm's length away."

"Nothing can—"

"Owayn, you know it can. You know the Pelbar has been working with the Balis on these lenses on the face."

"Manny, you are certainly aware that we can't get involved with him. We'd be sent right home if he didn't poison us."

"Sent home? Good. I can think of no better place to be. Did you see that painted Coo here?"

"Weeks ago. This position is an honored one, bound to lead to status at home. And it's necessary. Now let me eat, please."

"If you're unwilling that your own daughter should see, well, I just don't know what I shall do." Manny Sovel covered her face with her ringed hands and began to sob quietly, her dark hair, piled in a mound, bobbing above her fingertips.

Owayn put down his spoon and stared at her. "We have a copy of the Pelbar explanations. We will have it studied and do something about the problem."

"You don't need to concern yourself with me," Ferth said.

"Yes I do," her mother cried, slamming her fist on the tablecloth, making her plate jump. "Owayn, here we have the chance and you make objections. The way you do to everything."

"He's the enemy, Manny. He's a killer, like the rest."

"Listen. I've seen him. He looks harmless enough. We could send Ervil with her. As to the Pelbar being killers, we both know Borund stumbled into that folly on his own."

"Leave my cousin out of this. As to the Pelbar, I've seen him at work with no shirt. His body is a mass of scars, some obvious sword cuts—one ugly one on the side. He's no innocent."

"He's funny when he talks," Ferth said. "I've heard."

"Well," Mz Sovel said with finality, "Ferth and I are going over there when the weather clears. I will not have her groping and squinting around like an owl in daylight."

Owayn threw up his hands. "I forbid it."

"Chain us up, then," his wife shrilled. "Make prisoners of us. You don't care about your own daughter. You want her to be another tool of Borund's policy. Before he's through, he'll have us all killed."

"I won't hear any more about it!" Owayn set down his spoon and rose. He strode from the room with only one reluctant glance at the pudding. Perhaps Ervil would bring him some later.

"I really don't know a great deal about this, Mz Sovel," Stel said four days later in the rooms the Baliganis had assigned to the project. "Celeste's pamphlet is a start. If you were at Pelbarigan, she would manage soon enough. But here in the primitive East..." He grinned. "I'm sorry. Here is what we can manage. As you see, we're making up a series of lens types. We'll just try them on, one at a time, until one clarifies things for her. Then we'll duplicate it. One eye at a time. Eyes can be as different as snowflakes, so I've been learning. Up until recently I thought I had a matched set. But they've been no match for what they've been through. And they've had to be reset."

Mz Sovel glared at him. He glanced over at Ferth, who was gazing at the floor as her gangly legs twined around each other. He judged her about twelve, a freckled redhead just entering the elongated sapling stage. "So far," Stel muttered, "we've been caught up in simply making simple lenses for older people who get farsighted. Like me. Our eyes have traveled so far they like distance. They are beginning to rummage around for eternity."

"Please get to the point. What can you do for Ferth soon?"

Stel paused a moment and said, "You're used to ordering people around, aren't you." Ervil stirred restlessly, and one of the Baliganis looked up from his lens grinding.

Mz Sovel leapt to her feet and said, "Well! I have never..."

"It sounded that way, you know," Stel said mildly. "Ferth, what do you think?"

Mz Sovel seized the girl's hand and started for the door. Then she paused and looked at her daughter, who had begun to cry. She whirled toward Stel and found him still seated, smiling. "It might take a while," he said. "I don't have to do it, though I'd like to help. You'll have to be civil, though. I'm not a Baligani. I'm not afraid you'll be down here with your army."

"See here, scum," Ervil said, walking toward Stel. The nearest lens grinder stepped between them. Ervil glared up at the man, turned to see the Sovels departing, and followed them quickly.

A week later Major Zimon found Stel trimming the rib on a new boat with a hand axe. "It's no use, Stel. They can't understand the system yet. You'll have to go back to managing the new lenses."

"I will?"

"We would prefer it," the major returned, his breath vapor whipped away by the winter breeze.

Stel sat down and rubbed his hands. "May I live down here with my boat?"

"Yours?"

"Rayker gave me that old hull. I'm fixing it. I've built boats, you know. Keel to mast, tight and fast. Show them all my stern in a race. Bow to nobody. All my tacks driven home to stay."

"Please, Stel. Yes, you can live here if you promise not to leave on me."

"I won't. No need to go. Major, you know the 'Ganis are arming?"

"Wouldn't you?"

"Building an army, Major. The fishermen have it from their fishermen."

"So they've told me."

"Major, is your son going to patrol next summer?"

"He's a soldier. Did him good."

"The 'Ganis weren't ready then. I'm worried. My son will be there, too."

"I thought he was . . ."

"No. Kendo was afraid for me if he said my son was a soldier. Takes after his mother."

"It's clear from your scars that you've been one, too."

"No. I've been in fighting, but only because it had to be done."

"Why are you telling me this?"

"Because you're trusting me."

"What would you say if I told you Owayn wants you back there to work on his daughter's eyes?"

Stel laughed. "Not Owayn. His wife. After she tired of being angry." Stel wiped his axe blade on a rag and laid it under the old hull. "You want me to start now?"

"Soon. Come to dinner tonight. But no puns. Use them up on the wind and seagulls."

Stel watched the major walking up the beach to where his orderly awaited him. It was strange—for a moment he thought he saw Ahroe in the Baligani's straight-backed carriage. His smile faded as he turned and called up to a passing gull, "Come to dinner so I can punish you. There'll be a dish of fish, though oyster is moister. You'll solve my major problem." The gull veered away and flew out over the water, delicately touching the air with its dipping wings. "Your perch is in the ocean, old bird," Stel shouted after it. Then he felt a strange melancholy settle on him. He longed to read again and, taking a stick, knelt to write a sentence from the old book in the sand. He stood still pondering as the sun went down, then rubbed it out with his boot and stooped under the boat to wash for supper with the major.

* * *

Two weeks later, in late evening, Ervil entered the Sovels' house with Ferth. They stamped off the ice in the anteroom, as Mz Sovel opened the door and said, "Where did you find her?"

"Just outside, coming."

"Where were you?"

Ferth mumbled something.

"What? Speak out."

"With Stel."

"With what? The savage."

"He's not a savage. Why can't you fix my eyes if he's a savage? He's . . . all . . ."

"Don't stand there, freezing the house. Come in. I forbid you to—Now stop crying. You're always crying."

"You're always so mean. I have to have somebody to talk to. I can't—"

"My dear child, all of Baligani society is here for you to talk to. You don't have to—"

Ferth stamped and shrieked. "They hardly talk to me since . . . since all of Baligan knows we are building an aaaaarmy! They look at me like—like an eeeeenemy." She sank down on the floor, crying.

"You may go to the lens shop with Ervil, and that is all."

"She wasn't there, Mz Sovel," said Ervil.

"Wasn't—"

"No, I was visiting Stel down at his boat, and he brought me home so I was safe enough," Ferth shrilled, squealing, from the floor.

"Aauuh," Mz Sovel choked out. "Ervil, you mustn't say anything about this to anyone. Not Owayn, certainly."

"No, Mz Sovel," Ervil said. "But she is right. She was safe enough. I've seen enough of the Pelbar to know he wouldn't hurt her."

Manny Sovel plumped down in a chair. "You're all against me," she said. "And that savage."

Ferth rolled over on her back, her arms outstretched, and said, sighing, "He's not a savage, Tammy. He's helped me learn my calculation and has told me all about the West."

"Lies, no doubt. All lies," her mother muttered.

XXI

THE black-eyed daisies were blooming as the patrol rode up the west bank of the Cwanto. Garet led. Garf of Baligan rode behind him, followed by Kendo the Shumai and seven others. They had passed the ford south of Tremai the day before and taken note of its expanded fort, but the west bank showed no signs of Innanigani incursion.

Someone whistled from farther back in the line of horsemen. Garet paused and looked back to see the Shumai, Kahdi, dismounting and stooping to examine the grassy bank with care. The big Shumai stood and waved Garet on, then knelt and spread his hands and moved them across the grass tips. Garet frowned, then touched his horse forward again. Kahdi would report what he had found if it was anything. Perhaps a wild cow had entered the water there, where the bank sloped easily.

The patrol climbed a hill back from the river ahead of him, then walked the horses down the north side of the hill to the bank again. The river was swifter there, and narrow. Something made Garet uneasy.

Across the river an Innanigani officer whispered to the man at his side, "The lead man is almost there. Remember, if he doesn't step on it, shoot anyway when I signal."

Suddenly Garet and his horse flashed up in the air with a roar. Instantly, from the east bank, four machine rifles began to pound, and the whole patrol went down. Two horses thrashed until the anxious gunners gave each an extra burst. Silence and stillness followed.

After several sunwidths the Innanigani officer stood and motioned behind him. Six boats were brought forward and shoved into the water. The oarsmen stepped out and slid into their positions just as they had practiced it. Quietly they began to row out into the current.

Garet lay half under his horse, breathing with difficulty, bright blood bubbling out his chest as he did. Vaguely he fumbled for the saddlebags, reached blindly in, and drew to his chest four large, egg-shaped metal objects. Then he lay back panting and listened.

He heard the quiet voices and watery sounds as the Innaniganis beached their boats. Biting his lip, he twisted the top of one of the eggs and lobbed it over the body of his horse, then threw the second, then the third.

As the first one burst up in a giant flower of white fire, he took the last, turned the top, still holding it down, and wedged it under his armpit, gripping that arm hard with the other, holding in the fuse, biting his lower lip until blood ran.

Screaming and burning Innaniganis fell and ran into the river, and the weeds on the bank, though summer damp, caught fire, as did nearby trees where the phosphorus stuck to the trunks. The grass burned toward Garet. He smelled scorched flesh and pressed his nose down by the dirt to clear the air he breathed as much as possible. He coughed blood. Before the fire reached him, his breathing grew uncertain. He inhaled deeply once more, trembling. Then he blinked and let his breath sigh out in death, his eyes open, staring at the dark belly of his horse a handspan away.

The phosphorus bombs had killed or burned all but two of the Innaniganis, and the survivors frantically waded and swam back toward the east bank, as two more boats rowed rapidly out toward them. When his men were clear, the Innanigani officer ordered the gunners to shoot again, and their fire kicked up dirt and pumped into the dead. Several more phosphorus bombs went off, spreading the fire further. Thick smoke rolled back across the river. The Innaniganis began to choke.

Behind them the party who were to convey the dead westerners back into Innanigani territory rushed forward to the riverbank. Meanwhile Kahdi, who had seen the action from the hill, galloped his horse south, back from the river, to the nearest patrol camp.

Finally, near high sun, the fire spent itself, and the Innaniganis once again set out across the river to view their hardwon victory. The fire-blackened area still smoked. The men were sickened by the charred bodies of horses and men, some their own, but began to search through the remains for whatever they could learn.

One hooked a stick around Garet's blackened body to pull it

free from the horse. It remained lodged under the animal. "This isn't a freaking party," an officer said. "Take hold of him." The soldier looked around in disgust, but reached for Garet's arm. As he pulled, another white flash erupted, covering the man, the officer, and several others with white fire. Others ran for the bank, some again burning, while the remaining men in the force ran along the riverbank.

Rifle fire began to crackle from the hill to the south, downing several men there before the others took cover. The four machine rifles answered it from the east bank, raking the woods with fire. The rifle fire ceased.

Standing back from the east bank, Onus said to another officer, "Borund's plan has not worked, new weapons or not. If you want to invade the Peshtak, you might as well go ahead. There can be no pretense of the move being defensive now."

The man said nothing for a long time. "All right," he finally said. "Tell the messenger to inform Exalt Peydan that we in the north have been attacked and sustained a number of deaths. Tell him to cross the river in the morning and proceed westward."

"The men know, Exalt Onser. It will get out. Too many know."

"Shut your mud-swilling, filthy, harzas face and do what I say. Don't you smell the filthy, burnt bodies of your own men?"

"And theirs," Onus said over his shoulder as he hurried away.

When he was informed of the attack, Exalt Peydan asked the messenger, "Where did this occur?"

"North of here, about fourteen ayas, Exalt."

"Prepare boats. I will go and see."

"It is dangerous, Exalt. They have killed our men with their firing weapons."

"When we near the place, you can warn me, and the whole squad can land and proceed on the east bank."

"Yes, Exalt. I believe that Exalt Onser desired you to proceed with the invasion of the Peshtak. I heard him mention that it was in his message."

Peydan frowned slightly, took a piece of paper, and wrote hurriedly on it. "Subdirect!" he called. When the man came, he handed him the paper and said, "Take this man to the kitchen. I am making him a cook's assistant. On your way get me the four lieutenants. We have to investigate an incident in the north."

When Peydan arrived at the scene, after high night, the northern force had already crossed the Cwanto and proceeded southwest to link up with his, as a sentry at the crossing told him.

He viewed the burned area and the place where the Innanigani soldiers had been buried high on the hill west of the river. He also examined the remains of the westerners and their horses, which had been spread out, stripped of a few metal objects, and left.

"Bring the torch!" Peydan said. "Here. Closer." He shaded his eyes. "That one," he muttered, pointing, "is a Baligani. We have managed to kill a Baligani observer. Stinking codheads. Another of Borund's botches. Will we never be rid of these stupid, guts-eating adventurers? Look. Even surprised, they killed more of us than there were of them. All right. Back to the boats. We are returning to the Tremai fort."

Two days later, when Peydan had refused to commit his force to the invasion, Onser's force returned to the fort, shot him, and moved west with the whole army.

The day after that Xord arrived, completely worn out, at Baligan. He had to be helped through the gate of the north outpost, and when Major Zimon came, he silently handed him a message, still supported by two soldiers. Zimon unfolded the paper and scanned it quietly, then looked at the sky and said, "No. It cannot be." He turned to Xord and said, "What do you know about this?"

"Nothing. They read it to me. I—nothing. I grieve for you, Zimon. And for Stel."

"Lieutenant, listen to this: 'On the twentieth day of the Month of Honey, the Innaniganis ambushed a patrol on the west bank of the Cwanto, about thirteen ayas north of Tremai. They had a terrible weapon. Garf, son of Major Zimon, was killed. Tell Stel the Pelbar that his son, Garet, was also killed. One escaped and came to the camp I was at. We responded. The westerners shot their rifles at the invading squad from a hill. They shot back with their weapon, killing three more. I was wounded on the arm. We then fled. The Innaniganis have invaded the west in force. As we agreed, this is a XS3579753 message. Subdirect Reaf.'"

The circle of men looked very grave. "Major, I'm sorry. What can we do?"

"Do?" Major Zimon laughed ruefully. "Lieutenant, take this message directly to the governor. Put it in his hands, no matter what he is doing or not doing. If anyone attempts to stop you, tell them it is yellow priority."

The lieutenant and two subdirects trotted out the south gate.

Zimon watched them go, looked at his hands, and said, "Subdirect, see to the comfort of the Coo."

"We must tell Stel," said Xord.

"He . . . we need not be in a hurry. It is not good news."

"Let me rest. I will drum for him the dance of bereavement."

Zimon straightened up. "Rest. We will go together." He wiped his forehead with the heel of his hand and rubbed it on his thigh. Then he turned away, saying over his shoulder, with a slight tremor, "I will be in my quarters."

The next morning dawned foggy. Zimon and Xord stood, an odd pair, on the sand and mud bank of the harbor, watching as a soldier rowed Stel in from his boat, which was moored with the others offshore. A small group of curious fishermen had gathered. The owner of the skiff took the bow and drew it up onto land.

Stel, barefoot, stepped out of the stern and waded up to the group, squinting a little in the pearly light. He looked from one to the other. "What?" he said.

Zimon opened his mouth and shut it. Xord held his small drum in silence, staring down.

"It is Garet, isn't it? My son? Is it war, then? And Garf, Major, how? . . ."

"Both," Zimon said.

"I am sorry," Stel murmured, covering his face with his palms. "You are better at this than I am, Major," he said through his hands. After a time he took them down and stared eastward into the fog. "Too soon," he said. "There would have been time. He has a daughter, you know. Just born. He has had a troubled life. I am the cause as much as anything. And not. I wonder where he is now, and if he is—if the clear-eyed skeptics are right, and he has simply ended. Or the faithful, those muddy-headed, persistent, unmoveable seers into what is not to be seen, are right, and he is making peace with his own nature somewhere, or seeing deep into the character of God. Is it God, Garet, or Aven, or perhaps Atou? No, you have a Shumai soul, and it is Sertine. I . . . am confused. I think I shall be muddy-headed. There seems little point in being clear-eyed in such darkness. He was . . ."

Stel turned again to face them, with a look of desolation.

"I will dance for your comfort, Stel," Xord said. "And for you, Major."

"Thank you," Stel murmured, as Xord began a toneless chant,

hopping and shuffling, tapping his drum in monotonous thumping.

Other fishermen came, attracted by the strange sight, and stood in a ring, as Xord continued his dance, singing, "Ha, huh, huh, huh. Oh, to, no, no, ta, ka, ma, ka." Stel looked up at Major Zimon's deeply lined face and gave him a slight, whimsical smile. Then he sat on the bow of the skiff and patiently watched the Coo sing his chant of comfort to the bereaved. It seemed to take forever, and the crowd was much larger before it was finished.

At last Xord stopped abruptly, and Stel embraced and thanked him. "You must remember to be hard," Xord said. "Death comes to all. Some sooner is all. When it sees we care nothing for it, it leaves us alone."

"Yes."

"What will you do now? Come with me and fight the Innaniganis?"

"No. They have enough to fight. Stay here and help people to see, I think. I . . . it . . . may I stay, Major?"

"Of course," Zimon said in a hoarse voice.

"Will someone row me out to the *Joseph*?"

A dozen men stepped forward, but Zimon himself took the oars and rowed Stel away from the crowd. They stared at each other as they glided through the water.

"The 'Ganis will say they were attacked, Stel."

"I know."

"They will demand our help."

"Will you give it?"

"I think not. Garf had to die for something. But they will come and try to force us."

"The Federation will not permit that, Major."

"Will they be able to do anything about it?"

"Yes. I will send a message if you would like. With Xord. You may read it first, of course, and make what changes you wish. I assume the governor will stall. Will Ferth be safe?"

"Ferth?"

"Owayn's daughter."

"Yes. We have a representative in Innanigan. It is established and agreed."

They arrived at Stel's boat, and he vaulted lightly aboard. "I—I will stay here a while. If you need me, send here, Major. Please thank Xord again for me."

"That insufferable moaning."

"It was important to him. Remember, he danced for Garf, too. Thank him. It will bind him to you. If the 'Ganis come, the Coo will stand between with us."

"It is . . . hard to believe that."

"True, though. Thank you, Major." Stel watched him row away, then turned and sat hard on the stairway to his cabin. Despite himself, his arms began to tremble uncontrollably. "Garet," he murmured. "My little Garet. How long ago I lost you to fighting and its so frequent end."

As dusk settled on the harbor that night, Ferth came down to the water's edge and shouted repeatedly out over the water, "Stel, Stel." Shading her eyes, with her new glasses she thought she saw his figure far out, sitting on his boat, his back to her. What was wrong? Did the wind keep him from hearing her?

An old fisherman appeared at her side. "Go away," he muttered. "Leave him alone."

She glared at him haughtily. Then fear crept in as she saw his face. "He . . . didn't come to the lens shop today. He . . . was going to talk to me."

"You're not wanted here. Go home. Stinking Innanigani."

Ferth stamped her foot in anger. "Who are you to talk like that? Is he all right? What's the matter anyhow?"

The fisherman gripped her arms and shook her. "The matter? Your freaking army has killed his son is all and is invading the Peshkies. We're in for a war is all. Now get!"

He plumped her down. She sucked in her breath. "Killed his son? Oh. No." She looked out over the water. "Is he all right? Take me out to him."

"Get out of here!"

"Quick. Ervil will be coming. There's no telling when I'll see him after this. Please. Please. We're friends!"

"You are crazy," the fisherman said. He paused a long time. "All right. Come." He scanned the bank for Ervil, then picked Ferth up and waded out to his skiff with her. "If he tosses you overboard, you've got yourself to thank."

"He won't do that, though."

"Yeah. I know."

When Ervil arrived on the beach well into the night, he squinted out at the dark boats, trying to remember where Stel's was moored, then took a skiff and began to row. He groped among the hulls for some time, finally hearing, "Here, Erv. She's over here."

Ervil's skiff grated along the hull of a black boat in the star-sparked water. A hand reached down and held the gunwhale as he reached up and rolled aboard.

"She went to sleep on the deck here. Be careful. Everybody has been bringing me food. Don't step in it. I haven't . . . eaten it."

"Where is she?"

"Over here."

Ervil stooped down and felt Ferth's form under a light blanket. Her side rose and fell slowly, rose and fell.

"You could stay till morning. It's dark."

"I know. I've just been through it. Her parents would be frantic. They are now."

"Parents are that way. I will light a lamp, then, for you to guide on."

"Stel . . . I'm sorry about your son. I've heard, of course. Ferth has benefitted from you. Anyone could see it. She won't be seeing you any more."

"No." Stel stooped and shook the girl gently. "Ervil is here for you, Pumpkin."

Ferth woke slowly and in confusion. The two men carefully helped her into the skiff. She still seemed disoriented, but before letting go of Stel, she reached her arms around him and hugged him fiercely. "All right now. Hang on tight to the seat. Remember, Pumpkin, if you scratch your head with your foot while flying, always keep your wings level."

"What?" she murmured.

Stel shoved them off. As Ervil rowed back, he saw the light of Stel's lamp out in the harbor and lined it up with three stars in the east to keep his way. It was still burning, a distant spark, as they trudged up from the harbor bank and between the sleeping houses of Water Street.

XXII

EXALT Onser watched the newly rebuilt village of Turnat burn again with some satisfaction. An occasional rifle shot spat from the hill to the west, but it was met each time with a burst of machine rifle fire and a mortar round or two. His army had sustained some losses, but they moved as a unit, with discipline, and maintained shielded patrols with rifles similar to those of the westerners. In fact, he imagined they were probably better. But the westerners seemed to shoot with incredible accuracy. Well, Innanigan expected some losses.

Four villages had been burned so far, and Onser looked forward to eradicating the Peshtak from most of their territory that summer. Let the westerners mount a sizable opposing force. They would be meeting an army far different from Exalt Peydan's ragged bunch.

A subdirect walked up and stood smartly by Onser, saluting and waiting. "Yes?" said the Exalt.

"Exalt, we have a problem. We are using the machine rifle ammunition at too great a rate. At this usage, we will be out of it in about fifteen days."

Onser frowned. "What about the mortar shells?"

"Not so bad, Exalt. But they are going, too."

Onser tapped his leg with his stick. "Thank you, Subdirect. You may go. Bring me your observations in figures, please." The man left. Onser would not fall into the same trap that Peydan had—splitting the force. If necessary, he would march the whole army east to resupply. Or march it far enough so a sizable supply force would be safe. He wondered how far west the other savages lived. It would be truly a victory to raze a Sentani town. Were they a seven- or eight-day march farther? Perhaps even fourteen days? His expedition could sustain that if they were careful. He wished he had better maps.

Another rifle shot flashed from the high ground and its echo rolled and bounced among the hills. Another of his soldiers fell. Onser found himself wincing at the long bursts of machine rifle fire that raked the hill in reply. He would have to send orders. He watched the aid team rush the man to shelter on a stretcher.

Meanwhile, some twenty ayas west, a large gathering of westerners conferred. "I don't believe any Peshtak should go with us," Tristal was saying. He looked around and raised his hand at the subdued murmur that arose from them. "You may be tempted to kill and torture. And we want them to see the diversity of the enemy they have made. We want to make the invasion so expensive the Innaniganis will have to take their army home. We have too little intelligence to know where they are making this new weapon, but we can burn out a good deal of their structural strength while their army is here."

"While they harzas burn out all of ours. And get the Balis to defend Innanigani land."

"We've sent Jestak to talk to the Balis again. We know they have evidence that the Innaniganis started it. We'll have to defend them if the Innaniganis get nasty about it."

"Wonderful. Harzas wonderful. Defending the Balis."

"That will tie them to us."

"Meanwhile," Ahroe said, "we have a force coming. Over five hundred men. More later, we hope.

"So far we have lost more property, but they have lost more men. If we keep our heads down after we fire on them, they tend to waste their ammunition."

"Now my force will engage them when we move out, then leave you most of the rifles, Hesit, and ride east. You'll have all our horses back after we cross the Leynap."

"You'll be running, Tris?"

"Yes. It has to be silent. We can't even give them tracks— nothing they can read, anyway. Remember. If you see messengers, let them through. After ten days or so, that is. They will be demanding the return of the army. We hope. It may be to report that we are all dead. We hope not."

The next morning, as the Innanigani army turned northwest, skirting the marsh, on their way to six villages they had scouted in previous summers, the rifle fire from the woods picked up. Their return fire was more selective, following Onser's warning. They were unsure how effective it was, but one armored patrol found nine bodies, six of them Peshtak. All but one had been killed by the raking fire of the machine rifles. The other had fallen to a mortar shell. They recovered rifles from all of them and fell back to pass them in to the commander.

"At this rate," Onser said, "they will arm us. They look like nice weapons. What do you think, Lieutenant?"

The officer had been examining a rifle. "The equal of ours at least," he said. "They must have fine powered tools. Like our new ones. I hadn't imagined it. Not the Peshkies, for sure. The others—the Pelbar maybe. We ought to go there, Exalt. Head direct west to freaking Pelbar country and burn them out."

"We don't know where it is, exactly, Lieutenant."

"On the Heart. Down the Oh and up the Heart."

"Our intelligence is too poor. We don't know how far that is. Our instructions are clear for this campaign. Burn out the Peshtak. All or nearly all of them."

A subdirect entered the barricade. "Exalt, the attack is over. They've pulled away.'"

"Good. What are our losses?"

"Nineteen dead, seven wounded."

"And theirs?"

"Other than those we found, we don't know, Exalt."

In the distance a rifle shot spat out, then another and another. The machine rifles replied with several short bursts.

"They are still harassing, I see," Onser mused.

"Yes, sir," the subdirect said.

Five days later Tristal's force crossed the Leynap, having given their horses over to the hundred Sentani who had accompanied them. Tristal commanded a mixed group of Shumai, Pelbar guardsmen, and Sentani, armed with a few rifles, a large number of the new revolvers, some shortbows, and a large supply of phosphorus bombs.

Both groups stayed well north of any action, but two days after an Innanigani runner trotted, sweating and panting, up to the gate of the fort at Tremai. He was exhausted and had to rest before he was able to report the signs of a large force of horses having crossed the Cwanto.

"How many?" the lieutenant asked.

"I don't know. A mass of them. Hundreds, I think."

"Hundreds? Going east?"

"Yes, Lieutenant. We have scouts following. Two. But the raiders were well ahead of us."

"Will the scouts report to Fort Sconet?"

"They talked of it. But that's near abandoned now."

The lieutenant looked around. "So are we. Hundreds could take us on. If it weren't for the machine rifles."

The lieutenant sent a runner to report to Innanigan, but not long after he trotted into the trees to the east, a single rifle shot rang out. The lieutenant wiped his brow. "I can ill afford a patrol, but we'll have to send one."

At the time Tristal sat high in a tree overlooking a pleasant valley among blue hills. They had scouted the area the previous night and picked their targets—three bridges, one covered, nineteen barns, a school, a furniture shop, a weaving mill, and a dairy and painting shop. He could hear a distant dog barking. He hated the whole thing, but the war would not end unless brought to the Innaniganis. His men would leave the houses. This time.

His scouts had picked out another community to the south, skipping over two others. They would try to hit that one, too, before news alerted it. He knew home forces would gather, watches would be set, their raiding would grow more difficult all the time. By skipping the western towns the Peshtak habitually had raided, he hoped to confuse and distress the Innaniganis even further. He wished there were a way to strike to the heart of Innanigan's war-manufacturing capacity and leave the people alone.

The first raid went off without a hitch, the only casualties five Innanigani guard dogs. Tristal's men watched the circle of flame from a hill, then began a slow trot southward. Once well away from the fireglow in the sky, they used the roads to make better time, until the stars showed the night was waning. Then they turned into the woods.

The next evening, in the village of Blue Mills, the people were greeted at supper, near dusk, by small bands of men, who roused them from their tables and held them in the yards, while they fired all the buildings. There was much shouting, and anger, which the raiders did not respond to. One farmer grabbed his scythe and rushed at a young Sentani, who shot him through the leg with his revolver. Then he stepped back from the general rush of furious family women. One reached for the scythe, but he pointed and said, "No!"

"You slimy mud snake!" she shrilled.

"Your army is burning villages," the Sentani replied. "We thought you ought to see what it is like."

"Painted savage. You deserve it."

The Sentani, straightbacked and typically reserved, made no reply. A distant horn sounded. He backed up and trotted out into the road. A large dog rushed him. He killed the animal with a single shot and ran off to join the others.

After high night Tristal squatted with his men on a wooded hilltop. Far off to the northeast they could still see the faint glow of the dying town. "Now," he said. "We arc to the west so they think we are fading off. Enves—tell us about the village with the white building. Maybe only that building this time—and the barns. Joss—how is your leg?"

"Fair. Not deep. I'll make it."

"You can hide with two or three others and then work your way west."

"No. I'll keep up."

The next night they fired the village with the white building and met their first opposition, but the villagers had no rifles and in the uncertainty of darkness and fire glow, their arrows wounded only one man, a Pelbar guardsman named Recon, in the arm. Tristal pulled away to their rendezvous and counted the men. Recon was weak and in pain. All the others were present.

"We'll move northwest the rest of the night, then rest all day tomorrow," Tristal said. "I want to reverse direction. It is plain the word is out. We need to give them a few nights off. I'm hungry. Wayl, did you get any of that cow?"

"All of us got three quarters of it, Tris. I could almost eat it raw."

"Yes. Tomorrow we'll cook it. Small fires. Light, dry wood. There's enough wild land so nobody will see—I hope."

Meanwhile, an old Innanigani officer interviewed the people of Green Court, who sat or lay amid a wide circle of bonfires in a stubble field. They were surrounded by men armed with bows, all facing outward. Only two others were soldiers.

"Tell me again what he shot with," the officer said wearily.

"Something small he held in his hand," a young woman said.

"And what did he say to you?"

"He told me not to pick up the scythe and then he said our army was burning villages so they were going to burn all the Innanigani villages."

"No, he didn't say that," a dark-skinned man said. "He said they'd kill us all."

"No. Only if we resisted," a fat, red-headed boy put in.

"Not a bit. He said he wanted us to see how it felt to have our villages burned," said an old woman, her frizz of kinky white hair burling up in a cloud. "I for one don't like it. And I think our army ought to come home and chase them out."

The officer threw up his hands. "What did he look like?"

"He was tall, with a painted face."

"That was just charcoal from the fire. He wasn't tall. His hair was cut very short and combed forward."

"You all agree on that?"

"That one, yes. But there were some tall men with long yellow hair in a braid."

"Any with it cut around like a bowl?"

"I saw one."

"What about Peshtak—long hair hanging down?"

"A lot of them."

"You fat eater. There wasn't one."

"Listen, let's see how good you see with my fist in your eye."

The officer continued his questioning all night. With dawn, they could see smoking foundations, but the houses were unharmed. The officer conferred with his lieutenants. "They haven't killed anybody yet. Only this man shot, and in defense. I don't think there are any Peshkies with them. Now, look at this arc. They may be leaving after a show of force."

"To go fight the army?"

"I don't know. I don't like it. We know they have Sentani, Shumai, and Pelbar. Peydan told me it is a wicked combination. Among them, they have all kinds of strengths."

"Peydan is dead."

"What? How?"

"Onser executed him for refusing to move his soldiers west."

The old officer tapped the rolled map against his leg. "I don't like this. Not at all. Lieutenant, I want you to send a message to Dupon. Tell him we need machine rifles and some of the other kind. And ammunition. Everything he has ready now."

"Yes, sir."

"Do it now. There will be time to rest later."

"Yes, sir."

Three days later Tristal's force burned a weaving town forty-four ayas to the north, destroying everything, and for good measure burned all the privies in a nearby farm hamlet. That night he took his first serious casualties—two Sentanis killed by arrows fired from a large textile factory. His men captured and lined up the people who ran from the building when phosphorus bombs exploded it into flame. "Who shot those arrows?" Tristal asked in a low growl.

"We all did," several shouted in reply. "You going to kill us all?"

"Your army hangs all the Peshtak villagers they catch," Tristal said in reply. "What do you think of that?"

"They deserve it. Savages!" one man shouted.

"Shut your fat yapper," another shouted at him.

"We do not do it, because we are civilized," Tristal said evenly. "Now. All of you. Lie down. Noses in the dirt. Don't move."

When they looked up a short time later, no one was in sight. They stood and walked away from the ferocious heat of the burning building. "They're weak," one man said. "They don't like to kill. We'll beat them. They're freaking weak."

Some of Tristal's men thought so, too, and he could feel the sullen resentment at his letting the killers go unscathed, especially from the Sentani. The next day he sent Joss and Recon home with an escort of four men. He gathered the others and told them, "I know you want to fight. I think we will, but if we lose men now, we may never convince the 'Ganis to bring the army home. That is our primary mission. The next is to find the weapons factory—but there is only a slight chance of that. Tomorrow night we'll travel back south and hit that river town we skipped. A lot of grain there, didn't you say? They won't expect us. I hope."

At the moment the old officer, with several others and some legislators, were meeting around a long table in Innanigan. "We can't anticipate them, Legislator Borund. We've tried plotting some path of destruction, and then we've tried outthinking them and anticipating where we'd least expect them. Nothing seems to work. They are as elusive as fog. We need the army home."

"No," Borund said. "We have to handle this. I may take it over myself. We'll have the Baliganis to help us soon."

"They have refused, Legislator," said a thin man who just entered the room carrying a message.

"What? What of their treaty? We'll—"

"It seems they had an observer with the western patrol that was ambushed. He was killed along with them. It was on the west bank of the Cwanto."

"Lies. They are trying to get out of it."

"This is a long letter from Owayn, just arrived. He says he talked with a Bali subdirect named Reaf who was wounded by our machine rifle fire. He even showed the wound to Owayn. The killed man was the son of a Bali officer. No mistake. There was no incursion from the West. Onser made it up."

"All lies. Give me that letter!"

"It is our only copy, Legislator Borund."

"I . . ." He looked around the table at the grave faces.

"You'd better read it all to us, Cassan," said the old officer.

"It doesn't matter now," Borund said. "The thing is done. We are committed. We have to see this through. What about the Seliganis?"

"They are held in check by the Lake Sentanis. And the westerners have no doubt told them there was no initial attack."

"But surely it is in their interest to preserve the city of Innanigan."

"Not if they are destroyed by that action. Now. Read the letter."

The next day Borund was still at home, brooding on what to do, when his servant announced a visitor. "Brod Ticent to see you, Legislator."

Borund frowned and turned to his aide, who whispered, "An eccentric. From that secretive family by the south coast. The timepiece makers. He's been trying to get to you."

Puzzled, Borund nodded and motioned. A tall, thin man entered. After greetings he said abruptly, "It may be that the time my family has prepared for so long has come, Legislator."

"What is that?"

"We have the ultimate defense for the city—if it can be delivered to some important place in the west."

"Yes? Please. Explain."

"My great-grandfather found an ancient structure deep in the sand. Near the sea. He and the family dug it out and built a building over it. It seems to be an ancient undersea boat, with all the information intact. We have spent three generations studying it."

"What? Why have you not brought this forward?"

"Too dangerous. It contains five of the weapons that seem to be the ones that destroyed the ancient world."

"What! But they will never work after all this time."

"On the contrary. They do. They will. We have studied them,

repaired them, revised them. But they were meant to fly high in the air and descend on their targets, and we do not have the means to do that."

"Well, what then?"

"But we have devised an alternative system. That has been the real aim of our timepiece business and our powered tools. The point is to have an ordinary explosion drive together two dangerous masses. This causes the giant explosion. We have arranged a mechanical way to do it."

"But we would have to carry it to some center in the West."

"The army could do it."

Borund frowned. "It might be too far. I would like to see these weapons."

Ticent stood. "Because of the raiders, it would be dangerous to go without a sizable force, perhaps. Were they to set off even one, it would wipe out the south angle of our population."

Borund chuckled. "Nothing is that powerful. However, we will take a contingent of men. You have trusted the right person."

"I thought so, Legislator. I know you have special connections with the army."

Arrangements were made for a meeting, and Ticent left. "This is it!" Borund said. "This way we will force the Baliganis to help. And if not, we'll destroy them."

"Destroy? The city of Baligan?" The aide seemed uncomfortable with the thought.

"They broke their agreement."

"What will we gain?"

"Scare sweat and tears out of the West. And get the Seliganis to help."

"I don't know, Legislator Borund. It seems mad."

"Masterstrokes often do. We can't leave the raiders wandering around burning everything. You'll keep it quiet, I know."

The aide frowned. "Yes. I will. I hope you know what you're doing."

"Of course. I have a private force in reserve. We'll go together in the morning to see this wonder."

In his raid on the grain town, Tristal lost two more men, and this time the Sentani killed nine villagers in revenge. Tristal pulled his men back to the west and held a conference. In a speech to them he indicated he would not permit gratuitous killing.

"Maybe you're not the only one to have a say in it," said a Sentani, Narl, an older man who had fought the Innaniganis the previous fall.

"The agreement was that I would be. And I am following our agreed-on orders."

"We don't think they are convinced by burning. We believe they aren't pulling the army back. And we aren't going to leave our men open to be killed. They'll have to know that if they kill, they'll be killed."

"We? Who's we?"

"The Sentani."

"You speak for them?"

"Yes."

Tristal pondered, scanning his force. "You're settled on that? All of you?"

"Yes."

"Any disagreements among you?"

No one raised any objections. Tristal could sense sympathy among the Shumai contingent as well. "If that's so, then it's time we struck deep east, near the city. If you want to fight, I'm sure we'll get a fight. It may do us in, of course, and nullify the mission. But I can only command what I've been given to command. And we may come on their weapons source. We'll burn the two houses an ayas south of here and the three to the west. Then we'll move east to the river again for today. Agreed?"

"Agreed," said Narl. "But with any trouble there, we'll do some killing."

Far to the west, Onser read the message from Innanigan requesting that the expedition return to protect the city. "Onus, they want us back. Seems there's a large raid. They've burned over two hundred and fifty buildings already—barns and homes."

"Then we'd better go."

"You never would have left. We'll go all right. It is a clear enough order, though Borund hasn't endorsed it for the Hegemony Party. But I want those two villages first. We need to resupply anyway. It's only a half day's march."

"Then you will turn east."

"Of course. I am here in obedience to orders. I will go there as well. I'm sure we can end the raiding and return, turning more to the south next time. Sixteen villages isn't bad so far. We'll add two more tomorrow."

* * *

Borund, meanwhile, had accompanied Brod Ticent to the south side of their settlement, near the coast. He had descended the stairway into the Ticents' building and viewed the ancient submarine, which the Ticents had opened from the top and from which they had removed the five warheads. "We will need a detailed explanation of how they operate," he said.

"It is all written out, Legislator. Specific instructions."

"You are sure it will work?"

"We believe so. Of course we have been unable to try it out," Ticent said with a nervous laugh.

"Yes. I can imagine."

They conferred for a good half day, as Borund's men stood outside in groups. Then Borund said abruptly, "All right. I'll take this over now. We'll need two of them right away. We have the double-wheeled carts outside."

"Now? Take it over?"

"Of course. It seems clear enough. You have done well. Innanigan will surely reward you. Right now there is no time to chew it all over in the legislature. There is an urgent need."

"But you said—"

"No matter. You will be given credit. I am sure the reward to your whole family will be great. Secut, please call the men now."

"Wait. I cannot allow—"

"The matter is out of your hands now. This is a state matter. You will be kept on hand for technical advice. Ench, seize him and bring him with us. Keep all the others off."

A small struggle ensued, but Ticent was tied and marched out of his own building, and as he went, he saw the heavy carts waiting for the warheads. He felt dizzy with betrayal. But it had been his own fault. He hoped now that somehow a broader authority would be involved. Perhaps they meant to cart them west to join the army. But without conferring? Without safeguards?

Three days later Tristal's raiders burned a small iron foundry and the surrounding buildings only six ayas south of Innanigan itself. It stood in a stream valley west of a line of hills that ran roughly north and south. The raiders had brought several of the Innaniganis up the hill to question them about locations.

The foundry manager, a short, swarthy man who refused to say anything, stood near him. Tristal smiled slightly at him and said, "Bring his wife."

"No. You hurt her and so help me, swine, I'll tear you apart."

"Yes. Then perhaps you'll tell me a few things."

"Nothing. Never."

"Tie his wife to that tree."

"I—" The man surged and struggled against the leather cords holding him.

"Let me go, rot," the woman shrilled, sinking down.

"What is that empty land to the east?"

"Destroyed land from the old time. Once a great city," the man mumbled.

"Do you go there?"

"No. Poisonous from the time of fire. Still."

"What is that town down there?"

"Not saying."

Tristal looked southeast, and through the haze saw sun shining on water. "And that? What is that water?"

"The Eastern Sea, of course, you stupid savage. Why don't you go jump in it?"

"Loy, don't anger him," the woman said.

Tristal didn't answer. He was staring at the water far to the east.

After a time one of his own men said, "What's the matter, Tris?"

He turned with a slight smile. "I am the first person in well over a thousand years to see both the Eastern and Western seas, Kure. What a giant land this is."

The Innanigani stared at him.

"Loy? It is Loy, is it? The Western Sea is over three thousand ayas from here. All beautiful country. Some mountains so high they have snow on them all summer. River, forest, prairie, desert—all empty, all with scattered ancient ruins. Why did you send your army west when there is so much for all of us?"

"He didn't send any army anywhere, pig," his wife said.

"It is your army and it went," Tristal said. "We're going to leave you tied here. Somebody will see the fire and get you soon enough. You may get bitten, though. These are the worst mosquitoes I've ever seen."

"Pig. Dung heap. Maggot-infested carcass. Fouler of all that is decent. Cannibal. Eater of rotten fish entrails," Loy spat out.

Kure shook him in fury. Tristal held up his hand. "That is artistry, Kure," he said. "Much beyond the standard foulbreath of Innanigan. I wonder what it was like to work for him? We ought to write all of this down."

"Men coming," somebody shouted from below.

"How many?"

"A large body. From the north."

Tristal shoved Loy over by his wife and whipped his cords around hers. "All right," he shouted. "Here's your chance if you want a fight. Kure, take your squad to the west. Take Narl's with you. Gage, take your rifles and follow the plan. Wayl, your men hold the road. I wish we had some horses. All right, to it then." Tristal brushed a mosquito off Loy's arm, then ran down the hill. Already he heard shouts and the sharp popping of revolver fire.

The Innaniganis fanned out as Tristal had thought they would. Narl worked on the west flank and the Pelbar guardsmen, with their rifles, on the right. From his vantage Tristal could see reinforcements coming from the city. He took out his small telescope and watched an older man in a uniform directing a group hauling something on a cart. A weapon.

"Mith," he called down. "Tell the others more are coming. They have some weapon, I imagine a machine rifle."

Mith, a Sentani, took up his horn and blew the message in Sentani horn talk, then repeated it.

"I fear Narl may try to take it," Tristal muttered. "Tell the guardsmen to move north and concentrate rifle fire on anybody around the cart," he called down. He frowned. This might split his east flank. Mith blew the message, and Tristal hoped that Narl would understand its implications; he could tell by the Sentani firing that Narl was pressing his fight forward.

"Tell Narl that they are going to bring their weapon to bear," Tristal called down. Mith began the message, but halfway through it, it was drowned out by the roar of the machine rifle raking Narl's position. Almost immediately the machine-rifle's gunner jerked and dropped, bleeding. Another shoved him aside and moved to take his place, but he too fell. The old soldier directed them to move the cart into the shelter of an unburnt building, but then he spun and fell, clutching his side, then the cart rolled over his leg as he writhed on the ground.

The fire from Narl's men began again, but it was scattered now. A Shumai ran around the building and leapt into the cart, swinging a short-sword around him. He stopped, jerked, and fell off the cart, but two more, behind him, leapt into it and swung the end of the machine rifle around, getting off a long burst of fire before they too fell. Tristal witnessed its carnage in dead and hurt Innaniganis from that one burst.

The Pelbar riflemen were now in position to keep gunners off the weapon, but more Innaniganis were now arriving from the city, and Tristal had Mith pull Narl's unit back, then the front men, and finally the Pelbar and Shumai to the east.

The Innaniganis pressed forward, and the westerners had to leave their dead and move up the wooded hill west of the burning foundry. The Pelbar riflemen had a hard time of it, but with Sentani support finally most made it.

"I want fifteen Shumai, with supporting riflemen," Tristal shouted. "Yoth, you head them. I want you on the cart with the third machine rifle before anybody knows you are around. Narl, you hold the 'Ganis back here. Keep your heads down. Yoth, turn their weapon on them if you can. Remember—no heroic shouting. Stalk in."

Tristal's men held on as the Innaniganis raked the hillside with machine rifle fire. The first weapon then fell quiet. The westerners could hear shouting below. "Mith, tell the riflemen if it is now out of ammunition, to keep any more from getting to the south weapon."

Mith's horn sounded its measured codes, and Tristal could hear the methodical firing of two Pelbar riflemen in response. Meanwhile, below, Yoth's men had worked north through the brush and surged out at the group around the third cart. The fight was sharp and deadly, but at last Yoth himself seized control of the weapon and turned it on the Innaniganis. His raking fire cleared the second machine rifle and many of the men near it. He took an arrow in his leg, and swung the weapon around, spraying an arc of fire to the east and northeast. Then the four surviving Shumai pulled him off the cart and tossed in a phosphorus bomb, dragging him away as it flashed and roared, sending up popping and cracking ammunition.

"Mith, tell Narl to take those other machine rifles at all costs and pull them to the foundry. Send a general signal to rendezvous there."

As Mith blew the signals, Tristal ran down the hill and out into the road. By the time he reached the first cart, the Sentani were tossing bodies off it. Tristal stooped and dragged the old officer out of the way. The man cried out, and their eyes met a moment as the Sentani got the cart underway. Some resistance was met at the second cart, and Tristal raced to help.

In a short, sharp fight, they gained possession of that one, too, and ran it south. Innanigani dead lay everywhere, most of them killed with their own fearsome weapon. Tristal halted the carts at the end of the street to cover the area so they could recover their wounded. For the moment the fight was over, but they knew more Innaniganis would arrive at any time. Tristal then whispered orders to six men and sent them into the woods.

The westerners took a heavy cart from the foundry yard and loaded their wounded on it, then started down the southwest road, keeping it between the two machine weapons. They distributed the remaining ammunition between them. A quick count revealed they had about three thousand rounds total. They also had twenty-two wounded men, piled roughly on the cart. And they had left behind fifty-three dead. It was clear the raiding was over, and their remaining job was to get out. If they hadn't convinced the Innanigani army of invasion to return home already, it would not happen.

 XXIII

ONSER viewed the burnt Peshtak village of Tule with puzzlement. The westerners had fired it themselves, along with the later crops they could not remove—pumpkins, winter squash, some beans. His men raked quickly through the remains of several buildings, harried only by a few riflemen from farther west. Some quick bursts of machine rifle fire halted all the sniping. Yet he felt uneasy. A planted explosive burst in the central street of Tule, killing three of his men. He immediately gave the order to pull out as soon as the water supply was replenished. One more village, within easy march, and they would set out for the East.

On the Innanigani coast, Borund watched his men carefully ease the first of the ancient bombs into the hold of a fishing boat. The strange device was surrounded by men, all with their hands on it, steadying it as it was slowly lowered onto a hastily built cradle. Borund himself was silent, narrow-eyed. His jaw worked. No ally would be permitted to snub Innanigan that way. He would handle the matter without the endless haggling of the legislature. Looking northwest, he saw Gafeer talking with a sentry. Tucked under his arm was his cousin's dirty white dog—tattooed, he hoped, as they had planned. He and Owayn had discussed such a way of sending a message. The dog had lived in Baligan and should know its way to Owayn's house. He hoped. If not, Owayn would be one of the many casualties of the war.

Tristal halted his men four ayas west of their fight. The road crossed a brook, and after they had eased the cart of wounded through it, he drew them up and posted sentries. "I want sixty men," he said, his hands up, "ten of them Pelbar riflemen. We need to return for the dead and give them a proper burial."

"We'll all go," Narl shot back.

"No. Sixty will go," said Tristal evenly. "I have six men back there already scouting. We'll need the rest to guard the wounded and perform some other functions."

"All the Sentani will go," said Narl, tight-lipped.

"Here are the reasons sixty will go," Tristal replied quietly. "As I said, we need to care for the wounded. We will need to be quiet and unobserved, and even sixty is too many for that, but they may be needed to carry or convey the bodies. If we all went and got into another fight, we might be annihilated, and if that happened, the Innaniganis would certainly not be inclined to make peace with us. They did damage enough with a home force of civilians against trained fighting men. Besides, it would be extremely useful for us to be able to use their own machine rifles against their army of invasion—not to mention that it is vitally important that we get these new weapons back to the West. We'll have to copy them."

"I say the Sentanis all go," said Narl. "We . . ." Tristal swept him off his feet, held him up and shook him, then slammed him down with a hollow thud.

"Sixty go," he said quietly. "If you want to settle this, then we'll do it at home. Not here. Does anybody want to argue with that?"

No one did. Tristal said, "Tarl, pick twenty-four Sentanis. Keyn, pick twenty-four Shumai. Each of you lead your unit. Andag, you take the wounded. You'll find a briary hill seven ayas west of here. Cut a path through the briars to the top. There's a woods there. Wait for us there. I need ten scouts and fifteen foragers. All the rest go with the wounded. If need be, does anyone object if we burn our dead in a building after proper ceremonies—but only if there is no other way?"

"We would prefer not," said Tarl. "But it has been done."

"Each group decide, then, with its own," said Tristal. "All right, we need to move."

That night, about three ayas north of the recent battleground, a squad of Innaniganis stood outside the barn in which all the bodies of the westerners had been thrown. "The plan is to parade these harzas hunks of buzzard bait on carts through the city tomorrow," said the subdirect.

"What about our own dead?" a man asked.

"Don't be stupid. This was a harzas victory. It needs to look like one. The war is getting less popular all the time— What was that?"

"What, sir?"

"That noise? Are they all dead?"

"Dead all right. Stiff as icicles. Haven't you looked?"

"No. Bring a torch."

Five of the guards accompanied the subdirect inside the barn. "That one," he said, pointing. "He hasn't been stripped."

"Some were too torn up."

"Look, though. He has gear on." The subdirect strolled over to a Sentani body, which suddenly rolled to his feet and ran him through with a short-sword. The subdirect turned, gasping, and saw the other men struggling with dim shadows. The torch fell in the straw. The subdirect strangely worried about this as he crumpled and fell unconscious.

The guards outside lounged at ease since the last townsmen had long since gone to bed. The group with the torch appeared from inside the building. Something is odd, one thought sleepily just before the arrow whacked into his chest. He turned and started a shriek, but his air was clipped off by a hand.

"Is that all?" he heard a voice say, dimly, as he died.

"That's all," a Sentani muttered. "Get the carts. We'll do the parading—through the night."

The burial party moved away without further incident, though without seeing the Innanigani who ran away in the shadows. Four men were left to fire the building about thirty sunwidths after the main party went.

In spite of their grinding fatigue, the westerners half walked, half trotted the carts toward the rendezvous, avoiding houses where they could. As the first faint hints of morning rose, the advance man came pounding back down the road. "A roadblock ahead. They know!" A distant shout echoed from behind. As the raiders prepared to abandon the carts and carry the bodies south through the fields, bursts of machine rifle fire sounded ahead. They heard more shouting—Tristal's men were behind the easterners, who returned their fire, but only for a short time. The Pelbar riflemen ran wearily down the road, weapons ready, almost colliding with fleeing Innaniganis. A short, sharp fight followed, but the enemy quickly dispersed, and the raiders surged forward with the carts.

Mith's horn sounded ahead, directing them to abandon the carts and travel south on a trail through the woods. The day brightened slowly, as they ascended a hill with their burdens of dead toward a white barn that stood alone on a slight ridge among fields of hay stubble.

Tristal's men greeted them on the path and took the bodies from the tired raiders. Inside they found a common grave, neatly dug, and laid the men in it. With guards posted, they said the appropriate ceremonies, group by group, each one unhurried, each complete. Then Tristal signaled, and with shovels and several boards, they filled in the hole and packed it down.

"Fire the building," Tristal commanded. "We don't want them dug up again." The men lit the hay in a score of places at once, and the flames roared up instantly in the new morning light.

As they retreated, they heard a shriek, and saw three children standing in the hay door up above the flames. Instantly they ran back. "Jump," Narl shouted. "We'll catch you. Here, into these shirts!" He and four other men stripped off their shirts and quickly knotted them into a net. Two more children joined the others, but they would not jump. Braving the heat and racing flame, several men built a human pyramid, and one climbed it and caught the floor by the door. They boosted him up. He took a girl and said, "I'll help you. Pretend you're sitting down." He pitched her outward, and the men below caught her, cheering. Then he caught a boy and gracefully shoveled him out after the girl. The next one, shrieking in fear, held on, so he let him cling while he dropped the other two.

"Are you all?" he yelled, over the roar of the fire.

The boy clung to him shrilling his fear, and as a timber fell near them, he jumped with the child still holding his leg. The men cheered again as they caught the two and stood them up. Tristal knelt by one of the girls and asked if they were all out. She held her fist in her mouth and nodded her head.

"Nodding means yes," said a man behind Tristal.

"Where do you live? We have to go. Can you go home?"

One of the sentries shouted, and Tristal saw a woman toiling and running up the hill toward them. "Who is that?" he asked the girl.

"My tammy. She'll be mad." She began to cry.

Tristal picked her up and said, "No. She'll be glad to see you." Turning, he commanded, "Narl, direct the men to the camp with the wounded. Tarl, stay with me, please. All of you get out of here. We'll be along."

As the woman neared, the girl buried her face in Tristal's neck and all but the boy hid behind the men. He ran to the woman and clung to her apron, entangling and nearly tripping her.

"My . . . children," she gasped. "Give me my . . . children, swine!"

Tristal laughed. "Did we get them all?" At that point the roof sagged and pitched inward in a giant shower of flame and sparks. They all moved away.

The woman tried to gather all the children to her, still panting wildly. She reached up to the girl Tristal was holding, commanding in a high voice, "Canti, let go. Let go!"

"You won't spank us?" the girl asked.

"We'll see about that."

"The answer of all mothers, Canti," said Tristal. "Better mind her for a while anyway and find a new barn to camp out in."

The woman took her daughter and sagged to the ground, still holding her, panting and crying. Tristal squatted by her and said, "Did we get them all?"

"Yes, swine!" the woman shrilled. Tristal stood. "What are you going to do to us?" she added.

"Nothing," Tristal replied. "We would all rather be in the West and would be there if your army hadn't invaded. Just remember that when you hear about all the destruction."

"You are all filth. Whatever you got, you deserved."

"And you. Did you deserve it? Did any of the dead on either side deserve it? The only ones who have deserved it are the one you call Borund and his friends. Somehow they've seen an advantage for themselves in it."

"Our power is expanding. You'll pay for this."

"Expanding? Maybe like a bubble on the way to breaking. Maybe to your own despair. We're going. When you see your men, tell them not to follow and we'll do no more burning. The point has been made and more than made. Violence works both ways. When one side raises the level, the other follows."

"You've got no rights here! You can't talk like this."

"What rights have your army in the West?"

"They had to go to protect our border."

"Nobody violated it. Your army invaded. Face it. You are a gang of invaders who didn't expect much opposition."

The woman stood and stamped her foot. "I never invaded anybody. I just work and raise children and watch you burn up our building and our whole hay crop."

"You just quoted a lot of Peshtak mothers. Take the message. Remember it?" Tristal turned away.

She said nothing, but watched the two men trot west in the new sunlight. Then she turned and looked at the ruin of the barn, still furious with heat and flame, and gathered the children to her. When she looked again, Tristal and Tarl were gone.

 XXIV

Onser's men spread out and walked in toward the Peshtak village of Ultum, a large settlement in a broad cove among the ridges. It was surrounded by fields of yellow grain and pumpkins. Lines of shale walls bisected the fields. A distant dog barked monotonously, and smoke rose from several chimneys, spreading and hanging in the sultry summer air.

"Bring the machine rifles to the front," Onser ordered as they walked into the sunlit quietude. "Scouts, approach that wall," he called.

In a line, seven scouts, rifles at ready, walked out of the brush toward the nearest long wall. They crouched and moved slowly, sliding through weeds and high grass, glancing occasionally behind. One walked ahead to the wall, looked over, and screamed as a shot threw him backward. More rifle fire dropped the other scouts. Onser's machine rifles began to pound, raking the wall, breaking off chunks of rock and kicking up dirt.

"All move ahead! Keep those machine rifles up with the rest," Onser shouted. Rifle fire began to peck away at both flanks, and some from behind, as the Innanigani charge broke into a run, the men yelling. About forty arms out from the wall, a line of explosives roared up as the men ran through it, and before the smoke cleared, heavy rifle fire began flashing out all along the wall.

The Innaniganis wavered, and the officers shouted to them to drop and crawl, and let the machine rifles soften up the enemy. They did, and the heavy pounding of the new weapons again churned into the wall. Mortarmen began lofting shells over the wall, looking for the range. Rifle fire from behind the wall nearly ceased. Encouraged, the Innanigani infantry crawled faster. Rifle fire from the flanks increased, though, aimed especially at the mortar crews, dropping men nearly as fast as they could be replaced.

"They're finally making a stand!" Onser shouted through his megaphone. "This is it. This is where we break them." Another line of explosives roared up near the wall, heaving the ground and sending more men and parts of men into the air. Some began to flee, but others rushed ahead and leapt over the wall to the cheers of those behind.

The machine rifles had to stop firing, and immediately a fury of rifle fire lanced out from the wall, dropping Innaniganis from the thinning charge so fast that the others turned and bolted in a body. A megaphone again sounded a loud command to drop down, but only some heeded it, so the machine rifles could not again fire. Now the men who had dropped began to get up and run, with rifle fire from the wall hitting many.

As the fleeing men rushed through the Innanigani line, others joined them, and Onser had to withdraw his whole force behind the screening leaves of the woods edge. Occasional shots continued from the hill to the east. Looking out, they could see no advance from the wall. Nor was there any sign of the men who had made it over the barrier.

A lieutenant approached Onser and said, "Exalt, we have lost nearly two hundred men. An estimate of the enemy fire puts them at over four hundred, not to mention the roving riflemen—perhaps another fifty."

"Spread a defensive ring," Onser replied, growling. "We'll shell that wall down and blow away all the swine behind it."

"Exalt, we have fewer than a hundred shells left."

"Then use them. It may work. If not, we will pull back. Away from that defense our machine rifles will protect our march back. Too bad. I had hoped to take this place. It looks as though they may have gathered a large enough force to block it."

"Maybe large enough to kill us all, Exalt. I suggest we leave now."

Onser frowned at him. "We'll go lighter without the shells to encumber us. We know the savages are there. The more we kill here, the fewer we'll harzas meet in the filthy woods."

"Very good, sir," the lieutenant said, bowing slightly.

Soon the mortars began firing, and methodical *thuds* were followed by explosions near the wall and cries from the spotters.

But shots from the woods dropped mortarmen until the officers had hasty earth barricades put up around them. Then the snipers began working on any visible soldiers. Bursts from the machine rifles did little to dissuade them.

Behind the wall the combined force of westerners dug grimly as the shells lobbed over at them. Knowing the weapon from previous fighting, they had prepared trenches and bunkers on three sides of the village, but were still losing men, and the Innaniganis were finding the range more and more accurately. Mokil finally crawled down the approach trench and passed the word to pull away from the wall all except a few riflemen in covered bunkers. At last only twenty men remained, gritting their teeth against the regular blasts from the woods.

From the protection of the woods, Exalt Onser pondered. He began to see the previous expedition's failure in a new light. "Alster," he said. "I am not going to risk a new charge. We're pulling out. Keep the mortars working while the rest of us back up the hill. We'll leave a guard on them and signal them when to come. We need all our men now to get out and fight the raiders at home."

"Yes, Exalt," Alster replied, hurrying away—a little too fast, in Onser's opinion.

As the Innaniganis began to move up the hill, horn messages sounded from the summit to the south and were answered faintly from the village. At that point Onser felt the first knife of real fear lance into his chest. He had underestimated the enemy and knew he would need every seedweight of cunning and energy to get home. Well, then, he would give it. They would make it. They still had the machine rifle—and would nurse the rest of the ammunition.

Before evening the farm wife who had talked with Tristal was brought before an old officer who lay bandaged on a padded cart. "Tell me exactly what he said," the old man commanded.

The woman recounted the incident as clearly as she could, adding that the children had watched the men bury their dead in the barn.

"I'll talk to them later," the man said.

"Who is following them?" the woman asked.

"Only scouts now, but we've lost them."

"You mean you're going to let them go?"

"We tried to stop them last night and lost sixty-two more men. They have the new weapon and seem to know how to use it. Our trained people are all in the West or on the border. We've been using retired and untrained personnel."

"Then they're wandering around loose and can do anything they wish?"

"They won't. We've hurt them. We did that at least. They lost many men yesterday. They have wounded. And the blond man promised you he would do no more burning if we didn't follow them."

The woman stamped and yelled shrilly, "They are the enemy. How can you say such a thing?"

"Did they kill you? Or the children? See my leg? My own men rolled a cart over it as I lay wounded. The blond man pulled me away or the cart would have gone over it again."

"They are the enemy."

"*We* would have killed the children. I've seen it done out in Peshtak country. It is our duty to protect Innanigan. Right now the best way we can do that is to let them go. We'll train and prepare a better defense, but to let them alone is the best defense now. The army will have to worry about them. They'll both have the new weapon." The old man shifted himself and looked up at the sky. "If there's an army left," he added, shaking his head and muttering, "Fools, fools. Utter, mud-slathered, slime-coated, moss-eating, hog-headed, harzas sombee fools."

The farm woman covered her ears in shock at his language. "You've told me all then?" the old man asked. "Bring the children."

Borund stood by the helmsman as the two fishing boats leaned away from the east wind, heading south toward Baligan with all sails set. The dog whined at his feet. He spurned it away. "Shut it up, Cream Puff," he growled. He watched his men repainting the boat name and city designation. If they came in at dusk and moored far enough away, they ought to fool the Balis long enough. Refuse to help? The Balis would learn. Treaties are binding. Well, the agreement with the so-called Federation—that was necessary to the plan. It had been forced on them by the defeat of that seedy fool, Exalt Peydan. Besides, they were scruff, the offscourings of civilization, living in the dumps and mudflats of a lost culture. Savages.

He looked at Brod Ticent, who lay tied and morose on the deck. That man is not dependable, he thought. But necessary. Only he could arm the bomb and start the timer as it ought to be. Keeping his family as hostages had been a necessary move, an exigency of war. He knew he could justify it when the time came. The army would back him.

Three days later Tristal crossed the Leynap, wading and swimming rafts with the wounded quietly in deep night, then burying a Pelbar rifleman on the west bank, high on a small hill, with the others standing around. The Pelbar sung the guardsmen's burial hymn in a near whisper:

> "True in his friendship,
> steady in mind,
> firm in his purpose,
> may he now find
> in Aven's presence
> those of his kind,
> duties to hold to,
> strivings assigned . . ."

As he listened, Tristal wondered for a moment if the un-assuming Pelbar guardsmen, firm, unyielding, and undemon-strative, might not be the toughest men in the whole raid. They had taken almost as many losses as the Shumai. When told to hold a position, they simply did not move. They bound the three groups together with gentleness and a quiet resolve. Yet the raiders also needed the Shumai verve and Sentani discipline. Tristal glanced at Narl in the dark. He was no longer afraid of trouble there—not since the Sentani sprang to the aid of the children. His rebelling had been frustration at the loss of his friends. No Sentani ever took that well. Nor did the Shumai. In the distance a tanwolf barked then howled. Another answered. He was glad to be west of the Innanigani—all, that is, except for the army and its posts.

 XXV

It was dusk as two fishing boats nosed in from the channel and moored at the far north end of the anchorage. Xord sat with Stel at his skiff on the shore. The Pelbar squinted through the darkness.

"What?" Xord asked.

"Those boats. I don't know them."

"Are they Eastern Islands trade ships? I hear they expect them."

"No. They are tall masted. Big. With floating green ensigns."

"What, then?"

"I don't know."

In the failed light they saw the shadow of a skiff make for shore, then touch it and turn back again. "What was that all about, Xord?"

"They let something out. Something whitish. Hard to say. Want me to find out?"

"Not our business." They ate for a time in silence. Then Stel said, "So Jestak thinks I should go west. He didn't say why?"

"Raydi wants it. He'd tell you himself except he's deep with the governor. Who's Raydi?"

"My daughter. My poor, long-suffering daughter, whose parents seem to be always abandoning her—Hello, who are you?"

A small, whitish dog came trotting busily down the beach, tongue out. He paused, left his sign on an overturned skiff, and began to smell around.

"Stel," Xord said in a low voice. "That's what they let out of the boat. Needs a walk, huh?"

"I know every dog in the harbor, but not that one." Stel pursed his lips and chirped at the dog, who pricked up one ear and returned to smelling. Stel chirped again and held out a bone from the rabbit he and Xord had been eating.

The dog came near, neck out, nose wobbling, then shied away. Neither man moved. The dog returned and took the end of the bone, then, with small growls, began to tug on it as Xord slipped an arm under him and lifted him up. The dog squirmed and whined, then wagged his hind half as Xord petted him and handed him to Stel, saying, "Know him now?"

"No. Never seen him." Stel stroked the dog, then his searching fingers stopped and felt. "He has something. A tick? Build up the fire a little." The dog whined. Stel soothed him, then laid him down near the fresh flames and parted the hair.

"Oh. No. Just some scabs." He smoothed back the hair, but Xord reached out.

"Tattooing? Fresh tattoos?" He chuckled. "Who would tattoo a dog?"

Stel frowned and parted the hair again. "You're right. It is. I can't read it, though. Here. Add a little cold water to that tea. Your knife sharp?"

Stel held the struggling dog as Xord poured on the lukewarm tea water and they shaved away the hair. They looked up to see a Baligani subdirect watching. "Subdirect. Somebody from that boat has put a message on this dog."

"Message? On a dog? What boat?"

"That one—one of two over there."

"Whose are they?"

"I don't know them. They came in at dusk and moored there."

"What does it say?" Xord asked.

"Move him over here," Stel said, as the three men squatted

around the dog. "Here," Stel said. "'Whole house and agents head NW. Burn rec. Aband. all. Inform any Innan. Do instantly. Bnd.'"

The three men looked at each other. "I'll take that dog to the major," the subdirect said.

"They must mean to invade," Stel said.

"Who?" Xord asked.

"The Innaniganis. Look. 'Innan.' That's Innanigani, right? And I'll bet 'Bnd' is that coffin lid, Borund."

"Freaking hogsbreath," the subdirect muttered, reaching for the dog.

"Wait, Subdirect. Either let the dog go and follow him or take him to the governor. One of us will tell the major, or get another soldier to do it. I have a bad feeling about this. We'd better move."

"You tell the major, Stel," the subdirect said, snatching up the dog. "I'll go to the governor. Xord, you watch the boats." He ran up the beach.

Xord looked at Stel with pursed lips and said, "Huh."

"You do the dishes," Stel called over his shoulder.

"What dishes?" Xord returned, wiping his knife on a bleached board. Then he threw sand on the fire and squatted down to watch the boats.

Major Zimon listened to Stel's story impassively. "Where is the subdirect?"

"He took the dog to the governor."

"And Xord is watching the boats?"

"That's right."

"We're going to board those boats. Lieutenant, run to the governor. Give him my regards and ask him on my behalf to let that dog loose. See if it goes to Owayn's lodging. Subdirect, I want two squads, one for each boat. Subdirect Ogis, take four men and watch Owayn's lodging. Lieutenant Oron, organize the men on the northern defense perimeter. Send four men to rouse the armed citizens. You, Stel. Come with me."

The subdirect forced his way into a dinner party at the governor's, and the chief executive was angry, refusing even to look at the dog until an aide verified that it was indeed tattooed. "It's probably a trick of that savage, Stel," he growled. "And on my wife's birthday. Major Zimon will hear about this. Where is this dog? Oh. I . . . know it. That's Cream Puff, Owayn's . . . Show me the marks."

They laid the dog on a table on its side, stroking it gently. The governor bent near and studied the marks closely. "Holy honeybuckets," he muttered, turning white. "Get the westerner, that Jestak. If they are coming, the westerners have to protect us."

Jestak was at the party and came immediately. "Why northwest?" he said. "Away from the harbor. Would the army come from the northwest or by water?"

"Either. Or northeast."

"I'd like to see those boats."

"Subdirect, take the Pelbar to the harbor."

Jestak and the subdirect arrived at the beach at the same time as Major Zimon. Xord met them, saying, "One left back out the channel without lights. The other is still there."

One squad roused the corpsman who manned the one boat in the service of the city and set out in pursuit of the fleeing Innanigani. A soldier was dispatched to summon the fishermen's guard to supply other boats. The other squad manned skiffs, rowed out to the dark boat, and boarded it. A quick search revealed the strange structure in the hold.

Xord put an ear to it. "It's making a noise, a clicking," he said.

Jestak knelt and listened. "Aven, it must be a bomb with a timer," he said.

"Why?" said a subdirect. "What good would it do way out here?"

Jestak stood up and regarded the device. He reached out a hand to the old warhead and ran it along the surface. "Oh, no. No, no," he muttered. "This is an ancient weapon. Look. It's been put together with this other piece."

"How do you tell that?" Xord asked.

"Nobody can do metalwork like that now. Look. It may be . . . no."

"What?"

"An ancient bomb. We have to dismantle it. Xord, Subdirect. Get tools. Anything. Get Stel. He always has some tools. Any on this boat?" As he explained his fears, Jestak had broken the tip from a boat knife and was furiously struggling with a screw. Others began work on other fastenings, unscrewing, hacking, even filing and sawing to dismantle the device. One man kept his ear to the Innanigani housing and could hear, in any lull in the racket, the slow, inexorable ticking of the timer.

"It's coming loose," Zimon finally shouted. "Do we have a boat derrick? Hurry."

"It's coming, Major," a soldier called.

The timer rolled slightly away from the warhead. "No time to wait," Jestak shouted. "Everybody. Lift it out of here. We'll throw it over the side and pull this boat away."

"I don't . . ." the major began as he joined the others straining to lift the heavy device out of the hold.

"It was explained to me," Jestak said, grunting. "By the Dome woman, Eolyn. An explosion is needed to trigger the other device. That one . . . will make—here now, lift together—another— empty place . . . of Baligan."

"Filthy . . ." the subdirect began, then together they heaved the whole device up, swaying and grunting, straining to hold it as men above looped ropes around it to help. Finally it grated and rolled up onto the deck, but caught on a cleat and hung there.

"I'll get a pry," Stel shouted, running forward ahead of the wheelhouse, just as the timer ceased and the device blew up in a giant roar and flash, tearing the boat apart. Stel was thrown out into the water as the boat sank, taking with it what was left of Jestak, Major Zimon, Xord, and all the Baligani soldiers who had worked on the device—as well as the unexploded warhead. Then the boat alongside with the derrick also listed and settled slowly to the shallow harbor bottom.

Stel rose to the surface, dazed and bruised, his head ringing. He turned and looked, seeing with anguish what had happened, but realizing that the city of Baligan was saved. He suddenly wondered what would happen to Owayn's daughter Ferth. The Baliganis would not accept this. Slowly he swam toward shore, picking a dark area north of the crowd gathering on the beach. He waded ashore and without hesitation strode through the streets toward Owayn's house.

He could see as he neared it that it was watched from the front and, he assumed, from the back. He ducked into a garden three houses down, wondering why he was getting involved. Was he confusing Ferth and Raydi in his mind? What difference? He would be of no use at the harbor now. He would warn them and let them make their way out to the northwest, as Cream Puff's message had advised—or any other way.

At last he rolled in behind Owayn's lodging and pushed at a low window leading to their winter wood dump under the house. A voice said, "Jaas? That you?"

"No. It's Stel the Pelbar. Quick. Where's Ferth?"

"Here!" she called.

Then Owayn's heavy voice rolled over hers. "Seize him. Here. What is this? Are there others?"

Someone showed a small light. Eleven people crouched together among the small wood supply for the kitchen.

"What?" Ervil said. "What happened to you?"

Ferth began to cry. "Listen," Stel said. "There isn't much time. You've got to get Ferth out of here. Borund brought a boat into the harbor with an ancient bomb on it. It might have taken the whole city, but we dismantled the triggering explosive before it went off. Then it went off and killed a lot of people."

"Is that what we heard?" asked Mz Sovel.

"Shut up," Owayn commanded. "Go on."

"When this is widely known, I don't think they'll be overjoyed with you. You'd better get out now while you can. The house is being watched."

"We know."

At this point Stel saw Cream Puff snuggled in Ferth's arms. "Oh. You have the dog. They must have let it go and followed it. You'll be held."

"Listen, Pelbar. We know that. We're waiting for the last of us. But we'll never make it anyway, unless you help."

"Me? Help?"

"Didn't you come for that?"

"I came to warn Ferth," Stel said quietly.

"You are sure it was such a terrible thing?" said Mz Sovel.

"Yes. I had my hands on it. I helped cut the Innanigani part loose from it. When that went off, I was blown over the side."

"You look it. But you have to help us. With your boat."

"How is that possible?"

"Listen. Don't talk. Just get out the way you came in and bring your boat to the end of the south barrier. We'll be there sometime after high night."

"How will—"

"Don't ask. Will you help?"

"Ferth, yes. If they catch me, they'll call me a spy and traitor.

My own friends have just died—Jestak and Xord, the major, others." Stel paused. "Yes. I'll do it. There's been too much killing. But you have to do something in return."

"What's that?"

"Tell your people what Borund has done. I can't believe they would agree with it. And let me talk to your governing body. Is that agreed?"

Owayn sighed. "I may not be able to." He paused. "Yes, I agree. Now, go."

Stel crawled out the window, almost bumping into Jaas, the last Innanigani agent to come. As he wormed his way along behind the adjacent houses, Stel wondered why he was doing what he was. Well, saving lives was important. He had destroyed enough of them. The old book talked about forgiveness. And if he could talk to the Innaniganis, maybe he could make them understand. If they let him. He trusted Owayn as much as he would a copperhead. "Never go to bed with a copperhead and you don't have to worry about getting bit," Tor the Shumai used to say. Stel knew he was violating an obvious rule, but somehow the action felt right.

As he finally stepped out onto the dark road and began to limp toward the harbor, he saw a crowd pass by on the next street carrying torches. He dodged over nearby and saw they were making for Owayn's house—rough men, mostly fishermen and harbor workers, angry and determined. Stel began to doubt that the Innaniganis would make the south barrier. He shut his eyes tight and prayed for Ferth's safety, then hastened along the black streets toward the harbor.

As he rowed the skiff out to his boat, he saw a circle of lights around the scene of the disaster. When he thought of Jestak dead, a fist of grief rose into his throat and almost choked him. What of Tia and the children? What loss to Pelbar society. He gripped the oars, determined that Ferth would not die. She had no part in this—perhaps she was dead now, or on her way to it. But Owayn had some plan. As Stel slowly drew up his anchor and shook out a single sail, a bloom of flame rose in the direction of Owayn's house. That would keep them all busy. He wondered how the Baliganis would contain the fire and prevent the other houses from going with it. That would keep them even busier. With a slight jerk the sea breeze bellied out his sail and the boat began moving slowly south in the night, toward Stel's strange rendezvous.

XXVI

EXALT Onser had force-marched his men eastward for the rest of the day and into the night, trying to reach the camp they had set up two days earlier. It lay in a natural meadow, near water, and well away from the surrounding hemlocks.

The soldiers arrived exhausted and somewhat listless. A lieutenant approached the exalt and said, "Sir, the men are sick. A lot of them have diarrhea and headaches. We've talked about it. We think it's that well water from Tule. We've scrubbed the barrels now and refilled them from this stream. We..."

He was interrupted by a sudden explosion and both whirled in time to see two men falling in the firelight. It was a planted mine. Onser shook his head. "No help for it. We have to move out of here. Carefully. Don't want to lose more men. Be meticulous. Do it, Lieutenant, no matter how sick the men are."

As they moved, rifle fire flashed from the trees in a line and the easterners returned several bursts from the machine rifle. Onser began to understand even further the nature of the last invasion. Borund had even been there. Why had he so misdescribed it? His own sense of fear and caution deepened. At least they had the advantage of a warmer season.

Late that night, after they had established and hastily fortified a new camp, those awake saw a strange fire high overhead, moving downwind. They watched it in silence, and as it passed, hundreds of broadside leaflets settled, spinning and gliding, into the camp. The men reached for them and stirred the fires to read them as a subdirect trotted one over to Onser's tent. They brought a candle and spread it on the table. Onser read it aloud to the assembled officers:

NOTICE NOTICE NOTICE NOTICE NOTICE NOTICE

The Heart River Federation understands that many Innanigani soldiers were deceived into this invasion and wishes to offer amnesty to any who surrender in the next two days. You will be required to rebuild the villages that you have destroyed, but will be treated humanely and returned to your borders afterward as were some prisoners from the last Innanigani aggression. If you do not accept this offer, it is likely that you will never reach home again.

> The Joint Defense Force
> Heart River Federation

Onser swore and growled to his officers, "I want the word passed now that anyone caught reading this slime will be given twenty lashes, and anyone caught attempting to desert will be executed summarily. Go."

The men ran from his tent shouting. Almost immediately quick volleys of rifle fire blazed from all sides of the perimeter of the camp, well back. Men near fires fell and hid. The machine rifles began spraying the darkness in return, but only in short bursts. A subdirect commanded a gun crew to lob the few remaining mortar shells out into the darkness. The attack passed like a gust of deadly rain, and aside from the cries of Innanigani wounded, the forest was quickly silent again.

South of the Baligani harbor, Stel nosed his boat quietly into the darkness near the rock barrier as a small light glowed briefly then disappeared. He adjusted the tiller and stood ready to slacken his sail. The light glimmered again. He released the line from its cleat and glided in slowly. Men quietly waded out to the bow and guided the boat in. Twelve figures climbed over the bow. Ferth came aft and put her hand around his arm.

Owayn also came aft and whispered, "Jaas and his men will push us off and turn you. We'll need to hurry. What kept you?"

"Getting here without being seen."

"We have to move."

"True. Any sailors among you?"

"Jaas and Rude only. But they can instruct the others."

The boat was poled about and all sails raised. A west wind, freshening slightly, moved them through the water northeastward toward the channel. As they passed east of Baligan, the flames from Owayn's lodging flared the whole western sky.

"Good. My neighbors must be burning now as well. That'll serve the murderers," Owayn said.

"And keep them all harzas occupied," Jaas remarked.

Far to the northwest where Onser's invading force lay surrounded, rifle fire again began, but this time, as though the westerners were playing a game, it started to the east and wheeled slowly to the south and on around the compass, one shot at a time. Again the machine rifles replied. No one in the camp noticed another fire gliding high overhead until small explosives started raining down on them in clusters.

"Riflemen, concentrate on that!" a subdirect yelled, but the surrounding fire increased in intensity until most of the men simply kept their heads down.

"It's sinking!" the subdirect shouted, squinting at the light now drifting off to the east. The glow seemed to blink out, then a short time later blazed up farther east. "Shoot it now," the subdirect shouted. A machine rifle began firing bursts out into the sky. The fire instantly blinked out. Then it seemed as though all the surrounding rifle fire concentrated on the machine rifle pits. Three gunners fell over the weapons, and the rest crouched low and let the hostile fire kick dirt and drive into the logs around the positions.

After this the surrounding forest again fell silent. Once more the Innanigani force collected its wounded and buried its dead. A lieutenant eventually reported to Onser. "We've lost another thirty-two men, Exalt, and twenty-eight wounded."

"Ox brains!" the officer shouted.

"And the last yoke of them as well," he added with a nervous laugh.

"Have them harzas butchered to eat, then."

"Yes, Exalt. It's being done. I don't understand the light overhead. Do they have some means of flying?"

"That's impossible."

"And yet . . ."

"We'll find out what it means. Something simple."

"Did you see how well printed those leaflets were? These people are not simple."

"No. But neither are we. Keep the men digging tonight. We'll stay here tomorrow, rest, and prepare. Then we'll make a very long march starting before dawn the next day. I want to make at least fifty ayas."

"Exalt, the men—"

"They will have to do it."

At that moment, in a circle of torches two ayas to the east, thirty men worked to bring the second balloon down from the trees into which it had settled. One man inside lay dead, his cooling blood slowly dripping through holes in the basket onto the men beneath. The other one, groaning, hung on the side. Blood ran from his torn shoulder.

Mokil looked up through the trees. "Ikdal's setting in the west. It's near dawn already," he said.

As Stel's boat nosed through the channel eastward, he noticed the first false dawn. By his side, Jaas said, "Can't you get any more speed out of this harzas barge?"

"Only way is for you and some of the others to get in the skiff and row with a line. Even so, I'm not sure it would help."

"There are some freaking Balis ahead of us."

"They're busy with the other boat. Borund's."

"How you know it's his?"

"The message on the dog."

"You saw it."

"Many did. Ease off on the foresail a little. Talk softer. Ferth is sleeping."

"Ferth. There are more important things."

"She just saved your life. No. Don't ask how. You seem incapable of understanding. Look. There's the open sea."

"About time."

"When we clear the channel, we can run north northeast. I assume the others all ran northeast, so I'd like to keep clear of them and toward the coast."

"Borund would have done that."

"I doubt it. He would have tried to lose them in the night, hoping to reach Innanigani fishing grounds in a day or two. Look. I see three sails out there on the horizon."

"Where?"

"Against the light. See?"

"No."

"They are there. Take it from my good eye. The other's gone awry."

Jaas looked scornfully at Stel in the dim light. Slowly they cleared the channel and headed out into open water, picking up the easy swell there and pitching gently.

After a few minutes Owayn stumped up the stairs from the cabin with two other men and nodded at Jaas, who swung a club, knocking Stel unconscious. Ferth shrieked from behind her father and tried to get around him, but he thrust her back.

"Over with him," Owayn hissed.

As the men dragged Stel to the rail and lifted him over, Ferth burst around her father crying, but Jaas pitched Stel's limp body over and Ferth desperately leapt over after it. Ervil came up behind her and jumped in after her.

"Pry the Pelbar loose and bring Ferth," Owayn shouted, as his wife reached the deck, shrieked, and began pounding him on the back and head.

"I'll never let go . . . of him," Ferth yelled, swallowing water.

"Throw a rope," Ervil shouted at the retreating boat.

"Loose all the sails," Jaas said as he ran for the skiff.

"Don't you dare hurt the Pelbar, you swine!" Mz Sovel shouted.

"What?" said Owayn.

"Swine, swine, swine," she repeated, beating him with her small, fat fists. He caught her hands and stared at her dimly seen, contorted face. "Swine," she said again. "My mother told me never to marry you. Swine. Filthy, swill-eating swine. After what he did for Ferth, your own daughter! And now for us. Swine. And you promised him. Doesn't that mean anything at all?"

Owayn shrugged. "Bring them all aboard," he called, shaking his head.

They came up dripping. Ferth shivered, but knelt over Stel, whose scalp wound ran watery blood onto the deck. He groaned. "The fading stars," he said. "They came back so quick. I think I feel a little . . . ill."

"Disgusting," Owayn muttered. "Tie him and put him below. Set the sails. We've lost time. Hurry. The light is growing."

About fourteen ayas to the east, Borund watched the Baligani pursuers with apprehension. "Where was your explosion, your grand explosion, Ticent? Didn't test it, eh?"

"They must have dismantled it. You heard the trigger explosion."

"Sure that wasn't the whole thing?"

"No, thank all that is good. To destroy—"

Borund backhanded him across the face. Ticent held his mouth, glaring. "You," Borund said to the boat owner, "will that small boat go faster than this one?"

"Under sail? Yes. But you can't abandon this one. I need it for my livelihood."

"There'll be no livelihood if we get caught. Lower it. Ticent, we're going to leave you with your precious toy. See you in Innanigan."

"You can't do that, you bug-bitten traitor!"

"Throw him below and leave him." Three men seized Ticent and bustled him down into the hold, throwing him against the ancient bomb.

"There." Borund laughed down the hatchway. "Cuddle up to it. You've spent your life with it. It might make a good desk weight. Slightly ungainly."

"If the Balis get it, they can use it on us!" Ticent shouted.

"If it worked. I'll let you worry about that. We need it as a decoy. Shove off now, Ohor. Quick. In the boat."

Ticent stood, dizzy, and ran up the steep stairs to the deck, only to see the smaller boat pulling away. "Indecent fly-specked obscenity!" he yelled. "Crazy man. Fool. You'll see!"

He jumped down in the hold again, took the setting key, and wound the timer, then ran back up and threw the key after Borund. It struck the mast and fell at the legislator's feet. He laughed, took it up, and threw it back. It fell into the water. Ticent looked down in disbelief, as though awakening, turned again to the bomb, ran his eye around the boat, grabbed a life preserver, and jumped into the sea, swimming desperately toward the nearest Baligani boat, now less than half an ayas off.

The lieutenant on that boat, shading his eyes, muttered, "What in Billie's worm-riddled apple is going on here?"

"I don't like it, Lieutenant," a subdirect said at his elbow. "I think they must have set the bomb."

The lieutenant stared at him. "Shear off!" he yelled to the helm. "Turn about. Head back. Quick."

Ticent, raising himself above the chop, saw the Baligani boats turn away and yelled in desperation. "Stop. Wait. Don't leave me here!" He began to swim frantically, quickly getting winded. While treading water he turned and saw the boat bobbing, its tiller unmanned, carelessly luffing in the light breeze.

Borund laughed loudly, looking back, watching the fleeing Baliganis. And then, instantly, his whole world turned into giant white fire. He had only a fraction of a second to glimpse his death before he vaporized.

The fire ran over Brod Ticent in the water, frying him into an instant cinder in a boiling sea. It reached out for the Baliganis and took them into its perimeter of roaring heat. Its light and searing blast stretched far out for Stel's boat. As Jaas, Owayn, and three others turned toward the unearthly flare, their eyes burnt out. The dark bands on the sails briefly smoked.

Below, Stel saw the glow and buried Ferth's eyes against his chest, shouting, "Shut your eyes! Ervil, cut loose the sails. Cut all the stays."

Ervil ran up the stairs, took in the writhing figures on the deck, turned east and saw a giant, roaring, cloud mushroom occupying much of the sky. He seized a boat knife and began hacking ropes as a shocking rush kicked the boat over hard, almost sliding him off the deck. He watched Jaas disappear, clinging and clawing, into the water and slip under. Ervil had cut the mainsail free, but the foresail split and broke the mast. Somehow the boat righted itself in a tossing sea. Eight of the eleven left lay on the deck blinded and seared, rolling and groaning.

Ervil ran down into the cabin and cut Stel loose. "It went. The giant bomb. Quick, Stel. Up on deck and help. We've got to get moving."

"We were too far. We'll probably be all right in this west wind," said the Pelbar rubbing his wrists and standing. He scrambled up on deck and stood stunned by the giant cloud to the east. "So much for Borund," he muttered. Then he ran for the tiller.

The weary Baliganis had the fire under control by morning, and at first few saw the sudden, fierce glow to the east, but some did, stared, then shut their eyes in pain. Opening them, dazzled, they saw the cloud rise in the distance, awesome even so far away.

"So," one man said, still holding a fire bucket. "That's what the 'Ganis had planned for us. Pity the men out there."

To the northwest near the Innanigani invaders, a radioman muttered and fiddled with his equipment. "Nothing will work!" he yelled. "I've checked everything, but it's all dead. I don't understand."

Far to the west of them, Pelbarigan still lay largely asleep, but their radioman also found himself cut off in the middle of a message. He, too, could not make the equipment operate again. Later, when they roused Eolyn, she found that none of her electronic equipment would function. She sat musing and after a long time said, "I can think of only one thing. No. That doesn't seem possible."

"What?"

"A thermonuclear explosion somewhere has sent an electromagnetic pulse that's overloaded everything. That would mean we've lost all our communications. All of them. We'd better start rebuilding it all now. We can't afford to be without it." She paused. "How . . . oh, no. What if . . ."

"Yes?"

"What if . . . it has destroyed our eastern army?"

"Destroyed? The army?"

"Yes. It could. This is what made the empty places. I think perhaps someone ought to set out for the East. Maybe me, too. I'll rouse the Protector."

In Innanigan no one knew of the great blast until, a day later, fishermen arrived home with consistent stories of a second dawn, south of the sun, brief but bright. The legislators put it all together and concluded that one of the bombs Borund had taken had been detonated. They seized the other three and brought them into the city under guard. The citizens objected in a mass, and the bombs had to be moved again away from the population center. Everyone was very uneasy until other fishermen returned and explained that the blast had come from too far east to be at Baligan itself.

Meanwhile, Onser's army made its forced march eastward, with snipers picking off men continually. They camped, exhausted, on an easily defended ridge and took another rest day. During that day they saw the Federation balloon, tethered to a rope, above them three-quarters of an ayas off, two observers in it watching. The Heart River flag emblazoned the facing side of the craft. Several men tried to hit it with rifle fire without success. Some advocated a foray of riflemen, but as soon as the fifty volunteers began racing down the slopes, they came under heavy attack. Eighteen were lost before the others regained their defense line.

"Exalt," a lieutenant reported. "Tonight we must watch. There are rumors of desertion, surrender. That thing in the air has unnerved them."

"Tonight we move out, Lieutenant. Twenty ayas, to Uscar

Mountain. Then we'll be in position to make it to the Cwanto in another long march. If any of the scouts made it, we should have a relief force there awaiting us."

"If they made it."

"They will. We sent five separately. Somebody always makes it, Lieutenant. Somebody. Even after the Time of Fire some made it."

The lieutenant looked at him in silence. At last he said, "Yes, sir."

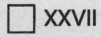 **XXVII**

THOUGH harried, Onser's force made it to Uscar Mountain and dug in for the day. A subdirect reported to the exalt that they had lost eighty-seven men.

"Eighty-seven! There's some mistake. There wasn't that much hostile fire."

"Eleven to the hostile fire, Exalt. The rest seem to have deserted."

"Stupid. So close to home. We can make the Cwanto tonight. Relief will be ready."

"Sir. The men are not certain of that, nor—"

"Yes?"

"That the Federation will stop at the Cwanto."

"That's the . . ." Onser began. Somehow it had not occurred to him that the Innaniganis would not be invincible in their own territory. But the Cwanto was not the Leynap, and even then there was a long walk east to the city and its settlements.

"Very well. Tell the lieutenants that they are responsible for the men under them and any further desertions will result in an execution of the officers in charge of that subsection. See to it."

The subdirect paused for just a moment, then said, "Very good, Exalt," and departed.

* * *

Stel jury-rigged a lateen sail out of the mast and remaining sections of canvas and limped northeastward. Manny Sovel manned the tiller, her husband lying at her feet, his chest seared in the pattern of the dark weave of his shirt. A wet towel lay over his eyes. Stel instructed Ervil and the others in handling the sheets and caring for the men who had been on deck during the blast.

Ferth hid her face and wept continually until Stel sat her up and made her look at him. "Little one," he said. "You'll have to hold that for now. We need too much help, yours included."

"I can't. Look at them all. Look at my father."

"It has to be faced, Pumpkin. We are going to get you home. And all them. You have to help. You have to tell yourself there'll be time to be horrified then. Push it away."

"I can't do that."

"There isn't a choice. And you can. I know you can. Look what you've done already. My wife always said 'Bite your lip and go on. There'll be time enough to cry.'"

"Oh, Stel, why did it have to be this way?"

"It didn't. It was a matter of choice. The trouble is that the choice was left to Borund. Most of us aren't interested in power and making choices for everybody. We have other talents. Other interests. So the Borunds of the world are left with choices they are less suited to make than just about anybody else. But we can choose, too. I hope you'll choose to help. That'll be a start. And you can begin by going down and checking the bilge to see we aren't leaking. The hatch door in the center of the cabin. Come on now. Up. Do it."

Ferth rose reluctantly and walked haltingly to the stairs down to the cabin. Her mother looked at Stel. He held out his hands, palms up, then returned to slowly working the shirt off a young man who lay tossing and groaning from his burns.

At dawn the next day Onser's force reached the Cwanto near the fort. His horn brought a return call from the fort, and soon men ran boats into the water and started across. Rifle fire picked up from the west, and a Federation balloon rose over ther trees.

When most of the men were across, Onser commanded the machine rifleman near him to fire at the woods.

"Not much ammunition left, Exalt, " the man said.

"Fire it all. We have enough at the fort, I'm sure."

The man ran the last half belt through the weapon, spraying

fire at the drifting smoke puffs that marked the hostile riflemen. Then as he opened the breech, saying, "That's it, sir," their position was raked by machine rifle fire from the south.

The Innaniganis still on the west bank hugged the ground as the bullets peppered the earth and trees around them. A second machine rifle opened up on the boats, raking them and toppling men into the river. The machine rifles at the fort began pounding the western positions, which fell silent.

Onser held his arm. Blood ran between his fingers. "They have the new weapon," he shouted. "All still here—dig in."

"Sir, they've stopped," a subdirect shouted. "Should we get over the river?" The man's tone sounded a little desperate.

Onser glared in his direction. "Yes. You go. Take twenty men who want to go." Onser had no patience with cowards and expected them to be killed, but the men ran for a boat on the bank and paddled it desperately across, using their oars and hands, and bailing with cupped palms. Much to Onser's chagrin, they all made it. He watched them run up the bank without their weapons.

Meanwhile, Tristal knelt over Narl, who lay gasping, one hand still on the machine rifle. "Lie back," he said. "Let me open the shirt."

"No . . . need . . . Tris," Narl whispered, then squinted his eyes and let out a final gurgle. A Sentani seized the weapon and frantically began to load their last ammunition belt. Tristal held his arms. The man struggled.

"No," Tristal said, through tight teeth. "This is a weapon of war, not a tool of vengeance. We have to set up the position."

"Get out of my way, Shumai," the man said.

"When we are ready, you can fire, Vendi," Tristal said. "Help with the logs."

The Sentani struggled, but couldn't free himself from Tristal's grip. Finally he relaxed, panting. "He's my cousin!"

"We're all cousins, Vendi. Even they are. We have only one more belt. The commander is still on the west bank. Wait for him. Wait until the weapon is protected."

The Sentani flashed him a final look of frustration and anger, then rolled back out of the position and went to help bring logs. Tristal laced Narl's shirt back up and looked down at his impassive calm. For a moment he put his cheek against the dead man's, then lifted him up and carried him back through the trees.

*   *   *

In the fort, the lieutenant muttered, "What does Onser think? That we have a thousand men here?" He turned to a subdirect who had just crossed the river. "How many men do you have now?"

"Four hundred sixty this morning, sir."

"Out of?"

"About a thousand."

The lieutenant whistled. "Together we have just over six hundred, then."

"We just lost a lot out there, sir."

"Where did they get the machine rifles?"

"Don't know. This is the first we've seen them."

"That must be the raiders, then. At least they're out of the east. But now they have those weapons, we can expect they'll make them, too. Did you bring your brass?"

"Brass?"

"Shell casings."

The man laughed. "No. All that weight when we were running?"

"Didn't Onser ask you to?"

"No, sir. Are they in short supply?"

"*Short* harzas *supply*? Yes. Already we've been melting harzas statues in the freaking city. They've begun going into the poison places for the stuff."

"Shouldn't do that, sir."

The lieutenant turned away without answering.

The Innaniganis on the west bank kept down for the rest of the day, which seemed to them endless. The tethered balloon rose higher, and when a few men tried long shots at it, return fire from the balloon made them duck.

"Exalt," said a subdirect. "That thing is almost an ayas away yet they are putting their shots on target. They've improved their weapons."

Onser regarded him silently, tucked in behind a hill of dirt.

Nightfall approaching the coast at Innanigan harbor found the watch gazing out over the water for the last fisherman. Nearly the whole fleet lay in harbor where it had been commanded to remain until the present issue could be decided. The watch shaded his eyes, squinted a long time, then blew a long horn blast. When the harbor guard officer ran out, he called down, "Strange sail, sir. Southeast. Short mast."

The officer trotted up the tower and looked where the harbor watch pointed. "Can't make it out. A fishing vessel. Baligani colors, right?"

"I don't . . . yes, sir."

"Blow the horn for alert. We'll go out to meet them. Hurry. It's near dusk."

Onser told a subdirect to signal the fort that they planned to cross the river in twilight. He intended to take advantage of the shield of darkness without allowing it to aid the westerners in closing in.

At the time Mokil was chanting the sacred words of Atou over the fresh grave of Narl. The raiders and many from the western force stood together. After the ceremony, Mokil said, "I suspect he would have liked a Pelbar hymn."

"While you sing it, I need to return to the position," Tristal remarked. "I suspect they'll try to cross soon." Vendi instantly followed, as did nearly all the Peshtak.

Night came on. A Sentani horn sounded. Sporadic firing started, and the fort began returning short bursts of machine rifle fire. The firelight from the balloon grew brighter as the craft ascended and drifted forward.

Over the river, the balloon released white phosphorus flares, and heavy firing began. "They're not in the boats!" Tristal shouted. "Look for heads in the water."

"There," Vendi yelled, and let loose a burst of machine rifle fire. The fort sprayed the woods in their direction and an occasional burst splatted into the logs of the bunker. As the flares died down, the last Innaniganis struggled out of the water and ran up the bank for the fort. Fire from the west bank grew thicker, and the machine rifles from the fort pounded out their return fire. Mortar rounds lofted out of the fort and slammed down on the west bank. Soon the firing died back.

Viewing the scene from the low branches of a tree, Mokil said, "All right. Let's collect our hurt and dead. Let's hope it isn't much of a job."

"Mokil. There's a Baligani here to see you," a man called up from below.

Mokil frowned and jumped stiffly down. "What? Here. We can walk back and have some light."

The Baligani runner, streaked with sweat and dirt, held a Shumai noggin of stew. "News," he said. "The Innaniganis tried to destroy Baligan with a giant bomb. It didn't work. But they did blow themselves up out at sea with a light brighter than the sun. Made a great cloud we could see twenty-five ayas off or more. Jestak is dead. Xord, too. Some of our people. Stel is gone. He was there. He may be dead, but we think he took away the Innaniganis in his boat."

"He what? Why would he . . ."

"A girl. Daughter of their representative. Wanted her out of it, we think. Took them all. Governor says Stel relieved him of a problem."

"Never know what Stel will do. But I've seen him do a lot of right things. Jestak dead, you say? That is hard. What—"

"The big thing is the bomb. We are getting one out of the harbor. I'll explain later. We're sending an army to join you. We need to know where to go."

"How many men?"

"Four hundred. And over a hundred Coo have joined them. On account of Xord."

"Where are they?"

"About seventy ayas southeast, near the Leynap."

"We'll send some of Arey's riders. Get them to go north up the Leynap. Either cut these people off or join us. A bomb, you say? That bad?"

"The kind, they say, that made the empty places. An ancient bomb. Unbelievable. A fireball an ayas wide."

"Atou and Aven help us. And you have one?"

"If it works. It's been underwater. We know nothing about it."

Mokil scratched his head. "Get Kahdi and tell him to mount some men and take an extra horse," he said. "I wonder. I'd like to talk to the enemy. There's a chance . . ." He paused. "Not much of one, though," he added. "How far west is Ahroe? Send Kahdi and some riders for her."

In the morning Mokil sent two boatloads of Innanigani wounded across the river under a white flag and invited the enemy to a talk on a nearby island. A lieutenant and a squad of men rowed across and met the westerners in the grass at the south end of the island.

Mokil questioned them about their knowledge of the bomb and the grave consequences of its use. They claimed to know nothing of it and would have regarded it as a hoax except for the presence of the Baligani scout, who confirmed the event and expressed the Baliganis' feelings on the subject.

"So you're going to join them? Violate your treaty?" the lieutenant remarked bitterly.

"All of Baligan would have been destroyed, and all the citizens killed, if the first bomb had worked," said the scout passively. "It seemes harzas odd to talk about treaties."

"You must permit me to doubt all this."

"Doubt it or not," said Mokil, "you have to realize what it means."

"What?"

"We can't chase you back to your borders this time and leave. We have to have a surrender of Innanigan so we can search out these bombs. Otherwise we all may die."

"You'll rot a long time first."

"I expect to rot a long time. But we could also do this peacefully. It ought to be in your interest as well to nose out these things." Mokil chuckled slightly. "At least then we could fight a normal war—or no war at all. War has gotten a lot worse during my lifetime. If everybody keeps inventing new ways of killing people, we may empty all Urstadge again."

"They're all old ways," the lieutenant said. "We're just finding them again."

"It seems the ancients weren't all that bright, and we're just following their example."

"So what are you asking? The surrender of my army? Here? Put all our men and munitions at your mercy, when we could sweep you away? Not likely."

"You've lost a lot of men trying to sweep us away."

"And killed a lot of scruff."

Mokil shrugged and ignored the insult. "We could go together and ask that the bombs, if there are any, be mutually destroyed."

"You could also jump over the moon."

"We have a bomb, you know. The one in Baligan Harbor."

The lieutenant paused. "It didn't work."

"We have no fear we could make it work. Then you would never rest, as we will never rest, because any boat entering your harbor may have it aboard. To roast the whole city like an overdone pigeon."

The lieutenant tapped his leg with his stick. "I will take your message to the exalt," he said, rising. "We will return at half after high sun."

Mokil watched them leave in silence. "Ahroe," he said. "I wish Ahroe would get here."

"I think we should send a force south and cross over. They may decide to leave now," Tristal said.

"Now? With all the wounded? Before the meeting?"

"Ahroe was right. They know that in that fort, this far west, all they can do is grow weaker and we stronger. We told them enough so they will understand that the Baliganis are sending a force."

"The men are weary, Tristal."

"Mokil, if Tristal leads, I'll go," Vendi said.

Mokil scanned the small group. "Tris, take the men you need. But all volunteers. Riflemen only. And cover yourself. They still have those machine rifles."

"And the mortars. You have any mines?"

"About twenty. Take them all."

At high sun the whole Innanigani force left the fort and quick marched eastward. The fort behind them burst into flames and burned fiercely. About thirty sunwidths later the lead men stepped into a minefield, and heavy fire from the south lanced into the columns. Machine rifle fire sprayed the area and the columns hurried on, making for a protected camp that had been set up earlier.

They received only scattered sniper fire until they were near the camp, exploding another pair of mines and taking more fire. In the camp Onser, still on his litter, beckoned to the fort commander. "It's worse now," he said. "We thought we'd steal a march on them."

"It's the raiders, Exalt. They're led by a big blond man who seems to know what we are going to do before we do."

"I was mistaken, Lieutenant. Dupon and Subish were so sure, and Borund's description of the fall expedition—how could I have been so misled? And that underpart, Crupp."

The lieutenant said nothing. "He told me what I wanted to hear," said Onser. "Maybe Peydan wasn't as incompetent as I thought."

"Peydan? He didn't have much chance with Borund interfering."

"What do you think about that bomb story?"

"I don't know, sir. Seems wild."

"But the Baliganis. We'll have to anticipate an army. How would they come?"

"Up the Leynap it's likely."

"They could cut us off. We'll have to pull out before dawn. And make some kind of heavy device to precede us to blow up those hidden explosives. Is there a relief force coming?"

"Made of what, sir? With the losses of two years ago, and the size of your force, we've drained away a lot of our manpower. Already we've lost one citizen from every twenty, and mostly young men. And from the folly of our leaders—many of whom have profited from it all."

Onser shifted himself painfully. "I wonder how much we can count on their mercy . . . if they do overwhelm us. But we cannot let that happen."

"I gather they are in earnest about this bomb, sir."

"I harzas wish I knew more about it."

"I suspect somehow Borund is at the bottom of it. Or Subish. Or maybe Amoc. Industrialists. We'll be drained of all our people. The raiders were really very bad, so the messages said. But they did little killing until they captured machine rifles."

"How will we recover and push them back? We must have a relief force. Perhaps the Seliganis—"

"Exalt, we have made ourselves stink in the nostrils of the Baliganis. If there is any truth to this bomb story, how will the Seliganis take it?"

"They might bow to our will."

"Yeah. And the wheat may never get bugs in it."

"Well, give the men fifty sunwidths of rest, and then we have to march to Bird Mountain."

"Tonight? The men—"

"Better tired than dead. We have to stay north of the Balis if they're coming."

The Innanigani prison was not large. The warden, a retired army officer, looked at Zard across the table. "What have you learned from the Pelbar?"

Zard recounted all Stel had told him about the bombs. Occasionally the warden glanced over at his secretary, who jotted furious notes.

"What do you think of him?" the warden asked.

"It sounded like the truth."

"It meshes well with what Mz Sovel said. What else?"

"About Stel?"

"You talk as though you knew him."

"I almost do. His son, Garet, commanded the horsemen who

captured me. I knew him well enough. He talked about his father—couldn't understand him."

"Can you?"

"He's the way Garet said. Very different. How many people would risk themselves to save their enemies, even though they try to drown him for thanks?"

"He's not the usual Pelbar, then."

"No. Not exactly. But Garet saved us, too. He was deadly enough as an enemy, but perfectly fair and merciful. I'm sorry he's dead. He had some of his father in him, too."

"Dead?"

"Apparently he was killed while patrolling at the start of the invasion."

"He was among the invaders we caught, then."

"Not according to Stel. Kahdi saw it, and the Baligani observer. Another observer, Garf . . ."

"Major Zimon's son. I know him."

"—was killed with Garet."

The old man winced. "This looks very bad."

"What?"

"Zimon dead. His son. Garf would not have been with an invasion. The other Baligani saw it?"

"Yes."

The warden leaned back and drummed on the table top. "Things are out of hand. This bomb, then. It's like the others we have. The Balis have one?"

"The bad part. Not the other bomb the Ticents made."

"Zard, we are in a mess. And, well, we want you to go to Lume Budde and tell him all this."

"What about Stel?"

"What about him?"

"Can he come? Owayn promised him he could address the legislature. That was a condition of his saving the delegation."

"Are you crazy? I have no authority. What do you want him for?"

"I have a strange feeling, Warden. He may be the key to the whole thing."

"He's locked up. I have the key. Go. Before I change my mind. This is a risk. They could have my job."

"The Federation could have it, too."

The two men looked at each other. "See Budde. Tell him," the warden said.

At the legislature a very thin, bald man was addressing the others, his head close to a sheaf of papers. "This year's military budget alone has been a third of our entire product, and another sixth has been destroyed by the raiders, totaling over two million raels. In addition, keeping the fleet in is depriving the economy of close to twenty thousand raels each day. And with the new price of brass from the Seliganis, and additional orders from the military, our economy . . ." at this point the man looked up and blinked around the room " . . . is nearly in ruins."

"The Chair recognizes Legislator Crupp."

Crupp leapt to his feet and leveled a finger at the bald man. "I've heard nonsense in my life, but never anything like this. The barbarians have been within five ayas of where we sit. They are even now marching on us from the west in force. We need to pull together, exert all our national effort for survival, and this lump of pond scum is worried about finances. Where will the economy be when the savages come howling down our streets? The point is we need the brass. We need the new weapons. And we need them now! Why are we here debating?"

The bald man regarded Crupp coolly. "We are debating because it is time to negotiate. These stories about the giant bombs need to be investigated. It is possible that we have done a great wrong."

"A great wrong! Survival is a great wrong?"

"Legislator Crupp, you must either contain yourself or vacate this chamber," the Chair said sleepily.

"It seems to me," said the bald man, regarding his fingernails, "that anyone who has personally made over eighty-two thousand raels on the war this year alone is in a poor position to call for more expenditures when there is an alternative."

"There is no alternative, you weasel-brained cow leaving!"

The bald man smiled slightly. "My niece talked to two of the raiders when they burned her barn. Her children were in the loft. The raiders saved them. She was angry, of course, and frightened. But they didn't hurt her—or the children. She thinks we can talk to them. You must admit that it cannot hurt. Even Crupp cannot wound with the slathered arrows of his filthy tongue. From what we—"

"I don't have to take this from a harzas lily-bellied slimewort!" Crupp shouted.

"Bailiff," the Chair called, "please assist Legislator Crupp from the chamber until he contains himself. We do maintain a modicum of order here. The enthusiasm of expression we can allow does have limits, and they have been transgressed. Yes, Legislator Amoc?"

"I cannot admit of a fellow member being muzzled, Mr. Chair. I wish the record to show a protest and call for a vote on the issue."

A shrill voice came from the gallery, "Listen, you harzas, frog-faced profiteer! My son died out there so you could fatten your odorous belly and you protest! You've got the gall of a scrub oak and the..."

At that point a bailiff put his hand over the mouth of the old woman and dragged her from the gallery.

"Perhaps we should clear the gallery, Mr. Chair," Amoc remarked.

"Mr. Budde?"

"I would object to that, Mr. Chair. The people need to know what transpires in these chambers. And I would like them to hear that I have been just handed a note that the Pelbar prisoner, Stel, was granted permission to address this body by our representative in Baligan, Owayn Sovel, as a condition of his getting them out of Baligan."

"Indeed? I don't believe Owayn had that right, Mr. Budde."

"Nonetheless, it would appear to me germaine to this issue that we hear the man in order to evaluate the enemy. He may have valuable things to tell us. It is clear we will have to make some accommodation with the enemy, and it would not hurt to know who they are. I might mention that my aunt, who is very old, also met the raiders. They burned her house, and when she refused to leave it, they simply carried her outdoors in her chair and left her in the open. I—"

"You are all talking as though they were friends!" Legislator Dupon shouted.

"Legislator Dupon has also profited from the government— at the rate of one hundred and ninety-seven thousand raels this year alone," the bald man remarked.

"Order! We will have order!" the Chair said loudly, pounding his stone.

"If I still have the floor," Budde said, "I might mention that this poor Stel has been wronged by us. First we almost blew him up. Then we gave him false promises. Then we tried to drown him. Then we imprisoned him on his own boat until the bomb went off. After which he brought the wounded home—

for which we have thanked him by imprisoning him again. I think we could try to make some of that right."

"Touching," Legislator Subish said. "Discussion of the appropriation is more important."

"Legislator Subish has been paid one hundred and twenty-three thousand raels this year by the government," the bald man said.

"You are out of order, Legislator Bloc. However, I thank you at least for your courtesy. This body stands in recess until half after high sun. Bring the Pelbar." The Chair rapped his stone and left the chamber amid shouts of protest.

Exalt Onser lay in his litter about eight ayas northeast of Bird Mountain. He could hear occasional rifle fire from the enemy, but they had not attacked for some time. The lieutenant from the fort came to him and knelt down.

"Yes, Nivel?"

"The men, Exalt. They want Lieutenant Oberly to take over the retreat."

"Him! Is he here? Didn't we get rid of him? He surrendered two years ago. Gave up. Is that what they want? Nonsense. Shoot him first."

"We don't have many reserves, Exalt. He was called up with our reinforcements at the fort. He knows the country from his love of fishing—even fished Peshtak country in the old days despite the danger. They claim he saw what to do in the west and did it. They think he'll get them out of this."

"By surrendering, no doubt. Simply tell them no."

"They all want it, sir."

"No matter. The answer is no."

The lieutenant stared off at the sky. "Yes, Exalt," he said.

"The point is that we get out, Exalt," said a subdirect, kneeling by him and smoothing his rumpled collar. "The men think Oberly can do it. I have watched him. He is a wily man, sir. You could always simply let it happen and take back authority later."

The exalt looked up at the man. He was out of line, but clearly concerned. Strange. He didn't know the man. He spoke in an odd way. His ear was torn.

Before Stel came to the legislature, he took a small detour to the harbor and gave the radiation detector that hung around his neck to the harbormaster, explaining, "You will know when radiation is present because it will chirp. If the radiation is massive, it will trill. You might want to try it out in the dead zone northeast. It did a lot of chirping on the way here. Ask the Sovels."

"Why are you giving it to me?"

"You have to examine all the fish brought in."

"With this?"

"Not with your nose. There was massive radiation out there. Some of it will have been picked up. Fish do migrate, you know." Stel smiled at him. "If we have peace, we'll get somebody to explain it to you. Most likely Eolyn, the Dome woman."

"She isn't a legend?"

"A good-looking one. A real legend."

"Come on, Stel. We can't keep them waiting," Zard muttered.

Later after high sun, the Innanigani force began to move dead north. The exalt leaned up from his litter. "What is going on?"

"We're going north," said the subdirect with the torn ear.

"I gave no order. This is mutiny."

"You have been relieved of command, Exalt, because of your wounds."

"By whom?"

"By the decision of the lieutenants, Exalt. Please. Let it lie. It can be sorted out later. Your authority is intact."

"There will be executions! I will not permit it."

"You don't want to come, then? Should we leave you?"

"I . . . no." Onser sank back down on the litter, wincing. He shut his eyes. They picked him up and swung him along.

By his shoulder, the subdirect said, "Sometimes, Exalt, strange tools have to be used to accomplish what is needed. Think of Oberly as one of the tools." Onser looked up at him, but he was looking away.

"Oberly thinks they went ahead, Exalt," one of the bearers said. "There is so little fire. Either that or they're as worn out as we are. If they are ahead, they'll link with the Balis and hold us at the ford. He says he knows another way."

The exalt didn't reply. He hated to admit it, but he saw the logic of Oberly's move. He tried to visualize the map in his head, but it wouldn't come clear. Behind them a rifle shot rang out and distant horns sang.

* * *

Stel stood before the Chair's dais and told the legislature as clearly as he could what he saw at Baligan and on the trip north. They questioned him extensively, and often insultingly, but he answered all the queries calmly.

"We understand you gave some sort of detector to the harbormaster, Pelbar. Please explain that to us."

"It's a radiation detector made for me by the Dome woman, Eolyn. I used it when I went north three years ago. It came in very handy. The whole of Urstadge is full of radiation ghosts, all of them dangerous. I have seen already that you have been building with a lot of fossil steel from the ruins. Much of the jail contains dangerous radiation."

"Impossible," said the Chair. "We are careful about that. All of it is contracted for as clean."

"Somebody has been lying to you, then," said Stel. "If there is peace, we'll see you are supplied with further detectors. So close to the dead lands, you need them when you contract with private citizens for things. At least in your society."

"No need to insult us, Pelbar."

"I meant no insult. It may be simply size. Or social organization. We're used to smaller societies in which mutual dependency promotes honor, and our traditions demand more of a sense of justice and less a juggling of rules. I imagine when we grow, we'll have plenty of problems, too. It has all been such a struggle so far it is easier to try to be honorable. There are plenty of exceptions, of course."

"You talk as though it's a simple matter, Pelbar. But to the point. You are certain you didn't exaggerate the bomb?"

"Did you talk with Owayn? Or Manny?"

"He is too ill. Mz Sovel's story agrees with yours, but she didn't know all you knew."

"It is certainly vital to eradicate these bombs," said Stel, "before they do more mischief. There will have to be trust. Mutual trust."

"We'll see about that."

"Yes. But after you have had your fill of death, we'll have to do what should have been done at first. Talk."

"And your side? What will satisfy their blood lust, Pelbar?"

"I know them. The warden described to me the leader of the raiders. He has often eaten at my table. He has had a wild and somewhat bitter life, but he is gentle as a sparrow—if you'll talk to him honestly. If your army is nearly spent, you have to know ours is, too. Let them all sit down together and talk. Of course there are now the Balis and the Coo."

"What do you mean?"

"I'm certain they're now committed—now that Borund has killed a Coo and tried to explode the city of Baligan."

"By 'committed' what do you mean?"

"I imagine they are moving north right now to join the Federation."

"You know no such thing, Pelbar," called a voice from the gallery. "We don't scare. Why are we taking time with this scruff?"

"Because it seems profitable. Now, Stel, what can you tell us of this Ahroe?" The Chair asked. "Will she be with the army—the one who burnt her own hand? Is she so indifferent to pain?"

Stel laughed nervously. "No. That was an act of mercy, you know. She wanted to share the pain so your men would not object. The Peshtak wanted some torture to requite them for their losses. It was symbolic. She simply tried to make it acceptable."

"How do you know this?"

"She told me."

"You know her then?"

"Yes."

"What do you think of her?"

"If anyone will be fair with you, she will. I have never seen her unfair when she knew how to be. She is completely devoted to her duties to society and will embrace yours as well as hers. Sometimes this makes her neglect individuals, herself included. You will not fool her easily. I wouldn't even try. She does have some limitations, of course."

"What are they?"

"The same as yours. She is fascinated by the existing methods of social action, and so she often doesn't see beyond them. This makes both you and her narrow your scope. Sometimes the obvious seems unthinkable, because the system has built in so many consequences."

"What are you talking about?"

"What could be plainer? The two armies should stop where they are, talk, then go home and dismantle all the bombs, collect the shells, melt them, and rebuild the statues, trade with each other, live at home and in peace. All the people want it."

"Would your side do that?"

"Likely not. They would want guarantees and concessions,

just as you do. The trouble is that only people interested in controlling other people's lives get into your business, or Ahroe's business. They get habits. The control becomes more important than the people. Systems take over. Injustice and murder are done because somebody has made a rule to legitimatize them. Soon the politicians can see no other way because they are fixed on the need to gain advantage.

"Meanwhile the people who are truly normal, who live in towns and on farms and make things work, are silly enough to let your sort run everything, and the result is awful—because politicians include a lot of really very weird people, only the normal ones are so used to them they forget to notice. So are armies strange. All made up of people who would rather be with their families—except for the true killers."

"We aren't getting anywhere. Tell us, Pelbar, how willing do you think you savages would be to talk? Plainly. Could this be done?"

"I really don't know any savages. But if you mean the Federation, of course. Why don't you go and ask them to talk?"

"I object!" said Legislator Subish. "We can't talk with that gang of murderers!"

"I heard some of us say that about you," said Stel. "If you'd like, I'll go and ask them to talk. Send Zard with me. The longer we wait, the shorter the trip will be. And the more death. You can send some negotiators—perhaps Legislator Budde. With such a prophetic and springlike name, who knows? He may succeed. I'd like to see Ahroe again one time. And I'd like Ferth to come."

"Why?"

Stel paused and looked enigmatically at the floor for a time. "For her education," he said. "And to give me courage. And to show Ahroe a gentle Innanigani. Pity runs easily in a gentle heart, and easiest when the object is so clearly worthy of it."

"I suppose you want us to march all our women and children out there for you to shoot," said Crupp.

"It wouldn't be a bad idea. You're learning. There would be no shooting—unless you did it. Or some misfortune. I know that. I mean know it. Not with Tristal and Mokil and Ahroe and Igant and Hesit even. They want this settled."

"Settled? What about the bombs? We haved three to your one. Want that settled, too?"

"What good are they? Suppose you set one off and destroyed

our army on the east bank of the Leynap. All that radioactive dust would drift eastward across all of Innanigan. That would be mutation and slow death for a lot of you. You know the poison in the dead lands. You want to invite that home?"

The legislators were silent for a short time. "What would you do with them? Throw them in the sea?"

"Of course not. Ruins the fishing—maybe not now, but when they began to leak. We should find a hill on our border and together dig a deep pit in the top of it. Pour some concrete in it. Line the bombs up on the concrete. Pour more on top. Then fill the hole with rock. And when anybody passed, he could add a stone. If anybody wanted them again, it would be no secret, would it?"

"You're joking. Mad. Give up the obvious ultimate defense?"

"Will it bring peace? No. While they are available, there will never be peace, only truce at best. This is a chance for real peace. Real peace. Don't you understand?"

"We're getting nowhere," said Legislator Dupon with disgust. "We need that appropriation now. This man is mad. When are we going to be serious? Is this whole body babbling loony? Does no one comprehend what is happening?"

"Why don't you appropriate your money and send us off to talk meanwhile? It can't hurt. If Legislator Budde is killed, the military profiteers will lose an adversary. If not, you will gain a peace and lose only profits. Lose a prophet or a profit. I will stake my life for his. No need to stew about it. You're in a pickle. I think I can get you out of this jam. Or give it a honey of a try—I've been bred to talk as you can see— Either that or your goose is cooked."

"Stel, you promised," Zard hissed.

"This man is a clown. We can't send off a clown!" Legislator Obil exclaimed.

"Why not? If you were a soldier and saw a clown coming down the road, maybe holding a bunch of flowers, what would you do?"

"Shoot him."

"Ah, but remember. It will not be you behind the rifle. It will be the Federation. They'll want to know what is going on. A hundred clowns would be better, but I don't suppose you could find fifty in all of Innanigan. Of course we could use women and children. But I don't mean to spoil this. Send me. Send Budde. We'll do our best. I promise. I know these people. I've eaten with them, worked with them, argued with them, fought by their sides, even made . . . I know them. It can't hurt, can it?"

"Send them," Legislator Subish said. "And then we can get on with the serious business of this body."

"Tell me, Pelbar," said a man hitherto silent. "How can you be so sure of your views?"

"I can't, of course. But I have traveled much, and have looked, and have no profit to make or self-interest."

"I can't believe that."

"No. I can understand you wouldn't. But a couple of years ago I lost everything. For a time I had nothing at all. Then as I thought about it, and took stock of what was left, I found it was everything."

"Talk sense."

"I found I still had the privilege of being honest, of courtesy, of kindness, of loving whatever was put in my way to be loved, whatever would accept it, and even some that wouldn't. Ferth accepted it because she was so lonely. Other people have accepted it. When I was helping your people get home, they accepted that. I am willing to help now because I have no private stake in any property, or honor, or position, or family. I am a free man. So I am free to try to help."

"You pile it high, Pelbar," said Subish.

"No doubt from your viewpoint, you are right," said Stel. "But what I do might help you, and if it doesn't, you don't have to accept it. So what can you lose?"

Late that night scouts brought the news to Tristal's men at the Leynap that the Innaniganis had turned north. "Fooled me," said Tristal. "I was so sure. Well, let's recross to our own side and rest. It may be just as well. We're really low on everything. Except fish. We've been emptying the river."

Some twenty-two ayas north, at Hutch's Crossing, the last of the Innanigani army waded up onto the east bank. "We made it, Oberly," said a lieutenant. "Now what?"

"Move about four ayas southeast. I know a hill farm with a nice well on high ground. Fields. Open ground."

"A farm? This far west?"

"Old army man. Married a Peshtak years ago. Peshkies never bothered them. I imagine the enemy is somewhere near Sconet Ford. We'll get a little rest, but not much. We want to pull back between the time their scouts find us and their force gets there."

"Their scouts?"

"Yeah. That way we can slip around them and cross the Oldvein and head southeast to the ancient road. I know a hill where we can wait for them."

"I . . ."

"We can set out our scout patrols to locate them, then the main force can hit them as they come along. Hard. That'll set them back. Then we can pull in our perimeter to something reasonable."

Later, coming north, Tristal received a new scout report. He leaned on a tree and thought for a time. "They have a new commander," he said. "I have to think like him. He's slippery. He's in his own country. I don't think we should chase him. I know we could get ahead of him. But we don't have the stuff any more. Soon we'll be back to bows again. I imagine that's all the Coo and Balis will bring. We'll move east now, slowly, and look for that ancient road. Let them set up. The men are nearly spent. We could use a rest. The Balis may catch up, too. It's been quite a pace. Ahroe must be far west."

"She'll be riding," said Mokil. "She'll be here."

A day later Kahdi's riders crossed north of Sconet Ford. With them were Ahroe and Miggi and a Pelbar guardsman. By now the two armies had completely lost each other, but lay only about eight ayas apart. The Innaniganis rested near the north ancient road to Innanigan. The Federation had skirted around a large lake and now lay on its south shore to the Innaniganis' west. Meanwhile, Stel and Legislator Budde were walking north-westerly toward Sconet Ford.

Lacking signs, Kahdi rode eastward, bearing north, hoping to find the trail of the Federation army. He was uneasy with Ahroe there in so fluid a situation, but she was used to travel and danger, and thought little of it.

At last they hit the ancient road and the signs of the Federation force, and rode east near the north shore of the lake. On a hill to their north lay one of Oberly's patrols watching.

"Hsst. Ongol," said one man. "Look. Horse riders."

"How many?"

"Only eleven."

"Only. There's just sixteen of us."

The subdirect commanding them muttered, "Pelbar. I see two Pelbar." He raised his rifled and sighted.

"Sir, we aren't supposed to reveal our..." The rifle crashed and one of the horses went down. Kahdi's men turned sharp and charged the hill shrilling their Shumai yells, then dismounted and melded into the cover as more rifle shots blazed out.

"Honeybuckets," one Innanigani said. "That freaking sub-direct. Where is he?"

"He's run off and left us. Quiet. We've got to get out of here."

"Who the harzas is he?"

"Don't know him. Talks funny."

A nearby shot knocked down one of the men, then two more quick shots to the east took down two more."

"Don't shoot. We surrender!" a man shouted.

"What are you filthy talking about? We freaking do not."

"We surrender!"

"Then all of you walk down onto the road," Kahdi called out.

"What'd you freaking do that, you mud-eating slime snake?"

"They'd of killed us, Ravo. The freaking subdirect messed it up and then ran. Why die for nothing?"

The Innaniganis arrived on the road, hands up, to find a woman kneeling by another, who lay half under a horse, which still kicked and struggled in its agony. The Shumai rolled the horse off the wounded woman.

Ahroe sucked in her breath. "Don't worry, Miggi. We'll get you to the others. It'll be all right. Here. Lie back. It went right on through the thigh. Didn't hit bone, I think. Horse didn't help much, did he?" She looked up. "Kahdi, we'll have to rig a drag. I...don't like this. Poor Mig. We'd better move out of here."

"We didn't do it. The subdirect did," said Oward.

"Shut your babble," Ravo hissed at him.

Ahroe looked over at the twelve Innaniganis, then turned away. "Did you get their weapons?" she asked Kahdi.

"Of course. How is she?"

"Can you leave four men to walk them in and send the rest with us?"

Kahdi didn't reply but jerked his head. Then he came and knelt by Miggi and wiped her sweat-beaded forehead with cal-loused fingers. "Destri," he said. "Take three men with these. Atlan, you and Brace ride ahead. We'll bring Miggi between." He looked at the Innaniganis and spat in the dust as the two point men rode off ahead.

Later, the subdirect reported to his officers on the encounter.

"There were fourteen, sir, all mounted. One of the men fired at a Pelbar. They attacked and killed some. I alone escaped. Some coward called out a surrender. Then the rest gave up."

"Where were you?"

"I hid when I saw what was happening."

"Weren't you in command?"

"Yes. The men gave up before I could do anything to stop it. They wouldn't listen."

"I suppose the shot missed, too."

"No. A hit. It hit a woman and her animal went down."

"A woman? A Pelbar woman?"

"No, sir. There were two. A dark-haired Pelbar and a red-haired Sentani."

Oberly put his palms to his eyes. "And . . . you . . . shot . . . one . . . of . . . them?"

"Yes, sir. My man shot the . . . redhead. I gave no . . ."

Oberly let out a cry.

"What in Billie's green apple is wrong, sir?" Lieutenant Nivel asked.

"He shot Miggi, Lieutenant. Miggi. The—of all the reports we've had, and all the disobedience of orders and all the incompetence and malfeasance, this is the—" He broke off and stared.

"I don't understand, sir," said the subdirect.

"By now I thought everybody knew who Miggi is," said Nivel. "Oberly met her on the last invasion. He—"

"Stuff it, Lieutenant," said Oberly. "We have to find that Federation army. Now."

"We've been trying to, sir."

Oberly shot another look at the subdirect. The man had a torn ear.

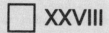 XXVIII

As Stel and Legislator Budde walked westward, they were met by an increasing crowd of desperate citizens, all of whom had now heard of Stel and wanted to hear the story of the bomb. He related what had happened and answered questions as factually as possible. Some people grew angry at what had happened without their knowing. Others railed at Stel and the "savages" of the west. But an increasing number joined the two on their westward walk. Budde could not understand it—except for a strange attraction Stel seemed to exert by his persistent gentleness and wry joking. The white-haired legislator grew increasingly convinced that something of importance was happening.

Meanwhile, Arey's riders had conducted the Baligani-Coo force across the Leynap south of Sconet Ford and marched steadily eastward.

Late in the evening Miggi was wounded, a subdirect presented himself to Oberly and saluted. "Lieutenant, we have located the enemy. They are camped south of Mayfly Lake."

"How far?"

"Not quite eight ayas from here, southwest."

Oberly whistled lightly. "All right. I want a truce party. I have a message. I need four volunteers and ten men to accompany me behind."

"What are you planning? Surrender again?" said Nivel.

"Surrender? No. Talk. Want to come?"

"No."

"Good. Assume command until I return. Keep the flanks out. Leave the fires lit. Rouse everybody and move the camp back over the Arit. Then take up the bridge. I'll see if I can learn anything. Remember we have a patrol out looking for the supplies from the city—mostly machine rifle ammunition. We're trying to get it in tonight. And . . . come aside." He and Nivel walked and stood by themselves. "That subdirect—with the ear? Watch him. There's something odd about him. You know him?"

"No. He was a late replacement to the fort at Tremai. I think he helped fight the raiders and came on. What's wrong with him?"

"I don't know. It's a feeling—and his story. A subdirect who is the only one to escape. Whose men fired against his orders. He always seems close to the center of things. He may have been one of Borund's pets. He's old for a subdirect, but doesn't seem that experienced. He has habits . . ."

"Yeah?"

"Of command. Do you see it?"

Nivel frowned. "No. I didn't notice anything."

"Maybe I'm skittish. No. It's something."

Near high night the Federation sentries reported a party with torches approaching from the east. Horns sounded and the force was brought to readiness.

Tristal rode out to the perimeter and there saw a party of four Innaniganis carrying a truce flag. He rode forward and dismounted. One of the men handed him a note without speaking.

Tristal opened it and walked near one of the torches to read it. It said:

> We got a report of a shooting. Was
> it Miggi? Is she all right?
>
> Lt. Oberly.

Tristal frowned, then laughed to himself. He got a piece of charcoal from one of his men and scratched a reply on the same piece of paper:

> Miggi is shot. Not all right. May
> probaly live unlike meny.
>
> Ttl.

He gave the paper back to the Innaniganis, who took it without a word, did a neat about face, and marched away without comment.

Tristal returned and reported the event to Mokil, who chuckled then said, "That crazy. Met him two years ago. A good officer, though, but they'd never see it. Not with this Miggi business.

Garet told me he fried the back of his hand to obscure the star brand so he could maybe return to our territory and see Miggi."

"What does she think about it?"

"Right now, nothing. She isn't doing well, Tris."

The horns sounded again, announcing the return of the four Innaniganis. Again Tris rode out to the sentries and took a note:

> May I see her?
>
> Lt. Oberly.

Tristal pondered. Oberly couldn't be far off. It could be a trick now that the easterners knew where they were. But it might be turned to advantage as well.

Taking the charcoal, he wrote:

> Com with the others. We wil admit you
> blindfolded. Garante safty.
>
> Ttl.

Tristal called forward some Shumai riders with handguns at ready. "Where's Destri?" he asked.

"Scouting."

"After all that riding?"

"Has it in mind to find the 'Ganis and tickle them some."

"Alone?"

"Him and Atlan. He's mad about Mig. Wants to do some damage. Feels responsible."

"Aven. What next? Here they come."

The four returned with Oberly, who looked grave. The Shumai blindfolded the easterner and helped him mount. "We'll send him back with a torch," Tristal told the volunteers. "You don't have to wait."

Oberly was helped down and admitted to a low tent dimly lit with two lamps.

"Hello, Oberly," said Ahroe. "Still featherbrained about Miggi? Be quiet, please. She's sleeping."

Oberly knelt down and touched her hand. It twitched. "A fever, then?" he said.

"It's not a hangnail."

"So I understand. I'm sorry. Look. She's on the ground. No bed or comfort here. Come on. We'll give you what you need, or take her to Innanigan. We have good doctors."

"This is not a cut or bruise. She'd die."

"What do you plan? To let her lie here in a stupid tent?"

"Shh. Please. Calm down. It hurts her if she wakes. Please talk outside."

"It wasn't our intent to injure her." He paused. "It's all mistakes."

Here Miggi blinked and looked. "You? You here? You?"

"We all are here," said Ahroe. "And him, too."

"I . . . got your note. All the way at Koorb."

"How . . . what can we do?"

"Look, Lieutenant, if there weren't a war," Ahroe said, "maybe we could manage something together. As it is, we can't. You always were somewhat bizarre, but you can't just lay aside the larger issue. Now if you can do something about that . . ."

"I—"

"Lieutenant," whispered Miggi. "I don't hold it against you. I can take my chances like everybody else. But . . . thank you for coming. And it was a nice letter."

"What . . . did you think . . . of . . ."

"It would have been all right. I've thought it over. But that is if . . . Now, please. This all is too . . . let me be."

Oberly dropped his eyes. "All right? It would have been all right? I'll go. But let me kiss you good-bye. Is that all right?"

"No, Oberly. It's too confusing," Miggi whispered, her eyes shut.

He looked at her, then at Ahroe. "Do you have any other business?" she asked. "We can go outside." She rose and took his arm.

Destri and Atlan had ridden east a good thirteen ayas, using the highway at first, then woods and footpaths.

"What's with you, Des? We ought to get back," said Atlan.

"No. The bastards. I'm going to get me some."

"Why? Because of Miggi? We did our best. Too bad, though. Hey, you aren't . . . She and you . . ."

"I just like her is all. All right. I thought . . ."

"Hsst. What's that?"

The two men stopped and dismounted, standing at their horses' heads. They could hear muffled sounds on a nearby road.

"Wish there were a moon. It's men with a handcart. No, two. Hey, Des, where are you . . . don't take them on alone. Wait."

Destri had mounted and moved out on the road behind the

men, then drawn his handgun and suddenly spurred forward, rushing in. One man shouted, just as Destri's gun began popping in rapid fire as he swept by. Suddenly in a heavy roar and flash both carts exploded, blowing away the Innaniganis and Destri. Behind, Atlan's horse shied and bucked, throwing him off. He hung onto the halter, dragging behind. When he got back, only one man remained alive. A small grass fire burned, almost domestically, around the fringes of the crater and debris.

Atlan dismounted and knelt by the man, who crawled in the road, dragging one leg.

"You," said Atlan. "Can you stand?"

"What?"

Atlan lifted the man and threw his arm around his own neck. "Come on. You're going to ride a horse."

Oberly was still talking to Ahroe when they heard the distant blast. "There go your supplies," said Ahroe.

"Umm. We've got enough supplies," Oberly said. "I'd better get back. I still say we ought to come to some truce."

"I'm sure we'd like that. But the bombs. We have to settle that. Without that there will be no peace."

"I don't know anything about them except the report of what the Pelbar said who saw the one go off."

"What Pelbar? What are you talking about?"

"The Pelbar in Innanigan. We just heard today. What was his name?—something like Sel, or . . ."

"Stel?"

"Yeah. That's it. So you know about him."

Ahroe sighed. "Oh, yes. I know some about him. So he's in Innanigan."

"That's what they said."

"Our men will see you out of the camp. Here. Hold still while I blindfold you. Remember, we would like a truce, but any peace has to include the bombs."

"Yeah, Ahroe. Do you think she—if we were to—"

"She has to live first, Lieutenant."

"Dear God, let that please happen."

Kahdi, who was standing nearby, spat. "Here, 'Gani," he said. "I'll take you back out."

* * *

Exalt Onser lay on his pallet talking with Lieutenant Nivel. "You can't let him take back the command. No commander goes off to see a girl in the enemy camp."

"I see your point, Exalt. But it's the men. Look. He's got us all this far without a fight. We've foxed 'em. He knows the whole countryside. The men aren't cowards, but they want a chance. I'm afraid—"

"Of what?"

"If I took the command back I'd be . . . killed. Accidentally, of course."

"My men are not like that. They've kept their steel through a lot this summer."

"And learned a lot, Exalt, about what doesn't work and whose ideas get them killed. We'll call a council in the morning when we're set up across the river. If we asked, Oberly'd give up the freaking command with no regrets."

"Well, then . . ."

"He's too good, Exalt. He can do it. Ah, here he is. Oberly— learn anything?"

"I heard the ammunition go up. What happened?"

"Don't know. We sent a patrol to see."

"How is the retreat?"

"Underway."

"Miggi was there and shot through the thigh. Ahroe the Pelbar was there, too. She said there was only one shot, and then they killed some and captured the others. I can see they want to negotiate. But they are in earnest about this bomb. They won't give up unless they give out. I can see they're about as exhausted as we are. Maybe we'll all give out together."

Shortly before dawn a patrol met the retreat with Atlan, whom they'd captured. He was walking, leading the horse. The one survivor of the blast rode, groggily clutching the tired horse's mane.

The subdirect saluted and explained the situation. They herded and prodded Atlan to a tree, where they tied him. The subdirect gave the Shumai's handgun to Lieutenant Nivel, who examined it carefully and laid it aside. Atlan shouted instructions on the care of the horse to the men who led it away, then promptly yawned and went to sleep. When Nivel returned the gun was gone, and a search didn't turn it up.

In the morning the armies, though repositioned, were still resting, with the Arit between. In midmorning Stel arrived at the Innanigani camp with Budde and a large crowd of citizens. Oberly, still tired, was exasperated, but the citizens, fired with Stel's idea, wouldn't move. They insisted that the armies talk.

Oberly threw up his hands. "Subdirect," he said to the man with the torn ear. "Get the horse. We'll send the Shumai back with a message."

The man looked at him and walked away. As he returned, he passed near Stel, who was talking to some of the soldiers. He stopped. They stared at each other. "What?" Stel said. "What are you..."

The subdirect started, then fumbled in his coat and pulled out Atlan's handgun, leveled it, and pulled the trigger. Stel spun around with the roar and smoke, and fell, holding his side, as the subdirect turned the horse, leapt on, and, kicking it inexpertly, galloped it down the riverbank before the sentries could rouse their wits.

Stel opened his eyes and saw a crowd of faces, with Budde's, frowning, by him. "What was that? Are you all right?"

"I... no. Not really. He..."

"Why did he do that?"

"He... his name is Terog. He's a Tantal. He was the Information Master of Ginesh. They... stole my daughter. Three years... ago. I got her... back. I and some... Peshtak... burned down Ginesh to get all the slaves... free. Stole his invasion... fleet. Fought him at the Bitter Sea. Won. Never expected to... see him again."

"Damnation."

The guards had brought Atlan, who said, "Stel! It's me. Atlan. How... what happened? That louse who took my horse shot you? Hey. How are you?"

Stel grinned weakly. "Atlan."

"Ahroe's over the river," the Shumai said.

"Ahroe?"

"Maybe they'd let her come... if you'd like that."

"What is this?" said Oberly as he returned from giving orders to the large party that had volunteered to go after Terog.

"Ahroe's husband. Stel," Atlan said.

Oberly mused a moment, then said, "Go get her."

As they waited for Ahroe and tried to make Stel comfortable, the Pelbar turned to Budde. "This is your chance. Ahroe can negotiate for the whole Federation. She did... it last time. Talk to her. Don't let her go. Look. Give up the bombs. If the legislature doesn't like it, too bad. It'll be done. Get the army to back you if you can. Look. . . . These people will. They're risking a lot for . . . a solid peace."

The crowd stirred with a murmur of assent.

"Don't talk, Stel. Just rest."

"I have plenty . . . of time to rest."

Meanwhile, Oberly stood on a rise taking reports from his scouts and trying to balance his retreat against the enemy force, while worrying about the sudden appearance of a crowd of citizens. In the distance he could see a Federation balloon rising up again and knew there was little he could hide from them.

"Sir," said a soldier who had come to his side.

"Not now. See your subdirect."

"It is of utmost importance, sir."

Oberly glared, but saw the man was in earnest. "What?" he said.

"The subdirect, Lieutenant. The one who shot the Pelbar. He was a friend of Borund's. He's a diehard. I've heard him talk about stealing and hiding the bombs if necessary. If you got soft."

"Huh. They're safe enough."

"Not sure, sir. And the patrol following him is almost all men who agree with him."

Oberly frowned. "He probably doesn't even know where they are."

"He says at Purth on the coast, sir."

Oberly blanched. "Well, thank you. I'll think of something. Now do your duty, soldier."

"Yes, sir."

What he was to do with the information, Oberly didn't know. Nothing at the moment. The bombs were well guarded. They were almost two days' march away. He had more immediate problems. He had wondered why the patrol volunteered so readily. He really didn't want the complication of Ahroe's coming to the camp, but there seemed little he could do about that at the moment. At least she could tell him about Miggi.

Ahroe found Stel lying under an old apple tree surrounded by a crowd of curious and frightened civilians. Sitting with him were Legislator Budde and Ferth, who stayed by him, silent and scared. Stel greeted Ahroe with a slight smile but made no move to sit up. She knelt by him.

"What are you doing here? How—"

"You're looking older, Ahroe."

"That happens. How are you? Is it bad?"

Stel sighed. "It is sufficient. It will do. But now that you're ... here, this is Legislator Budde. And this is Ferth Sovel, my young friend. This is Ahroe, the Federation diplomat. I hope you can talk this mess out."

"Sufficient?"

"Yes."

"You can't just give up like that. It just went in your side, didn't it?"

"Yes. But after it got in, it did a good deal ... of snooping around in there. Please get ... to the issue. As I see it, the territorial lines presently established ... should be maintained." Stel sighed and blinked. "You tell her, Lume."

"Perhaps we could go to the command tent."

"I ... want to stay with Stel."

"Hey, Pelbar, we could move him," a nearby farmer called.

"Or set up a tent right here. Move him only ten arms or so," said a woman in a white work shift.

"No," said Stel. "I want to be here. Everything has been done. I'm comfortable. . . . Ahroe, you go and talk to Legislator Budde. Ferth will stay."

Ahroe covered her face with her hands for a time, then took them away and said, "This is too hard. How can I talk about a peace while you are lying here like this? I haven't even asked you anything about your life, how it was you got here, or ... Can't you leave me with him for a few sunwidths? It won't be long. Don't worry. There'll be no attack. Not yet. Maybe not ever if we can settle this."

Silently they moved back away from the couple, all except for Ferth, who sat still, her thick glasses smeared with tears.

"He shot me ... with a handgun," said Stel, smiling. "Like from the cave. I think it was ... Atlan's. So everything comes full circle. And circles ... have an end, after all. My past has lain in wait for me."

"There must be something we can do for you. You can't give up like this."

"I'm not giving up. Maybe Eo could have done something. Or maybe I could have ... under different circumstances ..."

"Stel, I'm sorry about the book. If you only could have waited, come back. There's a community on the bluff, just south of

Pelbarigan. We set it up. They have free access to the old book and full religious freedom."

"No. You were right as usual. Taking the book from me made me desperate for . . . a little while. Then I realized how many Pelbar . . . read and sing their words of Pel all their lives, to no effect. It is . . . because it is easier to do that, even to study deeply, than . . . to pray. And that is the whole key."

"They pray."

"They say prayers, Ahroe. When you don't have all those words, you reach deeper. You make the whole thing come alive inside you. It becomes all . . . there is to you."

Ahroe stared at him. "So you didn't come back. Because of that. Because we have become irrelevant."

"He talked about you," Ferth said. "All the time." She began to cry again. Ahroe put out her hand to the girl and felt her shoulders shaking.

"There was the man I hurt. At Eolyn's. But forget that. Don't you see how important this is, Ahroe? There may never be any . . . more fighting if you can work this out. The 'Ganis are an arrogant people. They've been the bloom on the sunflower stalk. I imagine now the Balis are coming with an army."

"Yes. I suppose it's no secret. And some Coo."

"If this . . . to me . . . has got you together with them, now that they are humbled some, it's . . . a small enough price."

"For you? A small price for you?"

"Yes. I know now, Ahroe, as clearly as I see you, this, to me, isn't going to end anything. There will be further journeys, more songs, a newer Urstadge, more love and growth. Oh, Ahroe, I . . . they need you so much. I still have one more thing . . . to do."

"What now?"

"To stay alive so you and Budde will talk. I know it can be worked out. The bomb, Ahroe. . . . It's like a ferocious sun fallen to Earth. All the fighting so far has been children's slings and rotten apple wars. People . . . let the thing persist because they haven't . . . seen it. Can't visualize how awful . . . Ahroe, call Budde back. I'll last it out. We can talk."

She looked at him dubiously, then raised her hand for the legislator to return. He did come back, with the crowd, who stood around as the two talked much of the morning about details of an agreement. Oberly came and went several times, but busied himself with his men.

At one point Ahroe motioned him over. "Lieutenant, I am concerned about the man who shot Stel. If it is as they say, he may have a faction prepared to steal the bombs. If he manages that, all our talk will have been useless. I'd like to get Kahdi, the Shumai, to confer with you about a joint force on horses to follow him. We can't let that go. And we need a Pelbar scribe."

"I'll see to it."

"She's a bit better."

Oberly brightened. "Good!"

When Kahdi returned with Oberly, he listened dubiously then asked, "How long ago? We will go all right. We may not be able to catch him. We can supply a good hundred horses not too worn out. But you better send the balloon. Wind's pretty much right. It could go to the city and warn them. Don't think the 'Ganis people want some Tantal wandering off with their doom weapon."

Oberly sent Nivel and a subdirect to ride the balloon with a two-man Pelbar crew. The Innanigani lieutenant gripped the basket in terror as the craft lifted and began to drift eastward. It crossed the river, still climbing, and passed over his army, and the crowd of citizens, who cheered them noisily. They looked so tiny and frail. He suddenly pitied human pretensions. It was a strange feeling. Looking west into the distance, he saw a force nearing the westerners' camp.

"What is that?" he asked.

"Look through this," said the Pelbar navigator, handing him a telescope.

"How?"

The navigator explained, a little condescendingly, and Nivel stared through it. In a few seconds he could make out the banner of Baligan. So that was it. Budde had better settle things with the Pelbar woman. It was too late to tell his men. What was that? Red roaches? Coo with them, marching with the Balis? Worse. Coo near his city? It was hardly to be borne.

"We're drifting a little north," said the Pelbar navigator. We need more height."

The lieutenant blanched and looked over at his subdirect, a dark-skinned young man who was grinning broadly and unconcernedly. "Look. There's the sea," he said, pointing.

"No. That's the deadwater north of the city," Nivel said.

"Toads and mud," the navigator said. "Should we take it down and walk?"

Nivel frowned. "No. We'll come across the harbor. Where we're going is Purth, on the coast. Hooks up northeast of the city. We can cross the water and hope the wind doesn't shift northerly, eh?"

"Your game, Lieutenant." The fireman added alcohol to the flare.

Stel sighed and interrupted. "Ahroe, I'm sure we can supply them with radiation detectors. I already gave . . . mine to the harbormaster. . . . Now, if you don't mind, I'm going to sleep for a little . . . but you must not stop talking. . . . You must not stop for anything. Ferth, if you could get me a little more of that water."

Ahroe fixed her gaze on him. Their eyes met and held. She set her jaw. Then she turned to Budde and said, "All right. I agree to the radiation detectors, but only if they remain sealed and are not opened and studied." She glanced at Stel. She had been holding his hand the whole time, her slender fingers encircling his thumb. She glanced at Ferth, who stared at Stel in fear.

"Ferth," Ahroe said. "Bite your lip and go on. There's always time enough to cry."

Ferth stared at her, then back at Stel. "We are each doing our part, Ferth," said Ahroe. "Now you do yours."

They talked on, and in spite of the warmth, Ahroe asked for a light cover for Stel. He didn't stir as Ferth silently tucked it around him.

It was half after high sun when they concluded an agreement and called Oberly to read it to him. He nodded at each point, asked a few questions, and quibbled a little, glancing now and then at Stel, then back to Ahroe. Finally he said, "I'd sign that, Legislator. Ahroe, perhaps you . . . we—I know a nice place for Stel . . . a hill west of here. I have a friend there."

Ahroe looked up desolately. "Stel is—"

"I know. So is my friend. He came back wounded from Borund's first fiasco."

"Here now, what are you saying?" Budde exclaimed.

"He's gone," Oberly muttered.

"Not asleep?" Budde whispered.

A woman from the crowd of civilians began to cry, and a general moan joined her.

"It's the way of war." Ahroe's voice trembled. "What did you expect? Many others on both sides have experienced the same. Some much worse."

"They were not Stel," Legislator Budde said. "Stel is ours as much as yours. This is his peace more than anyone's."

Ferth sobbed quietly, and Ahroe drew the cover up over her husband's face, hesitating just a moment. Then she set her jaw and said, "Let's sign this thing."

 XXIX

THE balloon drifted near the bay shore north of the city, near the dead lands. The fireman had let it cool so it sank low, skimming over trees and dunes. Dead ahead people were dragging driftwood near the shoreline.

"Quick, look up," Lieutenant Nivel yelled as he threw down the line. They turned, looked up, then scattered. "Stop. Please, grab the line." Two women and a man turned and reached for the line but the balloon began to drag them. "More men!" the lieutenant shouted. Two more men chased them and caught it by the water's edge.

"Over you go, Subdirect. Right to the city. Warn them. Be careful who you tell. The harbormaster, Legislator Ustis, the warden, and then Exalt-emeritus Alwar. He's at the hospital I think. To it now."

Laughing, the young subdirect surged over the side of the basket and slid down the rope. "Let go," the lieutenant shouted, and the fireman added a torch under the mouth of the balloon bag. It slowly rose, drifting out over the water, trailing the rope as they slowly drew it up and coiled it. Below the subdirect was gesticulating and talking. Then he started to jog southward, toward the city. The people on the shore stared after the drifting balloon.

They rose high enough to see the land hooking northward ahead of them. "We're shifting north," the navigator said. "We may not make land."

"What can you do about that?"

"Not a mud-covered thing, Lieutenant. We go where the wind goes."

"Ahead," the fireman said. "What's that?"

"A ship? How can we . . . we're going to be close. Let down the line."

"That's not one of ours," Nivel mused. "I'll . . . it's from the Eastern Islands—that's their ensign, the green-clad volcano."

"We won't make it to them, Lieutenant. Too far south. I'm going to dump it near them," the navigator shouted. Without hesitating, he undid a cord and opened the top of the bag. The balloon sank rapidly, and they heard shouts from the ship, which began to turn even before they splashed into the choppy water.

"As soon as we hit, swim out from under!" the fireman yelled. "*Phhhfff!* This stuff tastes awful."

"I can't swim!" Nivel cried.

"Lie back. I'll take care of you," the fireman called.

The ship's sails loosed and fluttered as it came alongside and picked up the balloonists. In just moments it was lifting their craft aboard as Lieutenant Nivel explained the problem.

An older woman listened gravely then spoke. "My name is Arthil. Welcome aboard the *Farleaf*. We shipped from Godspalm. We're here from the islands because we detected a nuclear explosion. We decided to bring the trade ship early and help if possible. Tell us where this Purth is and we will take you. Here. Dry off and tell me what has been happening."

"It would take days, Arthil," the lieutenant said. "Turn your ship toward that tower far to the south. If you have fighting men, prepare them. I don't know what we'll find."

The *Farleaf* dropped its parties in small boats, and once ashore they began walking the two ayas south toward the Purth lookout, where the army had stored the three remaining bombs. Soon they heard heavy bursts of machine rifle fire ahead, and they began to trot, Nivel gaining ground on the island sailors, who carried some strange kind of weapons.

Finally they neared the last dune before the tower. Nivel heard shouting just ahead and he motioned the Pelbar down while he himself crept forward for a look. Before him an arc of about a hundred men, a mixture of soldiers and civilians, had dug in to face the tower. They had two machine rifles mounted in hastily dug pits, and Nivel recognized Legislator Crupp in a pit with one of the weapons. Suddenly there was an explosive thud and a mortar round arced up then slammed into the stone tower, spraying masonry on some of the attackers.

Arthil bustled up behind, and Nivel frantically waved her to a crouching position then explained the situation.

"Do you mind if we remove those weapons?" she asked.

"Remove? No. How?"

Arthil waved forward the panting men with the strange weapons and indicated the two machine rifles. Long tubes mounted on their shoulders, the two men snuggled down in the dune and aimed carefully.

"Clear to the rear!" Arthil called. "All right, volunteers. Let them rip!"

With a roar, two rockets lanced out and converged in showers of fire in the machine rifle pits. Much shouting followed, and as some of the attackers showed themselves, rifle fire spewed at them from the tower's defenders. Lieutenant Nivel pulled Arthil down as the attackers began shooting in their direction.

"It's almost dark. We'll have to pull back," Nivel said. "They have us outnumbered. How many men have you?"

"Thirty-two available. We can wait out the night near the sea, Lieutenant. I think we can keep them off. We can hope for help."

They pulled back to the shore dunes after firing two more rockets to cover their retreat, then they snuggled into the sand and set a watch. "Now we have time to talk, " she said. "Tell me what has been happening, please."

Nivel tried to fill in the overall story, with interruptions from the Pelbar navigator when the recollections got too partisan. Finally Arthil asked, "Have you heard of a man named Jestak?"

"Jestak was killed while dismantling the bomb left in the Baligan Harbor, I have heard," the navigator said. "I've known him since we were children. Did you meet him on his eastern journey? A small world."

"Killed?" Arthil was silent a long time. "While dismantling the bomb." Again she paused and stared at the stars. "I had hoped to see him. Well, someone must dismantle the bombs. There is always the cost. Yes, I knew him. When we were both young. What is your name?"

"Tanbar. From Pelbarigan. I have been in all this from the beginning. I hope we are nearing the end. I want . . . to quit the guard."

"What for, Tan? Want to farm?" the fireman asked.

"No. I want to start the first balloon service in the new world," Tanbar said. "Think of what can be done with it."

"Not a bad idea—say, what are those lights?"

Nivel ventured a look. "Torches. From the direction of the city. It must be well past high night."

"I have a bad feeling about this," the Pelbar fireman said.

"I'm sure it's all right," Arthil said. "Surely the attackers would not announce themselves this way."

Soon a crowd of over four hundred angry and tired citizens roused by the subdirect plodded through the sand directly toward the tower. The attackers, who had surrounded the tower by then, fired warning shots, scattering the newcomers, but they knew the game was up, and soon most had fled southward. Eventually the crowd surged up to the tower and joined the islanders who had taken refuge there. It was soon decided that all would remain there guarding the ancient weapons until reinforcements arrived. Some of the newcomers had thought to bring food and soon amid the signs of combat and slaughter, a strange party developed.

Toward dawn some distant rifle fire was heard but nothing else occurred until midmorning, when a mixed band of Innanigani and Shumai horsemen walked tired mounts across the sand.

Kahdi greeted Nivel with a raised eyebrow. "See you made it. A fight here? We caught up with Terog and his gang. He's dead. I'm dead tired. I've about ruined my horse. So that's the Eastern Sea. I could use a little of it." He dropped his horse's halter and stumbled toward the beach, shedding clothing a piece at a time as he went. The crowd watched him wade in with only his pants on, tumble in the surf, swim out, and then wave his pants like a flag. Laughter ran along the group of people on the dunes and with it an immense feeling of relief.

☐ Epilogue

THE peace Ahroe and Legislator Budde had hammered out held, and as time passed, Innaniganis wondered increasingly why they had invaded the west at such cost. With the peace they received horses, steam power, the radio, and new agricultural products, as well as an array of lost knowledge. They themselves contributed metalworking skills, several vegetables, further knowledge, especially of past literature and music.

The Federation remained a separate sovereignty, not being comfortable with the rule-oriented system of law of the Innaniganis, but that too grew milder under the influence of the western sense of trust and justice.

After Stel's mountain burial Ahroe returned to the west to become president of the Federation, but in five years she journeyed east again as its minister to Innanigan. She brought her daughter, Raydi, with her and lived at first with Manny Sovel and blind Owayn. Raydi read to him often, as did Ferth, and the two young women became close friends.

As Stel had proposed, the bombs were taken by a large mixed group to a shaft that had been laboriously dug into the rock of a mountain east of the Cwanto. When Eolyn arrived in the East, the Dome woman supervised their safe dismantling. The remains were spaced out and sunk in concrete. The shaft was then filled with broken rock, and thereafter travelers would often come just to add a stone to the growing pile on the mountain.

Not long after the initial peace, it became the custom for veterans of the conflict to ask for burial there. Stel's grave was already entangled in briars, but eventually the place had a caretaker and became a spot for national reverence.

On the way west by carriage eleven years after the conflict, Ahroe and Raydi stopped to visit with Kahdi, who lived near Stel's Mountain, having gone back to Innanigan to teach the raising of horses and then settled with a war widow. Ahroe found him balding and heavier, but surehanded as ever with his horses, and still whimsical.

It was late summer. The quiet fields chirred with insects and the maize had begun to sound dry as it rustled. Ahroe rode out to the mountain with Kahdi's nine-year-old son, Kendo. The boy was awed to be with Ahroe and was reticent, but as they turned a curve in the road, he said, "That's Stel's Mountain over there."

"It's only a hill."

"Yeah. But it's a mountain to us. I've been there before. Stel is in the center, with everybody all around. They say that God stood at his elbow when he made the peace."

Ahroe snuffed. "That was only Legislator Budde."

"He's there, too." Kendo paused and frowned. "Maybe God was on the other side."

"I wish She'd held out Her hand, then, when the Tantal shot him."

Kendo frowned again. "I suppose God must have wanted it that way."

Ahroe felt a despair she had not known in a long time. "No, Kendo. I can't think Aven wants such things. It is our own folly. Some people try to stop evil acts, and sometimes they do it by stepping in the way of it. Jestak did that, too. And Sima Pall and Brudoer and Gamwyn and Lume Budde and a lot of others. Your father and I did, too, I think, but it didn't strike us down. Maybe we were lucky. Maybe we were too careful. I don't think it was skill."

Kendo looked at her, not comprehending. "Why wouldn't Raydi come with us?" he asked.

Ahroe set her jaw. "Even now she didn't think she could stand it," she said a little strangely. Then she smiled and added, "But I have seen a lot and know that things have to be stood and accepted—and even loved. Stel said to me as he was dying that I should not worry. It was as though he was sent out ahead of us for our benefit. I'm not sure of that. He didn't do it alone, this peace. We were all exhausted. It was obvious. But..."

"Yeah?"

"We might have gone right on if he and his crowd had not come. And... if he had not proved his seriousness by getting shot. And insisting we go on talking. I could hardly stand it, you know, but I knew we'd never worked more closely together than then." She looked at him. "It was a great moment. I knew it then and still do." Ahroe wiped the corners of her eyes.

They arrived at the cemetery and easily found Stel's grave, a simple marker stone that read:

STEL WESTRUN

I'm not really here, you know.
Why should we have a stone lie so?

It was an epitaph he had asked for long before his death, though Ahroe had objected to its frivolousness. Now, looking at it, she wondered if it might not be just right. Of course, for those who believed in eternity, Stel was not there. But in another sense he was wherever people knew of the war. Everyone in the Federation know his place in the struggle even if they knew little else of it. It seemed to Ahroe strange that he should stand so in the center of his culture, he who always seemed to be escaping authority, playing his flute from a distance, maintaining his separateness. Jestak was like him and had shared his fate. They weren't statesmen. They were inspirers—poets of action. Ahroe sighed, realizing that it took people like her to organize the changes the poets catalyzed—at the cost of weary years of talk, compromise, thought, and labor.

She turned to Kendo and said, "All right. Time to go." Her voice was almost steady, and she held her head up, almost overcome by memories and the strange, elegiac songs of the late summer insects in the dry grass.

Miggi's volume about the Wars of Federation and Innanigan, published twelve years after the great crisis, remained the standard for many years. It included most of the primary source material for all later studies, and while some disagreed with its conclusions, none faulted its scholarship except a few Innanigani nationalists. Her husband, Legislator Oberly, always defended it.

Another decade passed. One rainy fall day, the Baligani harbormaster received a strange, crackling radio message from a fishing boat out in the sea beyond the eastern channel. He thought it said, "Strange vessels approaching the channel. Be alert. Don't know what they are." The rest was garbled.

The harbormaster sighed. Out of bureaucratic prudence he

called his coast guard to alert and sent a steam launch out the channel to meet whatever it might be, if anything.

They reported three odd and foreign ships with vertical rotating vanes that seemed to propel the ship without normal sails or steam power. At that point the harbormaster called the militia. After a very long wait, he saw the ships coming in sight, escorted by the coast guard. His mounted telescope showed one of his officers aboard the lead vessel, standing by an oddly dressed man with strange eyes. They were both gesturing. Another radio message announced that they had some illness aboard and needed to make some repairs.

The harbormaster called for his own launch and set out for the lead boat. As he drew closer he could see it was beautifully designed. Each of the rotating vanes bore a red circle, which flicked dizzyingly as the vanes slowly turned. He came alongside and boarded, and the coastguardsman said, "Sir, I can't understand any of them—except an old one-armed man in that cabin. He's a Shumai. Not well. I gather they are worried about him."

The harbormaster ducked into the cabin and saw the old man, very thin, in a reclining chair. With him was a black-haired man with almond eyes, straightbacked and wary. "Hello. I am Tor, of the Bowbend Shumai," the man said, softly. "This is Yukanna. We won't stay. Only to repair some rotors. I will talk for us."

"Zimonson, Tor. Where are you from? Who are these people?"

Tor gazed out the cabin window. "It's a long story, Zimonson. I've been . . . around the whole Earth."

After the boats anchored, Tor was brought ashore, with Yukanna ever watchful by his side. Tor insisted on walking through the crowd, sustained by Yukanna and another man, up the cobbled harbor slope toward the statue at the top.

He paused and regarded it. The green mottling on its rain-glazed surface partly obscured the faces at first. It was a group of bronze men, gazing out at the harbor, most of them standing soldiers. One, with a strange headdress, knelt. Nearby a Pelbar stooped, smiling whimsically. He held a small dog.

Tor frowned. "That looks like Stel. And Jestak. What has happened here?"

Later, as Tor lay in bed at the harbormaster's house, he wondered aloud to the harbormaster's wife if he might not have had a greater adventure staying home. A coastguardsman entered with a radio message from Innanigan.

"Please read it to me," Tor said.

The man read, "'I am here in Innanigan and am coming to see you. I am bringing Willton, son of Tristal and Fahna. Tristal is in the west. Do not dare go anywhere before I get there. Eolyn.'"

Tor repeated the message to Yukanna in a strange tongue. He replied briefly, then turned away, containing some sadness. His hand rested on Tor's shoulder.

Eolyn and Willton arrived three days later by steamboat. She wasted no time in visiting Tor. As she entered the room she was shocked by his appearance. "Tor," she said. "Look at you. What have you done to yourself? This is Willton, your grandnephew. Here. I'll have to examine you. Willton, where's that bag?"

Tor looked at her and at the tall young man behind her, seeing in her a sadness and richness of experience that graced her age lightly, and in him Tristal again, with a certain flicker of the eye that let him know the old Shumai spirit was not dead. "Hello, Eo," he said. "I've only got a little old is all. This is Yukanna." He spoke to his young friend in explanation. Then he turned back and said, "I'm glad you've come. We have to go soon enough. We want to catch the warm season in the southern hemisphere. I've seen ancient maps. It's a long way around the continent and cold at the south tip in any season."

"You can't go anywhere. Look at you."

"I have nothing to do but rest. The Hitobito do it all."

Eolyn sat on the bed. "I know better now, Tor. If you go, I am going with you, and I can't go."

"What does that mean?"

"It means you are staying with me. Do you understand?"

Tor gazed at the ceiling. "That would be good, Eo. But I can't disappoint my friends."

Willton, who had been looking at his great-uncle with some awe, blurted out, "Send me. I'll go in your place. Look, I have no connections. It'll work."

"Your father would never forgive me—if he has yet for last time," Tor said.

"Father? He and mother are out in Forman country arranging for further trade. He has been all over. I was born by the Bitter Sea and have been to the south islands."

"You'd have to learn the language."

"Better start teaching me now."

"Not now, Willton," said Eolyn with some asperity.

Twenty days later Eolyn and Tor stood on the harbormaster's motor launch and watched the three Hitobito ships sail southward in the open sea. Yukanna had cried a little as he embraced Tor, and Tor had looked very grave.

"He doesn't know what he's getting into," said Tor.

"Willton? He'll do better than you would. Look at you."

Tor shaded his eyes and watched the receding ships. "If you are so worried about me, Eo, maybe you ought to marry me."

"That goes without saying," she replied softly.

A fall cold in the breeze made the pilot turn up his collar. Mists blew between the launch and the ships, and gulls overhead glided and turned, crying their restless souls to the wind and to each other. "Helm, come about," the harbormaster called, hands behind him.

"There is an end to everything, Tor," said Eolyn. "Now that you're home."

"And a new beginning," said Tor wistfully, watching the vanishing ships.